Stephe Smith

Romance and Humor of the Rail

A Book for Railway Men and Travellers, Representing everyday Life on the Railroad

Stephe Smith

Romance and Humor of the Rail
A Book for Railway Men and Travellers, Representing everyday Life on the Railroad

ISBN/EAN: 9783337274269

Printed in Europe, USA, Canada, Australia, Japan

Cover: Foto ©Andreas Hilbeck / pixelio.de

More available books at **www.hansebooks.com**

"HE HAS NICE MUSTACHES" PAGE 304

ROMANCE

AND

HUMOR OF THE RAIL.

A BOOK FOR

RAILWAY MEN AND TRAVELLERS,

REPRESENTING

EVERYDAY LIFE ON THE RAILROAD,

IN

𝕰𝖛𝖊𝖗𝖞 𝕯𝖊𝖕𝖆𝖗𝖙𝖒𝖊𝖓𝖙 𝖔𝖋 𝖙𝖍𝖊 𝕽𝖆𝖎𝖑𝖜𝖆𝖞 𝕾𝖊𝖗𝖛𝖎𝖈𝖊,

WITH

SKETCHES AND RHYMES OF ROMANCE,

AND

NUMEROUS ANECDOTES AND INCIDENTS.

EDITED BY

STEPHE SMITH.

NEW YORK:

G. W. Carleton & Co., Publishers.

LONDON: S. LOW, SON & CO.

M.DCCC.LXXIII.

Stereotyped at the
WOMEN'S PRINTING HOUSE,
56, 58 and 60 Park Street,
New York.

TO

Hon. FRANCIS COLTON,

FORMERLY

UNITED STATES CONSUL TO VENICE,

AND LATE

GENERAL PASSENGER AGENT

OF THE

UNION PACIFIC RAILWAY,

THIS BOOK IS

Inscribed, as an Earnest Tribute of Respect,

TO A

WARM FRIEND

AND

COURTEOUS GENTLEMAN.

CONTENTS.

PREFACE.

I I.

WAY-BILL.

USTOM has decided that no book can start safely upon its travels without a learned introduction. No experienced Engineer will "pull out" without first sounding his bell, nor will a prudent Conductor leave the depot without the final "all aboard." To this limit would the author confine his Preface. Having made up his train, and received his orders, he has only to give the signal, join his passengers, keep a "wild eye," and leave the rest with Providence. If there should be a defective axle, a flaw in a wheel, or an imperfect box, he must endure the anxiety and suspense, from which the conscientious Conductor is never free, and be ready for the reproach and abuse which is his constant portion.

The author presents this little volume to the Railroad public, believing that it will be of interest to employés

1*

in every department of the service. It is not designed as a book of horrors, hairbreadth escapes, or impossible adventures; nor does it attempt to recount the fearful accidents and disasters which go to swell the record of every railroad year. Its mission is to entertain, rather than to instruct; to represent Everyday Life on the Rail as the author has found it. To the Traveller, it presents scenes and incidents which may serve to recall his own experiences.

A few of the sketches, rhymes, and incidents, the author has already given to the public in newspaper correspondence from different parts of this and other countries; but one never loses his relish for a palatable dish by having it twice served. Prepared in intervals of active duty upon the Daily Press, it makes no claim to literary merit or elaborate polish. If it shall present the Railway employé to a prejudiced Public in a more favorable light, or contribute in the slightest degree to the pleasure of the Railway Traveller, the author's object will have been fully attained.

He feels honored in being permitted to dedicate his work to the successor of W. D. Howells and "Ik. Marvel" at the U. S. Consulate of Venice. A man of letters, an experienced Traveller, and a worthy type of that refined element which has elevated the Railway business in this country, his name deserves to be recorded on a worthier page.   S. S.

SMITHVILLE, *Sept.* 1, 1872.

III.

FOGYVILLE AND THE BRANCH.

Fogyville, the last Anti-Railway Corporation—Its prominent Characters—Threatened Advance of the Branch—Opposition in the Interest of the Stage Line—'Squire Jones—The Man who couldn't see it !—How it became visible at last !

EFORE introducing the reader to the Men of the Road, and the personal experiences that go to make up Everyday Life on the Rail, the author begs permission to present the town of Fogyville, the last respectable village that opposed the advance of the inevitable Railway.

Without describing its exact location, it will suffice to say, that it is situated in a thriving State, about forty miles distant from the metropolis in which I resided, and at the time of my frequent visits, it was in the hands of our dear old Stage-coach friends that we all loved so well. I liked the town because it was somewhat faded ; in an undecided state of transition ; uncertain whether to accept the insidious advances of the proposed branch from a remote main line of railway in a friendly spirit, or simultaneously close its shutters and emigrate West in a compact body, to grow up with the place.   It was attractive to me, because it was a sulky coaching chrysalis, determined not to develop into the railway butterfly without a severe struggle.   It was a pleasure to take my pipe into the public room of the leading hotel of the place, and hear the proprietor of the "National Stage Line," hotel-keepers, liverymen, and other oracles converse upon the probability of the railway ever reaching Fogyville, and the injurious effects which it would have upon trade, if the infernal thing ever came so far.   I could ask for nothing more refreshing than a discourse from such men upon the destiny of railway enterprise, its operation upon the country at large, and its final operation upon Fogyville itself.   It was amusing, for instance, to see Thompson— who owned three buggies, one gig, and a hearse—driven almost mad at times, when some commercial traveller would arrive with fresh and strengthening rumors of the advancing iron road.   And again, when inflated with an extra quantity of local beverages, he would draw himself up to his full height, expand to more than his full breadth, and resolve to oppose, single-handed, if need be, the tide of the threatened improvement.   One portly gentleman, known as 'Squire Jones, gravely shook his head and expressed a doubt whether, with all his capital, Thompson was equal to the task.   Others—I remember the brave fellows well—expressed the hope that Fogyville would some day become a Railroad Station, but the dismal sentiment was soon crushed by a storm of doubts and misgivings.

I went to Fogyville every season to angle for trout. The town boasted a trout stream that, as a true sportsman, I would not exchange to-day for the best-paying railroad in this broad land.   I am not therefore bound to give the true name of my retreat, nor does it concern the reader whether it lies at the East or the West. To reach this retreat in those days, it required a six hours' journey and an outlay of between five and ten dollars. I can run out now in less than two hours, at almost any period of the day, for the matter of a dollar and a half. It has not the same air of seclusion now that it wore in the old staging days; and sometimes, as I lie upon the sloping grass watching my float, I fancy I can see the smoke of the metropolis, rising and floating above the trees, and hear the roar of the humming city life. In the evening I return to the little white hotel, take a fresh pipe, and listen to the conversation of the wise men of the village. When I first went there, Fogyville was in the full pride, profit, and glory of the old Stage-coaching days. From ten to fifteen highly painted, well-horsed rolling stages passed through from an early hour in the morning until a late hour of the night. The principal hotel was then a sight to see. Horses standing outside in the road; porters rushing to and fro with baggage; hostlers busy with bright and complicated harness; passengers, both male and female, alighting from the vehicles, assisted by obliging drivers, the proprietor himself, or mine host of the "Union Hotel." Buxom landlady and neat chambermaids standing at the doors, under the broad whitewashed porch, ready to welcome the guests.

The commercial traveller of those days was a steady, easy-going, time-taking, pioneer of trade, who drove his own team, or rode his own horse. Not the bustling, high-pressure, watch-consulting, New York or Chicago maniac who is left to us now. He was known as an "Agent," with no authority beyond the task that had been given him to do, and he gloried in the appellation, without having the ambition to be regarded as a commercial gentleman.   To obtain the favor of a choice seat in the coach, or indeed a seat of any kind, was an affair of many days' booking and quite a fee in silver or gold. The keepers of toll-gates were ready, obedient, and respectful; hostlers at roadside houses, where we "changed horses," were filled with admiration approaching veneration.   It was the height of their ambition, you see, to be called upon some day to fill a position of such imposing and heavy responsibility as that of a driver of a four-horse coach over a first-class road.   Some such conversation as the following was frequently heard between the two men who led the relieved steeds up the yard :

"Tom knows a thing or two about hosses, eh, Bill ? "

"As well as any a man on the road, Jack."

"There ain't the driver on the road as can git over him when he's a-mind."

"Not exactly, Jack."

Sometimes, if a driver happened to be new, or a little verdant and ill liberal, the remarks were not so full of admiration.

"Why, he's no more use for four on 'em, Bill, than my little finger."

"No more he ain't, Jack.   I'll bring a boy as will lick him any day, with his own team on his own run."

"Ony boy, ony infant, Jack."

This was about the status of things when I first began to visit my country town.   At this period the first rumors of a great railway enterprise began to dawn upon the world, and, after a decent interval, upon the town of Fogyville.   It is not my purpose to call up the barber of this village ; the keeper of the corner grocery who dealt out fresh meat twice a week ; the dealer in dry-goods and queen's-ware, and several important agriculturists, and the usual nightly visitors of a country hotel, in order to ridicule their opinions upon what was at that time the incomprehensible wonder of the age. They spoke according to their lights, and if these were not brilliant, they had many in authority whose intellects ought to have been sharpened by early training and intercourse with the world, to keep them in arguments for their nightly gatherings. The local papers of my country town copied everything that was launched in type in the metropolis against the new gigantic scheme, and every citizen wandered about armed with these silent but formidable weapons.

Mr. Ross—Major Ross I believe they called him—the proprietor of the "National Stage Line," was the central figure in our little arena of tobacco-smoke and discussion. He owned nearly all the vehicles and horses running to and from my country town, as well as the necessary arrangement for traffic on the National road. A tall, powerful man, with a red face, a loud voice, and a splendid capacity for the leading local beverage. He had not created his present position—he had been born in it. The frequenters of my country hotel gave the Major credit for possessing a vast fund of wisdom, but he kept it to himself. During the discussions on the great railway question, I never heard him speak but a few words. I record his favorite and oracular remarks here, because they have since been distorted into a vulgar phrase. "Well, it may be very good, but I can't see it." Then, after a little reflection, he would add, "No, I can't see it."

In this way a few years rolled by, and I still paid my regular summer visits to my country town. The barber, whom I had indoctrinated with my views upon railways, had died with opinions far in advance of his village and his age.   He left his business to an only son, with these memorable words : " Joseph, my son, a great movement is a-comin', keep an eye on't ! "

Major Ross still held fast to his coaches of the " National Line," in the face of several tempting offers.   He drank, if anything, a little more of the local beverage, and could not see it.   In another year the main line approached nearer, and as I said at the start, the enterprising directors had mapped out a branch to my country town.   It was at this time that I saw one of the early surveyors seized by the indignant villagers and ducked in a horse-pond, but I dared not interfere.

There was much excitement and an unusually strong muster at the hotel that evening, with a flattering disposition to rally around Major Ross as the representative of the coaching interest.   Saluting the sympathy expressed or implied, with a stage bow, the Major refreshed himself with another draught of the local beverage, and merely remarked that he couldn't see it.   What he thought he would not say, but he rested his faith, I think, with other interested townspeople, upon 'Squire Jones, to turn back the advancing tide of railway encroachment.   This gentleman was the largest land proprietor in the whole county.   He indulged in profanity occasionally, patronized horse-races, got a little groggy every night, and visited the theatre on State occasions in the metropolis. He owned extensive acres and many farms.   No branch line could possibly reach my country town, unless it passed for several miles through the property of the popular 'Squire.   The faith of the townspeople in the 'Squire's anti railway sentiments was very great.   The silent

Major Ross shared in the general feeling. He knew, indeed everybody knew, that the 'Squire's favorite recreation was to meet Major Ross' "Lightning Express coach" and relieve the driver for a ten-mile dash, handling the ribbons with a grace and skill, that the drivers professed to believe was the height of perfection. Knowing this, no one could hesitate about the nature and extent of the 'Squire's opposition to the proposed branch railway.

Another period of a few years. 'Squire Jones did oppose the railway, and prevented the extension of the branch to my country town. A majority of the inhabitants believed that principle was at the bottom of this. Some of us thought that it was because the worthy gentleman had not been offered his price. Railway pioneers were very liberal in those days, but ancient home-places and family acres were not to be cut up to encourage rapid communication, like a common, plebeian farm. The 'Squire, therefore, remained shrewdly passive.

In the meantime, the road came on apace. It had reached a point about five miles distant from my country town. At this point the directors also assumed a passive position. This had an injurious effect upon the National Line, still Major Ross couldn't see it. Two hours' walk, or one hour's drive, brought the traveller to the station, and two hours more by rail, with a trifling fee, carried him to the metropolis. For a time the people of Fogyville looked shyly upon this new and cheap mode of conveyance. Exaggerated stories of dangers to be feared, and fearful accidents that had already occurred, began to circulate. I regret that I am compelled to believe that these horrors were peddled about through my country town in that gentleman's interest. He couldn't see it, it is true, but he had been wise enough to reduce his fares, to meet the new competition.   One or two advent-urous spirits were finally induced to try the experiment of a railway journey to the metropolis.   They returned uninjured, with a favorable report of the sensations they had experienced.   Others followed, and the railroad rose steadily in popularity, in proportion as the novelty and the fear of danger wore off.

Then came the severest trial to Major Ross.   His own family began to turn against him.   One morning the sad intelligence reached him, that his nephew on the wife's side, had started off without the knowledge of his parents, to make his first trip upon the railway.   The mother came around with tears to explain and apologize to Mrs. Ross.   This excellent lady in her turn conveyed the apologies and explanations to her solemn husband. He did not say much, he never did; but it was plain that he felt the terrible affliction.   His passengers dropped off, day by day, his baggage-carrying was entirely gone; his daily consumption of the leading local beverage in-creased, and he was again induced by the advice of friends to reduce his fares.   Major Ross, proprietor of the " National Line," began to see it !

I continued my trips to Fogyville, clinging with the tenacity of a first-love to the old " National Line." There were numerous melancholy changes for the worse. The horses were old, ill-fed, and slow.   The toll-keepers were less admiring and respectful.   Gradually the little hotels on the line began to close their shutters.   This compelled an alteration in the arrangements for changing horses.   The drives were made longer, and the relief-horses were brought to us from wretched way-side barns. The proud hostlers had given way to old men in dirty, fluttering blouses, who seemed as much in need of food and rest as the worn-out horses. Things in the hotel had also vastly changed. It was still neat and clean, but lacked bustle, customers, and life. Death, bankruptcy, and emigration had thinned the company in the public room, but the same engrossing topic was discussed with the same earnestness, but with less obstinacy, and a little more knowledge and experience, than before. Many who had doubted with energy whether they would ever see a railroad within a hundred miles of Fogyville, now appealed to me to know if they had ever had the slightest misgivings about the ultimate establishment and development of a railway enterprise. " Major Ross," said they, confidentially, " had not seen it, could not see it now, but they had seen it all along."

Then came the sudden death of 'Squire Jones. It occurred just as he was on the point of acceding to the renewed offers of the railway directors, and allowing the road to come up to the town.

Major Ross, after renewed draughts of the leading local beverage, declared the death of 'Squire Jones a splendid stroke of Providence. The eyes connected with the decaying, coaching interest were now turned with anxiety to young Jones, the 'Squire's son and heir. The anti-railway interest had its doubts about the young man, and they were well-founded. Before the remains of the late lamented 'Squire Jones were decently covered, the pickaxes of the railway navigators were rooting up the turf of his sacred acres. Major Ross could not quite see it yet !

Another period passed by, and we arrived at last within a day of the opening of the railway from my country town to the metropolis. In the afternoon of the previous day I took my seat upon the box of the " Lightning

Express," the last coach of the "National Line."   I
desired to honor with my patronage the last journey it
was intended to make.

Major Ross mounted by my side to take the reins; he
had been his own coachman for many weary weeks.   It
was no ordinary journey.   It was a funeral of a four-
horse coach, performed by its ruined but obstinate proprietor.   As we moved slowly out of Fogyville, persons
stood looking at us with various expressions of triumph,
pity, and contempt.   Major Ross was well stimulated
with the leading local beverage at starting, and refreshed
himself at every opportunity.   The harness was old, and
Major Ross had frequently to get down to make repairs.
We arrived in the metropolis three hours behind time.
We had but two inside passengers, a pudding-faced boy
and a dog.   These were received at our journey's end by
eight females of various ages, sizes, and shapes.   They
made some cruel remarks to Major Ross about the uncertainty of stage travelling compared with the railway,
and I retired, just as symptoms broke out of a serious
quarrel.   I did not see or hear anything of Major Ross
for some years.

I still go down to fish in the outskirts of my country
town.   It is much altered, and has grown into a thriving,
prosperous place.   I get down at a small, clean, Gothic
station-house, and give my check to the agent, who is
baggage-man as well.   I recognize in him an old coaching hanger-on, who has gone over to the enemy.   I take
a seat in the short, thick railway omnibus, and jolt up
to my old hotel.   One day, when I arrived as usual, I
noticed a peculiar expression in the face of this agent.
As he took my check, he said to me confidentially :

" He's come back, sir ! "

"Who, Dick?" I asked.

"Mister Ross!"

As he said this, he pointed to the driver's seat of the omnibus, and glancing up, I saw the Major, looking much older, with the reins in his hand.

"He can see it now, sir," said the agent, quietly.

"Yes," I replied, "he can see it now, Dick ; so can we all."

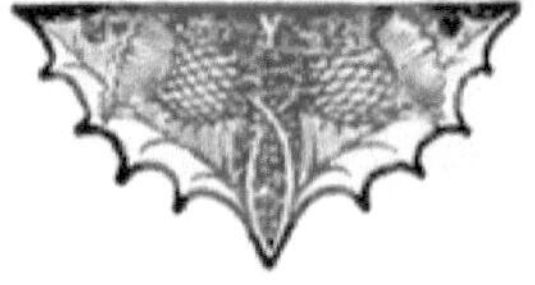

I V.

THE POETRY OF THE RAIL.

Voices of Steam—"Darn your Nonsense!"--The Wine-colored Gentleman—A Corpulent Man's Idea of the Poetry of the Rail—A Lady's Idea—The Commercial Traveller's Idea, etc., etc.

WE used to hear Poetry sing in the hedges, among flowers, and on the bosom of rippling streams. Now it hisses in the boilers of Number Five, Erie Road. It is audible in that demon scream—terrible as the shriek of death to tardy travellers, strolling animals, blundering old men, and rusty switches. Unconsciously seizing an angry fireman's hand at Turner's Junction, I exclaim—

"Voices of Steam! Ye are many-tongued voices of a coming age, a golden one, perhaps; maybe one dyed all crimson with bl———"

"Darn your nonsense!" broke in the genius of Number Five, "here's the one twenty-five starting"—and I went for my ticket. This secured, I took a seat in a first-class coach.

A wine-colored gentleman sat in front of me with a bow-window stomach. He was wrapped as if for a journey to the north pole, with an apoplectic voice that forbade all conversation. After a treaty of legs, I fell to musing on poetry—by-gone and present. "You may talk as you like," I said to myself, "I believe it is all here, just as much as ever it was."

"Listen! friend of the redundant stomach!"

"Oh! curse the noise; I want to go to sleep. Here's the *Tribune*, wonderful article on the Mexican War—Great man, Polk—splendid head—of—hair!"

"Snore, as thou wert wont to snore, O friend of the port-wine countenance; but know that that sound of the engine is like the champ and trample of a thousand horse. It might be Tamerlane riding to conquest, or Alaric thundering at the gates of Rome. Look out, friend of the exuberant bowels, and tell me what you see!"

"A miserable, ugly country, and four iron rails, like black lines ruled in my ledger."

"This, my friend, is the vision of the son of faith. We are gliding on golden rails, that the sunset shines on, and are just about to thread an arch. As we lean back, great clouds of smoke roll around us and grow crimson in the sunlight, and it seems as if we were in the car of the Indian Mythology, gliding away to Paradise."

My friend here presented his flask, with the remark, "Stranger, I think you need another drink!"

That is a corpulent man's idea of the poetry of the road.

I leave him to apoplexy and the *Tribune* newspaper, and move on to a seat nearer the engine. Away we go, with a battling tramp, and whistle and whiz past aston-ished laborers in green meadows; past telegraph wires upon which sit wry-necked sparrows. The smoke of the engine flies like a white banner, rolling away, stooping at last to join the white fog, that wingless sits and broods about the damp autumn fields. We rush through the dark caves of the tunnels—through the barrenness of high and bare embankments, with the force of a steam catapult, or a huge case-shot that is never spent ; like a battering-ram on a long race, for this steam-horse with fire for blood never tires. Swift round curves, up low hills—swift by village church, farm-house and wood, over the river, through fat and lean, rich and poor, meadow and street—for this mad horse never wearies, never tires.

I try another car, containing what seems to be a less aristocratic class. I find merriment here, and wayfaring people who are less afraid to show their honest feelings. They have more feeling, perhaps, and see more of the poetry of the Road. Are they listening with rapt ears, and gazing with steadfast eyes ? No ; a party with high cheek-bones, red, hungry whiskers, and a Western accent, is reading, " Dreadful railway accident near ——— ; fifteen lives lost ; list of killed and wounded." I look out and wonder at the lightning fashion in which we rush into the tunnel !

" This train going east, agent ? "

" No ; goin' west, ma'am ; there's the bell."

" Why didn't you say so before ? Oh, my bundle, give me my bundle ! "

" Too late, marm ; next train west at 2.40 ; three hours to wait. Ladies' waiting-room this way, marm."

That is a lady's ideal of railway poetry.

On we go again ; and presently the baggage-man, in half-overalls, enters our car, and approaches the spruce-looking gentleman in the seat adjoining my own.

"Over a hundred pounds, sir; have to charge you extra baggage on that box."

"Extra charges! why, I've carried that box of samples with a trunk check over every road in the country."

"See here; that's too thin; you hand over the extra dollar, or I'll dump that box into the ditch."

That's the commercial traveller's idea of the poetry of the Road.

"Damp seats, Lord help us! dusty, too—this a first-class coach—it's a stock car. Here, brakeman, do you call this a coach? Curse such a line—give me the narrow-gauge! Window won't go up; d—n the window—door won't shut; curse the door—draught above my head enough to drive a windmill. Here—say—what does the company mean by such a draught? Can't smoke here, eh? Give me the old stage-coach, say I."

That is the old gentleman's ideal of the poetry of the Road.

"Lord bless us, Betty! such a hissing and squeaking and clatter! and that whistle—like a devil's baby! Lor' sakes, how it went through my poor head. An' then getting out at the wrong station to wait four hours for the next train. Say, Betty, give me the old oxen and wagon at home!"

That is the rural lady's idea of the poetry of the Road.

"Ah, sir," said an old gentleman, roaring the words in my ear, "ah, sir, I remember, when I was a boy, being three days and nights on a journey that you do now in four hours. Those were the times, sir, the happy times. No hurry-scurry; no chopping up decent people with trains; no gambling in railway shares, with all the bully-ing and bearing you hear of to-day; no—dear me—such jolting—one can neither sit nor stand—" and the sudden stoppage actually threw the old gentleman into the lap of a spinster near by.

"Sakes alive! Mercy on us! Conductor! brakeman! take him off; the villain is crushing a poor, innocent female!"

And this is the ideal of the poetry of the Road these ancient people take to their homes.

They will not hear me, if I say I saw poetry in the life of the engineer or fireman. On rough days, say, when he cowers behind his screen, and looks out long and steadily through the rain and storm. A divinity? Bless you, no! No Diomed or Hector, but plain Mart Mason, of Number Five, Erie Road. Every crimson star that shines at stations is as familiar to him as the shining taps his fireman keeps so bright and clean. Every emerald fire, and white circle, and red globe, and all the silent voices that speak from headquarters to the brave men on the Road. When the great wind blows, and the lightnings flash, he grasps that handle or throttle there, and you know that power and courage and skill are at the helm. Firmly he holds that helm on those noisy nights, and drives his strong, swift steam-ship on its flaming path, scattering the red-hot ashes of its wrath, as it ploughs on and on. If the rain drives its liquid arrows at him, while you survey the storm from a comfortable seat, he only wipes his great spectacles, and looks out ahead. Then he screws the engine up till it gives a shriek of pain—a long, startling scream, that wakes up the sleepers in the next town, makes them mutter, only to turn again to slumber.

Perhaps the sense of novelty and poetry has left railroads forever, and the humble pen that attempts to record it now may have only its labor for its pains. The sight of a train growing out of a cloud of smoke, the terror of its march, and the battling of its rush, have grown familiar now. The obedient readiness of a train is now a thing of course. The propulsion of lightning, the comet speed, the strange contrast of such spiritual power, controlled by a soiled fellow in overalls—Caliban ruling Ariel—is lost sight of now by the great busy world that is so grossly sunk in its six per cents.

Would it not be better for us to do good, to be kindly and open-hearted ; to see some poetry in life, and not call the air blue fog, and the rose a vegetable? If that railway whistle could have been interpreted to you by an angel, you might have known that its meaning was as prophetic and dreadful as the Judgment trumpet.

Wake up, then ! unlock your cellar, and send a dozen of port to the brave engineer who risked his life to save the train that was bearing you to wife and little ones. And a substantial tribute to the brakeman, who leaped from the train and turned the switch on that awful night in September. Do something for the widow's son, while the father lies a mangled corpse at the scene of the recent accident. Above all, look reverently henceforth at all railroad men, of whatever station—and peace be with you.

V.

EVERYDAY LIFE ON THE RAIL.

AMONG THE ENGINEERS AND FIREMEN.

A Much-abused Class—At the Round House—Engineers' Gossip—
Anecdotes and Incidents—Personal Adventures—Romance and
Humor—A Joke on Bristol—Manning and the Deaf Man—Carter
and the Collector—A Narrow Escape—"Me Pay Pilot, 'ven you
Pay Pig"—Two Disciples of Münchausen—Stedman's Black Cat
—Mort Thompson—Charlie Burlingame's Sermon—"Dutch
Jake" and Princeton Bill—Patty on the Pilot—A Ride for Life—
A Song—A Female Fireman—A Rhyme of the Rail—The Dying
Engineer—How Buxton got up Steam—The English Engineer—
The Locomotive—An Acrostic.

CONFESS that I have long entertained an in-
dulgent feeling towards several classes of men
who are dealt hardly with by common report;
these are hackmen, baggage-men, conductors
of street-cars, and railroad men generally. While I am
willing to admit that these fraternities contain their proportion of black sheep, I am not aware of any peculiar
contagion attaching to their dinginess. I cannot believe
that the extra coat of soot so freely laid on by that ex-
travagant colorist—Public Opinion—can be justified by
appeal to any ordinary models. Few realize, perhaps,
the extent to which they think evil of good neighbors

and industrious public servants. Hackman 1006 occasionally uses language which he regards as merely vigorous and forcible rhetoric—or endeavors on strictly commercial principles to enhance the price paid for his exertions.

A railway conductor invites an impecunious passenger to leave the car at a certain station, and learns with horror that he has insulted a village alderman returning from a metropolitan debauch. Or a brakeman refuses a single gentleman admission to the ladies' car, and is reported for rudeness to an embryo Congressman. An engineer, running a "wild" engine out to some wreck, refuses to take a brace of pedestrians into his cab, and he is called up to answer the complaints of some agricultural committee. Devotion to rules and instructions brings these persons before their self-constituted enemies in an unenviable light, and straightway all hackmen and railway men are condemned.

I once attended a popular lecture upon temperance, illustrated by numerous highly colored prints representing, or professing to represent, the stomachs of drunkards.

The theory appeared to be, that redness is the greatest of all evils, and the stomachs depicted became redder and redder—from the rose-colored blush attached to that bane of teetotalism, the moderate drinker, up to the rubicundity, at once deep and bright, discovered in a man who had died of delirium tremens. At this point there still remained a stomach unaccounted for—one far redder than the rest. The intensely vivid scarlet of its centre passed gradually into maroon on one side, into purple on the other. There was no inscription to show the potatory sins which had been followed by such signal punishment.

At last the lecturer pointed his wand towards this appalling object. The expectant audience was hushed into breathless silence. A pin might have been heard to drop.

"This, ladies and gentlemen"—very slowly and deliberately uttered, as if in enjoyment of our suspense; "this, as I may say, heart-rending diagram presents to you a faithful and accurate delineation of"—pausing again, "a *railroad-man's* stomach!" And then, giving time only for the expiatory sounds, and for the rustle of subdued but general movement which accompany the release of an assembly from highly wrought attention, he proceeded to denounce those persons who, by riding on railways, afforded to the attachés thereof the means of rubifying their digestive organs.

I am not prepared to say as to the effect he produced upon others, but for myself, I was sufficiently struck by the injustice of the sweeping accusation which the words conveyed, to turn with no small disgust from the glib fanatic through whose lips they passed. From this small incident, I date the origin of an involuntary regard, since confirmed by many incidents, for a worthy class who have suffered unduly in the estimation of their fellow-men. I am always ready to defend them from so silly a charge, for it should be known, that no person given to excessive indulgence in any of the small vices, can find employment to-day in any department of the railway service. There are black sheep now and then, as we confess further on in these pages, but these are exceptions to the rule. There are traces of the Divine hand of the Creator in us all. Whether we look upward or downward in society, if we will only see each other rightly, we can come to no truer conclusion, than that men are good fellows in the main. The bond of fellowship clips all society together, and is a law of Nature, much more powerful than all the laws of all the lands.

With these paragraphs by way of introduction, the reader is invited to mingle with the men of the Road at their various places of rendezvous. We will hear them relate their adventures and spin their yarns in the vernacular of the Road, which, if rude at times, is none the less forcible.

Engineers and firemen are wont to sun themselves, when off duty, at the Turn-Table or in the Round-House, and it is not uncommon to find a score of these brave fellows gathered at a single sitting. A majority are off duty, a few may be waiting to "go on," but there is always time for a yarn, and some one to tell it. If there are no tables to set in a roar, the joke at least goes round. The better class of engineers begin life as apprentices in the shop, and developing into master machinists, go into the cab, familiar with every part of a locomotive, and thoroughly trained in the method of its construction. They are regular subscribers to the various publications that issue in the interest of their branch of the service, and, as a general thing, keep themselves well informed as to current events. The fireman, who goes through a severe apprenticeship, with the hope of some day getting an engine of his own, is usually much attached to his engineer, and the two are inseparable companions. He has little time for intellectual cultivation, and if given to reading at all, rarely gets beyond his local paper, or the cheap sensational novel. But his brasses must shine, and his rods glisten, though even food and rest have to be ignored. Both engineer and fireman become much attached to their engine, and usually christen it with some pet name, by which it becomes known all over the line. They vest it with human faculties, and not unfrequently expect it to give evidence of reciprocal affection. The confidence of the engineer in his locomotive is of the same character as that which binds the lover to his sweetheart, and he will follow it, in time of danger, with the most heroic devotion.

The author finds human nature very much the same on all roads, and everyday life on the Road strikingly similar on all the leading lines. The groups, therefore, that he has gathered, are composed of representative men of many leading lines of railway, the names and characters being genuine in every instance.

"I used to run a locomotive," said Bristol, "on a road branching out from the C., H. & D. at Hamilton, Ohio, and running into Indiana. John Lincoln was superintendent, but I've forgotten what they called that line. Podunk was on that road, a town in Posey County, not unknown to fame. Stopping there one night, I noticed two green-looking countrymen inspecting the locomotive, and giving vent to expressions of astonishment. Finally, one of them looked up to me, and said:

"'Stranger, are this a lokymotive?'

"'Yes; didn't you ever see one before?'

"'Haven't never seed one afore. Me 'n Tom come down to the station to-night, puppuss to see one. This is the feller, ain't he?'

"'Certainly.'

"'What yer call that yer in now?'

"'We call this the cab, and that's the driving wheel.'

"'That black thing yonder's the chimney, 'spose?'

"'Yes, that's the chimney.'

"'Be you the engineer what runs the merchine?'

"' I am the engineer.'

"'Tom,' said the fellow to his mate, after eying me closely for a few minutes, 'it don't take much of a man to be an engineer, do it?'

"That joke was on me."

"I came over from Liverpool," said Manning, when the laughter had subsided, "and gets a engine on the York Central. A bit of a accident 'appened at the other end of the line one day; that is to say, I run my engine over a very respectable gentleman of the neighborhood. When I gits to the end of my run, seems like everybody in the town was at the depot to bother me with questions. I don't say what town it was, as how I don't want to offend no man's feelins. One old gentleman 'arassed me very much, and wouldn't take no hexcuse, so, good-natured like, I told him as how it was.

"' I seed the old gentleman upon the line,' says I, 'walking along with his hands in his pockets, about 'alf a mile ahead, quite comfortable, and I dare say thinking o' nothink like—certainly, not of me, behind him, coming along with a couple of thousand tons at forty miles the hour. So I whistles away merrily—'

"'Good heavens!' cried my listener, 'do you tell me that you whistled when a fellow-creature was placed in circumstances of such imminent peril?'

"' I made my engine whistle,' I hexplained. 'I often speaks of the engine as if it was me, sir. I shrieked, I say, in a manner as was a caution to cats; but not a bit would the old gent get out of the way or turn his head, by which means, I can't help thinking ever since, that he was somehow deaf. We reversed, put our brake on, and turned off our steam, but bless ye, it was ne'er a morsel of use, for we couldn't have pulled up under a

2*

mile at least, and just as we neared him, the poor old
gent turned round and threw up his arms like this—'

"'Gracious goodness, my good man,' says my listener,
'do you mean to say that you ran hover 'im?'

"'Lor' bless ye, sir, why of course we did. We was
down upon 'im in a minute, like one o'clock!'

"The crowd was awful still now till a young commercial traveller observed quite dryly—

"'Yes, sir; the incident as which you have so graphi-
cally described, 'appened to my uncle.'

"My old listener wiped the spersperation from the
top o' his 'ead.

"'He was killed, of course?' he says.

"'No. The hentire train passed over 'im, merely re-
moving the skin from the top of his nose. The engine
threw him on his back between the rails, into a hollow
part of the ballast. If he hadn't been deaf, he would
perhaps have gone mad with the noise.'"

"My name is Carter, and I am an engineer on the
Rondout and Oswego Road. I was bringing in the eastward-bound train not long since, and stopped at Shokan.
I don't know what was up, but the Collector of the town
was on hand with a *posse* of men and a chain, to prevent
the train proceeding any further. The chain was passed
through the back end of the rear car, but before it could
be fastened to anything substantial, I got wind of how
matters stood. I threw the throttle wide open and
started the train with a jump. The effect on that Collector's *posse* was the same as that on the Indians who
attempted to capture a train on the Pacific Road with a
lariat."

"On a certain Tuesday in the year 1871, the down
train on the Bangor and Piscataquis Road was being

made up at Oldtown for connection with the E. and N. A. train. A locomotive of the former line was moving quite swiftly at a short distance from the depot. My name is Watford—Jack Watford, and I was in charge of that locomotive. A lad about seven years of age walked into the centre of the track, unconscious of the approaching engine. Busy with my inside brasses at the time, and moving, as I thought, merely at a depot pace, I failed to keep an eye ahead. The locomotive came rushing along, and the bystanders, horrified at the peril of the boy, shouted wildly to him to run. The discovery of his peril seemed to paralyze his limbs, and terror seemed to root him to the spot. I looked out now— saw the trouble, and shut off, but it was too late. Just as the engine reached the lad, a young man rushed from the crowd to the rescue. He seized the boy as the pilot of the locomotive was within a few feet of the spot; threw him by main force to the platform beside the rails, and by a mighty effort sprang, almost at the same time, clear of the track, apparently grazing the front of the engine as it thundered by. The cheers which greeted his humane achievement were well deserved. The brave fellow who performed this noble act is a young man named Luther Soaper, still living in Oldtown, Maine, about eighteen years of age. I need not tell you why I shall never forget either his name or the brave deed."

"Talking about pilots," says Crotter, "that reminds me of one. Jauriet is master mechanic of the Chicago, Burlington, and Quincy Road, stationed at Chicago, Illinois. He is of French extraction, one of the most accomplished machinists in the country, and the inventor of many valuable improvements in the locomotive. 'Ditto' is the pet name of an engineer on the road, also of French descent.   One time 'Ditto' sold two pigs to Jauriet, but never received his pay.   Well, along came Jauriet's order that every engineer should pay for every pilot he broke.   Two years after the sale of the pigs, 'Ditto' went into Chicago with a broken pilot, and the 'old man' hinted at the pay.   'Ditto,' who was always able to pilot his own canoe, replied—

"'Me pay pilot ven you pay pig!'"

Two of the most incorrigible disciples of Münchausen the author has met in his travels, are now to be found on this same C., B. & Q. Road.   These are the engineers Stedman and "Doc." Merriman.   These men have had many a tilt in the way of spinning yarns, but the boys are as yet unable to decide to whom the ribbon belongs.

"Doc., how about that fast time on the B. & M.?   I heard of it, when I was running into Albany."

"Well, the 'old man'* came to me, and says he, 'Cap, can you make it?'"

"'I kin, if the wheels 'll stick on,' says I.

"'Go ahead then,' says he, 'and I'll get on the way-car.'

"I looked behind after I let her out, and saw his coat-tails sticking straight out, and he standing on the hind steps.   When we reached the down grade, the trucks came off the hind end of the way-car, but we never stopped!   I made it, and the old man said it was the best time ever made on that road!"

"What kept the hind end of that car up, boy?" asked Stedman.

"Well, you see, we was going so fast, that the *wind* held her up all the way!"

---

* This term is always applied to the head of any department.

"Just so," rejoined 'Sted;' "that reminds me of our old black cat. She had twenty-two lives. She used to go down in the cellar and lick up all the old woman's cream. I thought I had her killed once or twice, but she managed to come round again."

" Which ? " inquired Doc.; " the old woman ? "

"No, you limping fool ! the old black cat. Well, finally I broke her to pieces one day against the cellar wall, so she couldn't come together again, and buried her in an old pile of rotten hay, near where some corn and punkins were planted. Next spring the corn came up and the punkins got ripe. One morning the old woman went down in the cellar for her cream, and there was the black cat, licking away as though she hadn't lost a day ! There was a little of the rotten hay sticking to her yet, and out of her body there protruded—"

"There what ? " interrupted Doc.

" Out of her body hung a punkin vine, and a little ways off was a punkin. Further along on that vine was another punkin, and then another, and so on all the way out to that hay pile ! "

"Say, Sted, how fur was it to that hay pile ? "

"Well, I didn't measure, but I should judge about a *mile !* "

" Doc." got down on his game leg, pulled off his cap, and said with warmth—

"Sted, that's an *infernal lie ! !* "

Charlie Clark, an old U. P. man, but now on the North Missouri, said they used to have " Doc's " match out that way. He wouldn't locate him exactly, now that the poor fellow was off, but if the boys had no objection, he would read them a rhyme, from which they could judge for themselves.

MORT THOMPSON.

AN ENGINEER'S RHYME.

" Time against the Pass'nger !
    No, but what's the odds ;
Fifteen minutes yet, you know,
    I'll make it, by the gods.
Throw off the brakes, my Sanders,
    Fill us a quart, my lout ;
Isn't old Sixty lovely,
    She'll jerk it for all that's out.

" You're mighty right, old pardner,
    She's never gin out as yet ;
' Up grade,' you say, my hearty,
    Well, what have you got to bet ?
' Orders,'—damn the orders;
    The fifteen ticks is mine ;
Fill up her belly, Sanders,
    And fetch us a drink o' brine.*

"Bully for you, that's lightning,
    Engineer's steam, you know ;
Afeerd ! get up, you scoundrel,
    Or I'll split you through and throug! .
Here's to you, my old sweetheart,
    Now take a good long breath ;
More fire, my lovely Sanders,
    Why, you look as pale as death.

" That's business, eh ? my Sanders,
    Hear, how she counts the rails ;
' Five minutes,' well, we'll make it,
    Old Sixty never fails.
Here, take your brine, you coward,
    How far to the crossing now ?
All right ; we'll take the chances
    For a fun'ral or a row.

* *Brine.*—The slang name for liquor.

> " What ! only one more minute !
>   Well, I've got another notch ;
> You say you heard 'em whistle—
>   More fire, you onery botch—
> There now, old Sixty's got it,
>   Got the throttle, sleek and clean ;
> Yer—shove us that ere bottle ;
>   What's the use in bein' mean?

. . . .

> . " We picked him up, some dozen rods
>   From where the two trains struck,
> Some twenty killed, I think ; and me,
>   Well, that, you see, was luck.
> I got his place, as was the rule,
>   When Mort went on the shelf ;
> A splendid Engineer he was,
>   But couldn't gauge himself."

" That was the way many a good fellow went in the old time," said Charlie Burlingame of the T., P. & W. Railway. " But the boys are side-tracking whiskey now, for it will beat the oldest man in the world. I ain't ashamed to say that I've quit it forever, and maybe you'd like to know what brought it home to me."

" If it's a sermon, Charlie, make it short, for in twenty minutes I must take old 110 North."

" Jim Styles is one of the oldest engineers in the country, and one of the best of men. He's running on the Ohio and Mississippi now. I fired for him several years, and he taught me all I know about a locomotive.

" It was common to drink at every station in those days, and some of us even went so far as to carry it in the box on the cab. Jim was very fond of his brine, and it often got the better of him. He was a widower with two children ; both girls, one about eighteen, the other eight.

I was a little sweet on the big one, and I believe Jim thought the road was clear, but—well, let me tell it my own way.

"We got to thinking seriously about this brine business at last, and one evening the little girl asked Jim and me to go to a temperance meeting in the town where we both lived. We laughed at the idea at first, but to humor his little pet, the father took her by the hand, and we were all soon seated in the church.

"The address was about individual influence, and pointing right at us he said : 'The little girl sitting on the workingman's knee in front of me, even *she* has influence !' Jim, as if acting under some sort of a spell, jumped on his legs, put the child on the floor, and then striking his hand against his thigh, exclaimed, '*That's true !*' Then, embarrassed at what he had done, took his seat, put the little girl again on his knee, and listened attentively to the speaker. Everybody was taken aback, of course, and some thought he was drunk, but I knew they would never have a chance to say that of Jim Styles again.

"Well, the meeting broke up, and a good many ladies came to kiss Jim's little girl. I pulled out a-ways, for, to tell you the truth, boys, I wasn't used to such scenes. After a bit, the lecturer came to Jim, and asked him what made him act so in the meeting.

"'I am an engineer on your road here,' said Jim ; 'and when I had the South run, I used to go for my brine every night, and seldom returned sober. I had a daughter then, about eighteen years old, a dutiful child, with a warm and affectionate heart. She used to come after me to the beer-shop, and wait outside the door in the cold and wet until I came out, that she might conduct me home. She was afraid, if left to myself, that I might fall and injure myself by the way. She caught a severe cold, poor thing, in this way; it turned to consumption, and she died. I felt her death very much, though I still went to the saloon. But somehow or other, I never liked to go that way alone after she died, especially in the night, and for the sake of company, I used to take with me the little girl whom you saw sitting on my knee to-night. But one night,' Jim went on, 'I was walking along with the little girl, she holding by my coat-tail; and when we got very near the saloon, there was a great noise within, and my little girl shrank back, and said, '*Father, don't go in!*' Vexed with her, I took her up in my arms and proceeded. Just as I was entering the saloon door, I felt a scalding hot tear fall from her eyes. It went to my heart. I turned my back on the saloon. It is now three months ago, and I have never tasted a drop since.'

"When I brought him his engine next morning, he got into the cab with a scrap in his hand. 'Charlie,' says he, 'take that, and learn it by heart.'"

"FATHER, DON'T GO IN!

" A father bore upon his arm
    A girl of tender years;
  She shivered sadly with the cold;
    Her eyes were full of tears.

"I paused to see why she should weep—
    A girl so young and fair—
  And why her father wore a look
    Of horror or despair.

"I did not need to tarry long
    Her tears to understand,
  For on the gin-shop's half-shut door
    The father laid his hand.

> "Loud was the wintry wind without,
>   Loud was the noise within;
> But o'er them all I heard her words,
>   'O father, don't go in!'
>
> "He turned him sternly from the door,
>   And strode along the street,
> Thanking his young deliverer
>   With words and kisses sweet.
>
> "Strong were the few and gentle words
>   The little girl did speak;
> But stronger far the silent tear
>   That trickled down her cheek!"

"Dutch Jake" is the railroad name of a Teutonic engineer on a certain Pennsylvania road that must be nameless here. "Princeton Bill" is the name of a worthy Scotchman, who attends the switches at an important point on the same road. He has been there ever since the road was built. A paralytic attack, or something of that sort, has affected the hinges of his jaw, and they work poorly. He can get up steam easy enough, but his rods are too tight. There is a heap of lost motion on the part of the jaws, before he gets a word out, and when it comes, it comes with a jerk. "Dutch Jake," on the other hand, stutters; his tongue always gets in the way when he talks, especially when he is excited. Jake first met Bill when the latter was fixing a switch to let his train in. Bill attempted to tell Jake that there were some cars to take on there. The jaws struggled, the mouth was all at sea, and the tongue forgot its cunning. Jake gazed first with awe, and hearing no articulate sound, imagined that the switchman was ridiculing his own infirmity. Boiling with rage, he set out to reply. "W—w—w—m—m—m—" was as far as he could get. His face red with the rushing blood, his lips kept moving, but not a word escaped. Bill replied in the same strain, after another "exhaust" or two. Jake was finally emptied of this struggling sentence :

"W—w—*what* i—i—in t—t—th—*hunder's* m—m—*mat*—ter m—m—mit *you?*"

Bill was sure Jake was mocking him, and went for him with both hands. If the boys had not interfered, there would have been a serious fight, for both were stalwart men. As it was, the scene was funny in the extreme.

"My name is George Guernsey, and I am an engineer on the East Tennessee, Virginia, and Georgia Railroad. My fireman's name is Joe Patty, and we both live at Morristown, Tennessee. Joe is just getting well of his injuries, and we think we can beat that pilot yarn one, anyhow. On a Sunday night, in February, 1872, we were coming in with the passenger train, due at Dalton at 7:33 o'clock, P.M. When within a mile of that village, Patty went forward to the front of the engine, to oil the valves of the steam-chest ; and just as he reached the proper place on the bumper, a beam to which the 'cow-catcher' is attached, the engine came in contact with a cow. The force of the train threw the cow upon the beam on which Patty was standing with his back to the cow, and his face fronting the cab. The shock threw him off his feet, but having a firm grasp upon a brace, he held on with the tenacity of a drowning man. He succeeded in maintaining his firm grip, until, with the use of his other hand, he regained his position. The cow, in the meantime, had fallen off into the ditch, dead. Patty's right shoulder and breast were badly bruised, and the

palm of his right hand cut entirely across.   I call that
a fearful ride."

"I think I can beat it," said Curry, "with one of the
most thrilling railroad incidents on record.   It was liter-
ally a Ride for Life.   It occurred on the Oregon and
California Road, between the cities of Portland and
Salem.   I had charge of the down train, and we approached the station at full speed, for we were some
minutes behind.   The road, at this point, runs through a
deep cut, something more than a mile in length, and in
entering it, the road makes a curve, so that an engineer
cannot see entirely through it.   So, as we thundered
along on that 10th of November, 1871, I little thought
what stirring times were upon me.   We had hardly
gotten into the cut, before I saw a woman riding
leisurely through it, and with perfect nonchalance, using
the centre of the track.   She was not more than half
way through the cut, and barely a quarter of a mile
ahead of me.   I whistled 'down brakes,' and then
sounded the warning.

"The woman hearing the peculiar death whistle of the
locomotive, looked over her shoulder, and saw the train
rushing at her.   She did not shriek or faint, nor give up
all hope, but like a true Webfoot, her courage rose equal
to the emergency.   She commenced swinging her riding
whip from one shoulder of her horse to the other, thereby
urging him to exert his utmost speed.   The whip, and
perhaps the shrieking of the steam-whistle, caused the
animal to make excellent time, but the iron horse gained
upon him every moment.

"The quick and nervous whistling caused the passengers to look out of the windows, and when they saw the
lady, the wildest excitement ensued.   Several jumped

forward and seized the bell-rope, as if that would help. The boys at the brakes were exerting all their strength, and you may bet, I was doing all I knew how to stop the train. The woman, too, was doing her level best to make that bit of horse-flesh rise to a Dexter's speed, but all in vain. The locomotive kept gaining on the horse and its rider, and there seemed no further hope.

"There were, perhaps, thirty feet intervening between the cow-catcher and the horse's heels, when, fortunately for the woman, she observed a place a trifle wider than usual, and with a steady rein, she guided the fleeing horse from the track, and endeavored to press him against the wall of the cut in order that the train might pass by without injury. In doing this, the woman was encouraged by Mr. Sam Winans, the conductor, who had ran forward and got out on the locomotive. A few moments more, and the fiery monster poked his nose past the rump of the horse. At this moment Mr. Winans threw his whole force against the animal, and held him until the train stopped. And then went up a rousing cheer of gratification and joy at the escape of the woman from a terrible death."

"Say, give us a rest on this escape and accident business," roared Cully, of the Baltimore & Ohio.

"Here, too," joined in Baker, of the Kansas Pacific; "out our way, we kill people by the score."

"What was that woman's name, Curry?"

"She proved to be a Portland belle, on a visit to a school-mate at one of the smaller stations; a beautiful, dashing, spirited girl, about—well, I think, sixteen."

"I say, what was her name?"

"Oh! ah! Well, her name is *Mrs. Curry* now!"

Whew-w! All right, John, let her out! [Sings.]

"Let her out !   Let her out !
   Sling care to the dogs;
Keep an eye on the throttle,
   And an eye on the frogs.
Watch the flags, and the signals,
   Red, yellow, and green;
We're on time, and as free
   A-as e'er Rover-r has been."

"Good enough," "bully for you," and similar expressions came with the applause.

Tounley, of the New York Central, said it was time for a little more romance.   "To begin at the commencement, I will state, that early in 1860, a young lady in the city of Auburn, N. Y., the daughter of wealthy parents, eloped with a young man named Niles, a railroad engineer, and the twain proceeded to Cleveland, Ohio. They were pursued by an infuriated brother of the young lady, and to avoid detection, after the marriage ceremony had been performed, the young lady arrayed herself in male attire.   In this disguise, and while selling apples on the street, she passed her brother several times without being recognized.   Early in the war, the couple went South to Nashville, Tenn., where Niles got an engine on the Nashville & Chattanooga Road.   His wife, still keeping up her disguise, shipped with him as fireman.   Between Nashville and Chattanooga, a shot fired by a rebel inflicted a serious wound upon the engineer, and he was taken to the Government hospital, at Murfreesboro, Tenn.   His wife followed, and to her careful nursing, Niles owes his life.   When sufficiently recovered to endure the hardships of travelling, they returned to Cleveland.   A few months later the alleged gold discoveries at Mandock, Canada, attracted them thither, and the wife accompanied her husband, still in masculine garments.

The vicissitudes of her career, exposed to hardships and accidents, were too severe, however, and a few weeks since, she died at Cleveland, after a brief illness. She wore male attire successfully for ten years. Niles, who now resides at Oshkosh, Wisconsin, is about 40 years of age, and does not refer to the heroic devotion of his wife but in terms of the warmest admiration."

"When a certain party sued our Company for damages," said a fireman, "engineers from all the roads were summoned to appear at the trial. Among others, Jauriet, our master mechanic. One of the lawyers asked the question :

" ' Can you get an engine up to a car, without moving the car ; if so, how ? '

" A number of engineers answered in various ways, until it came to Jauriet.

" ' Well, sir, I should just get a couple of pinch-bars, and *pinch* her up.' "

"At another time," said Malone, "there was a suit against the road at Peoria ; something about damages for setting fire to somebody's hay. Our Billy Wilson was a witness, and what he don't know about a locomotive ain't worth knowing. Well, the lawyer for the farmer wanted to have some particular point about an engine explained. Wilson had gone over it two or three times, but couldn't get it through the lawyer. The lawyer finally confessed that he couldn't understand it.

" ' I am not at all surprised,' rejoined Wilson. 'Anybody can become a lawyer, but it requires brains and experience to learn a locomotive.' "

Chilson, an engineer over fifty years of age, was killed on the C., B. & Q. Road, October 14, 1869. Jones said he would try and give an account of the sad occurrence.

" It was during the Fulton County Fair, and extra trains were the order of the day. Our train was the regular passenger, running from Galesburg to Rushville, with orders to meet the extra passenger at Canton ; then to run to Bryant for No. 20—Kimbal's freight. We side-tracked at Canton, and while there the telegraph operator received orders to hold passenger for No. 20. He started out with the order, and seeing the passenger coming, thought it was Kimbal's freight. He returned, failing to deliver the order—for if it was the freight, the order was useless. But it was the passenger, and the operator did not discover his mistake until the passenger came up to the platform, and had pulled out again. He ran after the train with the order, but, of course, it was a useless chase. We had orders to run to Bryant and 'hurry up,' and the freight had orders to 'hurry up' to Canton. Both trains were running at full speed ! They met on the short curve in the timber, about three miles below Canton.

" They saw nothing of each other until separated by only fifteen rods. Chilson called for brakes, and Brooks, his fireman, jumped off. He reversed his engine, and with one foot against the boiler-head, and both hands firmly grasping the throttle, he braced himself for his fate, and stood there until they struck !

> " ' Down brakes ! '   One splendid, hard-held breath,
>   And lo ! an unknown name,
>   Strode into sovereignty from death,
>   Trailing a path of fame.
>   .   .   .   .   .
>
> " Home—but his foot grew granite fast ;
>   Wife—yet he did not reel ;
>   Babe—ah, they tugged ! but to the last
>   He stood there true as steel.

" When we picked him up, life was not extinct. His

face was mashed, and his body fearfully scalded, presenting a horrid spectacle.   We carried him to a hotel in Canton, just across from the depot there, and laid him on a cot in the office.   The landlord complained of being full, and that it would injure his trade to have this man here.   He had friends in Canton, rich and well-to-do, but they refused to take him in.   Finally, we bore the sufferer to an old vacant house, where he died in great agony in four or five hours.   His conductor, baggage-man, and brakemen were with him to the last.   His last words were, 'Has the old man no friend in Canton who will give him a bed to die on?'

"Both engines were smashed up, and two or three ladies were slightly bruised, but I believe the Company thought poor Chilson was the greatest loss.   The telegraph operator went crazy, and Mr. Hitchcock assisted his family out of his own private purse.

"No, he refused to jump; he had often been heard to say that it was an engineer's duty to stand by his engine under all circumstances."

"I think," said Phil Potter, feelingly, "that we have as brave men, men as much devoted to duty, all about us, as those who have been celebrated in prose and verse. Here are some verses appropriate to the death of Chilson.

"INTO THE JAWS OF DEATH.

" The wind blows cold, the stars shine bright,
  The ice-bound river glistens,
Where flying onward, into night,
  The life-train madly hastens.

"On, on, past hamlet, town and wood,
  That fringe the frozen river,
As some infuriate demon would
  Glide, roaming on forever.

8

"On into night, with fiery eye,
    Its sinuous body dashes,
With iron muscles, pulse of steam,
    It plunges, screams, and crashes.

"Yet a great soul inspires the hands
    That guide its onward motion,
As starting from Atlantic lands,
    It seeks the Western ocean.

"And steady stands the engineer,
    True to his fearful duty;
And glancing back among the cars,
    Where rides babes, age, and beauty.

"He feels that loving human hearts
    Are in his watch and keeping;
And though he guides to joy or death,
    They trust him by their sleeping.

"Then firmer grasps the iron bar;
    His noble heart thrills faster—
Great God! is that the signal light
    That tells of near disaster?

"Then on the air the whistle shrieks
    Like some lost soul despairing,
And onward to its death-doom flies,
    Past earthly aid and caring.

"The Spartan hands reverse the valve—
    'Put on the patents, Nick!
We'll do the best we can to save
    Our passengers; be quick!'

"The crisis comes, 'Say, will you jump?'
    A glance, but no replying;
Then fixed his eyes where duty called,
    Though his path led to dying.

"A crash ! a flame leaps into air,
 And laps the sundered timbers,
And wailing voices echoed there,
 Where souls died with the embers.

"And babes and youth, and kindly age,
 And manhood's stronger glory,
Returned to him who seals the page
 · Of each such frightful story.

"And he who clasped the guiding bars
 To death, unswerved from duty,
Shall wear in Heaven the crown of stars
 That waits heroic beauty.

" For Christ, who died that men might live,
 And dying claimed our loving,
To man who dies for men, will give
 His welcome and approving."

"Say, Doc.," asks one, "what was the name of that locomotive you run on the B. & M. Road, two years ago? I heard that you were on that road awhile."

"Why," replies Doc., "that was the old ' *Ottumwa*,' 16+24 inch cylinder, 4 foot 6 in. wheel. You may talk about your rides and your fast time, but just let me tell you what happened to me once on that road."

The boys wink at each other and get into position.

"Well, I was put onto the 'Ottumwa' one day, and as the boys told me she wasn't very slow, thought I would try her a string or two. My conductor came around, and says he—

"'This time has got to be made, and you'll have to let her out to do it.'

"So I started. She moved off quite easy, and after we got out of town, I let her out a little. I had been jogging along I thought about on time, when Hilton, my conductor, came over, and says he :

" ' Old man, you will find by the time you get up the next grade, that you won't have much time left to go to L——for the passenger.'

"So I gave her another notch, and when I got to the top of the grade, I see, about a mile ahead, a good half mile of solid beef.*   I took out my watch and saw that I was forty-five minutes late.   Says I to myself : Doc., faint heart never won fair lady, and I told my fireman to shove in some more diamonds.†   I gave her a little of what goes through the boiler and opened her feed-box. When we passed through the beef it was all ready for the butchers.   I cut it up to order.   Superintendent said I was too much of a butcher."

"You don't mean to say, Doc., that you went down the grade so fast that you killed the stock ? "

" No, I don't say so, but I know the foreman of the Round-House ordered some of the wipers to drive off that *steer* that stood by the coal chute.   He mistook the ' Ottumwa ' for a steer.   They took eleven skins off the pilot !

"I've got to finish this packing now, boys, but *that's so !*"

"When ' Doc.' left the road here," said Stedman, " I took his engine, the old ' 51.'   That locomotive could drink more and do her work under it, than any critter I ever drove.   But I never could get her by Jim Aiken's at Mendota, until she had her *brine*.   Doc. had her pretty well trained.   I tried her one day, working her wide open,

---

* " Solid beef."—Cattle.   † " Diamonds."—Coal.

with 150 pounds of steam, but she stalled at Jim's sure. Couldn't get her by until we had our *brine !* Ask Frank Stone !"

"There are little incidents occurring on the Road," said Charlie Cossom, "as well worth the telling as the latest history of adultery and murder. A little girl wandered on the track of the Delaware Railway as a freight train of nineteen cars was approaching. As it turned the sharp top of the grade, opposite St. George's, the engineer saw the child for the first time, blew 'down brakes,' and reversed his engine. But it was too late to slacken its speed in time, and the poor baby got up, and, laughing, ran to meet it. 'I told the conductor,' says the engineer, 'if he could jump off the engine, and running ahead, pick the child up before the engine reached her, he might save her life, though it would risk his own, which he did. The engine was within one foot of the child when he secured it, and they were both saved. I would not run the same risk of saving a child again, by way of experiment, for all Newcastle county, for nine out of ten might not escape. He took the child to the lane, and she walked to the house, and a little girl was coming after it when he left." The honest engineer, having finished his day's run, sits down the next morning and writes the homely letter to the father of the child, "in order that it may be more carefully watched in future," and thanking God "that himself and the baby's mother slept tranquilly last night, and were spared the life-long pangs of remorse." It does not occur to him to even mention the conductor's name, who, he seems to think, did no uncommon thing in risking his own life, unseen and unnoticed, on the solitary road, for a child whom he would never probably see again. The moral of the story to him was, apparently, that mothers should keep their children off the track.

"Some one has put the incident very cleverly in rhyme, which I have carried in this old book ever since:

"A RHYME OF THE RAIL.

"BY A RETIRED ENGINEER.

"Now my running days are over,
  The engineer needs rest;
My hand is growing shaky,
  There's a queer pain in my breast;
But here near the old turn-table,
  I'll tell a tale of the Road,
That'll ring in my head forever,
  Till it rests beneath the sod.

"Lumbering on in the twilight,
  The night was dropping her shade,
And the 'Gladiator' labored,
  Climbing the top of the grade.
The train was heavily laden,
  So I let my engine rest;
Making the grading slowly,
  Till we reached the upland's crest.

"I held my watch to the lamplight—
  Ten minutes behind the time!
Lost in the slackened motion
  Of the up-grade's heavy climb;
But I knew the miles of the prairie
  That stretched a level track,
So I touched the gauge of the boiler,
  And pulled the lever back.

"Over the rails a-gleaming,
  Thirty an hour or so,
The engine leaped like a demon,
  Breathing a fiery glow;

A RHYME OF THE RAIL
PAGE 54

But to me—a-hold of the lever—
　　It seemed a child alway,
Ready to mind me ever,
　　And my lightest touch obey.

"I was proud, you know, of my engine,
　　Holding it steady that night,
And my eye on the track before us,
　　Ablaze with the drummond light,
We neared a well-known cabin,
　　Where a child of three or four,
As the up-train passed oft called me,
　　A playing around the door.

"My hand was firm on the throttle
　　As we swept around the curve,
When something afar in the shadow
　　Struck fire through every nerve.
I sounded the brakes, and crashing
　　The lever down in dismay ;
Great God ! within eighty paces
　　Ahead, was the child at play.

"One instant—one moment, and only
　　The world flew around in my brain,
I smote my hand on my forehead
　　To keep back the terrible pain.
The train I thought flying forever,
　　With mad, irresistible roll;
The cries of the dying—the night wind
　　Swept into my shuddering soul.

"Then I stood on the front of the engine,
　　How I got there I never could tell,
My feet planted down on the cross-bar,
　　Where the cow-catcher slopes to the rail.
One hand firmly locked on the coupler,
　　And one held out in the night,
While my eye gauged the distance, and measured
　　The speed of our slackening flight.

"My mind—thank God !—it was steady,
  I saw the curls of her hair,
And the face that, turning in wonder,
  Was lit by the deadly glare.
I know little more—but I heard it—
  The groan of the anguished wheels,
And remember thinking—the engine
  In agony trembles and reels.

"One rod ! To the day of my dying
  I shall think the old engine reared back,
And as it recoiled with a shudder,
  I swept my hand over the track.
Then darkness fell over my eyelids,
  But I heard the surge of the train,
And the poor old engine creaking,
  As racked by a deadly pain.

"They found us, they said, on the gravel,
  My fingers clutched in her hair ;
And she in my bosom struggling
  To nestle securely there.
We are not much given to crying,
  We men who run on the Road,
But I wept o'er the little darling,
  And sent up a prayer to God."

Hank Fales, of the Hudson River Road, hoped the boys wouldn't pull out until he had his turn. "We may never meet again," he said, and he wanted to offer a tribute to brave old Jake Vaughn, his old engineer. "He was lost in a frightful accident on our road, and his death was singularly affecting. When he was told that he could not survive, and that it was impossible for his wife to reach him before he died, he called Bill, his fireman, and asked him to write a letter for him to his wife. Bill thought a great deal of his engineer, and he afterwards put it in rough rhyme, and I keep the slip by me all the time. Jake called his engine 'Fleetwing,' and sometimes his 'wife.' He begged us, with his dying breath, not to blame *Fleetwing*, but the broken rail.

"THE DYING ENGINEER.

"A FIREMAN'S RHYME.

"Bill, I'm on the down grade now,
  And can't reach ary brake ;
Guess old '*Fleetwing's*' time is up,
  Leastwise, it's up with Jake.
Jake Vaughn—yes, write it down in full,
  She'll know what to infer—
You see I called ' Fleetwing' my wife
  Before I married *her*.

"Torpedoes—never mind—no use,
  Nor Sand—I'm running wild ;
Say, Bill, just scratch another word,
  One for our little child !
'Pull her over '—no, what use,
  On our side of the hill ;
Just hold her level for a spell,
  What! you ain't *crying*—Bill?

"' Broke '—you're right.   It seems to me
  She's lost a rod or beam ;
No fire, no water—say, my boy,
  How can you get your steam ?
Head-light's all agog, besides,
  And swimming in the wind ;
Say, Bill, afore you write that out,
  What's comin' on behind?

"Them bridges—no, the Hudson Road
  Ain't much on bridges, eh !
There'll be an awful smash-up, boy,
  Right here, some other day.

3*

> An' tell her ' *Fleetwing* ' ain't to blame,
>   Only she come it strong;
> Down grade, you see, yes—name in full,
>   Your'n truly, Jacob Vaughn.
>
> " Bill, I'm on the down grade now,
>   There's no way now to stop;
> The order's come for Fleet and me
>   To hurry to the shop.
> ' Lay off a trip,' you're right, my boy,
>   A long trip with the dead ;
> Just tell her, Bill, Jake ain't afeard
>   Of anything ahead."

" I formed the acquaintance of Mr. Tom Hoyle in the air, at an altitude, I should conjecture, of about 5,000 feet. We were sent up as *avant courriers* by a locomotive that subsequently retired from business ; so when we returned to Mother Earth, both employer and employment were gone. I was not allowed the pleasure of a formal introduction to Mr. Hoyle during that brief journey, but having been picked up in his embrace, I have always hugged the impression that he had a hold on my friendship for life. He was an English engineer, or 'driver' as they are called there, and I had been allowed a few miles on the stoker's seat, in order to watch Hoyle at his work. He was a little over anxious to make a good display of his skill and the power of his engine, and his original ideas exploded, with the result as hinted above.

" We were carried to a farm-house near by, where every care and attention were extended. It was during this forced confinement that I learned much about driving engines. Hoyle would get his splinters arranged comfortably, and sometimes go on for hours, in this way :

" 'When a man has a liking for a thing, it's as good as being clever. In a very short time I became one of the best drivers on the line. This was allowed. I took a pride in it, you see, and liked it. No, I didn't know much about the engine, scientifically, as you call it; but I could put her to rights if anything went out of gear— that is to say, if there was nothing broken—but I couldn't have explained how the steam worked inside. Starting an engine is just like drawing a drop of gin. You turn a handle and off she goes; then you turn the handle the other way, put on the brakes, and you stops her. There's not much more in it, so far. It's no good being scientific and knowing the principle of the engine inside; no good at all. Fitters who know all the ins and outs of the engine make the worst of drivers. That's well known. They know too much. It's just as I've heard of a man with regard to his inside; if he knew what a complicated machine it is, he would never eat or drink, or dance, or run, or do anything, for fear of bursting something. So it is with fitters. But we who are not troubled with such thoughts, we go ahead.

" ' But starting an engine is one thing, and driving of her is another. Any one, a child, almost, can turn on steam and turn it off again ; but it ain't every one that can keep an engine well on the road, no more than it ain't every one who can ride a horse properly. It is much the same thing. If you gallop a horse right off for a mile or two, you take the wind out of him, and for the next mile or two you must let him trot or walk. So it is with an engine. If you put too much steam on to get over the ground at a start, you exhaust the boiler, and then you'll have to crawl along till your fresh water boils up. The great thing in driving is to go steady, never to let your water get too low nor your fire too low. It's the same with a kettle. If you fill it up when it's about half empty, it soon comes to a boil again. Another thing : you should never make spurts unless you are detained and lose time. You should go up an incline and down an incline at the same pace. Sometimes a driver will waste his steam, and when he comes to a hill, he has scarcely enough to drag him up. When you're in a train that goes by fits and starts, you may be sure there is a bad driver on the engine. That kind of driving frightens passengers dreadfully. When the train, after rattling along, suddenly slacks speed when it ain't near a station, it may be in the middle of a tunnel, the passengers think there is danger. But generally it's because the driver has exhausted his steam.' "

" Barney Butz is the oldest locomotive engineer in the United States. He now runs an engine on the Reading (Pa.) Railroad. He was born in Conyngham, Luzerne county, Penn., about the year 1835 or 1836. In 1847 he was running an engine from Parryville to Weatherly, the 'planes' being then in operation. The cars were drawn up to the planes by a stationary engine. I am on the Reading Road now, and they tell a good story of Barney's readiness in case of an emergency. One day his engine would not steam well, and he was likely to be overtaken by a passenger train before he could reach the switch. Seeing a good-sized porker beside the track, he jumped from the engine—the train moving slowly— seized the pig, cut its throat, and stuffed it into the furnace. The fat of the pig was better than kindling wood, and in a very short time, Barney and his train were out of danger."

ACROSTIC.

Lo! the long railway train winding and narrow,
  Over the tressle-work into the city,
Coming too sure with the speed of an arrow,
  On to its wreck without warning or pity.
Moments seem passing the mastery of mortal—
  Only a miracle retrieves the error ;
Thunders the bridge at its innermost portal,
  Increasing and nearing and deepening in terror,
Voices would reach to the gateway of heaven
Ere this wild roar by a cry could be riven.

Even now, steady now, swift go as lightning,
  Nerving his arm with its mightiest force,
Gigantic the sinews like iron thews tightening,
  In driving the mad engine back on her course.
Now answers the signal of danger already—
  Easier backward now, safer and faster—
Every soul blessing the courage so steady,
Redeeming their awe-stricken lives from disaster.

VI.

GUELDEN'S LAST DRINK.

HAVE travelled this road every day of my life, ever since it was laid, in charge of the San Francisco, the prettiest and best engine on the line. It was a South-western road, running, as we will say, from A. to Z. At A. my mother lived, at Z. I had the sweetest little wife in the world, and a baby, the very image of its pa. I had always had a dollar or two put by for a rainy day, and the boys spoke of me as an odd kind of a man. To be shut up with an engine, watching with all your eyes, and heart and soul, don't make a conscientious man talkative, and I never squandered my leisure, spinning yarns and listening to railway jokes in the Round-House. My wife's name was Josephine, and I called her 'Joe.'

"I never belonged to any of the railway clubs or other organizations, and never should, if it hadn't been for Granby. Granby was a nephew of our division superintendent, and it's a failing with we men of the Road that we like to be noticed by the fellows at headquarters, if only permitted to touch the hem of their garments. Granby was a showy fellow, and often rode with me from A. to Z. He had a good opinion of me, and as far as I know, we were good friends. Once he said to me :

" 'You ought to belong to the Railway Scientific Club, Guelden.'

" ' Never heard of it,' said I.

" ' We meet once a fortnight,' he replied, 'and have a jolly good time. We want practical, thinking men of your sort, and I'll propose you, if you like.'

" I was fond of such things, and I had ideas that I fancied might be worth something. But the engineer don't have many nights or days to himself, and the club would have one evening a fortnight from Joe, I said.

" ' I will ask her. If she likes it, yes.'

" ' Ask whom ? ' he said.

" ' Joe,' said I.

" ' If every man had asked his wife, every man's wife would have said, "Can't spare you, my dear," and we should have no club at all,' said Granby.

" But I made no answer. At home I told Joe. She said :

" ' I shall miss you, Ned ; but you do love such things, and if Granby belongs to it they must be superior men.'

" So I said yes, and Granby proposed me. Thursday fournight I went with him to the rooms. The real business of the evening was the supper.

" I had always been a temperate man. I did not know what effect wine would have on me, but coming to drink more of it than I ever had before at the club table, I found it put steam on. After so many glasses I wanted to talk, and after so many more, I did.

"I seemed like somebody else, the words were so ready. My ideas came out and were listened to. I made sharp hits and indulged in repartee, told stories, and even came to puns. I heard somebody say, 'Granby, by George, that's a man worth having. I thought him dull at first.' Yet I knew it was better to be quiet Ned Guelden, with his ten words an hour, than the wine-made wit I was.

"I was sure of it when three months after I stumbled up-stairs to find Joe waiting for me with her baby on her breast.

"'You've been deceiving me,' said Joe; 'I suspected it, but wasn't sure. A Scientific Club couldn't smell like a bar-room.'

"'Which means that I do,' said I.

"'And look like one,' said Joe, as she locked herself and baby up in the spare-bedroom.

"One night I was dressed in my Sunday suit, ready to go to the Club, when Joe stood before me.

"'Ned,' said she, 'I never had a fault to find with you before. You've been kind and good and loving always; but I should be sorry we ever met if you go on in this way. Don't ask what I mean—you know.'

"'It's only Club night,' said I.

"'It will grow,' said she.

"Then she put her arms around my neck.

"'Ned,' said she, 'do you think a thing so much like a bolted and strapped down demon as steam is, is fit to put into the hands of a drunken man? And some day, mark my words, not only Thursday night, but all the days of the week will be the same. I have often heard you wonder what the feelings of an engineer who has about the same as murdered a train full of people, must be, and you'll know if you don't stop where you are. A steady hand and a clear head have been your blessing all these years. Don't throw them away. Ned, if you don't care for my love, don't ruin yourself.'

"My little Joe. She spoke from her heart, and I bent over and kissed her.

"'Don't be afraid, child; I'll never pain you again.'

"And I meant it; but at twelve o'clock that night I felt that I had forgotten my promise and my resolution.

"I couldn't get home to Joe. I made up my mind to sleep on the Club sofa, and leave the place for good the next day. Already I felt my brain reel as it had never done before. In an hour I was in a kind of stupor. It was morning. A waiter stood ready to brush my coat. I saw a grin on his face. My heart seemed ready to burst; my hand trembled; I looked at my watch; I had only just five minutes to reach the depot!

"Joe's words came to my mind. Was I fit to take charge of an engine? I was not fit to answer. I ought to have asked some sober man. As it was, I only caught my hat and rushed away. I was just in time.

"The San Francisco glistened in the sun. The cars were filling rapidly. From my post I could hear the people talking—bidding each other good-by, and promising to write and come again. Among them was an old gentleman I knew by sight—one of the shareholders; he was bidding two timid girls adieu.

"'Good-by, Kitty; good-by, Lue,' I heard him say; 'don't be nervous. The San Francisco is the safest engine on the line, and Guelden the most careful engineer. I would not be afraid to trust every mortal to their keeping. Nothing could happen wrong with the two together.'

"I said, 'We'll get through it somehow, and Joe shall

never talk to me again.   After all, it was easy enough.'
I reeled as I spoke.   I heard the signal.   We were off.

"Five hours from L. to D.; five hours back again.   I
knew now, that on the last run I should be myself again.
I saw a flutter, and never guessed what it was, until we
had passed the down train at the wrong place.   Two
minutes more, and we should have had a collision.
Somebody told me, and I laughed.   I heard the share-
holder say, respectfully :

"'Of course, Mr. Guelden, you know what you are
about ?'

"Then I was alone, and wondering whether I should go
faster or slower.   I did something, and the cars rushed on
at a fearful rate.   The same man who had spoken to me
before was standing near me.   I heard the question—

"'How many miles an hour are we making?'   I
didn't know.

"Rattle, rattle, rattle !   I was trying now to slacken the
speed of the San Francisco.   I could not remember what
I should do—was it this or that—faster or slower?   I
was playing with the engine like a child.

"Suddenly there was a horrible roar—a crash.   I was
flung somewhere.   I was in the water.   By a miracle I
was sobered, not hurt.   I gained the shore.   I stood
upon the ground between the track and the river's edge,
and there gazed at my work.

"'The engine was in fragments, the cars in splinters ;
dead and dying and wounded were strewn around—men
and women and children—old age and youth.   There
were groans and shrieks of despair.   The maimed cried
out in pain ; the uninjured bewailed their dead ; and a
voice, unheard by any other, was in my ear, whispering
'Murder.'

"The news had gone to A., and people came thronging down to find their lost ones. Searching for an old man's daughter, I came to a place under the trees, and found five bodies lying there, all in their rigid horror—an old woman, a young one, a baby, and two tiny children. Was it fancy—was it pure fancy, born of my anguish— they looked like—oh, Heaven! they were my wife, my children—all cold and dead.

"How did they come on the train? What chance had brought this about? No one could answer. I groaned, I screamed, I clasped my hands, I tore my hair, I gazed in the good old face of her who gave me birth, on the lovely features of my wife, on my innocent children. I called them by name; there was no answer. There never could be—there never would be.

"*A whistle!* Great God! Onward up the track thundered another train! Its red eyes glared upon me; I threw myself before it; I felt it crush me to atoms!

.   .   .   .

"'His head is extremely hot,' said somebody.

"I opened my eyes and saw my wife—

"'How do you feel?' said she; 'a little better?'

"I was so rejoiced and astonished by the sight of her that I could not speak at first. She repeated the question.

"'I must be crushed to pieces,' said I, 'for the train went over me; but I feel no pain.'

"'There he goes about that train again,' said my wife. "Why, I tried to move—there was nothing the matter with me. I was in my own room; opposite to me a crib in which my child was asleep. My wife and child were safe. Was I delirious, or what could it be?

"'Joe,' I cried, 'tell me what has happened.'

"'It's nine o'clock,' said Joe. 'You came home in such a state from the Club that I couldn't wake you. You weren't fit to manage steam, and risk people's lives. The San Francisco is half way to A., I suppose, and you have been frightening me half to death with your dreadful talk.'

" And Joe began to cry.

" It was only a dream ; only an awful dream. But I had lived through it as though it were a reality.

" 'Is there a Bible in the house, Joe?' said I.

" 'Are we heathens?' asked Joe.

" 'Give it to me this moment, Joe.'

" She brought it, and I put my hand on it and took the oath (too solemn to be repeated here), that what had happened never should occur again. And if the San Francisco ever comes to grief, the verdict will not be, as it has so often been, 'The engineer was drunk.'"

VII.

THE MANIAC'S RIDE.

BY A RETIRED ENGINEER.

T is ten years ago, boys, since that little affair happened near the P—— Bridge, but it never comes back to my mind without making me shudder. I was running old No. 20 between H—— and B—— at that time, and was regarded as a careful and reliable man. The road was in splendid condition; my engine had just come out of the shop, thoroughly repaired, and altogether the duties were pleasant and easy enough, as duties in our line go.

"It was on a Sunday morning, I remember, and I had backed down from the round-house to the station at H——, coupled on to my train, and was waiting for the passengers to finish their breakfast. My wife had brought the children down to the depot, as was her custom every Sunday morning, and I was playing with them on the platform, while the passengers came hurrying out, one by one. I was just giving one of my youngsters a parting hug, and wondering why my fireman stayed so long at his breakfast, when all of a sudden I saw a man —a stranger to me—jump stealthily but quickly upon the engine and pull the throttle ! The wheels creaked, the train moved, and the loiterers on the platform jumped hurriedly on board. Quick as thought, I placed the child in its mother's arms, and in another instant was face to face with the intruder.

"A single look sufficed to tell me that he meant mischief. A man of herculean stature, bareheaded, and scantily attired, with eyes glaring like coals of fire, with long hair falling down upon his shoulders, with sleeves rolled up above his elbows, displaying brawny, muscular arms, and with a wild, excited laugh upon his countenance, was before me, pulling the bell-rope violently, and taking apparently but little notice of my presence. In less time than I have been telling it, I had closed with him.

"'What are you doing ? Are you crazy ?' I cried.

"He looked at me for a minute, with that same devilish leer in his eye, and pushing me back as if I were a feather, said, abstractedly :

"'Don't annoy me now, I beg of you ; I'm busy.'

"I summoned all my strength, and rushed upon him again, for by this time the train was well in motion, and the rate of speed was momentarily increasing.

"He let go of the bell-rope, and, as I seized him by the arms, grasped mine in turn, and holding me in a vice-like grip, looked me full in the face.

"'Didn't I tell you,' said he, in a harsher voice than before, 'that I didn't wish to be annoyed.'

"I glanced into his face closely as he spoke, and then, for the first time, the horrible truth broke in upon me— *the man was mad !*

"I felt a shudder run through my veins, and great drops of cold sweat stood out upon my face, as in a single moment I realized the dreadful danger before me. I thought of my little children, whose kisses were yet warm upon my face, and of that long train behind us, full of passengers so little suspecting their peril. All the stories I had ever heard or read of crazy people and their freaks flashed through my mind in that instant, as I felt myself pushed backwards to destruction.

"But no; quietly seating me upon the bench, on the other side, he loosened his hold, and returned to his post, saying, in the same abstracted voice as at first:

"'There, now! I don't want to be bothered!'

"By this time we were dashing along at a pretty rapid rate, and I could see that he knew how to handle the engine almost as well as I did myself. I jumped to my feet, and a third time he leaned forward to reach the throttle lever.

"'For God's sake, stop her!' I exclaimed. 'Who are you?'

"'Me?' he answered, with a quiet laugh. 'I'm a practical engineer, working in the interests of science. I've studied for years, and years, and years, and now I want to make an experiment! Don't interrupt me!'

"He gave me another look, full of wild determination, and then burst into a fit of hilarious laughter.

"'Good! good! good!' he cried. 'But she'll do better, better, better, by and by! Now—she flies!'

"He gave the throttle lever another jerk; the engine shot away faster than ever, and trees, telegraph poles, fences, and houses went by like lightning.

"For a moment I sunk down upon my seat in utter despair. To measure strength with the madman was, I saw, simply suicidal.   A struggle could only result in certain destruction to myself, and probable destruction to the train and all on board of it.   But one possible chance of regaining control of the engine presented itself, and that would require all the nerve and coolness I had in me.   I must draw him into conversation, and watch for my opportunity to gain advantage either of his credulity or his vanity sufficiently to induce him to give me his place.   Once there, I must trust to Providence and my own courage to prevent further mischief.

"I scanned him closer than ever for a moment or two. He seemed to have entirely forgotten my presence ; now jumping up, and laughing, and clapping his hands ; now letting more steam on ; now looking eagerly out ahead, and murmuring : 'Better, better, better still !'

"My heart was thumping against my chest, as I said :

"'You seem to understand your business pretty well, anyhow, my friend.   Been long at it ?'

"He looked at me, looked away again, but did not answer.

"'I see you are a good practical engineer, as you say,' I continued.   'How long have you been at the business ?'

"'Years, and years, and years, I tell you !' he answered.   'It was I who fitted out Pegasus, the winged steed.   I who gave that fellow, Icarus, the wax wings ; but he flew too near Old Sol, and they melted and let him down into the water.   Ha ! ha ! ha !'

"'I wish I only had your experience at it,' said I ; 'what a team we'd make together, pulling in the cause of science, eh ?'

"A new light, an expression of unspeakable delight, lighted up his face as, catching my words, he turned toward me and, looking me full in the face, answered, but no longer abstractedly :

" 'Are you for science, too?'

" 'Science, every inch of me!' said I.

" 'Give us your hand!' and he shook mine with a fervor which sent a tingle to my very collar-bone. 'Hurrah for science. You're the man I've been searching for with a lantern these thousand years. You can help me. But' —and he leaned and whispered in my ear, so distinctly that I could hear every word and letter of it above the racket around us—'can you keep a secret?'

" 'Certainly I can,' I replied, while a sort of creeping horror stole over me, as I felt his hot breath upon my face.

" 'You swear you can?' he continued, looking inquiringly into my face.

" 'I swear I can!' said I, with a desperate effort, looking back at him.

" 'Because,' he grated out, between his teeth, 'if I thought you meant to betray me, I'd tear your tongue out!'

" 'Never fear one man of science betraying another,' I answered, with a sickly attempt at bravery. 'I'm your man!'

" 'Well, then, mind what I say,' said the madman, apparently reassured, and pulling from his coat pocket a bunch of dirty papers, scrawled all over with lead-pencil marks. 'Here's my secret, the result of five hundred years' hard study. To you, as a friend of science, I will impart it. But remember your promise!'

" By this time I felt terribly uneasy—not only in apprehension of my strange companion's intentions, but on account of the alarming rapidity at which we were moving.   The madman was crafty enough to keep his position upon the foot-board, and I saw there was no hope of stealing a march upon him in that direction.

"'Now, you see,' he went on to say, 'a tangent from a parabolic curve goes on to infinity,' and he held up one of the soiled scrawls before me, pointing out the marks upon it with his long, craw-like fore-finger; 'and infinity is what? Do you know? No; but you shall. Do I know? Yes; and, in the cause of science, I am going to show you. Speed, in locomotion, tends toward infinity. Infinity is unknown. The higher the speed, consequently, the greater the proximity to the unknown. Down where I've been studying, they wouldn't let me build my engine to make this experiment with. So,' and here his voice fell to a horrid whisper again, 'I came away secretly the other night, and now—ha! ha! ha!—I've got a good engine of my own! Speed, speed, speed is what we want! By and by we'll be ready for the tangent; then infinity, and then our fortune is made forever!'

"I saw that hope was fast disappearing. His intention plainly was to put the engine to her highest speed, and send us whizzing over an embankment at the first short curve. We had gone nine miles already, although only thirteen minutes had elapsed since we left H——. I nerved myself for a final effort.

"'Come,' said I, 'your secret is a wonderful one, and now that I know it, I will give you all my help to carry out your plan. But you have overlooked one important point. The tangent which will quickest bring us to what we are after—infinity—must be directed from a point as near as possible to the base of the cone. That point we cannot discern, unless you, with your superior insight into the principle involved, take a position upon the outside of the engine, and give me the signal when to send her off.'

"The idea seemed to strike him.

"'Good! better! best!' he exclaimed, clapping his hands, and shaking mine. 'But mind, don't take your eyes off me!'

"'That I shan't,' I said, fervently, as he opened the window, and made a movement as if to pass out upon the *running board.*

"My heart beat high again, but this time with hope and anticipation. Once outside, he would be at my mercy long enough for me to whistle down brakes, shut off steam, and reverse the engine.

"Alas! suddenly he turned, slamming the window, and then, glaring upon me like a demon, he hissed :

"'You've betrayed me! What did I tell you?'

"I trembled with horror.

"'Come, come,' I said; 'no I haven't. Go ahead. See! there's the curve just ahead. Hurry, be quick, or the chance is gone!'

"'I say you've betrayed me, and I'm going to kill you! I heard you whisper my secret a moment ago!' and he came toward me with all the frenzy and savage cruelty of a maniac.

"'Now,' thought I, 'one last struggle for life or death,' and mustering all my force, I struck him a fearful blow with my clenched fist upon the forehead.

"Still he neared me. I felt his long, bony hands in my hair. I staggered. I fell backward ; my head struck against something hard, my eyes grew dim, and I lay insensible."

The narrator paused for a moment, and passed his great rough hand across his forehead, as if to drive away the terrible memories his story had recalled. His companions, mute with eager interest, only drew themselves nearer as he resumed :

"I couldn't have lain there half an hour—for, when I came to, the first object that met my view in the distant landscape was the white tower of the Methodist Church in N——. I was lying on my side, between the engine and tender, with my head half over the edge.

"Weak and exhausted from loss of blood, which was still flowing from the wound on my head, I lay there helpless and hopeless. My eyes wandered to where the madman was still standing. I saw him with heightened wildness on his countenance, his long hair floating in the wind behind, his eye glancing eagerly out ahead, his lips muttering words to me incoherent and meaningless. Now and then he would dance, and clap his hands with a fiendish joy, then settle quietly down again to his sullen mutterings.

"The rate of speed at which we were moving was absolutely frightful—not less, I should think, than a mile a minute—and I feared every instant the crash would send me, madman, engine, everything, whirling to perdition.

"As each moment my faculties grew stronger, I began to realize, in all its force, the horror of my situation. What if he should discover in me signs of returning life ? He would, without a doubt, throw me from the train, or dash my brains out. Meanwhile, where was the conductor ? Perhaps he had been left behind at H——. The brakemen—could not some of them come to rescue me ? Had not our wild speed, our neglect of the usual stoppages, told those on the train that something was certainly wrong ? And why, then, did they not come to see what it was? Surely an end must soon come of this horrible affair, in some way or another.

"Heavens! of a sudden I remembered a circumstance, the thought of which chilled me to the very bones, and well might make me cry out in expostulation and terror to the terrible being before me. We were rapidly approaching P—— bridge, spanning the awful chasm through which, far below, the T—— river leaps and plunges, in three successive falls, to the quiet level of the valley below. I had in my pocket at that moment a copy of a telegraphic order from the division superintendent, stating that the westward-bound track on the bridge would that morning be taken up for repairs, and directing all trains to switch off on approaching the spot, and cross on the eastward-bound track.

"In a moment all the horror of the impending disaster broke upon me. Should this maniac persist in his mad purpose only ten minutes longer, he and I, and all of us, would be precipitated headlong downward through the air, crashing through the timbers, cars and engine with us, to be dashed to atoms upon the pitiless, jagged rocks below. Oh, how I prayed in that moment for forgiveness for all the wickedness of the past! With what unspeakable tenderness I recalled the parting words of those dear ones whom I might never see again, and how I inwardly asked God to watch over them after I was gone! I wondered whether they would ever find us, or know the real cause of the catastrophe. Eagerly, I watched the familiar landmarks flitting by, as on, on, on, we dashed, faster and faster, toward the death and destruction which now seemed all but inevitable.

"I heard a cry of wild joy from my companion, as, gliding like lightning around a curve, the valley, and, in the distance, the massive bridge, were first disclosed to his view.

"'Now! now!' he shouted. 'Here we are come, at last! Science, and infinity, and all the unknown, are mine, mine, mine, forever! He betrayed me, did he? and he died like a dog! Ha! ha! ha!'

"And he danced and screamed with a horrid zest, which, mocking my anguish and terror, only made me more desperate. I tried to move—a pang of agony shot through every nerve, and muscle, and fibre in my body. I sunk down again, in utter despair, and closed my eyes, waiting for death to come and end it all!

.　　.　　.　　.　　.　　.　　.

"Crack—crack—whiz—whiz—a scream—a shout—another crack—another whiz! I opened my eyes once more. The madman had fallen upon his knees, and with the expression of a demon incarnate upon his face, his two bared arms stretched above his head, his power-ful form writhing in horrible contortion, was gnashing his teeth, while his eyes protruded from their sockets, foam oozed from his lips, and a stream of blood, ever so small, trickled down his shirt front.

"'Come! come! come quickly!' I called out, as loudly as I could; but my feeble voice was drowned in the clatter, and I saw the monster, weak and wounded as he was, turn and crawl upon his knees toward me.

"'Come! for God's sake, come!' I screamed; but by that time his clutches were upon my throat, and I looked upward to the clear blue morning sky above us, to feel my breath growing slower and slower, as the cruel grip grew tighter and tighter upon me.

.　　.　　.　　.　　.　　.　　.

"The coarse, talon-like grip relaxed of a sudden, the

din grew less and less, and the welcome shriek of the whistle for down brakes sounded in my ears like the voice of a messenger from God, calling me back to life, and loved ones, and all that was dear. I felt myself lifted up like a child in two pairs of stout, friendly arms. I heard sobs, and shouts of joy, and the movement of many feet about me, and a voice whispered lovingly in my ear :

" ' SAVED !' "

VIII.

EVERYDAY LIFE ON THE RAIL.

THE author makes bold to affirm, that there is a "Jack Short's" on every respectable American railway. A pleasant, quiet place, where there are light wines, and ale on draught, in the front room, and a constant draught of fresh air in the rear apartment. Pipes, tobacco, cigars, an easy-chair, and a place for your feet. In winter, a warm fire, hot water, heavier wines, and oysters stewed and fried. An institution as necessary to a road, as important a part of the running gear as the turn-table, round-house, or switch. Here conductors side-track when off duty, and run into a cosey little round-house of their own. At these places of rendezvous, time-tables are ignored, special and general orders powerless. The edicts of the train dispatcher cannot enter here, and invitations from superintendents to "come" or "go" are of no avail. The conductor is king, and this is his palace. He is running on his own time, with plenty of margin; no wild trains on his track, nothing to follow or to flag. His engineer, fireman, and brakeman, surround him, bound together by railway ties, stronger than wood, and firmer than steel. It is his little court, where manhood, experience, and faithful service command homage, and right gallantly do these brave hearts yield to each that which is his due.

"Jack Short's," a popular resort for Western conductors, has numerous branches. At Chicago, Indianapolis, St. Louis, Omaha, Cincinnati; at "Jim Turner's," on the Erie; Jersey City, or the West End; at Mills', on the Hudson River; Jewett's office, or the St. Nicholas, at Kansas City; in Mr. C. N. Lee's room at Quincy; at "Billy Thompson's," at Dayton, Ohio, etc., etc.,—wherever there is a railroad and a "run," there is a "Jack Short's," where conductors meet to gossip and joke, and mayhap, live over the horrors of hairbreadth escapes.

So we join the conductors of various roads at "Jack Short's" to-night, and, getting a good seat, will ride with them as far as they go. The author does not give the names of roads represented in every instance, his object being merely to introduce the men themselves, who relate their incidents in their own way.

"Beer for the boys, Jack—some matches, and we'll commence our yarns."

 "'That seat is engaged,' said a pretty young maid,
  As I entered a carriage one day;
 'To whom?' 'A young gentleman,' pouting, she said;
  'Then where is his baggage, I pray?'

 "Her ruby lips opened like rosebuds in spring,
  Her face in deep blushes was dyed,
 As muttering crossly, 'You hateful old thing!
  Why, I am his baggage,' she cried."

"'That was on my train," said Howland, "coming out of Burlington; but I never supposed it would be told in that way."

"I run out of Indianapolis, and you may call me 'Major' for the want of a better name. I am as fond of dogs as Cole Wilson is of cats. Lately I came in possession of a Newfoundland, which didn't turn out well, and I was at a loss to know how to dispose of it. In this emergency a happy thought struck me; and on my next trip the dog occupied a berth in the baggage-car, till the train reached a little station away down the road.

"As the station-agent appeared, I said, 'Here, Jones, take out this dog, and keep it till the owner calls for it!'

"'All right! any charges?'

"'Collect fifty cents; you can keep the money if you want to.'

"Next time I passed that way the agent hailed me:

"'Look here, nobody's called for that dog yet!'

"'You don't say so! Well, the owner 'll be along soon.'

"'What's his name?'

"'Name? Oh, his name's Smith.'

"'But 'spose he don't call?'

"'Oh, if he don't call, you can just keep the dog, you know.'

"At last accounts, Jones was keeping the dog and cursing the delinquent Smith."

"My name is Nelson, and I run out of Albany. I don't mind telling the thing now, but I felt pretty cheap at the time. I sometimes think the Company ought to allow a conductor a little heart and judgment occasionally, but it's the safest plan, perhaps, in the long run, to obey the rules.

"As my train was approaching the Suspension Bridge near Niagara, on this occasion, I found a young man who could not pay his fare. The poor fellow was evidently in the last stage of consumption, and emaciated to skeleton proportions. He sat by himself, and his eyes were red, as though he had been weeping. But the laws of the Company could not be transgressed, and he must leave the train. No conductor knows when a detective may be watching him, so I led him with a heavy heart from his seat. He was all shivering with the cold, and no one moved or spoke until we reached the door. Here a beautiful girl arose from her seat, and with bright, sparkling eyes, demanded the amount charged for the poor invalid. I told her eight dollars, and the young and noble girl took that amount from her pocket-book, and kindly led the sick youth back to his seat. The action put to shame several men who had witnessed it, and they offered to 'pay half,' but the whole-souled woman refused the assistance. When our train arrived in Albany, the young protectress gave him money enough

to keep him over night, and send him to his friends the
next morning.

"'What was her name, Nels?'

"Well, as I said before, I felt a little cheap over the
part I was forced to play in the affair, so I hunted her
up, and on the first leisure evening, called to return the
eight dollars. This she indignantly refused, but I subsequently persuaded her to accept of a suitable present
at my hands.

"'Well, what else?'

"I finally persuaded her to take *me* too, and she's just
the best wife and mother on the road."

"My name is Peters, for that matter, and I am only a
country conductor, running a train that is freight one day
and passenger the next. I am brakeman and switchman besides. A couple living at Le Mars, Iowa, a station
on our road, were anxious to have their child baptized.
One day I had a priest aboard, and seeing him on the
platform as we came into Le Mars, this couple got on the
train, and the child was baptized while we were going at
the rate of thirty miles an hour. The happy couple got
off at the next station, and took the first train homeward-
bound."

"You remember Littlejohn, don't you, boys?" asked
Neal Ruggles.

"Yes, he's running now on the Central California,
Bob Matteson's road."

"Littlejohn was coming down the grade pretty fast
one trip, with his sweetheart aboard, when the engine ran
into a lot of solid beef, throwing her off the track, tem-
porarily, but doing no other damage. Fragments of one
of the animals came through the window, door, or some
opening, and lodged in sweetheart's lap.

"'Oh, Littlejohn's killed!' she screamed, jumping frantically to her feet, and surveying the bloody reminders. 'Oh, Littlejohn's killed—he's *killed!*' and she refused to be comforted until Littlejohn made his appearance, and took her in charge."

"I am on the Pittsburg, Fort Wayne, and Chicago Road," said Watson, "and we have a station called 'Hanna' in honor of a deceased citizen of Fort Wayne.

"When we stopped there the other day, my brakeman thrust his head inside the door, as usual, and called out 'Hanna,' loud and long. A young lady, probably endowed with the poetic appellation of Hannah, supposing he was addressing her, and shocked at his familiarity on so short an acquaintance, frowned like a thunder-cloud, and retorted, 'Shut your mouth!'

"He shut it!"

"'Old' fatty Hurlbut, of the New York Central, used to carry a heap of brine with him on his trips, both inside and out. He was finally discharged, and going home one day, found that his wife had caused the lightning-rods to be taken off his house and sold.

"'Why did you do that?' said he; 'ain't you afraid you'll be struck with lightning?'

"'Not when you are around,' she replied; 'ain't you a non-conductor?'"

"Here, Jack," said one, "bring us the slops on that; it's a little too old and thin."

"I am a brakeman on the Erie Road, and they call me 'Ambrose,' for short. I thought I would turn in a joke on Horace W. Whitaker, my conductor, for you may bet he'll never tell it on himself. He was collecting tickets one day from his passengers, and all handed over their pasteboard, save one old lady who sat next the door, near where I stood. She seemed to be reaching down to get something she had dropped on the floor. When her time to pay came, she raised her head and thus addressed the blushing conductor :

"'I allurs, when I travels, carry my money in my stockin', for you sees, nothin' can get at it thar, and I'd just thank you, young man, just to reach it for me, as I'm so jammed in that I can't git to it. I forgot to git a ticket at the depot.' 'Whit' glanced at the other passengers, some of whom were laughing at his plight; one or two young ladies among them blushed scarlet, and he beat a sudden retreat, muttering something about not charging old ladies, etc. His cash was short that trip the fare of one passenger."

George Alexander—" My run leads into a temperance town, which I will call Alesburg, division headquarters. Nobody drinks there, and every man, woman, and child is an apostle of temperance. Every citizen of any promise is a temperance lecturer, and the wayfarer, bibulously inclined, must get a prescription before he can get a drink. Colic prevails there to an alarming extent, and the heathen go about armed with blank prescriptions ready for immediate service the moment the first symptom comes on. This model town is out of Chicago about 160 miles, and I have known leading citizens to lose confidence in the Alesburg prescriptions, and hurry to the metropolis for relief.

"Not long ago, a well-known citizen of the 'Burg,' somewhat noted for his crusades against saloons, hunted me up in Chicago, and wanted to know if I was going to take the train to Alesburg that night. Told him I was, and noticed that the symptoms of Prairie Colic were rapidly developing. He had come in with some of the boy, she said, and staying longer than he had intended, his pass had run out, and his money too, and his friends had gone off and left him.'

" ' Very bad predicament indeed,' I said, ' for a respectable temperance man of Alesburg, but I don't see what I can do for you ; the rules are very strict.'

" He replied ' that if he was made acquainted with Mr. Harris, our general superintendent, he would return his old pass and ask for a new one.'

" What entitled him to a pass I never knew, but I told him I would introduce him to Mr. Harris at once, for I feared the colic was on him in full force. He left me and returned in about fifteen minutes with at least two more colics ahead. I accompanied him to Mr. Harris' office, introduced him, and he presented his pass, asking politely for a new one.

" Mr. Harris seemed much perplexed in his examination of that pass. Finally he returned it, remarking, with a peculiar smile, ' Sir, there is some mistake. This seems to be a prescription from Dr.——, asking Mr.——, a druggist of Alesburg, to give bearer one quart of what I suppose stands for *whiskey*—for colic. You have given me the wrong paper.'

" I left my fellow-citizen searching nervously in his pockets for his pass, but never learned how he got home."

" I was going to tell you," said George Boynton, " about the fellow that couldn't come it over Ed. Sadd. We had a very energetic waterman named Spielman, who got in the very bad habit of doubling on his pass. The boys on the main line passenger resolved to stop it, by punching the pass every time it was shown. The consequence was, Spielman had to make application for a new one. The boys, not at all discouraged, soon punched up pass No. 2.   When S. got his third pass, he procured a piece of sole leather same size as pass, and about a quarter of an inch thick.   On this he pasted his pass, and Mr. S. was ahead.

" It so happened that he got on Ed. Sadd's train. Our conductor, intent on ruining Spielman's pass, asked, as usual, to see it. The weighty article was brought forth, and the conductor's countenance dropped. The waterman saw his discomfiture, and said with a smile,

" ' I think I have stopped that punching business, Mr. Sadd—there's been a conspiracy against me, you see.'

" ' Yes, I see,' replied Sadd, scratching his head. ' Please raise that window a moment, Mr. Spielman, and I'll punch your pass ! '

" Mr. Spielman raised the window—the train being in full motion—and Sadd, drawing a small pocket pistol, put a hole through the centre of the pass.

" ' How's that for a punch ? ' said Sadd, as he went on down the car.   The boys call it a Sadd affair."

Major Martin, of the Cincinnati, Hamilton, and Dayton Road, has a good one on Billy Eckert of the same run :

" Eckert was a telegraph operator in the Burnett House at Cincinnati, and was very popular with railway men, many of whom stopped at that elegant establishment. Different influences were brought to bear, and he finally got a passenger train on the Cincinnati, Hamilton, and Dayton, without going through the usual apprenticeship.

" Ira A. Wood was general supt., I think, though Eckert had never seen him. · John Lincoln, who ' learned ' Eckert the road, told him the Company was a new one, and very jealous of its rules.   Nothing would advance him so rapidly in official favor as a strict adherence to and enforcement of all rules.   ' Billy ' felt a little proud of his conductor's silver badge, and when he stepped on his first train at the Cincinnati depot, he felt that he owned considerable stock in the C., H. & D. As he approached Glendale, he ran into his first obstruction. This was a corpulent individual, seated modestly in the rear end of a car, who was without a pass or a ticket. Eckert told him the rules were very strict, allowing the conductor no margin whatever.

" ' How long have you been on the road ? Have you a card, sir ? '

" ' Yes.' Billy had a fresh bunch of cards just printed. Gave the fat man one ; adding that this was his first trip.

" ' Ah ! I thought as much. Well, sir, my name is Wood ; I am the general superintendent of this road. Sometimes carry a pass, but left it to-day in another coat at my office in Cincinnati.'

" ' Sorry, indeed, sir. But there are so many with the best of excuses who are put off. The Company assures me that every one entitled to a pass will have one with them, and that excuses will not balance my account. I do not know you, sir, and have no right to know you without your pass.'

" ' Young man, you are right. I am only going to Hamilton, twenty miles. The agent there is my brother. When we get in, we'll go together and see him. Here is my fare.'

" Eckert took the fare with a trembling hand, with a vague idea that he had gained a victory, though what sort of a one, was yet uncertain.

" Now everybody in Hamilton knew old Yankee Wood, a regular Connecticut wooden nutmegger ; six feet five in his stockings, weighing 300 pounds ; with a nasal twang that could be heard for miles. This was the agent, and Eckert had learned about him as soon as any other big point on the road. When they got to Hamilton, 'Yankee' was on the platform talking to old man Earhart, the ticket-agent. Billy's passenger stuck to him, and as soon as he got out, 'Yankee' and Earhart rushed up to him with friendly greeting. Another moment, and 'Billy' was formally introduced to the general supt.

"From that time forward Eckert rose rapidly in the estimation of that Company, and was gradually promoted to a high position. Lincoln, for like fidelity to rules and regulations, was appointed supt. of the branch line, running from Hamilton through Oxford, to Crawfordsville. Groat and Pettybone, formerly conductors on the same line, are now at the head of prominent railways.

"This was at a time when railway men looked upon superintendents as a species of deity to be worshipped and feared, and Eckert's adventure was then considered remarkable in its way."

Wiers—"It is the safest policy in the long run to obey the rules. This is what my Peanuts * thinks about it.

"A PEANUTS' RHYME.

" 'I've been a Peanuts now for several years,
   I'm running here with—maybe you know him—Wiers.
   I keeps my eyes wide open, and sometimes—
   Picks up an idea, with my little dimes.

" 'I ain't no learning, so to speak ; you see,
   The old man got killed in 1863.
   And mother she was poor, and I was strong,
   And so I've been a Peanuts, right along.

* " *Peanuts* "—Train Boy.

    " ' I've seen how things are run, on these 'ere roads ;
       I've seen good fellows carry heavy loads ;
       There's Coleman—passed his only brother in,
       And got discharged, for helping his own kin.

    " ' And there was Hawley, he was sent adrift,
       For giving a old lady a free lift—
       A conductor's mother and a friend o' his—
       You see perliteness ain't the payin' biz !

    " ' And so to all employés I would say,
       Hog up a pass, or else you pay your way.
       The Company's got to hev some sort o' rules,
       If you don't obey 'em, you're the derndest fools.

    " ' Whole families sometimes come to want and woe
       By conductors failin' to spit out a " *No.*"
       On this ere road you dasn't pass your mother,
       And if it doesn't suit, why, try another.' "

"There is nothing so funny as the newly arrived son of the ' Green Isle of the Sea,' who is sure he is not going to be done, and determined to show the Yankees that he is as sharp as any ' wan uv 'em.' I am a ticket-agent, and my office is in the International Hotel at Suspension Bridge. One of the class mentioned stepped into my office the other day, and the following dialogue ensued :

Pat—" Shure is this the road to Dathroit ? "

Agent—" Yes, send you right through."

Pat—" Shure it's the rale road I mane, an' none o' thim chatin' turnpikes."

Agent—" You want to go by the Great Western from Suspension Bridge or the Grand Trunk from Buffalo ? "

Pat—" Divil a bit ! I've no clothes for a trunk, let alone money for the buyin' uv wun."

Agent—" Well, you want to go to Detroit and M——— ? "

Pat—" Shure I do."

Agent—"Which line will you take?"

Pat—"Och! any line, shure—a fish-line for a throut or two, perhaps."

Agent—"No, no; how would you like to go—which way?"

Pat—"How would I like to go? Shure, like a gentlemon, an' the same way me cousin, Mick Dolan, wint."

Agent—"And what way was that?"

Pat—"Shure he said it was a mighty quick way."

Agent—"Then you want a ticket on the express line; give me ten dollars."

Pat—"Tin dollass! What would I give yees tin dollass fur?"

Agent—"For your ticket by the express."

Pat—"Shure it's no express I warnt at all; it's the way to Dathroit."

Agent—"I know that; but there are three 'ways,' as you call 'em—Express, Trunk line, and Central; what will you take?"

Pat (puzzled)—"Ah—eh!"

Agent (leaning over the counter)—"Come, my good fellow, what will you take?"

Pat (glancing at a big ink-bottle that stood on the counter)—"Shure I'll take a dhrop o' whiskey, if it's the same to yur honor."

(This reply elicited an explosion of laughter from half a dozen other ticket-agents who were in the same office, one of whom, thinking to better matters, took Pat in hand.)

Agent—"You want to go to Detroit?"

Pat—"You may say that."

Agent—"And you want to buy a ticket?"

Pat—"Divil a bit."

Agent—"What do you want, then?"

Pat—"Shure I warnt to know the way to go to Da-throit."

Agent—"Well, buy a ticket, and that will show you the way."

Pat—"But won't yure show me the way?"

Agent—"But how can you get there without the ticket?"

Pat—"Shure I mane to walk."

There were two ticket-agents, but no ticket was sold by this operation.

At the next gathering—occurring perhaps a thousand miles away—Barton began:

"I was running on the Cincinnati and Indianapolis Road, when I came across a queer customer. This was a tall, awkward Hoosier, who got on at Lawrenceburg with a heavy valise. I had not been on the road very long, and Hoosiers were still a novelty, so I watched my passenger with more than usual interest. He took his valise to a double seat, and sitting down in one, emptied the valise in the other. There were yellow-covered novels enough in that seat to have started an Indiana book-store. He found room somewhere for his feet, and taking up one of the books, was fixed for the trip. When I called for tickets he showed me a life-pass from the general superintendent, written in the form of a letter, and of course I thought my passenger was a man of some consequence. All railway superintendents try to write illegible hands; they seem to look upon such an accomplishment as an evidence of genius, but the general superintendent of that road beat them all.

"When I came out of Indianapolis on the return trip, my Hoosier was on the train in a double seat, books and all.   So it was for ten or a dozen trips.   He was the first to mount the train, and the last man to leave it.

"Finally I accosted him one day with—

"'Stranger, which way?'

"'Any way,' he replied, without taking his eyes off the book—'Any way, damn the odds!'

"'I mean which way are you travelling; ain't you in the wrong train?'

"'Indianapolis Road, isn't it?'

"'Yes,' I answered.

"'Wal, that's my road; drive on!'

"Being a constant customer, I got acquainted with him at last, and this was his explanation:

"'You see, this darned road runs through the old man's farm, down there near Lawrenceburg.   When the fellers was buildin on it, the old man he fit 'em.   He sued 'em, and the gineral super. sent him a family pass for life, and *I'm a-ridin' on it out!*'

"I couldn't get it through me at all, and when we got to Cincinnati I persuaded him to accompany me to headquarters, where I assured him the 'gineral super.' would do the fair thing.   An expert there translated his life-pass, which read as follows:

> "'OFFICE GEN'L SUPT. CIN. & IND. R. R.
> "'*May* —, 18—

"'J. VAN BUSKIRK, *Lawrenceburg.*

"'Don't disturb the men, as you value your life; let them pass through.   Come or send one of your family to this office, and the matter will be satisfactorily arranged.

"'Conductors will recognize this as a pass.

> "'———— *Gen'l Supt.*'

"As nobody could read but a word here and there of

this scrawl, the fellow would have been riding to this day if I had not brought about that translation."

"I am Charley Nourse, conductor on the New Jersey Central. During the recent Small-pox terror in the Eastern cities, the trains out of town were running very full. I have pulled out of the depot at the foot of Liberty street (N. Y.) many a time, and left crowds of anxious people who were unable to get on.

"One trip, after every seat was occupied, an old gentleman entered the middle coach and stood up near the door. As we approached the first station, it was noticed that there were several suspiciously red spots on his face. As he stood where every one must see him, the alarm soon spread. One inquisitive chap asked him if he had had the small-pox, and he said 'Yes.' There was a general scramble among the passengers, all of whom wanted to get out right there. Another moment and we were at the station, when the old gentleman had the car to himself. I heard of the trouble, of course, and at this juncture cautiously peeped into the car.

"'How long has it been, my friend, since you recovered from the small-pox?'

"'Well, sir,' replied the victim of the disease, 'I cannot exactly say, but as near as I can recollect, it was about thirty-five years ago.'"

"If there is no one to sing a song, I'll read you this rhyme," said Frank Hughs, of the Quincy run.

"Good, who is it from?"

"Well, the incident occurred in 1869. It is told by a well-known conductor—Joe Cormick—now running on the Illinois Central."

This promised something extra, and the boys filled their pipes again.

"BRADLEY'S GIRL.

"A CONDUCTOR'S RHYME.

" On the Central Road in '69—
	Time midnight—snowing hard,
The plough ahead, in six-feet drift,
	Four hours behind—by card.
The rails all water—thick with ice,
	And a high old prairie air,
Our wood and coal fast giving out—
	Ah! that was a time to swear.

"Some sixty miles from Augustine,
	The point to meet my mate—
Change engines and obtain supplies,
	Then leave him to his fate.
And there to meet the young girl's friends,
	But would they bear in mind
That wind and snow were in our front,
	And we—four hours behind ?

"The berths on Pullman's car were full,
	Before we left the Lake ;
And half a dozen Throughs stood up,
	All swearing to keep awake.
And every coach had twice its load,
	As much as we could pull :
You see the Christmas times were on,
	And trains were running full.

" The cold increased, of course, when wood
	And coal were getting low ;
My people shivered, and I knew
	The worst was coming now.
I felt concerned about the girl,
	Though I saw she still slept on ;
I did my best—but then, you know,
	The odds were ten to one.

"Maybe you know old Bradley, boys,
  Who runs on the Central Branch;
As true a man as swings a lamp—
  Well—this was his daughter—Blanche.
A fair young thing in feeble health,
  From a ' Water-Cure ' somewhere,
Now coming home at Christmas time,
  And riding in my care.

"I got his message, and the girl,
  Where we met Jule Coleman's train;
Just time enough to lift her in,
  No leisure to explain.
A way-man kindly gave his seat,
  The best that we could do;
She thanked us, went to sleep, and then
  The snow-plough's whistle blew.

"That was the way it was, you see,
  We got four hours behind;
Snowed in—some fifty miles, at least,
  From help of any kind.
Maybe the tale is old to you,
  But you never heard the end—
That's kept a secret with us three—
  Old Brad.—his wife, and—friend.

" Eight-twenty was the time, I think,
  Yes, Brad. and *her* friends were there ;
Young girls in black—a white-plumed hearse,
  And a preacher with a prayer.
God ! what a Christmas Gift was that!—
  All for the best, 'twas said—
—The Christmas bells are ringing now,—
  Maybe some young girl's *dead !* "

Charlie Fox, of the Erie Road, said that " Jim Turner's
was the first ' Hash Shop ' out of New York on that road.
5

A passenger stopped there one day and put away twenty minutes' worth of refreshments.   Calling for his bill Jim struck him for a dollar.

"'Little high, ain't you, Mr. Turner?' asked the innocent passenger.

"'Sir, no, sir.   I never drink.'

"'No, but ain't a dollar a good deal for a meal?'

"'Not where a man eats a good deal and takes a dessert besides."

"'All right, sir,' and the passenger answered the 'All aboard.'

"When we got in, my passenger asked me to show him to the telegraph office.   He told the operator he wanted to telegraph Mr. Turner in regard to meals for himself and friends, and wrote an unusually long message.   The operator said Mr. Turner would be glad to pay the expense at the other end.   So the message went through, and must have cost Jim four dollars and a half!   Good deal for a meal!"

Fenton—"I am only a common express messenger, but I reckon I've a right to put a word in here, to be checked off with the rest."

"Certainly, only it is about time now for some more of that slop.   Yes, ten mugs."

"I was running on the Baltimore and Ohio Road the year before the rebellion, into Parkersburg, West Virginia, every night.   I stopped at the 'United States' Hotel, kept by a Mr. Tefft, who had a pretty daughter. I was kind o' sweet on the girl, and would have brought the package through all right if it hadn't been for the old man.   He didn't like a man who worked for a living. One night there was to be a big dance at the 'United States,' and I didn't get a bid.   It was the town talk for weeks, and was to be a big affair. The crack band of Harper's Ferry was to furnish the music, and the road and country were scoured for table luxuries. At Harper's Ferry the agent put two heavy packages on my run ; one, a corpse going to Parkersburg for burial, and the other, a big fiddle—double-bass, or whatever they call it—going to the same place. It was marked 'care of the U. S. Hotel,' and had been forgotten, probably, by the band. Both freights were boxed in the same way, and, to look at them, one would have thought that it was a pair of something going somewhere together, which was true. Of course, one was a trifle heavier than the other, but that could only be told by hefting.

" I swung my lamp over those boxes pretty often as we neared Parkersburg, for I had resolved to play a joke on that dance. I scraped the marks off the boxes, and changed the addresses ! As the dance would be under way when we got in, of course the leader of the band had arranged to receive his package at the cars, without waiting for it to go through the city office. Same with the friends of the corpse.

"After satisfying myself as to these points, I calmly awaited the last whistle.

" There were two crowds at the depot waiting for me. As soon as the leader of the band received an affirmative answer to his inquiry, he gave directions to his men to 'take it quick to the orchestra in the ball-room and open it, for the music was waiting ;' and after signing my book, he went away. The friends of the corpse had brought a hearse, and after scanning the address, lifted the box in, remarking incidentally, that it 'must be much decayed, it was so light.'

" I had drawn my month's pay that morning, and after

making out my report, sat down and wrote my resignation; giving it to the boys to forward to Baltimore, and telling the manager that I was ill, and that he must put an office man on my run in the morning. Then I gathered up my traps at the U. S., left a note for my sweetheart, and took a room down at the 'Exchange,' near the river.

"There wasn't much of a newspaper there then, but it managed to get a report of the affair next morning. They opened the corpse in the dining-room, when the dance was going on, and there was a scene. Musicians tumbled over each other—for there was a dead body there instead of a fiddle—women screamed and rushed from the room; lamps fell from the walls—well, it just broke the whole thing up. On the other hand, the bass-viol was buried with great solemnity, and tears of grief were dropped upon its silent bosom.

"When I left for Cincinnati, arrangements were being made to resurrect the one and bury the other; but whether there were tears and grief enough left for the second act, I never cared to inquire."

"On the Camden and Amboy, I am known as Bob Morris. I have noticed that railway companies generally have quite as large a 'dead-head' interest to look after as they care to have. They are continually beset with applications from a thousand and one sources for free transportation; and deal out their passes as liberally as they may, there seems to be no abatement to the multiplicity of demand. Newspapers want to be passed free (which is but just and right, as they always return a hundred-fold); clergymen have their stereotyped pleas—impecuniousness for gratuitous travel, which no Christian ticket-agent can withstand; educators, engaged in the

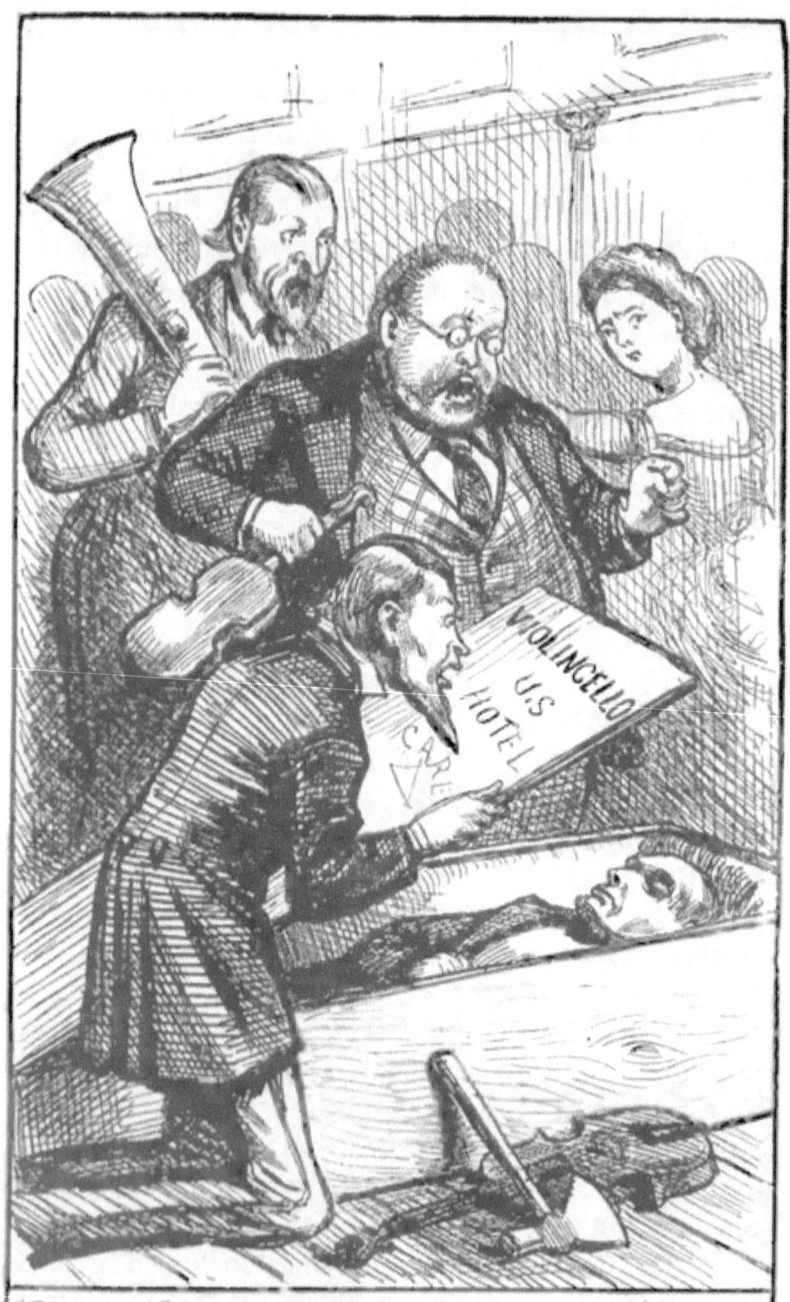

"THEY OPENED THE CORPSE IN THE DINING ROOM, AND THERE WAS A SCENE?"
PAGE 100

great work of informing the human mind, must, of course, have complimentary tickets, else what would become of the 'institutes'? Missionaries to frontier circuits are also to be duly provided for, or our border civilization goes up the spout. Then there is the never-ceasing procession of poor widows, peregrinating aldermen, crippled soldiers, Sunday-school excursionists, blind beggars, editorial celebrities, and dead-beats of every pattern, who have standing and irresistible claims to a first-class passage, which few superintendents are healthy enough to deny.

"There was a Methodist Conference somewhere on my line, and delegates were to assemble from all parts of the State—I don't know but from all parts of the United States. Half-fare round-trip and complimentary passes to dignitaries were the order, and trains were crowded to overflowing. In taking them up from day to day, I had no suspicion of foul play, until I came upon a countenance that I am sorry to say I had seen often before. I could not be mistaken; in spite of the Presbyterian whiskers and white choker, I was sure this countenance belonged to Captain ——, the courteous bar-tender at the Brevoort House, No. 11, Fifth Avenue. A quiet, handsome man, of portly form, dignified in manner, well-fed, and always clad in unexceptionable black, slow of speech, and of excellent address, he was well calculated to deceive as a representative of spiritual affairs.

"'I'll tell you how it was,' he explained, when the affair was all over. 'A number of those clerical gentlemen stopped at the house here, over night; and one of them, suddenly seized with cramps, rushed in here, begging for burnt brandy. I gave him a sling, and he emptied all his pockets hunting for the shekels with which to pay. He took your train before I was up next morning; and when my boy swept up, he found the gentleman's pass to and from the —— Conference. He proved to be a big gun, and I thought I'd shoot her off once, just for a lark.'

"I remembered then, that the Reverend Dr. —— had told me of his loss on the train, and when I explained at headquarters, and came upon the pass, the joke was on me."

"Mr. Morris, I salute you," said Mr. J. C. Mullen. "I was once a conductor on the Camden and Amboy, myself. I am now General Agent of the Burlington and Missouri Road, with headquarters at Coneston, Iowa. We have a little more romance out our way I think than you have on Eastern roads. We have a peculiar way of serving it up too, as witness the following:

"Passengers on Johnnie Miller's western-bound train were treated recently to an immense sensation. In a first-class coach were a man and woman, the former, judging from his appearance, about forty-five years of age, and evidently a working-man. The woman was a really pretty girl, not over twenty-one. The twain took the train at Chariton, Iowa. Soon after leaving that station, they commenced gradually to lean towards each other, and 'eyes looked love to eyes that spoke again'"—

"And all went merry as a marriage bell, eh John?"

"Yes, for a while," answered Mullen. "She was reposing with her head on his shoulder, and their hands were clasped together, as if they feared they would lose each other during the night. Their overflowing affection attracted the attention of every other passenger in the car. They slept sweetly, and all unmindful that Mr.

Man's true and legal wife was in the first car ahead of the one in which they were riding.

"I ain't worth a cent on a yarn, but of course you understand that this man was eloping with the handsome young girl. His neighbors in Chariton knew of his plans before he left, and raised a sum of money. With this they purchased a revolver for Mrs. Man, and a railroad ticket, which would enable her to follow her runaway husband. So, when they stepped into a first-class coach at the station, she walked into a second-class car, and they left Chariton on the same train.

"The situation can now be readily comprehended. Mrs. Man waited until the train had passed two stations, when she prepared for action. She walked boldly into the car where the elopers were still in the embrace of Morpheus.

"The guilty pair were suddenly awakened, and there stood Mrs. Man, with a revolver pointed straight at her husband's head. The girl jumped up and rushed into the sleeping-car, claiming protection from the Pullman conductor, who locked her up in the state-room. At the stopping-place, Mrs. Man, who kept guard over her husband, walked him out of the train, and when they were on the platform of the depot she actually kicked him, beat him, and stamped on him until she had him thoroughly subdued. They took the return train for Chariton, and Mrs. Man is now looking for that girl."

"I am a sleeping-car conductor," said Slossom, "and if we weren't sworn to keep all secrets, I might give you boys many a good thing. We have to keep everything under cover, you know. A country couple, evidently just married, got on at —— station, Michigan Central Road, and I gave them the best room I had. Passing through afterwards, I could just hear enough of the whispering to know that they were discussing the novelty of a bed on the cars.

"Arriving at the end of their journey in the morning, I entered the car as they were leaving it, just in time to hear the rustic bride say:

"'Wal, Josh, ef that's wot they call a burth, I ain't afeard, be you?'"

"I am Henry ——, —well, never mind the rest—of the New York and Erie. Three miles out of Jersey City you strike the great 'Bergen Tunnel,' one mile long, through solid rock. If an Irishman were telling this story, he would say that he had seen a great many funny scenes occur in that tunnel, only you can see nothing at all for the darkness. At the same time I am satisfied that such scenes do occur. Once a gentleman, for some unexplained reason, undertook to change the lower portion of his apparel, during those dark seconds, but made a wrong calculation as to time! But kissing seems to be the choice sport. Kissing in a tunnel, think of that! I have been told by a friend that the charm is in the novelty of the thing. It is the darkness, the rank burglary; the nice calculation as to time; the sudden assault and desperate defence; the acute agony of the skirmish line hair-pins; the carrying of the outer works; the fierce struggle at the scarp; the sweetness of the surrender; the questionable honor of the victory. Then the horrid repairs, and the impossible attempt to appear serene before the other passengers. There's a short lifetime in the kissing of a girl in a tunnel!

"I had a newly married couple out with me, not long ago, on the Cincinnati express. I have had a great many just such couples in my time, but somehow or other these youngsters attracted my attention. Young man, curly hair, of course; young lady, blonde, you know, with that sort of hair that when you and I were young used to be called tow. Rosy cheeks, full lips; well, I should say, a very kissable girl. He was 'awful sweet on her,' as my brakeman suggested, and she—well, I thought I could see her saying, 'James, be still, everybody's looking at you.' We were coming to the cavernous grove, and James became fidgety. It was plain that there was a conspiracy, and that the tunnel was to be made a party to it. Lady thoughtful and evidently unconscious. Then the wheels rattled and whirred louder and louder, and in another second we were in the tunnel; James, his bride, and all of us!

"We came through all right; and James was through too, the bride not quite. The wreck was fearful! Very little hair left on the head, but quite a bunch on the seat, with a lesser wad on James' shoulder. The color had faded from one of her cheeks, and lodged on his nose. His neck-tie was swinging from her brooch. She commenced the work of reconstruction, looking up at him under her uplifted arms, as if to say—'See what you have done before these people.'

"James went for a drink of water; I saw him with one hand on the nozzle of the cooler, and the other on a flask. Half the hair-pins were gone, and when she came up from the floor, looking so woe-begone and friendless, I was rude enough to smile. I couldn't help it. She saw it, and smiled in return, as if to say, 'You know how it is yourself.'"

"I judge," said a brakeman, "from a rhyme I have here, that tunnelling of that sort is getting quite common:

5*

"IN THE TUNNEL.

" Riding up from Bangor,
  On the Pullman train,
  From a six weeks' shooting
  In the woods of Maine.
  Quite extensive whiskers,
  Beard, mustache as well,
  Sat a ' student feller,'
  Tall, and fine, and swell.

" Empty seat behind him,
  No one at his side ;
  To a pleasant station
  Now the train doth glide.
  Enter aged couple,
  Take the hinder seat ;
  Enter gentle maiden,
  Beautiful, petite.

" Blushingly she falters :
' Is this seat engaged ? '
  (See the aged couple
  Properly enraged,)
  Student, quite ecstatic,
  Sees her ticket's ' through ; '
  Thinks of the long tunnel—
  Knows what he will do.

" So they sit and chatter,
  While the cinders fly,
  Till that ' student feller '
  Gets one in his eye ;
  And the gentle maiden
  Quickly turns about—
' May I, if you please, sir,
  Try to get it out ? '

> "Happy 'student feller'
>   Feels a dainty touch;
>   Hears a gentle whisper—
> 'Does it hurt you much?'
>   Fizz! ding, dong! a moment
>   In the tunnel quite,
>   And a glorious darkness
>   Black as Egypt's night.
>
> .   .   .   .
>
> "Out into the daylight
>   Darts the Pullman train;
>   Student's beaver ruffled
>   Just the merest grain;
>   Maiden's hair is tumbled,
>   And there soon appeared
>   Cunning little ear-ring
>   Caught in student's beard."

"That reminds me of an adventure," followed Drury, "of a little 'circumstance,' I might say, if there hadn't been more than one. I run the Pacific express train on the Pan-Handle Road. We left Columbus, Ohio, one night, and everything went on as usual, until we got between Dennison and Steubenville. Then one of my brakesmen notified me that a lady desired my presence in the rear car. Now, I am a married man, and proof against the tricks of fast girls, but I always try to make ladies comfortable on my train. I found the lady in some trouble and embarrassment. First, was I a married man? Told her I was. Then it transpired that she was on her way from Cincinnati to join her husband in New York, and that a crisis was impending, involving the appearance of an additional passenger. I was taken back some, of course, but I set to work to make the lady comfortable. First, to clear the car of all male bipeds; next, to summon from the forward cars all the female assistance that could be had. The result was a fine girl, weighing, I should judge, about nine pounds. I always carried a change of underwear with me, in case of accidents, and from this supply the ladies soon improvised a wardrobe for my new passenger. This was all well enough, if the fates had been satisfied. The train left Steubenville on time, and was soon thundering through and around the hills of West Virginia, when I received another shock from the same battery. This time it was a 'bouncing boy,' as the old ladies have it—twins, by all that is out! One a Buckeye and the other a Pan-Handler. The remainder of my underclothing went to start this young rascal on his first trip. Then for fear something might happen, I sent word to the engineer to hurry up, and we reached Pittsburg ahead of time. These two half-fares had no tickets, it is true, but you will admit that it was but half fair to bring them through! We conveyed them tenderly to the Union Hotel at Pittsburg, and forwarded a telegram to the husband at New York. What effect the joyful (?) tidings had upon him, has never transpired."

Johnnie Richardson, of the Hannibal & St. Joe, thought it was his turn.

"If you have ever been over our road, you must remember Smith's 'Coupon Shed,' where we stopped ten minutes for a bowl of sweet milk and a chunk of brown bread, price ten cents. Nothing could be more refreshing at a late hour of night; and I have heard many a passenger assert that they relished it better than the most elaborate meal.

"Well, I knew one duck to get too much of it! On account of the uncertain ballast of our road, we are required to be more particular in enforcing that old rule : 'Passengers are not allowed to stand on the platform.' This duck *insisted* upon riding on the platform, and as fast as I hauled him in off of one, he would dive through for another. To all my expostulations his only reply was :

" ' Sir, I am looking at the Missouri moon !'

" I got tired of following him from one platform to another, and finally, getting him by the arm, I said :

" ' Say, done out here yet ? '

" 'Sir, no, sir ; I am looking at the Missouri milky-way, now !'

" ' Well,' I replied, ' we are on the down grade now, and if you stay out here much longer, you'll get into a milky-way, yourself, and see stars, too.'

" ' The joke had no effect upon him, although I think it's about as good a thing as any of you fellows ever got off !' "

" But you didn't get him off," retorted one.

" No ; I sent for a bowl of milk, and sucked him in. He was an insane conductor, just discharged from the T., P. & W."

" I was a country pedagogue for awhile, but am now with the Eastern Express Company. I remark, that the imagination has an extraordinary influence on the human mind and body. For instance, we received on board a Boston boat a long box, addressed to Halifax. It was marked ' *head* ' and ' *feet ;* ' and those who had anything to do with it drew their own inferences. The hands, in putting the box on board, detected an unpleasant smell issuing from it, which was considered nothing unusual. The smell increased during the passage, so that everybody shunned the box, and it was got rid of as soon as the boat reached her wharf. So offensive was the odor that it would not be allowed in the warehouse.   The first teamster sent to remove it from the wharf would not put it into his wagon, and a second one was so affected by the smell that he became sick and giddy.   Finally, it was got into the wagon, and hurried to the office, where somebody determined to investigate.   A hatchet was procured, and one of the boards lifted.   A very handsome carved Indian figure in wood was disclosed to the gaze of the crestfallen teamsters, everything about it as clean and as sweet as a new-planed board.   It was intended as a sign for some enterprising tobacconist.

"Well, if you propose to take the express train, here is another package.

"Mr. C. S. Pomeroy, better known as 'Brick, No. 2,' is the transfer express clerk at the depot in a railroad centre, which of course must be nameless here.   He has charge of all trains in his line, sleeping in the depot, and retiring after the departure of the last train.   Not long since, trifling depredations were being committed in the transfer office ; sneak-thieves found means of entrance, and opened barrels of crackers, boxes of fruit, etc., baffling all attempts at detection.   'Brick' finally resolved upon a grand *coup*.   He piled up some long narrow boxes, containing light freight, with a few boxes of fruit, and on top, a coop of game chickens, arranged so that the slightest careless touch would bring them to the floor and awaken him.   This done, he secured a heavy club, put out the gas, and went to sleep.   It was not long until the crash came, and in a moment Brick was on his feet.   Moonlight through a crack or window revealed an outline of the situation.   The boxes lay partially opened, the chickens were abroad, and in the midst of the *débris* lay the thief !   Not a boy, or a woman, but a Swedish man with the national hair, and florid countenance. Anything but a Swedish thief, thought 'Brick' in the excitement, and though the enemy was prostrate, he laid on his club with frequent and vigorous blows. There was no cry of pain, no effort at resistance, no sound or echo save the sickly thud. 'Brick' concluded that the thief had been killed by his fall. So he lit his gas, and checked off the result.

"*He had killed Gen. G. Washington*, the father of his country, and a hero for '76 years. The General having been done in wax, was on his way to Wood's Museum at Chicago, to join his staff. 'Brick' had introduced him at a *Matinee* before his time.

"Of course, 'Brick' waxed warm, and it sticks to him to this day."

"I am on a Southern road, and once had a load of editors on their way to Winona, to attend the Press Convention there. It is not always safe to joke editors; and, in getting this off, I don't want to give either my own name or that of my road. Dr. John Woods, of the Scooba *Spectator*, took charge of Mr. Stevens, of the Columbus *Index*, on this occasion, and had much difficulty in getting the young gentleman to Jackson. Like most editors, Stevens' baggage consisted of only one extra shirt, and that a *checked* one. The baggage-man accosted Stevens with:

"'Any baggage, sir?'

S.—"'Yes, sir.'

B. M.—"'Let me see the checks!'

"Stevens cautiously unravelled the bundle, and, holding up the forlorn shirt, asked the man if he could see the checks. An umph! in *basso continuendo*, and the expressman was gone!"

Sandy Burrrell, of the I., B. & W. Road, stroked his famous whiskers, and said:

"I had a baggage-smasher running with me once, who had his old-fashioned idea of running baggage exploded in a peculiar way. Jim had ruined two or three trunks for a certain commercial traveller, whose route lay along our line, who resolved to teach him a lesson. This gentleman, who was in the hardware line, packed a carpet-bag full of loaded revolvers, and handed it to my man Jim. He took it, and, as the owner went away, threw the bag up against the wall of the car savagely, then drew it on the floor and stamped on it as usual. At about the fourth jump, firing began along the whole line. Forty-two revolvers went off in rapid succession, distributing bullets around the car with disgusting carelessness, the smasher's legs running against six of them before he could get out of the car. He rode upon the platform during the whole of that trip; and when he did enter the car, he encased his legs in stove-pipe, and ran an iron-clad snow-plough in front of him, to push the baggage out with. He is running on our main line now, and I believe he smashes fewer carpet-bags than he did in the blissful past—much fewer, and he wears a melancholy air. The only boon he craves, so Billy Smith tells me, is that he may be present when that carpet-bagger calls with his check. He threatens to check his career."

"Not quite so much style and dignity out on those Kansas roads as they put on further east," says John Minckler. "Ed. Jewett, who used to be on the C., B. & Q., is ticket-agent at Kansas City. His office is a sort of headquarters there. I was sitting there with him one day, when a rough-looking, portly fellow came in and sat down by the stove. His pants were rolled up, and he wore a seedy, slouch hat. I wondered who he could be, and what he was doing behind the scenes. Ed. had to get up to ticket somebody, and when he sat down again the rough-looking fellow broke out with—

"'I've got the most penurious set of conductors and men in the world. Here I am without money, and no way of getting any—can't even get a drink.'

"Ed. smiled, as though he was used to such interrogations, and, turning to me, said:

"'Mr. Minckler, this is "Uncle Ben," assistant superintendent of the Leavenworth, Lawrence & Galveston Road.'

"Of course, we all went over to Joe Hunt's and took some 'brine.'"

"Now make room for one of the oldest ticket-agents in the United States. I was conductor on the Little Miami Road, and the C., H. & D., in Ohio, for a long time; and left the track on account of my health, or for the want of it. Opened a general ticket-office, on my own account, adjoining the 'Burnett House,' in Cincinnati, just above the Vine Street entrance. Name—ah! I forgot, Pettybone—on the Road, 'Pet.'

"Rush one day for tickets; everybody going everywhere. My clerk had gone to a funeral. Of course, there will be mistakes, when one is in a hurry. About an hour after it was all over, a well-known lawyer came in and returned me a one-dollar note, overpaid him in making change. I was speechless; then, as my eyes moistened, I grasped him by the hand, and exclaimed:

"'Judge, stand still a moment. Let me look at you —and you a lawyer, too.' We went in and had a cobbler.

"When I made up my cash that night, I threw out a

one-dollar counterfeit bill.   That was the bill I got from Judge C——."

"Joe Reevy said he used to be agent of the Terre Haute Road, at Pana, Illinois.   Had a ticket-clerk who was a little tricky.   One week the Western roads were flooded with well-executed counterfeit $5 notes on the *Chippewa* Bank, and my clerk got stuck on one.   This was returned to us, with a printed description of the counterfeit, and directions for detecting it.   This we pasted up outside, near the window.   That counterfeit Chippewa laid on the clerk's desk for a long time, waiting for a call.   Next night, portly gentleman came along, asked for ticket to ——, handing the clerk two five-. dollar notes, Chippewa Bank, both genuine.   Clerk took them in quickly, dropped one on his desk, and threw out his counterfeit.

"'Sorry, sir, but that is not a genuine bill!'

"'Not genuine!' exclaimed the astonished gentleman, 'I gave you two, both alike!'

"'Beg pardon, sir, here they are.   One is good, the other is not.   You will find a description of the counterfeit near you there on the wall.   Do me the favor to examine for yourself, as others are waiting.'

"The gentleman 'examined,' was convinced; gave another five, and received his ticket.

"The audacity of the thing, and the extraordinary coolness of the clerk, made me powerless to interfere, and I allowed him to 'get even.'   The last time I heard of that clerk, he was running for Congress against an honest soldier, with the chances two to one in his favor.   Yes, sir, I am residing now in St. Louis."

Henry Tristan said that when he was a conductor on the Hudson River Road, one of his brakemen came into possession of a "blessing" in a singular manner, and he thought the fact ought to be recorded. He tells it in rhyme, and being a long-winded "cuss,"-the account is somewhat tedious, but the point comes in at the right place:

"LEFT BEHIND.*

"A BRAKEMAN'S RHYME.

" 'Oh, sir, my box—the black one there,
　　Oh, would you be so kind,
　It's all I have in this wide world,
　　And that is left behind.'
　I pulled the rope, and Number Twelve
　　Backed slowly to her place ;
　I can't forget that oblong box,
　　Nor, indeed, that lady's face.

" Now if things that lose their owners,
　　All our sympathies so bind,
　How much more should living creatures,
　　Who, forlorn, are left behind.
　See the dog in some strange city,
　　Who has lost his master, kind,
　I confess an honest pity
　　For a cur that's left behind.

" With his nose upon the pavement,
　　How he threads the mighty throng,
　Lifting anxious eyes to faces,
　　Whining out his lonely song.
　Kicked and cuffed by every idler,
　　Set upon by his own kind ;
　I could hang the man who strikes him,
　　A poor dog that's left behind.

* See " No One To Blame," page 128.

"For I can't forget the school-days,
    Those first days at Abbott Lawn;
When the shadow of a mother
    That bent o'er me was withdrawn.
Or the utter desolation,
    The despair that filled my mind,
When she left me with the master,
    Left her little boy behind.

"So I pitied this poor lady,
    Travelling alone that night,
With the box that held her wardrobe,
    Scarce a dozen pounds in weight.
Seeking friends in some great city,
    Or a lover there to find,
Or perchance a friendless maiden,
    Whom love had left behind.

"So I turned my brake and fixed it,
    Then looked her up a seat,
Gave the fire an overhauling,
    Then sat down to warm my feet.
And my heart went towards that lady,
    For her weeping made me blind,
So I went and sat beside her,
    Though I left a wife behind.

"By this time we reached the station,
    I believe I touched my hat,
When the lady came and asked me—
    'Would I have an eye to that?
I expect to meet my brother,
    If the telegram went through;
Then '—she sobbed—' he'll come and get it,
    With many thanks to you.'

"Henry Tristan, our conductor,
    Now came through the crowded train;
And I told him why I signalled,
    And we both went back again.

> Taking up the oblong bundle,
>   We could find no plain address,
> So we put it by for orders
>   To return by next express.
>
> "But that 'order' never reached us,
>   And that 'brother' never came,
> So I took that bundle with me,
>   And it found a home and name.
> He's as bright a little youngster,
>   And as pretty as you'll find,—
> But my wife will never tell you
>   How that boy was left behind."

Charlie Lee, known far and wide as the courteous Assistant Superintendent of the Hannibal and St. Joe Railway Company, stationed at Quincy, Ill., has persuaded his line to adopt a plan that seems likely to rid that road of the three-card monte swindlers.

Each conductor is provided with a number of large cards bearing this inscription: "Beware of three-card monte and confidence men." Whenever any of these gentry are discovered aboard a train, the conductor goes into the car and puts up the warnings over the door, where everybody can see them. It makes the manipulating gentlemen wince and swear and beg, but the sign stays there to their sad discomfiture. If all the roads would adopt some such plan, there would be fewer robberies by these men to report.

Jule Coleman, a conductor on the same road, thought it was a good time and place to slip in a good joke on "Ox-Horns," of Galesburg, Illinois. "Ox-Horns" is the trade-mark of John A. Marshall, the Illinois clothing man, who gets up the "harness" for all the railway men in the Northwest. His establishment in Galesburg,

Illinois, is a sort of railroad headquarters, where Greenhalgh cuts and Gowdey swings the style. "John" is a leader in the Methodist Church, a practical wag, and incorrigible joker. In passing the contribution-box in his church on one occasion, he came to a seat crowded with conductors, and saluted them thus:

"Tickets, gentlemen, tickets. You can't ride on this train unless you pay. Salvation is free, but it costs like h—l to run the church."

"John" met with his match once. He used to pick up a friend or two and run out to Brookfield, on our road, to enjoy a few days with Blossom, of the Passenger House there. On one of these visits he met with the advance agent of a concert troupe, who rode into Brookfield in a gay vehicle resembling a pedler's cart. "John" offered to go ahead on his route and bill a town or two, and it was agreed that he should start with the wagon next morning. A few miles out of town, old lady rushes out of the house, when the following colloquy ensues:

Lady—"Say, what have you got to sell?"

John—"I am a travelling agent, madame, for the great menagerie of ancient and modern times, which is shortly to be exhibited in this section."

Lady—"Have you any elephants?"

John—"We have, madame, six elephants; but these constitute a comparatively unimportant part of the show. We have living specimens of bipeds and quadrupeds, who roamed the earth not only in the antediluvian, but also in pliocene and postminocene periods, embracing the megatherium, with six legs and two—"

Old Lady—"Well, I declare."

John—"But, madame, the greatest curiosity of our exhibition is a learned and classical-educated monkey, who was brought up by a Mohammedan priest in the region of the great Desert of Sarah. He wears one of Ox-Horns' best suits ; a hat fitted to his head by the famous Charvat,* and he speaks with fluency all the modern languages, besides Latin, Greek, Swede, and Cesky. While being exhibited in Washington, he actually repeated Grant's—"

[Beautiful young lady suddenly sticks her head from the window and calls out :]

" Mother ! mother ! Ask him why they let the monkey travel so far ahead of the other animals !"

" I am a passenger conductor," said Palmer, " on the road running from Covington to Lexington, in Kentucky. I have a love-passage to communicate, for the entertainment of the ladies. If any one doubts its authenticity, I refer to Halstead, of the Cincinnati *Commercial*, and Bloss, of the *Enquirer*. These gentlemen were on a voyage at the time, looking up the Know-Nothings, and were on my train when it occurred.

" On the Orange Road was a newly married couple, who got on at Arrington depot, in Nelson. They were billing and cooing every five minutes, to the infinite disgust of the females and the amusement of the other sex. I admired one favorite posture. He was sitting at the window, and she was anxious to see the country, and leaned across his knees to look out. Of course he wasn't going to let her fall out and be left, so he got a good Kentucky hold round her body, and never broke his

---

* This refers to Mr. Charles H. J. Charvat, of Spear Bros., a native of Tennessee, and one of the most popular and accomplished young merchants in the City of Galesburg. He is familiar with the languages named, and this explanation is given, lest he be confounded with Mr. Marshall's questionable animals.

grip for an hour. The pressure at times must have been about seventy-five pounds to the square inch. Then he would slack up. She was 'mighty' afraid of dropping out of the window, for she never whimpered, even when he tightened his arms to the last notch ; that is, when going across the river and ugly high banks. After she had seen the country enough, they began to whisper to each other, and after each whisper bite an ear, holding it a little while and 'chawing' like puppies do your fingers, in fun. He would make out sometimes she had bit him too hard and tousle her for it. The tousling was the best part of the performance. She knew she had done wrong in the auricular matter, and ought to be tousled. Most of the men in the car thought so, and if she hadn't submitted they were ready to help in this act of justice.

"Several of them stood up every now and then, to be ready if their services were needed. Some were interested to such extent in suppressing, with marked and repressive punishment, this unlawful compression of the male acoustic organ between the incisors of the female, that first refreshing themselves by passing to the ice-cooler and swallowing deep draughts and then returning to the neighborhood where the sufferer was avenging himself, keeping their arms in position for immediate use in case of emergency. The vanquished was doomed to support the head of the conqueror till he should recover from the fatigue of asserting his rights. I could tell you more."

"I am a brakeman with 'Cotton' Smith, the handsomest conductor on the Toledo, Peoria, and Warsaw Road. The Wabash fellows call it the 'Tired, Poor, and Weary.' We run from Peoria to Warsaw, a little town on a high bluff, overlooking the Mississippi river."

"Oh, well, go ahead, or give the track to somebody else."

"Well, one trip, as we were about to pull out of Warsaw, an old man came down to the cars to see his daughter off. 'Cotton' helped him to secure a seat for her, and he went round to the window to say a parting word, kind of private like, you know. While he was passing out the daughter left her seat to speak to a friend, and at the same time a prim-looking lady, who occupied the seat with her, moved up to the window. Unaware of the important changes inside, the old gentleman hastily put his face up to the window and hurriedly exclaimed, 'One more kiss, sweet pet!'

"In another instant the point of a blue cotton umbrella caught his seductive lips, accompanied by the passionate injunction : 'S'cat, you gray-headed wretch!'"

"I think I had that same blue umbrella in my train once. Its owner was named Miss Polly Partington, who, at the mature age of fifty-one, made up her mind to visit New York for the first time in her innocent life. Railroads had been unknown in Aroostook county until that summer, and she had never seen anything of the kind. The old farm-house in which she lived was seven miles from the station. Taylor, the station-master, was telling me how she sat calmly upon a seat placed on the great wooden platform which surrounds the country depot, and gazed with amazement upon the train that arrived, paused a few moments to take on passengers, and then proceeded upon its journey. As she gazed after the train, Taylor inquired :

"'Why did you not get on, if you wished to go to New York?'

"'Git on!' said Miss Polly, 'git on! I thought this whole consarn went!'

"Taylor explained that the platform was stationary,

6

and when we came up with the express train I found her
a seat by the side of a benevolent old gentleman.   I was
curious to know how my unsophisticated passenger would
act, and after awhile made it convenient to be near.
Clutching fast hold of the seat in front of her, she was at
first much alarmed at the speed at which we were going,
but gradually became calm and much interested in the
novelty of her surroundings. The old gentleman answered
her many inquiries very civilly, and among other things
tried to explain the use of the telegraph wires, and told her
that messages are sent over the wires at a greater speed
than they were travelling. 'Wa'al, wa'al,' said Miss Polly,
'you don't ketch me a-ridin' on 'em, for this is as fast as I
want to go, anyhow.'   She saw so many wonderful things
that she concludes at last not to be astonished at anything.
A misplaced switch sends us into the train that preceded
us, and our friend is thrown to the end of the car, among
a heap of broken seats.   She supposes it to be the ordinary manner of stopping, and quietly remarks, 'Ye fetch
up rather sudden, don't ye?'   I returned after a time,
and found that the old gentleman had provided her a seat
in a forward car which was uninjured, and she arrived at
her journey's end without further accident.

"Here she was surrounded by a crowd of eager hackmen, and listens in wonder to their oft-repeated call of
'Hack!' 'Hack.'   Grasping her umbrella in one hand,
and her bandbox in the other, she looks down into the
face of the loudest driver with the compassionate inquiry,
'Air you in pain?'   She is rescued from the consequences of his wrath by her nephew, who came to the
depot to look for her."

"I was the party who conducted Mr. A. Ward from
Providence to Boston, though you may have heard of it

before. The famous wag was feeling miserable and dreading to be bored, when a man approached him, sat down, and said :

"'Did you hear the last thing on Horace Greeley?'

"'Greeley? Greeley?' said Artemus. 'Horace Greeley? Who is he?'

"The man was quiet about five minutes.   Pretty soon he said :

"'George Francis Train is kicking up a good deal of a row over in England; do you think they will put him in a bastile?'

"'Train? Train? George Francis Train?' said Artemus, solemnly.   'I never heard of him.'

"This ignorance kept the man quiet for fifteen minutes; then he said :

"'What do you think about General Grant's chances for the Presidency?   Do you think they will run him?'

"'Grant? Grant? hang it, man,' said Artemus, 'you appear to know more strangers than any man I ever saw.'

"The man was furious; he walked up the car, but at last came back, and said :

"'You confounded ignoramus, did you ever hear of Adam?'

"Artemus looked up and said : 'What was his other name?'"

"Jack Haney, known as 'Old Flat-wheel,' formerly of the Prairie du Chien, is now a popular conductor on the Union Pacific.   He had charge of the famous excursion train, composed entirely of Pullman cars, on lightning time, from New York to San Francisco.   He had orders to see how fast he could go !   Old Devant, President of the road, was aboard, and, remonstrating with

Jack, told him to decrease his speed, or he would kill every one on the train.

" ' My orders are,' replied Jack, ' to take you over this division of the road as fast as steam can carry you. You needn't be alarmed about so small a train as this. When we kill any out here, we always kill enough to make it an object ! ' "

" Hank Argentine, a popular conductor on the Rock Island Road, says he likes to see a commercial traveller taken down occasionally. On a recent occasion, one of these gentry got on his train, and, as usual, spread himself and baggage over two seats. A lady afterwards entered, apparently a young and timid thing, and, after some trouble, I got her crowded in among the travelling man's baggage, on the opposite seat. Then my commercial began to do the agreeable ; they are always so knowing, those travelling men. He began to suggest to the young lady that the spring season was approaching, when she hoped there would be no collision. ' Fine weather for vegetation,' continued Commercial. ' Yes,' said the lady, ' green things were growing bold.' ' Which way was she going ?' ' Going for him, if he didn't keep a proper distance.'

" ' Ah, see,' he said, not at all discomfited, pointing to a calf through the window—' See ! what sort of an animal is that ? '

" ' I should judge, from its resemblance to you,' she replied promptly, ' that it was a travelling man looking for his baggage.' "

" ' I wanted to put in a word before we go,' said Cleveland, " for ' Billy ' Smith, one of the first and most popular conductors on the T., W. & W. Road. An old lady coming from Iowa was put on the train at Clayton. She was ninety-two years old, deaf, and partially blind. It was one of the coldest nights of a severe Western winter, and the old lady was but thinly clad. She had no ticket or pass—nothing to show where she wanted to go. She could only tell that her son put her on the train, but, with tears, refused to divulge any names. When the train was well under way, the lady had occasion to leave her seat for a moment, when the humane conductor, searching everywhere for a clue to the mystery, found a slip of paper under the seat, upon which were these words, written in a clerkly hand:

" ' This woman wants to go to Salem.'

" 'Billy' carried her to Bluff City, put her in charge of the agent there, with instructions to send her to Salem next morning. She was found cold and stiff near the Salem depot next evening, having perished from cold and exposure. There was some excitement and suspicion of foul play.

"Mr. Smith asked the Company for leave of absence, which was granted. He then went back over the route to the point in Iowa supposed to have been the poor woman's starting-place. It was never known how, inch by inch, he made his way to the unnatural son's very door. Nor did it ever transpire how much of his own money Mr. Smith expended in that long and uncertain search. Suffice it to say, that the son was brought to justice. It turned out that the old lady stood between the son and the possession of a splendid farm which he was to inherit from a deceased father at the mother's death. With the deliberate coolness of a villain, he sought to anticipate death, that had already called through slow but sure decay. When asked why he gave time and money to a matter that concerned the State, rather than himself, Mr. Smith replied with feeling :

"'The law is very slow, boys, and I could not help thinking, that perhaps that poor old woman was *somebody's mother*. I have an old mother at home, myself!'"

"One or two conundrums, boys," said "Fatty," of the Ohio & Mississippi, as the party arose to go. "Little Mary Wenner, of York, Pennsylvania, discovered a broken rail in a railroad track the other day, and swung her apron to the engineer of an approaching train in such a manner that he stopped, and saved the train from destruction. Now how much money did that Company pay this little heroine in cash?"

" Eighty-five cents."

" One stick of peppermint candy."

" One new Chinese fan."

" One York shillin'."

"Not a penny," resumed "Fatty," "but the boys on the train, headed by Billings, the engineer, and the passengers, raised her a purse of $200 before the train resumed its run!"

Charlie Clark, of the Union Pacific, came in with another :

" A baggage-master on the New York Central has, in the last twenty-eight years, travelled almost a million and a half of miles. What was his run per day?"

Parker, of the Cincinnati & Marietta Road, took a hand :

" Mr. Julius A. Sumner, of Akron, Ohio, claims to be the first man to ride on a passenger car in the United States, and that he sailed on the first steamboat on Lake Erie. What relation is he to Charles Sumner, and if so, how much?"

" Brake, brake, brake !
    Oh ! where can the brakeman be ?
And in ladies' ears I cannot speak
    The thoughts that arise in me.

" Oh ! well for the ' Railway Arms,'
    Where the brakeman is smoking, they say,
Quaffing huge draughts of ale,
    And forgetting the 'permanent way,'

" While the stately train goes on
    To destruction under the hill,
And the blame is laid on a vanished hand,
    Or a signalman's fickle will.

" Brake, brake, brake !
    I hope no collision may be,
For compensation when I am dead
    Will bring small comfort to me."

IX.

NO ONE TO BLAME.

[The reader is referred to the rhyme on page 115, entitled "Left Behind." The following verses were subsequently found pinned to a portion of the child's clothing. It was supposed that the young mother intended to leave the little waif on some particular door-step, on an appropriate occasion, but afterwards changed her mind.]

EFT on the door-step, 'mid lightning and rain,
The same old story told over again;
Of love unrequited, desertion, and shame,
Left on the door-step, no home and no name.

Robes all embroidered, fine flannels and lace,
Who could have left it alone in this place?
Some fair and fine lady, with tears and embrace,
Left it here sleeping—a smile on its face.

Or some friendless maiden, with no one to blame,
Whom poverty crush'd, then gave over to shame;
Whose stricken heart prayed for love and a name—
Left on the door-step, and no one to blame.

Perhaps these fine laces were woven in tears,
Each thread a new heartstring, that tells of her fears—
Fears of the villain who gave it to life,
And made her a mother, but never a wife.

See those initials, how splendidly wrought,
No coarse, clumsy fingers e'er shapen'd that thought ;
Two syllables outlined—of some broken name—
Whisper them softly—there's no one to blame.

Whisper them softly—the rest are entombed
In a heart that is broken, a soul that is doomed ;
I would not awaken that sorrow again,
By a word rudely spoken, or a thought to give pain.

Take it up, lady, there's no one to blame,
Tho' the fop in your parlor has the poor mother's name ;
Flatter his graces, tell daughter to come,
He has wealth—and the secret need never be known.

Hunt down the mother, go blacken her name,
Don't mention her sorrow, but tell of her shame ;
How she has fallen, that others might rise,
Keep her well under, till the stricken thing dies.

Send love to the heathen, in Charity's name,
Ask God to bless Pagans in some foreign clime ;
But crush the poor sister, without a friend near,
She loved and she trusted, no help for her here.

See ! it is smiling on you and on me,
While the mother is praying, where no eye may see ;
Take it up, lady, there's no one to blame,
Maybe the angels will give it a name.

X.

THE RAILWAY POSTAL SERVICE.

Advantages of the New System over the Old—The Standard Road
in the Western Service—At the "Gem City"—Pointless Jokes
—Impecunious Swindlers, etc.

DISTRIBUTING Post Offices are now to be
found on all first-class lines, the system of route
agents having been abandoned. A handsome
car, constructed especially for the purpose, is provided, and has a place next the express car, on all express
trains. There are two compartments or divisions—one
for letters and another for papers. A recess in the forward part of the car is for mail-bags, that contain both
"through" and "way" mail. There are two postal
clerks to each car : the responsible chief, who presides
over the letter department, and the assistant, who
"learns" the routes and serves his apprenticeship, among
the papers. Both are sworn into the Government service,
and the car itself has no direct communication with the
rest of the train. No one, save a sworn Government employé is allowed admission into this car, and the plebeian
railroad employé is always given to understand that a
portion of the American Government is abroad.

It was formerly the custom to have the distributing done in local post offices. Everything had to be "billed" and "booked," and accounts kept of letters sent and received. Now the local office has but to "bundle" its letters, fasten with string, put them in bags, and send to the route cars. The postal clerks then distribute them while *en route*. There is no longer any necessity for the vast quantities of complicated books and miscellaneous stationery, the stock-in-trade being stout string. All mail-matter used to be sent to the leading metropolis, marked "D. P. O.," for distribution. By the new arrangement the force is reduced in the local offices and increased on the road. This prevents all unnecessary delay. For instance, Western letters used to stop twelve hours at Chicago or Buffalo for distribution. By the new system they are bagged through. Leaving the hands of the writer, a letter never stops until it reaches the person to whom it is addressed.

It is calculated now that a letter will travel as fast as a human being, which every one will acknowledge to be a vast improvement upon the old method.

Of roads running out of Chicago, the Chicago, Burlington, and Quincy is called the Standard, in the Postal Service, in the West. It carries more mail, by actual weight, than any other Western road. As the department weighs the mails once every year, this fact can be readily ascertained. The next road is the North-western, and so closely were they matched, that at one time they indulged in the most bitter rivalry.

With the Government seal upon the door of the railway postal car, as well as upon the lips of the officials, the author found it difficult to learn much of their Every-day Life by actual observation. Their places of rendezvous are at the junction of two or more lines ; at the beginning or terminus of long "runs," where a night intervenes between the arrival and departure of trains. But three or four can come together on these occasions, and the leisure hour detracts but little from the monotony of the busy day. If it is at Quincy, a few jokes and "drives" over a mug of beer at the "Gem City," send them to their bunks for a few hours' rest. Notwithstanding a frequent poultice of wine and beer, the jokes are usually dry, and without point. For instance :

Hank Boblett says the H. & St. Joe Road is one of the heaviest of mail routes, but the work consists chiefly of hauling in butter, eggs, and potatoes.

Then Poole tells of Bonham's mistake in regard to Dilge, and how the latter escaped the mistake his victuals made.

Then Moore of the Wabash tells how Hartman wanted a double house, and Hartman gives the details of how Moore was seized with diphtheria in his off ear. Moore is the "wag of the Wabash," and his comrades throw a bag at him whenever one comes in their way. On one occasion, a clerk was transferred from the C., B. & Q. to the Wabash, and placed over Moore and his associates. This was a bit of "red tape" of the wrong color, and did not "distribute" worth a cent. They turned the boxes on the new man. "How do you like the new run?" they asked, after a trip or two. "Oh, it's a bore," was the reply. "When I was over on the C., B. & Q., all I had to do was to throw 'North' in front of me, and 'South' behind, but here you throw North to the West, and South to the East." Porter advised him to buy a compass, but he was removed before it arrived.

Palmer tells of a fellow who handed in a letter at the

State Line for the Pump Works in La Fayette. It was said to contain $12, but never reached its destination. A "tracer" discovered that the letter went through all right, but that the writer in his haste had neglected to enclose the money. Another man came to him and wanted $5 returned, claiming to have mailed that amount in a letter that had never been received. Beard, a special agent of the Money Order Department, thereupon started over the route to investigate the matter, spending time and money in a fruitless search. It was the opinion of experienced clerks, that persons pretending to pay debts in this way never enclose the money at all. The blame therefore falls on postal clerks, who frequently forfeit lucrative positions, at the demand of some impecunious and unprincipled adventurer.

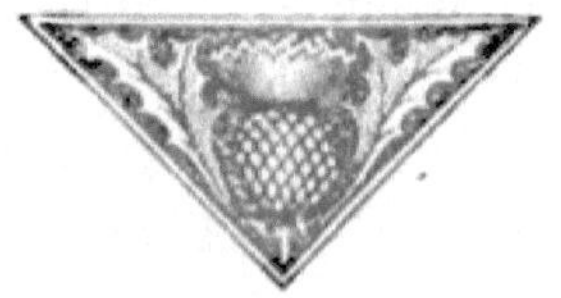

XI.

THE NIGHT EXPRESS.

HALF AN HOUR till train time, sir,
    A fearful dark night, too ;
Look at the switch-lights, Tom, my boy,
    Fetch in a stick when you're through.
" On time ! " why yes, I guess so,
    Despatch says " left all right ; "
She'll come round the curve a-flyin',
    Sime Murray comes up to-night.

Don't know him ! well, he's engineer ;
    Been on here all his life ;
I'll never forget the mornin'
    He married his little wife.
The summer the mill-hands struck, sir,
    Quit work there, every one ;
Kicked up a row in the village,
    And shot old Donavan's son.

Murray was there say an hour,
    When up came an order from Kress,
Ordering Sime to go up there,
    And bring down the Night Express.

He left his gal in a hurry—
  A pity to spoil the fun—
Thinkin' of nothin' but Mary,
  And the train he had to run.

And Mary sat by the window,
  To wait for the Night Express;
And sir, if she hadn't 'a' done so,
  She'd been a widow, I guess.
For it must 'a' been nigh midnight
  When them mill-hands left the ridge,
They come down, the drunken devils,
  Tore up a rail from the bridge.

But Mary heard 'em workin'—
  Guessed there was somethin' wrong—
And in less than fifteen minutes
  Murray's train would be along.

She couldn't come here to tell us,
  A mile—it wouldn't 'a' done—
So she just grabbed up a lantern,
  Then made for the bridge alone.
Down came the Night Express, sir,
  And Sime was making her climb,
But Mary held up the lantern,
  A swingin' it all the time.

Well, by Jove ! Sime saw the signal,
  And stopped the Night Express;
And he found his Mary cryin',
  On the track, in her weddin' dress.
Cryin' and laughin', for joy, sir,
  And holdin' on to the light—
Hello ! here's the train—good-by, sir,
  Sime Murray's on time to-night.

XII.

HEN the smoke blew and the sparks flew, and we stopped to put off or take on, you could hear the church-bells ringing, and the katydids chaffering and interrupting each other, like gossips over their tea. The noise and hurry of the night express, and the peaceful, sleepy country life blended for an instant in a kind of harmony, and then, by contrast, went wider and wider of each other than before.

Now that the moon came out to keep an eye on the world, I felt I might drop it all off my mind. So I put down my bag and my water-proof and my head, and shut my own eyes. But my ears were wide open, you may be sure.

Pretty soon, something went wrong with the box of one of the wheels, and there was a flurry of lanterns and oil-cans and men, for a little season. Then "Pooh! pooh!" screamed the whistle, and we were off again. The moon now began to see something worth seeing. *Myself*, you understand, comfortably settled for the night, after having secured the monopoly of a whole seat, voluntarily giving up half of it to a stranger. And before the night was over, I witnessed a romance a hundred times more absorbing than sleep.

The woman who sat by me was elderly, with a sharp, handsome face, worn and marked with time and trouble. A man followed her into the car, and presently found a seat before us. Directly he turned about to my seat-mate. "He is really your husband, you know, Mrs. Evans," he said, in a low, but perfectly distinct voice.

"He is *not !*" she replied, with sudden emphasis.

Instantly how wide-awake I was !

"I beg you not to be hasty," continued the man, persuasively. "I do not pretend he did right in leaving you and his child for so many years without a word. And his second marriage is more inexcusable yet. But this second Mrs. Evans has been worse treated than you have, and if *she* will overlook her wrongs and permit him to leave her for you without making any trouble, it seems to me *you* may find it possible to forgive him ; for the sake of your boy, if you would not for yourself."

"For the sake of my boy !" broke out Mrs. Evans, passionately. "A great gift such a father would be ! I tell you, Mr. Crafts, every drop of blood in my body flies into motion thinking of such cowardly meanness and terrible wrong ; and you may be perfectly sure I will never acknowledge or even see him. This is my final answer, and you may take it now."

The handsome face grew handsomer and more immovable at every word, and I wondered at the man's hardihood in persisting any farther ; but he turned still more in his seat, with a determined and thoroughly business air, as though he had just so much to say, and should say it in any event.

All this time the man who occupied the seat before

me with Mr. Crafts, was sitting leaned against the window, with his hat slouched over his eyes, apparently asleep in his corner, but in fact listening all over, as his whole attitude in some indescribable way showed. Mr. Crafts and Mrs. Evans were both too absorbed and too excited to notice him; and indeed I suppose he had as good right to listen to what was none of his business, as I had, if it was forced into his ears.

"But, Mrs. Evans," began Mr. Crafts again, "your husband is very penitent, and ready to make any promises you may require, and to submit to any conditions whatever, if you will only acknowledge him *as* your husband. The other woman will never intrude or interfere. You shall have what property you possess secured to yourself personally, and you cannot ask any more humble confessions than he is willing to make. Besides, although he has showed lamentable and even criminal weakness in neglecting to send for or to you, yet I believe he was never really base at heart or intentionally a scoundrel. He kept hoping his business affairs would brighten, as he says, and was ashamed and discouraged about letting you know of his failures. So time passed along in this way until the woman beguiled him into a marriage, quite unconscious of what she was doing. Indeed, Mrs. Evans, your husband has apparently been more weak than wicked; and I do not think you show a Christian spirit of forgiveness in refusing to see him, at the very least."

"Mr. Crafts, I *have* no husband. He was lost to me twenty-one years ago, and I have no wish or intention of seeing or hearing anything more respecting the creature who wears his name," returned Mrs. Evans, cold and immovable as Bunker Hill Monument.

We halted a moment as we neared the next station, and she took the opportunity to pass into the next car. I never saw Mrs. Evans again, though the story did not end here.

She was scarcely gone, when a voice came from under the slouched hat in front of me. "Crafts, are you going to let her go so?" it said, in a tone startling in its woe and despair.

"I can do nothing with her, Evans. I told you so before. You have heard her talk now for yourself, and can't you be satisfied?"

"You *won't* desert me now, Crafts. I don't care so much for her, but I want my boy," said the voice in pathetic and agonized entreaty.

"I can do nothing more for you. You have sowed, and now you must reap. You hear what she says," he added, in an indifferent manner.

"Then why did you tell me at the start, she had left England with my boy, and say you would intercede for me? Why did you not leave me with Marianna and my farm in peace? Marianna was kind and cheerful and made me comfortable enough, and I should have been contented and satisfied all my life, if you had never come and told me Eugenia and my boy were living and on this side of the ocean; and then persuaded me I could come out into the world and take my place among men once more. Marianna has left me, and Eugenia will not come to me. You have lost me both my wives and taken my money besides, Marianna's boy is dead, and Eugenia's is lost to me. There is nothing for me in this life or the next," said the unhappy man.

"Business is business," returned Mr. Crafts. "I must live as well as the next man, and you cannot say but the bargain was fairly made, and the money fairly earned. You were to give me the farm outright, and in return I was to inform the second Mrs. Evans that she was not, and never had been, your legal wife; as well as do my best to bring about a reconciliation with the first Mrs. Evans—none of which was desirable work. I have closed up with Mrs. Evans the second, and made suitable and comfortable provision for her future; and I have tried my utmost with Mrs. Evans the first. But it is not my fault that she declines to have anything to do with you. I did not engage to furnish a character for you; that was beyond my power, as well as not in the agreement. It is a pity about you, but I can do nothing more; and you must admit I have fulfilled all my engagements, and done all I promised, which it appears is more than you have always done."

The man seemed already too wretched to mind this cold-blooded thrust. He only crushed his hat lower on his forehead, and settled back in his seat, a living image of forsaken and hopeless desolation. So we whirled along past sleeping villages, over long reaches of open country, under the quiet stars, and into the heart of the great, waking city, where he left the cars, disappearing from me in the gray morning among the crowd of men gathered about the station.

We need not the voice of the great archangel to tell us that " to be weak, is to be miserable." And this man who had evidently been sinfully weak all the way, and who doubtless deserved the woe he had brought upon himself—I pitied with my whole heart.

XIII.

THE LITTLE CRIPPLE.

[A machinist, killed by an accident in the shops, left a widow and two children
—Jim ———, a young engineer, and his little brother Ned. Jim was very fond
of this little brother, and frequently amused him with a ride in the yard on his engine. On one occasion, in an unguarded moment, Ned fell, one leg being crushed
under the wheel. The leg was amputated, and he lived but two years after the
occurrence. The little fellow, going about on his crutches, became a general favorite, and his sad death occasioned universal sorrow.]

IN a city of the prairie, where uncertain waters flow,
    Stands a modest little cottage, that the winter winds well
            know;
    Here and there a ragged clapboard, or an idle hinge was
            seen,
But within that shattered cottage all was wondrous neat and clean.

Everybody knew the cottage, for the little children said,
Here lived a widowed mother, and her little cripple—Ned.
On this night the storm was raging, and the prairie winds were wild,
As the mother, pale with watching, smooth'd the death-bed of her
          child.

It was not some fair, fine lady, with white and jewelled hands,
And a host of cringing lackeys to obey her least commands;
But a poor mechanic's widow, robbed by death of every joy,
Who had known no other fortune, save this little crippled boy.

In the corner were the crutches, and the toys he put away,
For he often tried to follow little comrades at their play.
On the bed he lay there sleeping, as the mother thought a prayer,
For she could not speak for weeping, and she knew that God was
           there.

She would not have him waken, and she dared not think him dead,
So she knelt and prayed in whispers, for her little crippled Ned.
Prayed that God would spare the suff'rer, and take herself in-
           stead—
But the little lips now open—" Mother, here is little Ned."

" I've been talking with the angels, and they took the pain away "—
Thus the mother's prayer was answered, thus she knew he could
           not stay.
" But they said they'd come to-morrow. Oh ! dear mother, don't
           you cry,
But give Ned a drink of water, for I'm going by and by."

With nervous step she hastened to take up the tea-cup near,
And the waiting water trembled as it caught the falling tear.
A mouthful feebly swallowed—" Mother, where is brother Jim?
When he comes from work, please tell him, Ned left good-by for
           him."

The door is softly opened, and the brother enters there,
But he hears no voice of welcome, only sobs and words of prayer.
Then the two kneel down together, in the presence of the dead,
And pray God that yet in heaven they may meet their little Ned.

XIV.

EVERYDAY LIFE ON THE RAIL.

AMONG THE FREIGHT-MEN, CONDUCTORS, AND BRAKEMEN.

The Freight-men—The Freight Conductor—The Accommodation Train—Sayre and the Lecturess—Packard's Conundrum—How Courtney got out against Brown—Conductor's P——'s great Fête—A Dollar for a Kiss—"Blazer, look yar!"—How Reddy got away with a Drover—Allison of Le Roy—"Notis!"—Promotion—Crawley's Scare—Frazier and the Swindlers—"Dutch Cooper"—Avery's "Lightning Stop"—The Dog Charmer—One Foot ahead—"Don't, John!"—Workins' Leap—Merrill and the Ku Klux—Rich Wine—The Phantom Brakeman—A Bore—In a Fog—A Coupling Pin—"Put Down the Brakes"—Dead—And No Name.

REIGHT-MEN, when off duty, usually congregate in a way-car or caboose in the yard. Their's is a rougher life than that of the more favored passenger-men ; yet it is not without its pleasures and attractions. The Company looks to the Freight Service for much of its material for advanced positions, and the rough fellow who "checks" freight to-day, may be your genteel Passenger Conductor to-mor-

row, or Division Superintendent next week. He is en-
thusiastic in extolling the merits of his branch of the
service, and dwells with ardor upon the advantages of
his own " Run ; " the power of his engine, the skill and
experience of his engineer, and the wonderful exploits
his " crew " have performed in the direction of " running
switches," "lightning stops," and dangerous couplings.
He is always ready to tell you, that any one can run a
passenger truck, but that the management of a freight
train requires great knowledge of the road, and vast executive ability. He is exceedingly jealous of his dignity
and authority, and will not hesitate to use force in the
protection of what he calls his rights. Unwilling at
all times to acknowledge superior merits in his cotempo-
raries, the conductor who is sent above him to a passenger train, becomes his mortal enemy. He sometimes
allows himself to be on speaking terms with passenger-
men, but he knew most of them when they were " freight
heavers," and he regards them merely as creatures of
luck, or the favorites of some corrupt system of promotion. When he becomes a passenger-man himself, he
regards the promotion merely as a tardy recognition of
his merits, and turns his back upon his old comrades who
spend their railway lives upon the outside rather than
within the cars. You who have travelled have met the
freight-man newly metamorphosed into the conductor of
a passenger train. He is the cross-grained, overbearing
tyrant, who answers your questions with a jerk as though
he were conferring a favor. Who has never time to be
polite or well-bred. He wears fashionable garments and
indulges in "loud jewelry." He treats those under him
as menials, and fawns with the supercilious air of a
courtier upon those who occupy stations above him.

When the smell of the freight wears off, he sometimes takes on a polish which comes of constantly brushing against travelled people and men of the world : and with a good heart within, he finally develops into "the most popular man on the road."

Those of his kind who refuse or neglect to help on the developing process, degenerate again, and we find them "running freight" on some other and distant line.

They are hardly as cosmopolitan, as a class, as passenger-men, and in meeting with a few to-day in a way-car, the author cannot promise an extensive assortment. A passenger-man of standing may leave one line and readily obtain a corresponding position upon another. A freight-man with a real or supposed prospect of promotion constantly before him, is quite apt to remain on one line, until this hope is realized or abandoned. Passing their railway lives upon the top of the train—so to speak —mingling with boxes, bales, and bundles, rather than with living, bustling human beings, their everyday experiences are dull and monotonous. The sunshine of Romance very rarely lights up the freight-man's sky, and if a joke or a bit of fun comes aboard with his merchandise, it is the exception rather than the rule.

A freight train with a passenger caboose attached is called on some lines an "Accommodation Train." It "accommodates" the Company rather than the public, and derives its chief recommendation from the fact, that it "stops at all stations." As this train has been side-tracked for the night, we find a number of the boys gathered in its caboose.

"As I was going through the car on my run to-day," said Sayre, "I saw a lady smoking a pipe very industriously in a rear seat.

7

"'Madam,' said I, as courteously as I knew how, 'we don't even allow *men* to smoke in this car.'

"'That is an excellent rule, sir,' she replied, with the utmost coolness; 'if I see any man smoking in here, I'll inform you at once.'

"I think she was some lecturess on woman's rights."

"Joe Packard, now of the Illinois Central, is probably the worst cut-up man on any road. Scarcely a portion of his body but has its scars. His last freak was an attempt to leap from a way-car that was off the track, on to a coal flat. Just as he jumped the coupling gave way, the car stopped, and he struck down in the road-bed, where there wasn't a particle of coal. He says he made a better jump since, all the way from the Erie to the Illinois Central. He used to come in every trip with a new 'religious conundrum,' as he called them. He would go up into the office and shoot them off at some one at headquarters. I remember the last one, very well.

"'How many boiled eggs could the giant Goliath eat on an empty stomach?'

"'Fifty dozen,' replied one.

"'No, sir, only a single egg. If he ate one egg, his stomach wouldn't be empty, would it?'"

Joe has a Sabbath-school now at Amboy, with Captain Wells, Rosenbush, and John Henry as pupils.

"Secoy said he was going to tell the boys how Courtney got out against Brown. He believed George would get off a joke if the Angel Gabriel should blow his horn. I was running the extra freight, with Courtney as my engineer, and Brown was pulling brother Bristol. We were pulling into Neponset, when we met 24 with her flag gone, and then went for Kewanee. When in the hollow, west of Neponset, met Bristol and Brown going for Neponset.

Thought something was wrong, and Brown was evidently of the same opinion. Courtney commenced to back up, but the grade was too much for him. I ran out after Brown to stop him. He was handling his engine with masterly skill, but still he gained on George, whose nerve failed him. He was on the last step, and his fireman on the other, ready to jump. For forty rods they ran within a car's length of each other, at a five-mile gait—we trying to get away, Brown trying to stop. Brown stood with one hand on the throttle and the other on the lever—while Courtney, at this hazardous moment, passed in one of his jokes.

"When he was in the army, he took a job at driving mules. He had a yellow mule in which he had no confidence whatever. One night, after eating up the bows of the wagon, this yellow mule commenced pawing Courtney out from under it, in order to eat him up. He thought his chances now were about as big as when the yellow mule was after him.

"All this danger was brought about through the carelessness of a brakeman who let his white lamp go out."

"Last fall," said Patch, "Tom Holdsworth had an Extra Stock East, on the Main Line. He stopped on the grade, and Len. Bassett, a brakeman, went back to flag. In starting up, the train broke in two. Bassett, seeing that he could not stop the train that was following, and gaining rapidly upon them, rushed for his own train, woke up his drovers, and jumped them out, saving a number of lives. He then put on brakes and stopped his train, the result being but a slight damage to the way-car. This was an exhibition of nerve that you don't see every day."

"Oh, I don't know as it beats Lucas much," said

Lowry. "Brakeman, Charlie Lucas, saw a head-light one night, coming pretty close. He took his torpedoes and red light, and went back. Arriving at the proper distance, he found he was flagging a belated farmer who was hunting up stray stock. There were no signs of any other pursuing train. Charlie's name has since been changed from Lucas to looseness, though he never gets tight."

"Do you know how near Bill P—— came to getting his foot in it?" asked "Pigeon."

"Didn't think there was anything big enough to hold it!"

"Yes, about ten years ago, he applied to Hammond for a passenger train.

"'All right, sir,' replied the colonel, 'only one objection.'

"'What's that?' asked P——.

"'Require an extra coach to carry your feet.'"

"Doc. Merriman says he was coming down grade once, to side-track for some train, when he saw obstructions on the track ahead. There were two or three inches of snow on the track, which made them more visible, of course. He reversed, called for brakes, and sent his fireman down to clear the way. Fireman returned, and said there was nothing there. 'Doc.' swore, and went himself. After surveying the obstacles a moment, he looked over to the switch, and there stood Patch.

"'Patch,' yelled 'Doc.,' 'the next time you cross the track in front of my engine, I want you to pick up your tracks. There ain't an engine on the road can git over 'em in three inches of snow.'"

"I think I can couple on to that," said Richardson, "and get ahead. Sam Young, well known in Truckee,

Nev., is conductor on a freight train running to Visalia, on the Southern Pacific Road. One night when the moon was full, his train was steaming over the broad plain near Visalia, just as the orb of night was rising."

" Orb of night is very good indeed," said Love.

" The moon," continued " Rich," "appeared like a locomotive head-light, in front of the train, apparently, at considerable distance ahead. The instant he saw the light, Sam yelled to the engineer to stop the train; 'for God's sake to reverse.'

" The alarm was given, the brakes whistled down in a jiffy, and the train stopped. The conductor jumped off and ran on ahead a few hundred yards as rapidly as possible on the track, and commenced swinging his red lantern as a signal of danger to the supposed approaching train. After worrying himself out in running and swinging his light, he stopped a moment, completely out of breath, and took a square look at the fancied monster in front. Sam Young saw the ' man in the moon,' and the truth flashed upon him that he was awfully bilked. He hastened back to his train, and told the engineer to go ahead, as the danger of a collision was more remote than he had calculated. The engineer, fireman, and brakeman discovered the mistake before the conductor did, and when the latter returned, there was such an explosion of laughter as was probably never heard before on a freight train. Sam promised to stand treat for the next six months if the parties who witnessed the blunder would agree not to make it public. But the joke was too broad and too good to keep, and, in spite of the promises made, it leaked out."

" Cook, of the P., P. & J., went into Chicago and paid a visit to the Dollar Store. After making some trifling purchases, he offered the pretty saleswoman a dollar for a kiss.   The lady agreed and delivered the goods.

"' Now,' says she, with a pretty foreign accent, 'give me another dollar, and you may kiss my mother.'   Cook was delighted with the adventure, and paid over the dollar.   The girl went out and returned, leading in a wrinkled old bleared-eyed female, hobbling on crutches.

"' Here she is !'

"' Not any, if you please, Miss—the fact of it is, I never mix drinks.   I am a freight conductor on the P., P. & J.   Send her to the depot, and I'll bill her through at special rates !'"

Bill and George Blazer are well-known on the H. & St. Joe, the one a conductor and the other a brakeman. It was never known what they did with that cotton, but every time they stop at a certain station, a colored girl pushes her way through the crowd, and cries :

"Say, dar! you Blazer boys—if you don't fetch back dat ar cotton, I call out your name loud as ever I kin holler."

Drovers, as a class, are the most impudent and tyrannical patrons of the Road.   It does the boys good to get away with one occasionally.   Ike Lowrey—known on the C., B. & Q. as "Champagne Charley"—went out with a stock train one day, with "Reddy" Blair as brakeman.   When they got to Altona, Ike sent Reddy back to tell the drovers that "now was a good time to get up their stock."   One of the drovers said to Reddy, "Is my stock down?"   "Yes, sir," replied the brakeman.   "You are a liar," said the insolent drover.   "You are a gentleman," responded Reddy, "which is the biggest lie I know of."   "Get out of this car," said the drover. "Who is running this car?" retorted Reddy.   "I can run it if I want to," said the drover, waxing warm.   "I

"COMPLETING THE JOB ON THE TRACK"
PAGE 151

came here like a gentleman to notify you that your stock was down, and you insult me. Now get out of this car, or there will be a piece of stock down that can't get up." Reddy then went for him, and put a Mansard roof over both of his eyes, punching him severely, and drawing him from the car, completing the job on the track. Then, calling assistance, the drover was carried back into the car, where the boys washed and dressed his wounds. The affair was subsequently investigated at headquarters, and the decision rendered that employés are justified in protecting their rights and dignity upon all occasions. This incident occurred about six months ago, and last week the drover's shirt collar was dug out of a coal-pit near Altona, and it now hangs in a frame in Roger's way-car as a bloody warning to all drovers not to drive too fast.

"I am sorry to learn from the Eastern papers," said Burton, " that my old friend Jim Allison has gone into the counterfeit-money business. Not that he was caught in the act of ' shoving the queer,' but that he had the 'queer' in his possession, there can be no doubt. Jim is agent at Le Roy, on the Erie Road, and is known all over that line as the prince of good fellows, and very fond of a joke. A short time since he received a valuable (?) package from those sharpers in New York—a small box of sawdust and $92 in bogus greenbacks. Upon paying the C. O. D. and examining his prize, Jim acknowledged that it was the first time he ever bought a 'sell,' and paid for it in cash, in his life. The papers of Le Roy thereupon published the facts, and warned the public to look out for Allison and his counterfeit money."

Simpson, of Buda, says there is a sign hung in a conspicuous place at a certain station on the T., P. & W., with the following, painted in gilt letters :

" NOTIS.

" *Aple bois are forbid to pedle thar stuff on these Platform.*"

It is feared the author of that " Notis " is subject to attacks of appleplexy.

" The system of promotion on some of our roads," remarked the Honorable Freeman of the Kansas Pacific, " if there is a system at all, is not very well defined. There is a passenger conductor on the C., B. & Q. Road in Illinois, that jumped all apprenticeship and rode into his present berth over the heads of good men who had been at the wheel for years. Another worthy fellow on the same road, Jim Howland for instance, recently got a freight train after braking on the same road for ten or twelve years. Sometimes, of course, it is the fault of the men, but it oftener happens that their claims and merits are overlooked.

" Now, there's Billy Murphy, running passenger on the Albany and Susquehanna. He was formerly a Justice of the Peace at Schoharra, New York—a man of few trials. Through the influence of influential friends, he got his present position, never serving a minute at the wheel. I'm all smashed up now, and can't get about much, so I'd like to ask Billy if he remembers when he pitched into my peanut stand at Schoharra, and if he has ever asked to be forgiven ? Also, if ' Fat Jack ' (he used to weigh 450, boys, as sure as that's a crutch)—if Fat Jack and Cas. Griffin, of the same road, remember that they were running as bounty-jumpers in the army when I was U. S. Deputy Marshal at Albany ?"

Collins—"Jack, tell us how you fellows scared Crawley out on the U. P., or whatever road it was."

Freeman—"Well; we thought it was a joke then; but it's hardly worth telling here. Johnnie Crawley was train despatcher then, good man, too. He is now train despatcher of the Lake Superior and Minnesota Road, headquarters at Duluth. We started out of Bear river with a gravel train; at the time I had charge of the pit. Crawley was on, and when we got near Aspen he thought we wasn't going quite fast enough. I told the engineer to let her out. In a few moments that train was flying. It wasn't certain that the wheels would stand that rate of speed. Crawley told me to hold her up, and Frank Brown, the conductor, tried to put on the brakes. I picked up a chunk of coal and told Brown to let her go, or I'd bust his head, until Crawley, pale with fear, yelled out:

"'This train will never reach the pit in the world; she's bound for the ditch.'

"And he got ready to jump; but we made the pit."

"Walbaum, a well-known railway-bridge builder, was travelling on a train not long since, when he was accosted by a couple of swindlers, who showed him a mysterious padlock. They were willing to bet $10 that he couldn't open it, after being shown how it was done. The trick, it seems, was in changing the key. Frazier, one of Walbaum's men, took the bet, put up the money, got a coupling pin, and opened it at a single blow. He took the money. I saw that myself."

"Dutch Cooper" was coming west on 25, and wanted to stop in the hollow near Wyanet for water. Frank Avery, the brakeman, proposed to give him a *"lightning stop"* right there, all by himself! Coming

7*

from Princeton to Wyanet, Frank fell asleep and failed to get out. The consequence was they ran by the tub, clear into Wyanet (you see it was down grade), Cooper just screaming for brakes. He was mad, and backed up to the tub, swearing like a streak.

In the meantime, Frank was scratching his head, and studying how he was to get·out of the scrape. While Cooper was taking water, Avery goes over on the engine and says :

"Cooper, I like to broke my leg back there."

"How ish dat?" asked C.

"Well, I got out on top, and tried to set the brake, but the derned dog broke, and threw me off—nearly killed me."

"Ish dat so? Vell, I wash pooty tam mad; but I feelsh better now, as you most broke your tam leg!"

That's the way Avery made the "lightning stop!"

Whenever a cur, be he of high or low degree, catches Satterfield's eye, that moment the cur is doomed. "Sat" is known as the "Dog Charmer," and he has charmed, captured, and winged 278 dogs since he has been running on the East End. It is a source of revenue not to be despised. His method is similar to that of the snake that is said to charm birds.

He catches the dog's eye, looks at him steadily for a moment, and transfixes him to the spot. Then, making a few passes, the animal is magnetized, and completely under his control. He has been known to draw a favorite dog to him in this way, while the master's hand was caressing his head, and the poor thing would glide to "Sat's" side, impelled by a force it was impossible to resist.

"Conductor P. ('now this is all among ourselves, you

know,' said Rogers) was sitting in his way-car, one day, with his legs crossed, one foot, of course, in air. A waggish passenger, who had been noticing the size and peculiar shape of the pedals, approached P., and taking out his pocket-book, said :

" ' I want to bet five dollars that that is the biggest and ugliest foot now living.'

" ' Put up your money,' said P., ' I take that bet.'

" A brakeman was called and the stakes placed in his hands. P. then coolly exhibited his other foot.

" ' The money is yours,' exclaimed the astonished passenger, and P. was five dollars ahead."

" ' Don't, John ! Don't, John '—These words tumbling off the top of a female voice, caused us to rush for Satterfield's way-car. There we found John hugging a Dutch girl, and kissing her in the intervals of her screams. After we got them separated, John explained.

" ' You see she had no monish, and no ticket, and I told her she must get off. Den she say, if I let her ride, she would let me hug her and kiss her. I was yoost gettin' my fare, boys—dat ish all. She not know de fare to Aurora, and she can no go at half price.'

" So ' Sat ' went for her again, claiming full fare ! "

Jim Workins was coming along with the way freight on the middle division. Arriving at Arlington, he found several trains there blocked up. Jim got his train stopped, and went back to flag the train following him. After stopping them pretty close to the way-car, he went inside, and feeling tired went to sleep.

Courtney, his engineer, oiled the rails in front of the drivers, got up on his engine, pulled her wide open, and called for brakes. Jim jumped to his feet, and sure that everything was going to pieces, leaped through the cupola, and lit on his hands and feet. Never pausing to look around, he kept up this leap-frog gait until he cleared the fence.

Merrill ran across a band of Ku Klux, with hook eyes, on the Buda grade. Much alarmed, he reported the circumstance at headquarters, describing their mysterious movements, and detailing all the facts. An order was issued immediately that all trains should run slow down that grade, and uncle Billy Hughes furnished extra lamps. George was complimented for working in the interest of the Company—when it was discovered that the Ku Klux were a number of coal-miners with lamps in their caps.

"Jim Richardson, or '*Rich*,' as we called him," said Lucas, "used to brake for Dan Elliott. On one occasion, when running on the Lewiston Branch, he discovered a leak, a fluid of an attractive color and odor issuing from one of the cars. He went for it with his best forefinger, sucking as he went. Pleased with the taste, and anxious to capture a bucket of the wine, he out with his key and went in. He found it a car of *green hides*, leaking; and 'Rich' has been hiding ever since."

Hackney, of the Fox River Valley Road, had a brakeman of whom he stood in the greatest fear. One time he got off the track, at Donner's Grove, on the East End. He was on the engine at the time, and in backing got her off. Having no flag, he had tied his coat on the back end of the train, but the circumstance had slipped his mind. Starting back, the wind blew the sleeves of the coat violently, and Hackney, thinking it was his brakeman on his muscle, broke for the prairie. That's an actual fact. He is frequently asked to explain about that Phantom Brakeman!

Crysdale—"We had a smash-up down near Du Quoin on the Ill. Central once, when S. M. Avery was Supt. of the Central Branch.   I don't know now how much stock was killed, but the next day Mr. Avery got the following letter :

DOOCOIN, Jan. 18—

SMAVERY

Sentralia.

I want you to cum yer at oncet theres bin a smashup i want you to bring six dollars to pay for mi hog —the hog squeeled, but the engine wouldn't stop its a bore.

. J. CERAMPLE.

"The old man thought it was 'a bore' sure enough."

Sayre—"About the only thing a conductor fears is the dense fog.   We were caught in one, one trip, and if you will let me spit it out in my own way, maybe you can understand.

"'Hank,' says I, 'you go over and tell Spielman (engineer) to keep a wild eye.   Second extra on No. 18, left Leland about five minutes ago.   Look back pretty often, see if they're coming.   Tell Spielman to side-track and let No. Four by, at Sandwich.   Tell him to get in out of the way, quicker than lightning, for No. Four will be whooping 'em up, by the time she strikes the whistling post.   I don't want to drop any torpedo on her to-night, for Si. has got 28 just out of the shop and he'd hate awfully to flag that engine.'

"Hank says, 'All right,' and rushes up the ladder, and over on to the engine.   Fog !   No, I guess not. On arriving at the switch, Spielman whistles down brakes. I call out from the way-car and ask, What's the matter ?   Si. says, Extra ahead on one side-track, engine disabled on the other.   About that time I could hear No. Four coming over the iron bridge, about a mile off!   I picked up red light and ran back with the flag.   Ran as far as I dared ; slapped down two torpedoes.   Ran a little farther, and could just see No. Four's head-light. Looked to be about forty feet in the air.   Could almost feel her hot breath, as she came tearing along, anxious to make up every lost minute.   Si. behind her—anxious for the reputation of his better half, as he styled his engine— was peering through the fog.   As he' see the red flag waved across the track, he whistled down brakes ; and without waiting to shut her off, hauled her over.   Rail being wet, she slipped, and as he struck the torpedoes, he slipped out between tender and engine, and took a look at things.   About that time his head-light shone on the hind end of a way-car, and four or five drovers were climbing off—boot in one hand, and a prod in the other —making for a corn-field.

"A miss is as good as a mile, so Si. felt greatly relieved, when he discovered that the only damage done, was the wetting of the 28 all over with that peculiar mixture of coal-dust and water, for which the boys have an appropriate name.   Believe *me*, I don't like those fogs."

When Foster was braking for John "Sat," on the East End, the train broke in two.   "Sat" sent Foster back for a pin, and the new brakeman returned with a common brass pin, that one of the boys had pulled out of his coat.   "Sat" was a little surprised, but he told him to take the pin and go back and couple the cars. Foster saw the point, and his knowledge of coupling-pins dates from that occasion.

"In regard to promotion," said George, "men who brake on freight trains are the first to rise.   The brakeman on a first-class passenger never looks out for any other train, while the brakeman on freight has to look out for every other train, especially if he is running extra. He must know the time-card thoroughly, and keep his eyes open all the time. A man who wants to learn railroading must begin with this practice. The freight brakeman goes through an experience, while the man on a passenger goes through nothing."

PUT DOWN THE BRAKES.

No matter how well the track is laid,
No matter how strong the engine is made,
When you find it running on the downward grade,
    Put down the brakes !

If the demon of drink has entered the soul,
And his power is getting beyond your control,
And dragging you on to a terrible goal,
    Put down the brakes !

Remember the adage, "Don't trifle with fire,"
Temptation, you know, is always a liar;
If you want to crush out the burning desire,
    Put down the brakes!

Are you running in debt by living too fast?
Do you look back with shame on a profitless past,
And feel that your ruin is coming at last ?
    Put down the brakes !

Whether for knowledge, for honor or gain,
You are fast wearing out your body and brain,
'Till nature no longer can bear the strain,
    Put down the brakes !

The human is weak, since Adam's fall ;
Beware how you yield to appetite's call ;

" Be temperate in all things," was practised by Paul ;
Put down the brakes !

Ah, a terrible thing is human life !
Its track with many a danger is rife ;
Do you seek for the victor's crown in the strife ?
Put down the brakes !

XV.

DEAD—AND NO NAME.

[December 18, 1867, several persons were burned to death in the disaster at Angola. A young lady was found in the rear end of a coach, seated upright, in a natural position—*Dead!* There were traces of fire upon the hat or bonnet, the hair was slightly burned, and a portion of the dress ; the eyes and lips wearing marks of violence. There were evidences of rare beauty ; the clothing was costly and elegant ; but there was nothing to lead to identification, save a single initial found upon her garments, the plain letter " M." There was no luggage, and Mr. John Fisk, the conductor, had but a vague impression that she was going to Le Roy. The car in which she was found was only slightly damaged by fire, and it was supposed that she died from fright. Others thought that some villain, taking advantage of the excitement and confusion, attempted a nameless crime, and she died through fear of a worse fate than death by fire. All efforts to obtain a clue to her name and history, were in vain.]

HERE is the face,
　　With marks of fire on it, remains of a bonnet,
　　A piece of veil round it, just as they found it,
　　　　But no certain trace.

　　Eyes all a blot ;
The torn lips remaining, a half smile retaining—
Closed with a prayer—could God have been there,
　　　　Or was she forgot ?

　　A bit of rare lace ;
Around the neck turning, saved from the burning,
Charged with a clue, to some lover true,
　　　　Who knew her embrace.

Handkerchief? Yes!
Richly embroidered, now soiled and disordered,
Here, near the hem, the plain letter " M,"
  The rest you may guess.

A torn glove there!
In it still lingers the shape of the fingers;
That some one has pressed, may be, and caressed,
  So slender and fair.

A ring here you see !
No name or date on it, yet love must have won it ;
A pledge of vows plighted, perhaps of love slighted—
  Where can *he* be ?

One heavy shawl,
On the seat near her, it could not be clearer ;
Spotted and soiled, torn and all spoiled
  And—that is all !

Under the hat,
With the bit of veil round it, just as they found it,
Rich golden hair—a mother somewhere,
  Would recognize that !

Years now have passed ;
And her sad history remains yet a mystery,
Attempts to obtain some clue were in vain,
  Till hope died at last.

 Dead—and no name !
Was it some sorrow, the dread of to-morrow,
Or was there foul play? There is no one to say,
  And no one to blame.

XVI.

HOW TO DETECT THEM.

BY AN OLD CONDUCTOR.

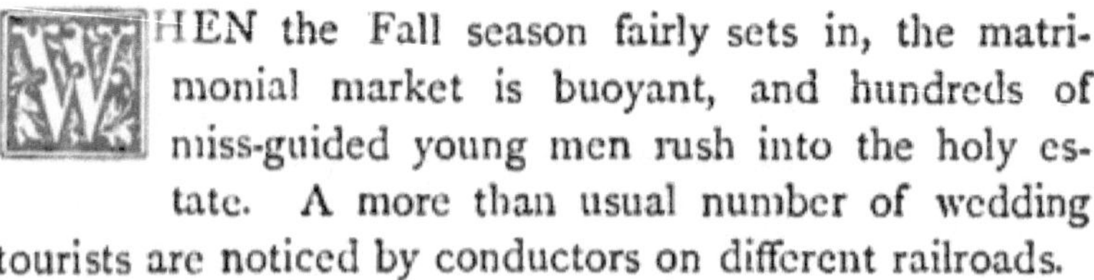

HEN the Fall season fairly sets in, the matrimonial market is buoyant, and hundreds of miss-guided young men rush into the holy estate. A more than usual number of wedding tourists are noticed by conductors on different railroads.

Of course, it is not on account of being ashamed of each other that they try to disguise their situation, but simply to avoid being criticised and remarked upon by profane strangers. Thus they lay the fond unction to their souls, that they are travelling *incog. /* But, good gracious! how badly fooled they are. It is one of the easiest things in the world, to the careful eye, to tell precisely how many days, or even hours, they have been spliced. They can sometimes be detected by the great pains they take to appear like old married people or cousins, as they sit demurely in the cars. In many cases their dress in part exposes them—it is so *apropos* to the occasion, being neat, symmetrical, and bran new.

In cases where the parties have good taste, there is no gaudiness or flub-dubbing about their attire. All glitter and display are thrown aside, and the city belle appears more like a Quakeress in her simple travelling dress of drab or mouse-color.

Sometimes the youthful culprits engage in playing at lovers, or affect a flirtation, but it is always a stupendous failure. Their eyes betray too much happiness for wit and repartee; there is such a peculiar softness and tenderness in their confidential whispers, and such a pride in the possession of each other, that none around them are deceived. It is generally the case, that the bridegroom makes the discovery first, and throws his arm carelessly around the shoulders of his wife, as much as to say defiantly to the envious, " Who's afraid? Who knows but we have been married many years?"   Not know?

The guilty slyness in the way that arm steals round, first on the seat-back, then gradually closer, while the bride evinces a silent pleasure as she acquiesces in a very unperceiving way. Indeed, it is she who lets the cat out of the bag, most quickly. The narrow-gauge seats are most preferable to the broad-gauge, and if you sit on the seat back of them, you will observe at first the lady's shoulders are not even—they incline just a little to her partner. After travelling in this position a few hours, her neck gets as limber as a washed paper collar, and her head gravitates to the broad shoulders of her husband, and there it nestles innocently and confidingly, in the repose of honest, pure, and truthful love. At times, in spite of all precautions, a tress or two of her golden locks will get loose and drop on her shoulder. But it almost seems that there is order and neatness in their very disorder and abandon.

So they go, fancying themselves lost in the crowd—unnoticed, unknown; with their secret locked up in their own palpitating bosoms.   Poor young people !

ON COMMISSION.

A CONDUCTOR'S COMPLAINT.

I wish to ask what I am to do for the abatement of a certain nuisance, to which I am much exposed.   The question is one of those which I feel sure that nobody on earth can answer, for which reason I am the more deeply impressed with the necessity of putting it.

Mine is the case of A. B., a single man, who says he is not likely to marry.   His age he refuses to state with precision, but admits that it is not under thirty-nine.   Is a passenger conductor, and not a wealthy man.   To make the most of his income, he has to exercise the most rigid economy.   He resides at a station on a road running into the city of New York—you may call it Poughkeepsie or Salamanca.   It was his fate to have been born and reared in that town, and to be personally acquainted with every man, woman, and child in it.   Is quite sure that he never takes his train from that station without being loaded with commissions.   Cannot be deceived in his recollection on that subject.   Said commissions have on several occasions broken his peace, and deprived him of the liberty of action to which he considers himself by law entitled.

He thinks it may be true, that as a general rule, a little commission taken singly is a trifle; but that little commissions become onerous by reason of their multi-

tude and variety. He doubts whether a conductor starting out on his run, be not an ass when he permits his pan-
niers to be laden to his own discomfort. His particular
misery is, that he himself knows not how to avoid being
such an ass, unless he be content that all his friends
should regard him as a good-for-nothing, disobliging cur-
mudgeon. He has thought of quitting Poughkeepsie or
Salamanca forever; he has also thought of never quitting
it for half an hour. The origin of A. B.'s grievance is to
be found, perhaps, in his possession of a certain reputation for the scrupulous exactness which is not uncommon
in bachelors; and for good-nature, as well as a conscientious desire to discharge himself honestly of any trust re-
posed in him. He has known young friends to keep
a commission in reserve three weeks, in order that it
might be his felicity to execute it.

A. B. further declares that he has one day of his own
between trips. On this day he is visited by numerous
friends—each with a commission. First, a small boy
brings a note saying that Mrs. Williams would be glad to
see Mr. A. B. at once, on important business. After the
ascent of a steep and not undefiled staircase, the deponent states that he knocked at Mrs. Williams' door,
which was inscribed with her name on a brass plate.
After a sufficient number of courtesies had passed, deponent made allusion to the "important business," upon
which there ensued, as nearly as he can remember, the
following conversation :

Mrs. Williams—" Oh, my dear Mr. A. B., you have no
idea how anxious I am that nothing will prevent you
from taking your train to-morrow. You know the state
poor little Hofer is in. His second teeth, I may say, are
all breaking out in a mob over the roof of his mouth, in-

stead of coming up in file out of his gums. You know Mr. Teether in New York?"

A. B.—"The great dentist?"

Mrs. Williams—"Oh, yes. You know every one. I have been told that if I would take a model of my Hofer's mouth in wax, and send it to him, he can have an instrument made which, when worn, will restore the teeth to order. I have already taken the model, and it will carry very nicely in this little tin box. How long are you in New York?"

A. B.—"One day."

Mrs. W.—"I am sure he can have it made in time, at least, for your next trip. I wish Hofer was here, that you might look into his mouth, then you would know how to explain it exactly."

Deponent further states that, having parted with this lady, with a promise to fulfil her wish, and the model of Hofer's mouth in his pocket, he called next upon Mrs. Ferguson. A. B. deposes that a discharge of cannon could not have startled him more than the production of a fragile box of card-board, which seemed to be about a foot and a half high, and of the same circumference—a muff and tippet box—which she placed sideways before him on a chair, and which she declared would take up no room at all in his car. That it was simply a muff and tippet that a relative in New York had commissioned her to send by the first opportunity.

A. B.—"Pardon me, madam, but would it not be better to send it by express. I should be obliged to carry it about loose."

Mrs. F.—"I dare not trust those rough expressmen, they are so careless. I should not object to your carrying it loose, if you will be sure and not lose it." (Afterthought, expressed with a sweet smile.) "It can sit on your knee."

A. B. felt bound to smile amiably, and further deposes that he took the muff and tippet, and was under the necessity of paying the expressage on the parcel out of his own pocket.

Mr. and Mrs. Comstock were next visited. This married couple had been resident during three years in my station.

Mrs. Comstock—"Ah, yes, to-morrow is your day. How I wish ladies could be conductors. It seems years since I have been in New York ; but then home is where husband and children are. By the bye, speaking of children, I must not forget a little commission I have to give you."

A. B.—"What is it ; anything in my power I shall do with all my heart for you, Mrs. Comstock."

Mrs. C. (laughing)—"Oh, I have only a very little, foolish thing to ask. You will laugh, perhaps, but I remember hearing my mother speak of the benefit her children derived from it. An anodyne necklace—perhaps two "——

A. B.—"Half a dozen, if you like."

Mrs. C. (playing with her baby)—"That will be too many. One can get nothing here. No, two. Then my little darling will not have the pain her sister had in cutting tooti-ittle-teethums."

A. B.—"Good-day, then."

Deponent adds, that he paid other visits, or rather replied to other notes in person and received other commissions. But the whole harvest of commissions was not reaped. In the evening there came a note from an old skeleton of sixty-five, who seemed to be fully persuaded

that cod-liver oil would bring flesh to her bones, and the
color of youth to her cheek ; and that cod-liver oil was to
be had pure nowhere but in New York. Deponent was
to bring some of that oil (which he utterly loathes and
abominates). The bottle was not likely to break if carefully packed in his valise or ticket-box. The next morning, A. B. further states, as he was about to start his train,
he felt his arm grasped from behind, and a soft voice
said, "One word, only one word." The voice was that
of our leading milliner. Her commission was, that I
should see a sister of hers and tell her that their very
amiable and esteemed friend Mrs. R. was in Poughkeepsie or Salamanca.

That trip was tolerably well got through. The message concerning the existence in Poughkeepsie or Salamanca, of the amiable and esteemed Mrs. R., was delivered to the fascinating sister in that lady's garden.

Sister—"How good and kind you are ! And this
charming Mrs. R., you will see her ?"

A. B.—"It would give me great happiness to do so."

Sister—"Ah !   Yes, yes" (with her hand on her forehead, in deep thought).   "And what have I—" (suddenly
very radiant).   "What happy ideas !"

The lady darted forward, and selected from a stand, a
tall flowering shrub, of what nature complainant (who is
no botanist) is unable to testify ; but it shot up to the
height of three feet from a large pot, and was covered
with blossoms of a powerful and sweet, but very sickly
odor.

Sister—"Dear Mr. A. B., I will send it ; you will take
it ?"

A. B.—"Utterly impossible, madam !"

Sister (caressingly)—"Yes, yes !   You are so good

you cannot refuse me. What do you say? It will be spoiled? Not one blossom will ever reach her?" (Looks very serious, calls a gardener, and gives an order in which A. B. catches the word pasteboard.) "Nothing is impossible, my kind friend, for you and for me. Good-day, sir. My kindest friendship for ——. Quick, Adolphe! quick!"

Adolphe was quick, and complainant testifies that he had scarcely reached the depot to take his train, when Adolphe appeared; that he had seated himself in a coach for a moment's chat with an old friend, when Adolphe succeeded in thrusting between his legs the detested shrub, so packed as to bear a strong resemblance to a funnel, and of such height that it reached to within not many inches of his nose. He pulled the rope and the train started. Before twenty minutes had elapsed, a young woman who was sitting opposite the said shrub, turned suddenly pale and then fainted; whereupon a man who seemed to be her husband, uttering many vile phrases, wrenched the said shrub from between A. B.'s legs, and without a word of apology, threw it out of the window! Did A. B. expostulate? Oh, no!

A. B. deposes that he fulfilled all commissions as his power served, but that he had firmly resolved on leaving New York to forget the cod-liver oil. Fancy his surprise, therefore, when only fifteen miles out, a brakeman came with a package that had been left with him for me, as the train was pulling out. This was a half-gallon bottle of that medicine which was to his mind so offensive and disgusting. The lady for whom it was intended had, with the prudence of age, despatched her order in a letter to Helmbold, to save her kind friend the trouble of a journey to his store.

I have set down my case as judiciously and temperately as I can, and now I ask what I am to do? What is any man to do who is in a position similar to mine?

XVII.

The Railway Telegraph Service—The Train Despatcher—The Six Spectres—Out on the Line—The Irishman's Telegram—Bixbie's Customer—The Loafer's Seat—A Negative Bliss—The Dot and Dash—How Operators carry them—Scene at a Dinner-Table— The Night-Operator's Ruse—The Superintendent and the Operator—An Incident—Telegraph Gossip.

NOW that trains are "run" by telegraph on all our prominent railways, only the most experienced and expert operators are employed. They must be "sound" operators and sound men in every instance. A visit to the train-despatcher's office at any railway headquarters, will cause one to wonder how admirably the system of railway telegraphy operates.

Here are, say, half a dozen of the oldest and most experienced of operators, giving their ears to the "tick" and their eyes to the card ; watching through the wires the machinery moving in all directions over the entire line, with a firm but invisible grasp upon each train. The "order" that requires but a moment in transmission may prevent collision, avoid delay and confusion, and save life ; while the ominous tick tells of the position of every train, and conveys to the superintendent of the road the tidings, "all is well ! "

These six spectres are enclosed in a wooden cage. You peer at them through gratings, and wonder when they will get out. You make signs to them, but they are busy with more important signs ; you offer tobacco, but they do not bite. No word is spoken, and there is no noise ; no sound save the irrepressible dot and dash. In instant communication with the whole world, they have no word for you. If you give them ten words, they look up the tariff, but they must be unspoken. The telegraph has a silent language of its own, current only with the battery that supplies the breath, and the magic key that gives it utterance. Ignoring space, its operators seldom meet except in the city offices ; and it may be said that they are never separated, save through the temporary inter-position of a broken wire, a storm, or ground connections.

While all orders for the running of trains issue from the train-master's office, the telegraphist who superintends their transmission is really the responsible agent. On many roads, he assumes the entire responsibility, while others receive both the credit and the pay. By constant practice and close observation, he acquires a knowledge of the road and the capacity of its machinery possessed by no other official to the same degree. There are two "sets" of telegraph train despatchers at headquarters, one for day and the other for night duty. Night and day operators are also employed at all junctions, meeting-places, and crossings. The day despatcher, when relieved by the night assistant, is glad to retire in order to recuperate for the next day. And the night despatcher, having brought his trains with their precious freight through dangerous storms, and the thousand and one unforeseen difficulties that threaten their safe transit, is only too glad to be relieved from the strain. Convivial meetings or gatherings for social intercourse in the language of the outside world, are as rare as they are dangerous. If the despatcher has an hour's leisure, he must not load it down with burdens that may compromise either his brain or his nerve. He is, therefore, a person of correct and exemplary habits, with the disposition and proclivities of a recluse. He never forgets that an unsteady hand upon the key, a bewildered brain, or confused faculties might damage the property of his corporation far into the millions, or sacrifice thousands of valuable lives.

His office wears the stillness and gloom of the powderhouse. No one not immediately connected with his department of the service is permitted to cross the forbidden threshold. His every sign is obeyed with scrupulous exactness, and he sends out his dot and his dash as though the "message" were the edict of a king. With one hand upon the key, and the other at the adjustment, the ear is bent to note the slightest change in the "tick," for the burden of its monotonous whisper is safety or disaster. He cannot leave it for a moment, and you may be sure a laugh or joke is rarely heard in the prison-house of the despatcher.

"Out on the line," however, where the duties are less exacting, the railway operator is frequently found sunning himself on the platform, always within hearing distance of his instrument. If he be located at a country station, he has both his leisure and his sport. He is not always the verdant person that he may seem to travelling eyes.

He may be fresh from some large city office, ripe in knowledge and experience, sent down to the country to supply some temporary vacancy. He is always ready to move, and knowing that ability in his profession is always in demand, he is not particular as to where he makes his home. You meet Mr. Charlie de Forest with Zantzinger at Mobile, Alabama, to-day, and next month he is working the Commercial " Circuit " at San Francisco.

Mr. Frank C. Jones, whom you left at the lunch-room in Savannah, Georgia, met you, in a fortnight, on the platform at Elmira, New York, with a telegram concerning your luggage. As a class, they were at one time the most industrious of travellers, but since the business has become more thoroughly systematized, and the pay about the same in all parts of the country, there is less disposition on the part of telegraphists to wander from place to place.

The railway telegraphist, in the pay of the " Company," is not eager to do a very extensive business in the commercial line. With him, this is rather a source of annoyance. It necessitates the keeping of complicated books, and adds but little to the railroad salary. He is not always as polite and courteous to the wayfarer as the travelling public have a right to expect.

An Irishman went into the depot office at Parkersburg, and directed a despatch for Baltimore. After watching the operator for some time, he modestly asked if he would soon send it. He replied that it was a half hour gone, to which Pat responded :

" How the divil can it be half an hour gone, while there it is hangin' on the hook, while ye were clickin' and fiddlin' with that little brass play-toy there ? "

The window was slammed in the poor man's face.

Another Celtic traveller struck Bixbie of the Erie at Elmira.   Bixbie is an innocent and truthful young man.

"Do yez charge enybody for the eddress, when yez sind a bit by tillergraft?"

"Never," replied the operator.

"Do yez charge for signin' the name?"

"Never, sir."

"Thin sind this, and my brother will know I am here: '*To James O'Brien, New York.   Signed, Michael O'Brien.*'"

The operators at division headquarters on the C., B. & Q. were much annoyed by loafers who gathered beneath the windows on the outside.   A box running the full length of the office had heretofore furnished a tempting seat for the *habitués*.   The telegraphists covered this with zinc and connected it with the batteries.   A person sitting on the box without touching it with his hands would not feel the electricity; but if his hands drop on the box or he puts them thereon to assist him in rising, he receives such a sudden and astonishing shock as sends him an unbelievable number of feet towards the roof or the adjacent tracks.   Any good day a person may see some of these unfortunates unexpectedly struck with this domesticated lightning, describing a fifty-feet parabola in the air.

Girls have recently "come on," so that what was once a "positive" blessing for a time promised to become a "negative" bliss.   But Woolsey says, "It's no use; they can't do it.   In Baden, the Government decided to employ women as telegraphers.   All went well enough for a while, but soon they began to talk with each other about parties, beaux, and Dolly Vardens, and kept it up at such a rate, that their clatter monopolized the wire.

The Government has permitted them to retire to private life."

The operator always carries his dot and dash with him. You will find him making a key of his knife at the table if his dinner is slow, and communicating with his wife in monosyllables, which he learns to believe save both time and money. It is the ruling passion strong in death. When a comrade was summoned to the death-bed of poor Phillips at New Albany, he had but an hour or two to live.

"No use, boys," said he; "no battery—no current—zinc all eaten away, and no time to galvanize. Guess I'll have to cut off!"

Bruch says—"Talking about fellows carrying the dots and dashes with them, I know two who made it pay. They left the Louisville office, and went down the Mississippi river on a sporting tour—playing cards for money. They managed always to sit opposite each other, and conversed freely with their fingers on the table. They won every time, and being apparently strangers, the trick was never suspected."

Charles Temple, of the Ohio and Mississippi Lines, tells of an adventure while on a recent visit to San Francisco. He was invited to dine with Swain at the Occidental. While at the table, they amused themselves by clicking upon their plates with their knife or spoon, in the language well known to telegraph officials, but unfamiliar to other people. One would pick up his knife and convey to the other a remark like this:

"Why is this butter like the offence of Hamlet's uncle?"

"I give it up," replied his friend.

"Because," he telegraphs, "it's rank, and smells to heaven!"

8*

At this extraordinary intimation given at the expense of the landlord, who sits by perfectly unconscious of the joke, the other is overcome with laughter, in which the first joins, while all wonder what may be the cause of their merriment.

A newly-married pair sat opposite these wags, whom they imagined to be from the country. The young lady, who was right good-looking, came next in order, as the butt of their telegraphic hits.

"What a lovely little pigeon this is opposite, isn't she?" clicked No. 1.

"Perfectly charming," answered No. 2; "looks as if butter wouldn't melt in her mouth. Just married, I guess. If that country fool alongside of her were out of the way, I would toss her a crust of bread."

"Never mind him," replied No. 1; "give her a nudge with your foot, under the table."

To the consternation of the foolish young men, the bridegroom picked up his knife, and on his empty glass clicked off the following despatch—his face flushed, and his brow set in a very determined manner:

"This lady is my wife, and as soon as she finishes her dinner, I propose to give both of you a sound thrashing."

This was enough to bring a very solemn look upon the two faces opposite. There was no more joking, and no appetite for the remainder of the meal. The offenders immediately arose and slipped out of the way, fearing to encounter the bridegroom, who was himself an expert telegraphist.

" I was night operator," says Wheeler, "down there at Centralia on the Branch, for awhile, but didn't know a soul on the line. Lewis was superintendent, but somehow or other I couldn't even get acquainted with him. Yes, my name is Bob. There was a plug at Du Quoin —a boy, I supposed—who went for me the very first night. There wasn't much to do but receive reports of trains, and the rest of the time '*Dn*' * and I fought like cats, though a good many miles apart.

"It went on that way night after night, until he called me a name I couldn't take. I replied with a worse one. Then he told me in a business-like way, that he would be down the next night to thrash me. Knowing that he couldn't leave, I told him to come on—that he would never get back alive.

"Next afternoon, I learned, to my horror, that '*Dn*' could take the passenger, run down to Centralia, remain twelve minutes, and take the next passenger back. The cheerful information also reached me, that '*Dn*' was a grown man, stout, and well-proportioned; while I was a light fellow, weighing scarcely a hundred pounds.

"We had a day operator, named Jones; he used to be manager of a New Orleans office before the war, and had been in the Confederate army. Good friend of mine, and I knew he would fight. I asked him what he was going to do that night. He said he was going to play billiards, up in the club-room, with Joe Cormick. I told him I expected a friend on the 9.30 train, and would like to spend an hour with him, if he would stay for me and watch the instruments. He said certainly, if I would come up and remind him. Of course, I reminded him, and when the train came in sight he was seated in my chair, taking reports. I then got out in a dark place and watched. I saw a strapping big fellow go into the office,

---

* "*Dn*"—the telegraph call for Du Quoin.

and I went round to the other entrance, to see the sport at a safe distance.

"By the time I got there the fun had commenced. '*Dn*' had struck the 'night operator' over the head with a cane, much to my friend Jones' surprise and disgust. Then Jones let him have a heavy paper-weight right in the snoot, which scattered him some, and made the blood fly. Then Cormick coming in on some errand, saw how the game was, and took a hand. I think '*Dn*' was the worst-licked operator I ever saw! Yes, he managed to get to the train, and resigned, of course, the next day. The best of it all was, I got the credit of trouncing him, and the 'night operator at Centralia' was a terror to the boys on that line for some time. Joe Cormick, who was a popular conductor, as well as an estimable citizen, was afterwards elected Mayor of Centralia.

"I resigned, too, and went on a line where they were just introducing girls. The current of business is more refined where girls are employed on a telegraph line, and there is less danger of personal collisions."

Marcellus, who worked at the next table, remarked, that he formerly ran a telegraph and ticket office on the same road. "I had heard that Mr. J——s, Supt. at Amboy, was a common-looking gentleman, of quiet manners, rather rough exterior, and that if you obeyed rules and orders strictly, you could get on with him well enough. Well, old Keeler gave us strict orders that no one should be allowed in the ladies' waiting-room, after the trains had passed at night. Loafers and dead-beats had been in the habit of slipping in there o' winter nights, and sleeping by the hot stove. Before I went there I was told some thieves, taking advantage of this looseness, had made a raid on the ticket-office one night—which was in the same room—and the old man had to make good the loss. So I was charged to enforce this 'order' strictly, and, if necessary, call in the night watchman and station baggage-man to my assistance.

"Well, the depot was a mile from any hotel, and there was no gas there then. One night we had a fearful accident at the Long Bridge at La Salle. Train got off at the steam shovel; engine and cars; couldn't get it on; nothing could pass; regular block. Conductor came over to telegraph J——s. J——s answered, would 'come out on wrecking engine.' It was about three o'clock in the morning—dark and stormy—when they got the track nearly cleared, and I went back to my office to go to bed. Unlocked the door of ladies' room; found a lamp dimly burning, and a man doubled up in one of the seats, sound asleep. Went out again; hunted up night watchman; woke up baggage-man—both strapping big Dutchmen—told 'em to draw that man out of ladies' room.

"'He say he vos von supertender,' said the watchman 'so I make him in.'

"'Superintendent! that's played out—he's over at the wreck, if he's anywhere. Come, get him out—that's Keeler's orders.'

"They went at it, and when they got him half-way out he was wide-awake.

"'Where is Mr. Keeler?' he inquired.

"'Gone to bed long ago,' I answered.

"'Where is the operator?'

"'I am here, sir, obeying orders.'

"'Don't you know, sir, that I am Mr. J——s, superintendent of this division?'

"'I do not, sir. Never saw you before. The fact of

it is, sir, Mr. Keeler's order does not permit us to know anybody.   Have you a pass, sir ? '

" ' Pass for what ? '

" ' Pass to sleep in the ladies' room ! '

" ' No, sir, I do not—'

" ' Well, sir, then you'll have to pass out.   It's a very old joke indeed, sir.'

" ' I tell you I *am* the *superintendent !* '

" ' Can't help it, sir, if you were the President; Keeler's orders must be obeyed.   Go on, boys.'

" And they went on.

" Nine o'clock, I think it was, same morning, they woke me up to send important message.   Opened office ; few minutes in came party of the night before.

" ' Morning, sir,' I said.

" ' Good-morning,' dryly.

" ' Where did you sleep last night ? '

" ' Partly in the ladies' room, partly in passenger coach. Give me a blank.'

" Gave him blank, and he wrote the following :

" ' J. R.—Amboy :

" ' Track clear ; leave in twenty minutes.   The operator here is all right.

" ' John C. J——s.'

" Here was a go, sure enough.   I tried to explain, but he took me by the hand and said :

" ' Young man, you are somewhat impulsive and profane, but you've got the right idea about *orders.*'

" Then he was off !   Bless his old soul, I would walk fifty miles to shake that hand again.   He is still superintendent of the two divisions at Amboy ; beloved by his employés, and endeared to them by a thousand deeds of kindness."

Hunter, of the Western Union Lines, relates the following incident concerning the early days of telegraphing, and the incredulity with which the first feats of that art were received by the public.

"The first telegraphic lines in this country were laid early in 1844, between Washington and Baltimore, after a long struggle with Congress for a $30,000 subsidy, which was finally granted. Among the first messages sent was an announcement of the nomination of James K. Polk by the Democratic Convention sitting in Baltimore. During the campaign of 1844 the establishment of this 'great line'—thirty-nine miles long—'connecting Baltimore and the national capital with electric wires,' was largely dwelt upon by the stump orators of both sides. The Hon. James J. Farran, at present one of the proprietors of the Cincinnati *Enquirer*, and at that time, I believe, a candidate for Congress, made a speech in Cincinnati, one night, in which he related as one of the marvels of the age that Polk's nomination was known in Washington within half an hour after it had been made. He was loudly applauded for this; but there was one man in the crowd, and it was no less a person than Mr. Washington McLean—then as now a prominent politician —who could not believe it. On the contrary, he jumped up and cried out : 'Jim Farran, you're the biggest liar I ever heard. You know very well that ain't so. It would take that long to copy off the message, let alone to send it forty miles on a wire.'"

As our best-informed telegraphists are in doubt as to whom should be awarded the chief honor of giving the magnetic telegraph to the world, the author goes out of his way to record here a few observations that may help to correct a popular error. The following curious passage occurs in one of Addison's essays, published in No. 241 of the first volume of the *Spectator :*

" Strada, in one of his Prolusions, gives an account of a chimerical correspondence between two friends by the help of a certain loadstone, which had such virtue in it, that if it touched two sewing needles, when one of the needles so touched began to move, the other, though at ever so great a distance, moved at the same time, and in the same manner. He tells us, that the two friends, being each of them possessed of one of these needles, made a kind of dial-plate, inscribed with the four-and-twenty letters in the same manner as the hours of the day are marked upon the ordinary dial-plate. They then fixed one of the needles on each of these plates in such a manner that it could move around without impediment, so as to touch any of the four-and-twenty letters. Upon their separating from one another into distant countries, they agreed to withdraw themselves punctually into their closets at a certain hour of the day, and converse with one another by this their invention. Accordingly when they were some hundred miles asunder, each of them shut himself up in his closet at the time appointed, and immediately each cast his eye upon his dial-plate. If he had a mind to write anything to his friend, he directed his needle to every letter that formed the words he had occasion for, making a little pause at the end of every word or sentence, to avoid confusion. The friend in the meanwhile saw his own sympathetic needle moving of itself to every letter which that of his correspondent pointed at. By this means they talked together across a whole continent, and conveyed thoughts to one another in an instant over cities or mountains, seas or deserts."

This was written on the 6th of December, 1781, nearly a hundred years ago, long before modern telegraphy was thought of. May not this passage have suggested to Prof. Morse the grand idea which he turned to such excellent practical account?

Discoveries rendering the electro-magnetic telegraph possible were made by Oersted of Copenhagen, in the year 1819; others were made by Arago, and Davy, and Ampère, in 1820, and by Sturgeon, in 1825. None of them, however, reached the point of discovering a means of making the wire practically serviceable over any considerable distance. The difficulty was deemed insuperable, and Mr. Barlow, of the Royal Military Academy of Woolwich, England, in his investigations, published in 1825, declared adversely upon the possibility of a telegraph. Nothing feasible in the way of discovery was made for two or three years after, though it seems to be established that Harrison Gray Dyar, an American, put a short working line of telegraph in operation on Long Island, in 1827 or 1828. He used common electricity and not electro-magnetism, and but one wire, which operated with a spark, that left red marks upon paper, chemically prepared. The device of working it by an alphabet, by spaces of time between sparks, was very nearly in principle that used by Prof. Morse; and it is noted as another curious coincidence, that Morse was the brother-in-law of Charles Walker, who was the legal counsel of Dyar, at the time of Dyar's experiments on the electric telegraph. Dyar asserts that Morse, who was not a man of any scientific attainments, got his ideas of operating a wire telegraph from his (Morse's) brother-in-law, the latter having derived them from him, while acting as his counsel years before. However, this question only affects the validity of Morse's claim to the invention of the mode of working the telegraph.

The great difficulty in the way of operating the wire at any distance had not been met until Prof. Henry made discovery of the fact, in 1828, that a galvanic current could be transmitted to a great distance with so small a diminution of force as to produce mechanical effects, adequate to the desired object, by means of a galvanic intensity battery. Prof. Morse subsequently availed himself of the discovery by Prof. Henry, to make telegraphy practicable, and profitable to himself. Prof. Henry, who took out no patent for his discovery, seems in this, as in his other invaluable scientific labors, to have sought for no other reward "than the consciousness of advancing science, the pleasure of discovering new truths, and the scientific reputation to which those labors would entitle him."

Up to 1848, Morse seems to have fully conceded that he was indebted to the discovery of Prof. Henry to enable him to make the magnetic telegraph successful. At that time, Morse got into litigation with other parties over his claim to the monopoly of telegraphic rights, and he appears to have deemed it necessary to his interest to depreciate the importance of Henry's discoveries. The concurrent testimony, however, of leading telegraphic authorities, and of the very men who were associated with Morse, in telegraphic patents, go to show, that he merely availed himself of Henry's discoveries and applied them to his machine. It does not appear that Morse ever made a single original discovery in electricity, magnetism, or electro-magnetism, applicable to the invention of the Telegraph.

Mr. F. Ives Scudamore, Superintendent of the Government telegraphs in Great Britain, relates an incident in his recent report upon the success of the system of employing male and female operatives. After showing how much the tone of the man has been elevated by the association, and how well the women perform the "checking" or "fault-finding" branches of the work, the gentleman goes on to speak of the friendships formed between operators, or "clerks"—as they are termed abroad—at either end of a telegraph wire. They begin by chatting in the intervals of their work, and very soon become fast friends. A telegraph operator at London, who was engaged on a wire to Berlin, formed an acquaintance with a female operator, who worked on the same wire in Berlin. This developed into a warm attachment, and without having seen her, made a proposal of marriage, and was accepted. They were married, and the marriage resulting from their electric affinities is supposed to have turned out as well as those in which the senses are more apparently concerned.

Affairs of this kind are not uncommon in this country, though the employment of females as operators is the exception rather than the rule. Operators are not rash ; there is something in the very nature of their work that makes them the coolest of men. They do not marry without due acquaintance. An operator at one end of the wire can readily tell by the way in which the operator at the other does his work, whether he is passionate or sulky, cheerful or dull, ill-natured or good-natured, sanguine or phlegmatic.

———

The progress of the electric telegraph within the past six years, has been very great in every quarter of the globe. Upon this continent, the electric wire extends from the Gulf of St. Lawrence to the Gulf of Mexico, and from the Atlantic to the Pacific Ocean. Three cables span the Atlantic Ocean, connecting America with Europe, and another submerged in the Gulf Stream, unites us with the Queen of the Antilles. Unbroken telegraphic communication exists between all places in America and all parts of Europe; with Tripoli and Algiers in Africa, Cairo in Egypt, Teheran in Persia, Jerusalem in Syria, Bagdad and Nineveh in Asiatic Turkey, Bombay, Calcutta, and other important cities in India, with Hong Kong and Shanghai in China, Irkoutsk, the capital of Eastern Siberia, Kiakhta on the borders of China, Nangasaki in Japan.

A direct line of telegraph, under one direct control and management, has recently been established between London and India, with extensions to Singapore, Hong Kong, Java, and Australia.

Europe possesses 450,000 miles of telegraphic wire and 13,000 stations; America, 180,000 miles of wire and 6,000 stations; India, 14,000 miles of wire and 200 stations; and Australia, 10,000 miles of wire and 270 stations; and the extension throughout the world is now at the rate of 100,000 miles of wire per annum. There are, in addition, 30,000 miles of submarine telegraph wire now in successful operation, extending beneath the Atlantic and German oceans; the Baltic, North, Mediterranean, Red, Arabian, Japan, and China seas; the Persian Gulf, the Bay of Biscay, the Strait of Gibraltar, and the Gulfs of Mexico and St. Lawrence.

More than twenty thousand cities and villages are now linked in one continuous chain of telegraph stations. The mysterious wire, with its subtle and invisible influence, traverses all civilized lands; passes beneath oceans, seas, and rivers, bearing messages of business, friendship, and love; and constantly but powerfully contributing to the peace, happiness, and prosperity of all mankind.

XVIII.

"COME HOME!"

DON'T fret, Mag, for the short time I shall be away," I said to my little wife, as I put on my gloves and great-coat.

"Couldn't you stay at home just this one night, Will? Do you know I felt so lonely and strange last night when you were away, and to-night I can scarcely bear the thought of your being absent so long !"

She looked up to my face with an anxious gaze, and a tear stood glistening in the corners of her sweet blue eyes.

"Why, you little goose," said I, kissing away the bright tokens of her earnestness, "why should you feel alarmed; do I not go every night to see that everything is '*O. K.*' on the line? I shall be at home by seven o'clock at the latest, and if you are really afraid to stay in the house alone, I will send up my brother Bob to keep you company."

"No ; don't do that ; it would look foolish, and Bob would only laugh at me when he came. He does not understand me. I think no one understands me—except you, dear Will."

"Thank you, Mag; I think I understand you. There is nothing to fear here in Cottage Grove, where the whole village is ready to come at your call. Here are the street cars, so good-by, and don't fret."

I was off, but my wife lingered by the porch, following me with her eyes; and so long as the house was in sight I could look back and see her white dress shimmering, ghost-like, in the light which streamed through the open door.

I was telegraph superintendent of the—well, we will call it the Willington Railway. The trains were run entirely by telegraph; and our despatcher having been taken suddenly ill, we had put a skilful operator in his place, who sometimes yielded to a desire for grog. I thought it best therefore to be near at hand in case anything should go wrong. I had been married but a few months, and was by no means reconciled to the necessity of leaving my wife home to pass the night in "that nasty old box," as Mag sometimes called my office. My dead father had left me the home-place at Cottage Grove, a village connected with the metropolis by a street railway.

A short ride brought me to my post. There was nothing extraordinary in the duty to which I had been called away, nor was it any new experience to me; but on that night my mind was filled with vague, indefinable fears, for which I tried in vain to account. The night was clear, and away in the north-western sky the aurora borealis was flitting to and fro in a thousand strange fantastic shapes. On entering the office, the night operator whom I had come to relieve was ready to depart.

"No use for two of us to-night, sir," said he; "a foreign

current has possession of the instruments, and not an office
has 'called' for the last hour.   Good-night!"

When I was left alone, I found it was as he had said.
The electric currents which are developed in the atmosphere during most meteorological changes, had rendered
the wires quite useless for the time.   Seeing that my
office was likely to be a sinecure, I drew my chair to the
stove, and taking down a book, tried to interest myself
in the story.   The volume which I had discovered was
" Jane Eyre," but it had no power to quiet my wild, wan-
dering thoughts.   While I was turning over the leaves,
the stillness was startled by the sharp, quick click of one
of my "sounders," as though some one was attempting to
" call."   With a shiver of alarm I turned quickly to the
adjustment, but soon perceived that the dot and dash had
been sounded by no earthly power, and I knew that it
had been produced by a current of atmospheric electricity
acting upon the wires.

Smiling at the nervousness which caused me to start at
so ordinary an occurrence, I turned from my desk, and
again sat down by the fire.   But smile as I would, and
reason as I might, I felt that I was fast succumbing to
vague, foundationless fears.   Thinking that the atmosphere of the room, which I felt close and hot, might have
something to do with my peculiar condition of mind, I
flung open the door, and stepped outside in the hope
that the cool air might scare away the phantoms of my
brain.   As I crossed the threshold, the midnight express
crashed past with a speed and force which shook every
timber of the building, and uttering a loud shriek, disap-
peared into the tunnel at the end of the steep gradient, on
the summit of which my station was placed.   When it had
gone, there was stillness, stillness broken—if I can call

it broken—only by the peculiar sighing of the air passing along the wires, which is heard even in the calmest of nights. I stood and listened to the strange, melancholy, Æolian-harp-like sound, now so faint as to be almost inaudible, and anon swelling into a wild low wailing. I looked up and saw Orion and the Pleiades, and thought how often on nights, not long ago, when I had watched for Maggie in the wood, I had gazed up through the tall sombre pines and watched their trembling fires. From that my mind reverted to the earnestness with which my wife had asked me to remain at home that night, and the unusual pensiveness of her manner when she bade me good-by. What could be the meaning of it all? As a general rule, I had a most profound disbelief in omens, presentiments, and all sorts of superstition; but in spite of it, I felt that I would have given a good deal, at that time, to be transported just for one minute to my home, to see whether all was well there. The express had passed, the trains were all hurrying "on time" to their connections, and it was not probable that any "orders" would be sent or received. So, I might have called up Gordon, my assistant, who lodged near by, but as I could give no good reason for going away, I resolved to stay where I was, and get through the night as best I could. I turned inside again, and poked up the coals with rather more noise and vigor than was necessary. I filled my pipe and lit it, but the weed had lost its tranquillizing power. As the wreaths curled upward, I saw my wife's face, looking at me tearfully as when I had left her. Again one of the instruments clicked sharply, but as before, with no intelligible sound. I leaned my elbows on the desk, and with head between my hands, watched the armiture as a cat watches a mouse.

9

An hour might have passed thus, when I was again startled by the instrument's nervous dot and dash. This time it was louder and more urgent, and it seemed to me, though I may err here, with a peculiar unearthly sound, such as I had never heard before. I am utterly unable to tell in what manner the impression was produced, but it seemed as if there mingled with the metallic click the tone of a human voice—the voice of one I knew. The armiture began to move more regularly now, and to make sounds that my practised ear understood. Slowly came two dots, a space and a dot, as if some novice were working the instrument, and then the letters "*C—o—m—e*" were signalled. No sooner had I read off the final "*e*," than to my amazement and terror I saw the "key" move as if touched by some invisible hand, and the signal "*O. K.*" was made, which the receiver always transmits at the end of a message.

A cold thrill ran through me, and I felt as if every drop of blood were leaving my heart. Could I have been the subject of an optical delusion? I knew that such was not the case, for I had plainly heard the click of the "sounder," and saw the armiture move in obedience to the current that made the sound. And now I could perceive that another word was being slowly spelt out. But so bewildered and terrified was I, that I failed to catch the sounds. With an overwhelming feeling of awe, I watched the lever intently while the letters were again signalled, and this time I read "*H—o—m—e.*" I stood petrified with fear and amazement, half believing that I was in a dream, for reason refused to accept the evidence of sense. Could that be a message for me? If so, whence came it? What hand had sent it? Could it be that some power higher than that of nature thus warned me

"A COLD THRILL RAN THROUGH ME"

page 194

of impending danger? Should I obey the mysterious summons?

Deliberating thus, the instrument again sounded, with a clangor seemingly imperious and unearthly. After a few uncertain movements, the words "Come home—come home—" reached my practised ear with unerring distinctness. I could remain at my post no longer. Come what might, I felt that I had no alternative but to obey. I ran to the house where my assistant lodged, and on rousing the inmates and gaining admission, told him he must take my place immediately, as I had been called suddenly away. The man seemed somewhat surprised at my excited and startled manner, but what he said or did, I cannot recollect. I rushed to the barn where a horse was stalled, and perceiving a saddle hanging on the wall, threw it on his back, and in a moment or two was dashing along the road in the direction of home. I shall never forget that ride. Although I urged my horse with whip and voice, until he flew rather than galloped, the pace was far too slow for my excited mind. At last, breathless and panting, we clattered up the street of the village near which I lived. Suddenly a horse and rider appeared at the other end of the street, and a hoarse voice uttered a loud cry of "*Fire!*" At the same instant, the church bell was rung violently, and at once, as if by a common impulse, the whole village started into life. Lights appeared in the houses, and an hundred windows were dashed quickly up. I saw white figures standing at these windows, and heard nervous voices cry —"*Where?*" Checking my horse with a jerk which threw him on his haunches, I listened for the reply: "The Woolsey House."

Great Heaven! my worst fears were realized. It was

my own home. I choked down the agony, which almost forced a cry, and pressing onward with redoubled speed, soon arrived at the scene of the fire. The house was a large old one, and when I reached it, smoke was issuing in thick, murky volumes from the windows of the second flat, while fierce tongues of flame were already leaping along the roof. A crowd of men were hurrying confusedly about with buckets and pails of water. In the centre of a group of women, I found our maid, Mary, stretched on the grass in a swoon. "My wife!" I exclaimed, as I rushed forward, "where is she?" "God knows, sir," said one of the men; "we have twice tried to reach the second flat, but were each time driven back by the smoke and fire." Without uttering a word, I entered the house, and ran along the lobby. The stair, fortunately, was built of stone, but the wood-work on each side was one mass of blazing and crackling flame. Before I had taken three steps, I fell back, blinded, fainting, and half-suffocated with the smoke. Two men who had followed me caught me in their arms, and tried to restrain me by force from endeavoring to ascend again. "Don't attempt it," they said; "you will only lose your own life and can't save hers." "Let go, you cowards!" I cried, as soon as I could speak; and with the strength of madness dashed them aside. I rushed upstairs, and this time succeeded in reaching the first landing in safety. The room which we used as our bedchamber led off a small parlor which was situated on this flat. Groping my way through the smoke, I found the door, but to my horror, it was locked! I dashed myself against it again and again, but it resisted all my efforts. To return as I had come was now impossible, and I knew that the only hope of saving even my own life was to go forward. Despair gave me strength; and lifting my foot I struck it violently against one of the lower panels of the door. It yielded a little. Another blow, and it was driven in. I crept through the opening, but so thick was the smoke in the parlor that I could distinguish nothing. "Maggie, Maggie!" I shrieked, "where are you?" but no answer was returned. Crossing the parlor I gained our bed-room door. To my joy it was open, and stretched on the floor I found the apparently lifeless form of my wife. I bent over her, and on placing my hand on her heart, I found that it was still beating. I lifted her very tenderly and gently, and carried her in my arms to the window, which I broke open. Of what followed I am only dimly conscious; I have a confused remembrance of men bringing a ladder, and strong arms helping us down, and the people cheering; but it is all very vague and indistinct. My next recollection is that of finding myself in a neighbor's house all bruised and weak, but with my own wife bending over me, and administering to my wants with loving hands.

On the evening of the next day, when the short winter twilight was fast closing round, and the first snow-flakes were falling, I lay thinking over the strange events which I have tried to relate. Maggie drew a little stool close to the couch. I had not mentioned a word to anybody concerning the warning which I had so mysteriously received. When questioned as to what caused me to return so opportunely, I had always made some evasive answer. I feared the reality would never have obtained belief.

"Willie," said the soft low voice of my wife, "if you had not come home—"

"Hush, my darling. Don't talk like that, for I can't bear even to think of it."

"But it might have been. And do you know, Willie, I had such a strange dream on that awful night?"

"A dream, Maggie? Tell me what it was."

"You remember," said she, drawing closer to me, "the evening you took Mary and me into the telegraph office, and told us all about the batteries, and magnets, and electricity, and a great many things which we couldn't understand at all, though we pretended to do so, lest you should think us stupid?"

"Perfectly."

"And you remember how I wanted to send a message with my own hands, and you threw the instruments into what you called 'short circuit'?"

"Yes."

"You made me take hold of the 'key,' and then you guided it while I sent a message to your brother Robert, who was in the office at Centralia. And the end of it was—'Come home—come home!' which I repeated over and over until I could do it quite well without your help?"

I turned quickly around, but she was gazing intently at the fire, and did not perceive the startled look I gave her.

"Well," she continued, "the night before last, when you were away, I could not sleep for a long time after I went to bed; and when I did sleep, I dreamed such a horrible dream. I thought I was in your office again, and had hurried there because I was afraid of some Terrible Thing. I did not know what it was, but it was close behind me, and I thought nobody could save me but you. But you were not there, and I seized the key, and wrote the words, 'Come home, come home!' as you had taught me, thinking that would bring you. Then, when you did not come, I felt its hot breath on my neck, as if it were just going to clutch me in its dreadful arms, and I screamed so loud that I awoke. The room was all dark and filled with smoke, so thick that when I jumped up, I fainted for want of air. And O Willie, if you had not come just when you did, I might—"

"There, Maggie, don't let us think of what might have been, but rather let us be thankful that we are spared to each other still."

XIX.

THE PHANTOM CONDUCTOR.

GIVE this little sketch to the public with the hope that some one may give me a rational solution of an event that has perplexed me for years. My address is "Mrs. Joseph Lorrimer, Harrisburg, Pennsylvania." My husband is overseer of the Crosby Iron Works, just outside that city.

I met the hero of this story during my bridal tour. It was a quiet wedding, and there being no money to spare on either side, after a family breakfast, we went directly to the cars, and started for our future home.

I was a young thing then, just eighteen. The trip—from Philadelphia to Harrisburg—was a wonderful trip to me, who had never taken an hour's ride on the cars before in my life.

I gazed with eager eyes upon the country through which we passed, and all that was going on around me. The passengers; the car and its fixtures; the conductor and the brakeman ; were all objects whose novelty gave me plenty of food for thought.

At Lancaster the cars stopped some time for dinner ; and just as they were about to start again, our conductor entered the car, ushering in an old lady in Quaker garb, beneath whose deep bonnet was visible a kind, plump, rosy face, with bright-spectacled eyes.

She glanced round on either side as she advanced up the aisle in search of a seat, and, in obedience to a nudge from me, Joseph rose, and beckoning to the conductor, said :

"There is a seat for the lady here."

Smilingly the old lady approached. I commenced to gather up the shawls and packages that lay upon the vacant seat, that it might be turned to its proper position, but the old lady checked me.

" Don't trouble thyself, friend ; I can sit just as well with the seat as it is ;" and without further ceremony she ensconced herself opposite me, while the one-eyed conductor deposited a large covered bandbox at her feet, and paid her so many little attentions, at the same time addressing her in so familiar and affectionate a manner, that I saw at once she was no stranger to him.

A glance at the kind old face opposite soon told me that they were mother and son, for the two faces were wonderfully alike, especially in the open, cheerful expression.

Drawn toward her at once, we soon became quite sociable. As I had surmised, the conductor was her son, and the old lady was very proud and fond of him indeed. He was a fine, portly-looking man, with genial brown whiskers and curly hair. He would have been really handsome, had it not been for the loss of one eye. This

9*

had been lost by disease, the exterior of the eye retaining its original expression. The remaining eye was blue and bright, as jolly and sparkling as the rest of his good-humored face.

He stopped to have a word with his mother, and as she was talking with us, we very naturally all fell into conversation together. He had seen a great deal of life on the rail, and his conversation to me, at least, was vastly entertaining.

Among other interesting things he explained to us the signs and signals used by railroad officials upon the road. One of these signals—the only one I need mention here —he said was as follows :

When a person standing in the road in front of or by the side of a car, throws both hands rapidly forward, as if motioning for the cars to go backward, he means to give information that there is "danger ahead."

"When you see that signal given, ma'am," said our conductor, "if the cars don't obey it by backing, do you prepare yourself for a flying leap ; for the chances are that you have to practise it before long."

He spoke lightly, but, noticing that the ideas suggested were not very pleasant ones to me, he changed the subject, and I soon forgot the little feeling of discomfort his words had occasioned.

The old lady did not travel with us far. She stopped at a way station some twenty-five miles west of Lancaster, where, she informed us, she had a daughter living. Her own home she had already told us was in Lancaster, where she lived with a married daughter, who kept a boarding-house. She gave us one of this daughter's cards, and Joseph promised if ever he had occasion to visit Lancaster he would try to find her out.

It is not my purpose to detain the reader with any details of my private history, further than is necessary to give a just comprehension of what is to follow. Two years had elapsed before I was called upon to take the second journey, to the events of which what I have already narrated forms a necessary prelude. This time I was journeying alone from Harrisburg to Philadelphia, upon a visit to my parents, whom I had not seen since my marriage.

I was very ill for some time after my baby's birth, and after I had regained my health, the little fellow was taken ill. After nursing him all summer, he finally died. I was so weak and miserable myself, that I could not struggle with my grief as I should have done; I pined and fretted and wasted away till the doctor ordered a change of scene; something to cheer me up, or he would not answer for my life.

It was not acceptable advice to me. I did not want to be cheered or amused. I did not want to leave home and the dear reminders of my dead baby. Above all, I did not want to leave my husband, for I felt a superstitious dread that he too would be taken from me. He could not leave his business now, but promised to join me as soon as he could. So he wrote to father that I would be in Philadelphia on a certain day, and having put me in the cars at Harrisburg, he knew there was very little doubt but that I should reach Philadelphia after a comfortable half-day's ride.

Ah! how different was this trip from the one I had taken two years before! How different was I—the wan-faced, hollow-eyed invalid in my mourning robes—from the shy blooming girl, in her bridal array, who found so much to amuse and interest her in that brief journey.

Nothing interested me now—all was wearisome and monotonous.

I did rouse up a little as the conductor approached to collect my fare—the remembrance of the one-eyed man and his nice little mother occurred to me the first time for many months. The conductor, however, was not my old acquaintance, being a sallow, dark-eyed, cross-looking man, as different as possible from the other one. I felt a little disappointed at first, but after he left me I leaned my head back again and thought no more about the matter.

After a while I fell into a dose, which lasted until the call of " Lancaster—twenty minutes for dinner ! " ringing through the cars aroused me and informed me that we were just entering that city.

I sat up then, sleepily and languidly. It was a warm day in early October, and the windows of the car were lowered ; I leaned my elbow upon the sash, and looked out upon the scene before me. As I was thus gazing, drowsy and indifferent, neither caring nor thinking much about what I saw, I noticed a man upon the roadside, a little in front of the car in which I sat, gesticulating violently with his hands and arms.

The next minute I was sitting bolt upright in my seat, my heart leaping almost into my mouth with sudden fright, for, in the gestures that were being made, I recognized the signal, which, two years before, the one-eyed conductor had told me meant " danger ahead."

The cars were not moving very rapidly, and, during the moment that we were passing by the man who had given the signal, I had a full view of him—his face being turned towards the cars, and his eyes meeting mine so directly that I could have spoken to him had I chosen. I recognized him at once—it was the one-eyed conductor ;

and, seeing that, I was worse scared than ever, being now quite confirmed in my belief that an accident was impending ; for I knew that he must occupy some responsible position upon the road, and could, therefore, have made no mistake in the matter.

No one else, however, either inside or outside of the car seemed to partake of my alarm. The cars were slackening their speed, but that was because we were approaching a station, and from no other cause that I could ascertain. I had not intended getting out of the cars until I had reached the end of my journey, but I had been so startled by what I had seen that I could not sit quiet in my seat.

I got out with the rest of the passengers, but did not follow them to the hotel. I stood upon the platform, gazing up and down the track uneasily, but could see nothing at all that could awaken apprehension.

The one-eyed conductor was nowhere to be seen, though I watched the road, in the direction where we had passed him, for some time, expecting every moment to see him come into sight.

A porter, trundling a wheelbarrow, passed me, and of him I ventured timidly to inquire—

"Is there anything the matter with the engine or with the track?"

"Not as I know on," he answered gruffly, and passed on.

I was still terribly uneasy; I was certain that I had not been mistaken in the man or the signal ; the latter, especially, I remembered—a forward motion with both hands, as if directing the cars to back. I could recall distinctly the face and gestures of the conductor when he had explained it to me, as also his words, "If you ever see that signal given, prepare for a flying leap, for the probabilities are you'll soon have to take it;" and the longer I dwelt upon what I had witnessed, the more convinced did I become that the signal had not been given causelessly.

I went into a waiting-room to sit down until I could determine what it would be best for me to do. I felt a most invincible repugnance to returning to the cars and continuing my journey; the excitement and worry had made me sick and faint, and I felt that I ran a great risk of becoming ill before I reached my journey's end, even if there was no other danger dreaded. What if I should stay over at Lancaster until next day, and telegraph to father to come to me there? And at the same instant I remembered that there was in my travelling satchel, in the little outer pocket where it had rested undisturbed for two years, the card which the old Quaker lady had given me, bearing the name and address of her daughter, who kept a boarding-house. That remembrance decided me; if I could find lodging at that place, I would remain over night at Lancaster.

There were plenty of conveyances around the depot; and summoning a driver to me, I showed him the card, and asked him if he knew the address.

"Certainly, mum," he said, promptly; "take you there in ten minutes; Mrs. Elwood's boarding-house; quiet place, but excellent accommodations, mum."

Thus assured, I entered his carriage, and he fulfilled his promise by setting me down, after a short drive, in front of an unassuming, two-story frame house, whose quiet, orderly appearance made it look very unlike a boarding-house. A boarding-house it proved to be, however, and in the landlady, Mrs. Elwood, who came to me after I had waited awhile in the darkened parlor, I traced at once so strong a resemblance to my old Quaker friend, as convinced me I had found the place I sought.

As she was leading me upstairs to my room, I ventured to state that I had met her mother two years before, and had formed a travelling acquaintance with her.

Mrs. Elwood's pleasant smile upon hearing this encouraged me to ask if her mother was living with her, adding that I should be pleased to renew the acquaintance if she was.

The reply was in the affirmative.

"You will meet her at dinner, which is served at two; and she will be glad enough to have a chat with you, I venture to say."

I wrote out my telegram to father, and Mrs. Elwood promised to have it attended to at once for me ; then, after doing everything for me that kindness could suggest, she left me to the rest I was beginning very much to feel the need of.

A tidy-looking little maid came to me when the dinner-bell rang, to show me the way to the dining-room ; and there the first person I saw was my little old lady, already seated near the upper end of the long table.

She bowed and smiled when she saw me, but we were too far apart to engage in any conversation. After the meal was over she joined me, shook hands very cordially, and invited me to come and sit with her in her own room.

I was glad to accept the invitation, for in my loneliness the kind face of this chance acquaintance seemed almost like that of a friend; and soon—in one of the easiest of low-cushioned chairs, in one of the cosiest of old-lady apartments—I was seated, talking more cheerfully and unreservedly than I had talked since my baby's death.

I expressed some surprise that she recognized me so promptly, to which she replied:

"I had always a good memory for faces, though names I am apt to forget; when my daughter spoke to me about thee, I could not at all recall thee to mind; yet as soon as thee entered the dining-room I remembered thee."

"And yet I do not look much like I did two years ago," I said sadly.

"That is true, my dear; thee has altered very much. I almost wonder now that I should have recognized thee so promptly. Thee has seen trouble, I fear," gently touching my black dress.

"Yes," I said, "I have had both sickness and death to battle with; I neither look nor feel much like the thoughtless, happy bride whom you met two years ago."

"Is it thy husband who has been taken from thee?"

"Oh, no, no, no!" I cried, and ready tears rising to my eyes; "I don't think I could have lived if I had lost him. It was my baby died; that was hard enough—the dearest little blue-eyed darling you ever saw, just ten months old."

My old friend's face betrayed her sympathy, as she sat silently waiting for me to regain my composure. After a little while she said, sighing:

"It is hard to lose a child, whether young or old. I can fully sympathize with thee in thy trouble, for I, too, have lost a son since I last saw thee, though I wear no outer garb as a badge of my bereavement."

I looked at her, a little surprise mingled with a sympathy I tried to express.

"I thought I remembered your telling me you had but one son?"

"That was all," she said sorrowfully. "God never gave me but the one, and him He has taken away."

I stared at her now in undisguised astonishment.

"Was not that gentleman—surely, madam, I was not mistaken in thinking the conductor—the gentleman who brought you into the cars when we met two years ago—was your son?"

"You are right; he was the son of whom I have spoken."

"The one-eyed man?" I gasped, forgetting delicacy in astonishment.

The old lady flushed a little.

"Yes, friend, I understand whom thee means; my poor Robert had lost the sight of his left eye."

"I saw that man this morning," I cried. "I saw him from the car-window, before we entered Lancaster. What strange misunderstanding is this?"

"Thee has mistaken some one else for him, that is all," said my companion gravely. "My boy thee could not have seen, for he died fifteen months ago the fifteenth of this month. He died of cholera after only two days' illness. Thee could not have seen Robert."

"I did though—I did!" I cried, excitedly; and then I related to her the whole incident, dwelling particularly upon the signal I had seen him make—a signal I had never seen but once before in my life, and then made by him when he explained it to me. "I was not mistaken," I concluded; "I could not be; your son was not an ordinary looking man, and I remember his appearance distinctly. Surely, as I sit here, I saw this morning the man who you tell me died fifteen months ago."

The old lady looked white and frightened, while, as for me, I was growing so hysterical with bewilderment and excitement that she would allow me to pursue the subject no farther.

She led me to my room and persuaded me to lie down, leaving me then, for she was too much agitated by the conversation we had to be able to soothe or quiet me.

I saw her no more that day. I did not go to tea. The restless night I passed, in conjunction with the excitement of the day, rendered me so seriously unwell that I was not able to rise until a late hour the following morning.

I was still dressing when there came a rap at my door, accompanied by the voice of my Quaker friend, asking admittance.

I opened the door and she entered, with white, awe-struck face, and hands that trembled so she could hardly hold the newspaper to which she directed my attention.

"Friend," she said, "thy life has been saved by divine interposition. The train in which thee was yesterday a passenger, in less than two hours after thee left it, was thrown over an embankment, at a place called the 'Gap,' and half of the passengers have been killed or wounded. Child! child; surely as thee lives that vision of my poor Robert was sent to save thee!"

That is all that I have to tell. I know nothing more about the affair than I have written, and I have no comments to make upon it. I saw that one-eyed conductor make the signal of "danger ahead;" I was so much influenced by what I saw that I could not continue my journey. In less than two hours after that warning had been given the danger was met, and death in its most appalling form was the fate of more than fifty of the human beings that danger signal was meant to warn.

YOUR HUMBLE SERVANT'S WIFE.

A FIREMAN'S RHYME.

'Twas my first run on the Hudson,
  And I had old Merrick's flame;
Though I won't stop now to tell you
  How she got her name and fame,
Leastwise 'twould be a slander
  On a good old chum of mine,
Who was killed there near Poughkeepsie,
  When he run the Forty-nine.

Well, of course he left his engine,
  For I'm sitting in his cab;
When he pulled out for New Hamburg—
  But I ain't a-going to blab.
A darnation clever feller,
  But a little on the brine,
Awful sweet on Mary Lawler,
  But that's no affair of mine.

She was waiter at Jim Foster's,
  Out of Rochester a-ways,
Where the passengers got fodder
  And the boys—well, Wilson says
There's more benzine shoved out o' there,
  In small, flat flasks, you know;
And—as I was just a-sayin',
  Merrick was this Mary's beau.

She came down to see his body,
  Just as though she'd been his wife,
And I never saw a woman
  Take on so in all my life;
Wrung her hands and cried—my Lord! sir,
  Tore her hair and yelled like mad.
I've been through some awful scenes, sir,
  Never one just quite so bad.

She kept at it for two hours,
    Till the crowd began to move ;
Some with eyes a little moistened,
    Some to tell of woman's love.
Then a lot of heavy fellows
    Came to sit on Sam's remains ;
Men of weight—say three parts tallow,
    And a modicum of brains—

Turned him over for inspection,
    Searched his pockets through and through,
Took his silver watch and wallet,
    And a locket, done in blue.

  .   .   .   .

Then a scream : and my fine feller
    With the trinket in his hand,
Found two arms around his collar
    And his body in the sand.
Then she hauled out on a side track,
    With the locket safe in tow,
For you see it held his picture—
    All there was of Merrick now.

" Where was I ? "   Why, right on hand, sir ;
    He had been a chum of mine
On the " Cincinnati Short-Cut,"
    In the year of Fifty-nine.
When I heard of this disaster
    I went out to lend a hand,
And was ready when his sweetheart
    Laid that fellow in the sand.

That was how I came around it,
    And made up to Merrick's flame ;
Told her now I had his engine,
    I must have *her*—all the same.
Then she spoke of poor Sam Merrick,
    And the time he lost his life ;
Of the locket—well, sweet Mary
    Is your humble servant's wife !

XX.

THE RAILWAY AT HOME AND ABROAD.

The Railway in America—Russian Railways—The Railway in England—A Wooden Railway—The Railway in India—Railway Fortifications—The Railway in Germany—No Smoking—New Method of Heating Cars—Why Accidents never occur on German Railways—A Peruvian Railway—Another Triumph for American Manufacturers—The Passenger Tariff on Railways in Europe—A Schedule of Prices.

HOWEVER important the changes which railways have introduced may be, we stand as yet only on their threshold. This subject must naturally excite the attention of those who solve social problems and compare the past with the present to a higher degree in America than in Europe. In the Old World the Railway follows the beaten path; connects cities which exist already, and serves only as a medium of communication between long-established centres of population. In the New World, creates the cities which it is to connect, and by penetrating into the wilderness, carries thither civilization and its concomitants. In our Western States, cities are not founded to meet the requirements of a surrounding population, but the surrounding region is populated to meet the requirements of cities, which have been imported by the locomotive. In all countries of Europe, England alone excepted, the railway is under the control of the Government. In many countries, this control is absolute and direct. In England the railway is left entirely to individual enterprise, and the result has demonstrated how inadequate a mere commercial control often is for the security of such vast industrial undertakings.

The development of the railway system in America is also left to individual enterprise. A power has thus grown up in our midst, which not only influences the political and financial measures of the several local governments, but threatens to make them subservient to its interests. Various causes bring about this result. First, the distances in the United States are so immense, that the lines which connect the main points of trade and travel are virtually monopolies. Then though private enterprises, they have received in most instances aid from the different States, either in money or credits, while Congress has donated to the more important lines large portions of the public domain. In this way, millions upon millions of acres have passed into the possession of private corporations, which not only own the lines, but are the lords of the whole contiguous territories. There are certainly plausible reasons for this liberality. Without the railway to fit them for settlement, the vast uncultivated regions of the West would be practically inaccessible, and of no more value than the African desert. By encouraging the construction of railways, which demands a heavy outlay of capital, with grants of alternate sections of land along both sides of the line, the remaining lands are brought within the reach of the settler, and find ready sale. At this writing, the matter is being viewed from a higher standpoint, by a class of people exceedingly jealous of the growth of this power. Experience teaches that landed property goes hand in hand with legislative influence, and even democracies are no exception to the rule. The consideration of the consequences of these immense grants of land and their attendant political power as regards private corporations, is left to the intelligent citizen, while the author proceeds with his gossip concerning the Railway abroad.

It is good for nations as well as individuals to be relieved of their conceit, especially in matters in which they flatter themselves they are superior. The Yankee carbuilder will hardly believe that the Russians, who have been regarded as half-reclaimed savages, are capable of teaching him a very seasonable lesson.

The first line ever laid down in Russia, extends from Moscow to St. Petersburg. The train usually consists of half a dozen cars of immense length. Entering by a broad, easy staircase and convenient platform, the astonished and delighted traveller finds himself in a saloon, with a table in the centre, surrounded by sofas and divans. Opening from one side of this saloon, is a passage leading to the farther end of the carriage, and passing on to an iron platform outside. Neither height, stoutness, crinoline, nor other moderate majesty of human proportions or ornament, creates any obstacle to the free movements of the passenger. Heavy curtains, when pushed aside, however, reveal three pleasant, private apartments, if he desires repose. Each is furnished with six cosey easy-chairs. Another passage leads to similar apartments reserved for ladies. A pretty winding staircase shows the way to a sleeping-saloon above. The view from this upper floor is quite charming in fine weather, and enables the traveller to observe the general aspect of the country, for miles in every direction. Everything is admirably arranged. The doors fit closely, yet open easily; and as on entering the carriage it is necessary to pass several—of which one shuts as the other opens—there are no drafts from the wintry air outside. Over the passage is a loft, where may be stowed away, within arm's reach, whatever a reasonable person can expect or desire to have with him. Double windows exclude the bleak air from rushing directly upon weak lungs; but there is so good a system of ventilation, through the roof, that the cars are never unpleasantly close. Lastly, there are washing-places, dressing-rooms, and other conveniences, handsomely fitted up, and scrupulously clean.

The amusements in this Traveller's Paradise, are numerous and varied. They beguile the tedium of a journey so effectively, that it seems like a holiday jaunt, rather than the usual term of imprisonment such journeys are in other countries. Portable card-tables, wax-candles, chess, draughts, cards, and books are to be had for the asking. Cheerful games and good reading are agreeably varied by festive stoppages, the speed being about twenty-five miles an hour, and a first-class station every fifty miles. Here is to be found, at a rational price, tea, such as scholars love, true nectar for philosophers; while ruder sons of Adam may choose other drinks from divers rows of curiously shaped bottles of wonderful wines, and richly-colored *liqueurs*. There are *bonbons* and beef, ducks and geese, partridges and venison, mighty sturgeon, and the doubtful Russian delicacies of *caviare* and *gelinottes.* There are even clean waiters, white linen, flowers, and bright lights. The cheer is so good that parties of fine ladies and smart officers travel from St. Petersburg and Moscow expressly to dine at these refreshment stations. When the traveller has plentifully regaled himself, according to his eating, and the night wears on, he has only to tell the railway servant that he is ready for sleep, and before he need take his place in the train again, he will find his berth ready. The berths on this railroad are superior even to those on any American line. They are as good as the berths in the state-cabin of an American steamer.

There was a time when the English railway was better than our own, but that time has passed. Take the fastest train on the direct line between Liverpool and London, and compare it with similar trains on the Erie. For this distance of two hundred and ten miles, through first-class fare is thirty-five shillings, or about nine dollars. From New York to Elmira, on the Erie, a distance of two hundred and seven miles, the fare is eight dollars in a drawing-room coach—this as a local rate. The coaches here are more elegant, and the rates perceptibly cheaper than in England. The rate of speed is about the same, thirty miles an hour. There is no comparison in regard to smoothness. The Erie gives you the motion of an easy carriage, the English road the rattle of a wheelbarrow. There are four wheels under the coach, while here we have twelve. On the English road, a failing wheel necessitates disaster. Here we may send off from one to four, and if judiciously selected, the coach spins on as smoothly as before. We talk and write with ease on our American lines; there both are next to impossible.

They surpass us, perhaps, in the division of cars into

10

compartments, in their system of taking fares, and in the politeness and attention of employés, and in other particulars that affect the traveller, but we shall match them in this, by and by. At every railway station in England, there is a stairway or platform or other means of crossing the track. Persons who disregard the prescribed way and step upon the track, are immediately seized, and fined twenty-five dollars. In this way the companies are saved many suits for direct and constructive damages. Another economic experiment was noticed. This is the Railway Savings Bank, to be found on all the principal lines. The Company brings the bank to the depositors, saving them the trouble of going to the bank. In this way they collect the small savings of their workmen when they are paid off, encouraging and enabling them to be provident without inconvenience, and without excuse for not becoming so. Great success has attended the plan from the start.

There are 599 railway companies in the United Kingdom. England alone has 434, Scotland 80, and Ireland 85 companies. The lines of about half of the total of these companies are either leased to or worked by the great leaders of our railway republic. The other half are independent. The London and Northwestern, the "King of Railways," represented by a length of 1,507 miles open, carried in the twelve months ending December, 1871, 32,340,610 passengers, being just about the total population of all England, Scotland, and Ireland.

China has not a mile of railway, and steadily refuses all applications and proposals in that direction.

Japan, not waiting for proposals, organized a railway system a year ago, depending altogether upon her native population. She is now constructing a road to her great seaport, Yokohoma, connecting it with Yeddo, the capital, and the principal cities of the interior. Part of the railway system in Japan is already in operation, and is being pushed forward with all the energy of American enterprise.

The Pasha, who is the Brother Jonathan of Egypt, after making the Suez Canal possible, has connected his principal cities by rail with the seaports on the Mediterranean and the Red Sea. This enterprise is not only in the interest of commerce, but the wily Pasha has military operations in view, as well. He is fortifying his little kingdom against the schemes of his master, the Sultan.

They are planning a railway now, up the Nile to the ancient City of Thebes. What echoes the whistle of the locomotive may start in those hallowed precincts!

Next in length of mileage to the London and Northwestern, comes the Great Western, with 1,387 miles open.

A wooden railway, four feet eight and a half inch gauge, has been constructed in the province of Quebec, Canada. The rails are of maple, four by seven inches, and fourteen feet long; the ties of hemlock and tamarac. The line is thirty miles long, and cost $5,000 per mile, including nine stations, car and locomotive depot, engine and repairing shops, engine and tender, two passenger cars, eight grain cars, and twenty-five wood cars. The trains run with remarkable smoothness, at the rate of twenty-five miles an hour. Mr. Brooks, in his "Seven Months' Run," says: "The railroads of India are doing more for the conversion of Hindoos, if not Mohammedans, than all the missionaries." He should have added, that England is doing more with these same locomotives to convert India into British gold.

You get a good idea of the railway in India, by starting from Calcutta for Benares, *en route* to Bombay, 1,407 miles distant by rail. You travel by the "East Indian R. R." line. During the long hours of your journey, you cannot better amuse yourself than by noticing and asking questions about the peculiarities of railway construction in India. Remember, that all the iron in the track, the locomotives and cars, were transported from England, a voyage by sea of from 15,000 to 20,000 miles. The ties or sleepers of the track are iron, the roofs of the freight cars are of corrugated iron, the telegraph poles are hollow cylinders of galvanized iron, all from the same country. Nearly everything in the way of railway material is also manufactured in England. The head of every department and work in the Indian railways—every conductor and engine-driver, is an Englishman, imported for the purpose. Educated Indians are made very useful in subordinate positions at station and freight houses.

The track is mainly ballasted with broken brick, burned in kilns along the line. The depot buildings and fences are constructed of the same earth material, and the roofs are covered with brick-tile, No insurance is needed. Every station-house is strongly built, and adapted for the double purpose of railway traffic and military fortification, where necessity demands. Every line of railway, therefore, becomes a line of forts—a clever scheme and of vast importance, when we consider the infinitely small number of English, compared to the native population. Clever people, these Anglo ancestors of ours, in spite of their antipathy to "Alabama" claims and consequential damages. They have most successfully bound India together with their net-work of iron, transported from its native English hills 15,000 miles away. They have ruled those millions of discordant Indian people with squads of unacclimated troops, counted only by scores in the comparison.

If you start from St. Goarshausen, for a dash over a German railway, you take the second-class carriage. Thus you avoid the soft cushions and red velvet of the first-class carriage, quite an advantage with the thermometor at 85° in the shade. Many, if not most, of the German railways have four classes of carriages, in the grandest of which by day sit only princes and fools. By night in an express train, where there are no sleeping accommodations, a first-class carriage is a matter of necessity, but at no other time. We endeavored once to escape the tobacco smoke of inferior company, by travelling first-class. While indulging in congratulations on having a solitary potentate as a fellow-passenger, the baron brought out a pipe, with a bowl as big as a coffee cup, and began to puff away, without so much as saying "by your leave." You find there a new method of heating cars. A preparation of wood, charcoal, nitrate of potash and starch, is employed. It is put in close iron boxes, placed under the seats, a double top being employed to prevent the seats of the cars from becoming inconveniently hot. The prepared charcoal is packed in boxes, in pieces four inches long, three inches wide, and two inches thick. On the line between Aix-la-Chapelle and Berlin, eight pieces constitute the quantity used for heating a compartment.

This serves to warm the car efficiently, during sixteen hours, the fuel being still red hot at the end of the journey. The prepared charcoal costs thirty-two shillings the hundredweight, and the expense of heating one compartment is about three farthings an hour.

In Germany, an accident has never occurred from the breaking of a rail. Not a person has lost his life, nor has a person been mutilated from this cause, in all the thirty or more years that steam carriages have been running on iron ways in Germany. The reason is plain. It is determined by scientific experiment how long iron will resist, on an average, the beating of wheels, and then the law requires the railway authorities to put down new rails periodically, whether those in use exhibit signs of weakness or not. While this involves expense, it is so managed as to be gradually distributed over a period of years, until the whole is completed within the given time.

The Peruvian Government is now constructing a railway 14,000 feet above the water. It goes over the Andes, 7,000 feet higher than the highest point of the Sierra Nevada, crossed by the Central Pacific Railway. This elevation is within 1,000 feet of perpetual snow. Mr. Edward H. Spaulding, of Bloomington, New Jersey, assistant engineer of the Montclair Railway for four years, is now in that country with some of our best American engineers, who were selected to accomplish this difficult undertaking.

This railway goes from Peru to Arequipa, forty miles; thence to Puno, on Lake Titicaca. This lake is partly in Peru and partly in Bolivia, and is one of the principal sources of the Amazon, which is navigable for nearly 4,800 miles. The combined railway and steamboat communication will cross the continent at its widest point. Mr. Meigs, the contractor, has had contracts in that country amounting to over $100,000,000. Our American styles of cars and rolling stock will be introduced on this railway, thus adding another triumph to our American manufactures.

The following statement of prices on the railways of Europe, per one hundred miles, in first, second, and third class carriages, and on express trains, may be of interest to Americans who visit Europe, or those who would contrast the expense of travelling :

RUSSIA—First-class, 14s. 5d. ; second-class, 10s. 10d. ; third-class, 3s.

PRUSSIA—First-class, 12s. 6d. ; second-class, 10s. ; third class, 3s. 2d. Express train—first-class, 14s. ; second-class, 12s. The Rhine—first-class, 11s. 10d. ; second-class, 8s. ; third-class, 3s. 10d.

NORWAY—First-class, 13s. ; second-class, 9s. ; third-class, 4s. 6d.

SWEDEN—First-class, 11s. ; second-class, 7s. 6d. ; third-class, 4s. 9d. ; Express trains—first-class, 13s. ; second-class, 10s.

BAVARIA—First-class, 10s. ; second-class, 7s. ; third-class, 4s. 10d.

BELGIUM—First-class, 10s. 3d. ; second-class, 7s. 6d. ; third-class, 5s.

WURTEMBURG—First-class, 10s. 3d. ; second-class, 6s. 8d. ; third-class, 5s. 1d.

DENMARK—First-class, 12s. ; second-class, 9s. ; third-class, 6s.

SPAIN—First-class, 14s. 7d. ; second-class, 10s. 5d. ; third-class, 6s. 3d.

AUSTRIA—First-class, 13s. ; second-class, 10s. 3d. ; third-class, 6s. 6d.

SAXONY—First-class, 11s. ; second-class, 8s. 3d. ; third-class, 6s. 8d.

SWITZERLAND—First-class, 12s. ; second-class, 9s. ; third-class, 6s. 8d.

ITALY—First-class, 14s. ; second-class, 10s. 6d. ; third-class, 7s. Express trains—first-class, 16s. ; second-class, 12s.

PORTUGAL—First-class, 13s. 3d. ; second-class, 10s. ; third-class, 7s.

HOLLAND—First-class, 14s. ; second-class, 10s. ; third-class, 7s.

FRANCE—First-class, 14s. 6d. ; second-class, 11s. ; third-class, 7s. 6d.

GREAT BRITAIN AND IRELAND—First-class, 18s. 6d. ; second-class, 13s. 4d. ; third-class, 8s. Express trains—first-class, 21s. ; second-class, 16s. 8d.

It will be seen that there are no third-class carriages on express trains, on European railways. Also, that Russia and Prussia accommodate the working classes at the cheapest rates, while the tariff of Great Britain and Ireland is the highest of all for first, second, and third class carriages and express trains. It must however be borne in mind, that in those foreign countries, where the railways do not belong to the State, the shareholders receive considerable Government assistance, in consideration of their being compelled to adopt a low tariff. The rates per mile on these roads, reduced to our currency, will not bring travel to as low a standard as in this country, unless we take their third-class carriages. On their first-class and express trains, the average is from four cents per mile, to six and a half cents ; on the second and third, from two and a quarter to three and three quarters per mile.

If you are limited to forty days abroad, the expense will be about $350. For instance, you leave New York July 20, and arrive in Liverpool on the 30th. In London three days ; to Paris *via* Southampton, visiting Metley, Cowes Rouden, two days, and home in ten days, costing as follows in gold: Steamer excursion ticket, $140; expenses on board, $10; four days in England at $10—$40; to Paris, via Southampton, $7; extras, $10; four days in Paris at $5—$20; circular ticket to Switzerland, $27.50; eight days at $5 extra, $40; to Liverpool from Paris, $35; extras, $5, on the voyage home —total, $344.40. The charge of $10 per day in England will cover railway expenses. The Queen's Hotel, St. Martin's Le Grand (opposite the post-office), London, is a good family house—rooms from 4s. to 7s. per day— order what you like. The best restaurant in London is the 'Gaiety,' on the Strand, near the Charing Cross Hotel —dinner admirably served, 3s. 6d., exclusive of wine.

XXI.

THE REAR CAR.

A COMMERCIAL TRAVELLER'S STORY.

Y father, who had been a prosperous merchant in the city of B., was ruined by the war. I took a position with a large New York house, and soon became a leading commercial traveller. Early in the fall of 18—, I took the ten P.M. train from B. for the city, having in my possession collections to a large amount.

I had learned that the safest place on the train is the last car, and as there is usually the most room there, I took my place in a double seat near its centre. There were but four other passengers in this car: an old gentleman trying to read a morning paper by the dim lamplight, two farmers, and a man who appeared to be an invalid—bundled up to his eyes in a large shawl.

The train moved off, and as soon as the conductor had been through the car, I fixed myself for a nap. I arranged myself with my back toward the front of the car, and with the aid of my overcoat and bag, made quite a comfortable couch. I was just dozing off, when I was

again awakened by the brakeman opening the door and
shouting the name of the station we were approaching.
At this place, the old gentleman and the two farmers got
out, leaving the invalid and myself the sole occupants of
the last car.

The train hurried on, and I again closed my eyes. I
soon succeeded in getting to sleep, and was enjoying
quite a comfortable nap, when I was awakened by an uncomfortable choking sensation and a painful feeling of con-
straint. As I attempted to move, I found that I was powerless, and I realized with feelings of surprise and alarm,
that I was gagged, and bound securely with fine ropes to
the seat in which I sat. My captor now came in front of
me. It was the invalid, whom I now recognized as an unprincipled villain by the name of Bradley Morgan. He had
been, a few months previous, in the employ of my father,
but had robbed us, and had been convicted, on account
of conclusive evidence which I had furnished against
him. He had broken jail, however, and his whereabouts
till now had been unknown to me. With these circumstances fresh in my memory, I knew I had little mercy to
expect at the hands of this man. With the utmost coolness, he now examined my pockets, and took from them
my watch, collections, and all the valuables they contained. He even took the gold button from my shirt
collar, and wrenched a large seal ring from the middle
finger of my left hand. This done, he blew out both the
lights of the car, passed out the forward door, and closed
it after him. Another moment, and I heard the rear door
of the forward car open and shut, and I felt relieved that
I had escaped bodily harm at the hands of the scoundrel.

He had not been gone a minute, when I felt that the
train was gradually lessening in speed. It drifted along

for a little, and slowly came to a stand-still. I supposed that we had stopped at some small station, and the conductor or some passenger would shortly come in and relieve me from my very unpleasant position. I twisted my head around as best I could, and looked through the front windows of the car. *I saw the lights of the rest of the train disappearing in the distance, away down the road !*

May I never feel again the horror of that moment! The awful nature of my situation flashed on me like an electric shock.

After successfully accomplishing the robbery, Bradley Morgan had uncoupled the last car, the brakeman having gone into the forward car, as the train did not stop again for almost an hour. For the same reason the absence of the last car would not be noticed for some time. And there I was left powerless in the last car, to be run down and horribly killed by the night express, which followed us in forty-five minutes !

At first I was almost stupefied with terror. I felt that I had but half an hour to live, and at the end of that time an awful fate awaited me. All my past life, even to trifling events, seemed to pass before me—a thousand things that I thought I had forgotten came back to me in that moment with wonderful vividness. I thought of my father and mother, and the dreadful affliction which was so soon to come upon them. It seemed as though I could see the once happy home of my childhood, now to be darkened with grief. Oh, how fervently I prayed that I might be saved !

Rousing myself, I strained the cords that held me with the strength of desperation, but though they cut deep into my flesh, they did not yield at any point. At last, after repeated exertions, I succeeded, to my great joy, in freeing my left hand. The ropes, however, still passed around my left arm at the elbow, and prevented a free use of it. I tried at first to loosen or untie the ropes, but I found that this could not be done. Then I managed with much trouble and some loss of time to get my jack-knife from my right trouser pocket. With the help of my teeth I succeeded in opening one of the blades, and with excited eagerness began to cut the ropes. Unfortunate haste! At the first stroke of the knife it slipped from my hands, and fell just out of reach on the seat.

A cold sweat burst out all over me, and it seemed to me as though my last hope were gone. I knew that at least twenty minutes had already passed, and that I had but little more than that left. I would have given untold wealth to have known just how much I had.

The knife had fallen on the seat, to the right of me, and I could not reach it with my left hand, strain as I would. For some minutes I wrenched and writhed like a madman, foaming at the mouth ; and then, exhausted, I sank back in despair. And there I sat—sat and waited and listened for the coming of the train. Twenty times I thought I heard it, but still it did not come. At last I really heard the rattle of the approaching cars ; very faint at first but gradually growing louder.

Again I strained every nerve to reach the knife, and this time the tips of my fingers rested on it. In another moment I had it firmly in my hand, and was cutting quickly but carefully the cursed ropes that held me. I had loosened almost all, when, raising my eyes again, I saw the head-light of the engine come tearing along toward me ! In an instant the last rope was cut, and scarcely another passed before I was leaping from the car.

Just in time, for a moment afterward the engine of the night express dashed into the car which I had left, crushing it into a shapeless mass of wood and iron !

The result of the smash-up was the total demolition of my car, almost entire destruction of the locomotive, and partial wrecking of most of the cars in the train. No lives were lost, however, the engineer being the only person seriously injured.

Measures for Morgan's apprehension were taken at once. He was in custody within a week, most of the stolen property having been found in his possession. He was arrested in New York, and while being conveyed by the same railway to B. he attempted to leap from the train. Slipping, he fell under the wheels, and was crushed to death.

XXII.

THE SNOW BLOCKADE.

The Night Express Snowed in—The Conductor's Cool Announcement—Making the Best of It—Personal Experiences of Travellers—Judges, Lawyers, Doctors, and Preachers—The Employé's Apprenticeship—The Polite Attentions of Conductors and Brakemen—A Superintendent Exposed—The Timid Traveller—The Consumptive Traveller—Lunches—Hints to Travellers—Reading on the Cars—Lateral, Vertical, and Diagonal Motion—The Hog Palace Car—Time-table in 1769—No Excuse for Ladies' Cars—Suits for Damages—An Item for the Ladies—Trains Behind Time—Editorial Passes—A Heathen Colony—Custom-house Annoyances—All Aboard!

 COLD morning in December, the severest of the year. The night express due in B—— at noon was still behind time, and now its passengers looked out through the narrow windows upon a landscape white with snow. The wind howled dismally, and the ominous roar could be distinctly heard above the endless clatter of the wheels beneath our cars. The snow was still falling, and the gale catching it up in clouds, dashed it in drifts against the train, enveloping roof and platform, and measuring its depth upon every

available surface. Now and then a jerk and a sudden pull forward would warn us that far to the front the great engine had encountered some snowy barrier. Yet through and on moved the long train, in the light of the early morning, until day gradually stole upon the travellers, now thoroughly awake to a scene, so cold and forbidding without as only to give a keener zest to the cosey comfort within.

The storm seemed to increase in violence as the hours wore on. Eight o'clock, and the breakfast station still twenty miles away! The snow-drifts grew more and more formidable at our front, and the engine gave signs of weakening before the increasing strength of the enemy. Passengers began to grow uneasy; looked nervously at their watches and peered anxiously out of the windows. Consulted their time-tables; assailed the conductor whenever he passed with all sorts of irrelevant inquiries, when suddenly—the train slackened its speed, again moved on, slackened again, and then stopped perfectly still with a jar and a rebound, which had well-nigh sent some unwary ones off their feet.

There was an immediate rush for the forward car to learn the extent of the trouble. One or two imprudent ones attempted to alight, but on finding themselves waist-deep, were only too glad to regain the solid footing of the platform. Meanwhile, the word ran down from mouth to mouth and from car to car: "*Snowed in!*" The situation was growing worse with every moment, and the possibility of extricating the train grew more remote with every keen blast that came to add a few more inches to the thickening wall around us. The barrier grew higher every instant, front and rear and on every side. Spasmodic efforts—now forward, now back, proved fruitless, and at length the great monster, weary and exhausted, ceased its fierce breathing, and the train lay still, half buried in the snow.

The conductor announced that the dining-car had provisions for two days, and that headquarters would soon discover the trouble and send a " working train to their assistance. The gentlemen could amuse themselves around the warm fires in the smoking and express cars, and the ladies could have sole possession of the sleeping and dining cars. It was best to prepare for a day and— perhaps a night in the snow." So we went forward to our seats, exchanged cards and introductions, lit our cigars, and fell to filling the hours with grunts and complaints, animadversions upon the management of railways, the alarming increase in the number of accidents, and all that sort of thing. There were travellers in the party who had been around the world by steam ; good-natured passengers, lymphatic travellers, timid travellers, curious travellers ; doctors, lawyers, and professors.

" Now if we only had a press and type," began the Professor, " what a jolly newspaper we could make. There is a newspaper in Scotland which is printed in a car, on the road from Edinburgh to Glasgow. The press, cases of type, and compositors are all in the car, and the news and telegrams received on the road, so that the edition for the provinces is worked off *en route !*"

" Attention !" exclaimed the colonel, rising and motioning with his cane—" Now see how that fellow slams the door ! I take it that the employé's apprenticeship is very short. A man is believed to be competent for the position when he can shut a door in such a manner as to lead the occupant of the tenth seat back to infer that it is too late to prepare for eternity."

"I may say, colonel," said the judge, "that it is hard-ly reasonable to expect too much in the way of polite at-tentions from conductors and brakemen on railroad trains, and no one is disappointed at not receiving them. I do not think it unreasonable, however, to ask any Company desiring the patronage of the travelling public, that they shall employ at least one man to a train who is able and willing to give a civil answer to a civil question. It might also be advisable for them to correct certain evils without waiting for suggestions from the public or the press. For instance, the custom prevalent among brakemen of thrusting their heads into the cars and growling out the name of a station, the last syllables of which are nipped in the bud by the premature slamming of the door, is particularly objectionable, and should be corrected. The only result accomplished by this calling out of the names of stopping-places, is to set people wondering what the man said, or tried to say. If this matter is left to the em-ployés of the road, responsible parties should see that it is properly attended to. But we see no reason why it should be left to them at all. An excellent apparatus for informing travellers of the names of stations is used on the passenger trains of the Ogdensburg and Lake Champlain Railroad. It consists of a small wooden box with a glass-front, surmounted by a bell. When a train arrives at a station the bell rings and the name of the next stopping-place on the route appears under the glass in letters three inches in length. Such an apparatus is a great addition to the comfort of railway travellers, and saves much anxiety arising from mistakes and uncertainty. We do not see why some such arrangement could not be adopted on all roads. A reliable indicator of this de-scription would relieve the public from the annoyance of questioning reticent conductors and surly brakemen, and save a great deal of trouble all round."

"I think," said the commercial traveller, "that I will expose one man who is worthy of notice. I wish to expose him to the admiration of the public in general, especially all those who journey by rail, and whose associations compel them to ride upon it. Mr. George A. Merrill, Superintendent of the Rutland, Burlington, and Vermont Valley Railroad, has issued this notice, and it is posted in the cars of his road. I carry it with me, and exhibit it on every road :

"'NOTICE.

"'Baggage-men on the trains, freight as well as passenger, are expected and employed by the Company not only to do their work well, but PLEASANTLY, and to give every facility to travellers by information and by ACTS. Any departure from civility of conduct, and that courtesy due to the patrons of the road, will render them unfit for its services, and they will be dismissed accordingly.

"'Travellers may be unreasonable, but that will be considered no excuse for any employé to be so in return.'

"You see it is printed in large type, so that he who rides may read. The result is, civility and polite attention to every want. If you ask a conductor a question, he does not throw the answer over his shoulder as he moves on, but replies succinctly and intelligibly. The brakemen are polite, and I will warrant there are not many trunks thrown end over end on that road."

"What a charming innovation?" said the tired traveller. "Perhaps the next train that sweeps from the north will allow us half an hour for dinner."

"That tempts me to remark," said the doctor, "that many persons find that the lunches they catch at railroad stations, or which they carry with them in their bags or baskets, give them headaches, and serve as very poor substitutes for warm dinners at home. It is probably because they are made up so largely of cake or pastry. The food is too concentrated, has not enough of waste matter and fluid about it, and so produces constipation, which is a sure cause of a dull head and general bodily discomfort. The vegetables and soups we eat with our dinners at home are valuable for their waste matter as well as for their nutriment. With our lunches we miss these, but fruit is still better for those whose stomachs are healthy enough to eat it uncooked, and fruit we can almost always have with us. For a substantial lunch to take from home, especially for one who is taking active exercise, cold chicken is good, or cold meat cut in slices. These, laid between buttered slices of bread, make very nice sandwiches. Thin biscuit is usually more acceptable than bread, and if cut open, spread with currant jelly, and put together again, is very nice. The less of cake, and the plainer that little, the better for the traveller's comfort. Fresh soda crackers and fresh apples make an excellent light lunch ; but the fine flour crackers are so concentrated that it is best for all who can do so to eat the accompanying apples without peeling them. A simple lunch of this kind, which you can buy as you hasten through the streets to the depot, is far better than the little sweet cakes and pastry abominations sold at stands near the depot. I doubt if women, who know how such things are made, are often caught buying them. Figs or raisins go well with crackers or gems ; but fresh, juicy fruit is preferable when you can get it."

"Here are a few hints to railway travellers," said the preacher, "that I have written down in my Diary :

"Do not travel at night if you can avoid it.

"Take your breakfast always before starting on a journey.

"Keep your ticket under your hat-band, or the inner lining.

"If an open window proves uncomfortable to another, you will close it.

"Obtain a seat near the aisle and near the centre of the car and near the centre of the train.

"Never stand an instant on any car platform.

"Purchase nothing whatever to eat on a rail train, unless it is a simple sandwich to be eaten at noon.

"Don't be disturbed if you find the best seats in a railroad car taken. As no one knew you were coming, of course they did not reserve one.

"When a car is crowded, don't fill a seat with your bundles. True politeness is not amiss, even amidst the confusion and bustle of a public conveyance.

"Avoid conversation while the cars are in motion, because the overstrain of the voice to make one heard above the noise of the wheels has been such that in many cases there has been such tension of the vocal chords as to impair the voice for many months.

"All reading in rail-cars while in motion is injurious ; but the injury will be greatly mitigated by reading only a quarter of an hour at a time, and for the next five minutes let the eyes be directed to very distant objects. This alternation from things near to those remote is a very great relief and rest."

"That reminds me again," followed the doctor. "Most if not all who read on railroads are sensible of weight and weariness about the eyes. This sensation is accounted for on high medical authority by the fact that the exact distance between the eyes and the paper cannot be maintained. The concussions and oscillations of the train disturb the powers of vision, and variation, however slight, is met by an effort at accommodation on the part of the eyes. The constant exercise of so delicate an organ produces fatigue, and if the practice of railroad reading is persisted in, must result in permanent injury. Added to this difficulty is bad or shifting light. The safe and prudent mode is to read little if any. The deliberate finishing of volumes in railway cars is highly detrimental.

"Sydney Smith complained that, in travelling from Exeter to London, in the stage-coach, he was subjected to no less than fifteen thousand jolts; and he naïvely asks if such jolting could be good for a man's stomach. Fifteen thousand jolts is a very excellent guess. It is this excessive jolting which plays the deuce with us; and whether five or fifteen thousand jolts are experienced in the course of a journey, we still suffer. Hundreds who have travelled long distances, feel it next morning, in the stiffness and soreness of their muscles, a soreness and stiffness for which they cannot account. Just consider for a moment the multiplicity of motions which accompany a railway carriage, spinning along at, say, forty miles an hour. There is a lateral motion; the oscillation of the wheels from rail to rail; the vertical motion, varying according to the fulness of the car; then there is a diagonal motion, which is easily perceived if we watch our fellow-travellers and the attitude they assume to preserve themselves against the impulse, or if we notice the direction which a loose object on the floor invariably takes. An eminent chemist declares that he counted ninety thousand motions in a first-class railway carriage from Manchester to London; how many more there were, he didn't reckon up. Reflect for a moment, my snowed-in friend, on the infinite concussions the frail body is thus subjected to. This shaking up of the system is by no means healthy; nor does the evil stop here. To balance one's self, to counteract, or at least to endeavor to counteract, the effect of the jolting and jerking of the lateral, vertical, diagonal, and impelling motion, the muscles of the whole body are strained. If we make an effort to keep our equilibrium, we are flopped to and fro, backward and forward, like a doll in a child's arms."

"Ah!" sighed the "snowed-in friend," "one sighs to be a pig, when one thinks of the Berg Hog Palace Car. When the swine wish to slumber, they blow a whistle made from the tail of a brother who has gone before, the conductors enter and conduct them to a hot Russian bath in the rear end of the car, after which they are rubbed down with rough towels, a lunch of old boots and ice cream furnished. Not a squeal is ever heard on these cars, nothing but grunts of satisfaction, and a skilled musician puts in from eighteen to twenty-four hours a day, playing on a cottage organ, and singing such ballads as the 'Ham Fat Man,' 'The Watch on the Rhine,' 'When the Pigs Come Home,' etc., etc. In fact, life is one perpetual holiday on the hog trains until they arrive within a few miles of Jersey City, when the train is stopped, a steam fire-engine throws a stream of chloroform into each car, and the inmates sink into a slumber from which they do not awaken in this world of trichinæ, butcher-knives, smoked ham, head-cheese, and death."

"How well the time-tables of this year compare with the following programme of a hundred years ago! I cut it out of Stewart's almanac for 1769.

"'The stage-wagons kept by John Barnhill at the

Golden-ball perform the journey from Philadelphia to New York in two days. They set off from Philadelphia and New York on Mondays and Thursdays punctually at sunrise, and change their passengers at Prince-Town, and return to Philadelphia and New York on the following days, passengers paying ten shillings to Prince-Town and ten shilling to Powle's Hook, opposite N. York, ferriage free.'"

"We're making about the same time, now," said the consumptive traveller. "Ugh! how cold it gets; express-man, fix up the fire!"

"There was some excuse for ladies' cars during the war," said the colonel, "but now there is certainly none, when all pay the same price for passage. Under the lock-car rule, all other cars are virtually smoking cars. There are many gentlemen who travel, to whom tobacco-smoke is extremely obnoxious, and yet these young men are held prisoners in these smoking cars. If any car is to be locked, let it be the smoking car, and put all the other passengers on their good behavior. If a man will smoke, let him go into the smoking car. If a man will chew, squirt his tobacco juice about the car, and soil ladies' dresses, let him be sent to the smoking car. Because an inveterate chewer and squirter of tobacco has his wife with him, it does not follow that he should have any better right to the ladies' car than a well-bred gentleman who travels singly. Gentlemen, take off your locks and put your passengers on good behavior."

"That reminds me of a case," said the lawyer, "that recently came into my hands. A few months ago, a man recovered heavy damages of a Western railroad company, in consequence of having been violently ejected from a ladies' car, so called, in which he had the audacity to take a seat, though unaccompanied by a lady.

The result of this suit probably encouraged Mr. B. H. Rugg, my client. He had purchased a ticket for the Cincinnati & Muskingum Railroad, and insisted upon taking a seat in a first-class car, instead of contenting himself with the accommodations afforded by a mean and dirty one filled with tobacco smoke, into which he was ordered by those in charge of the train. For his effrontery, he was promptly put off the train by the conductor, and now brings suit against the Company for $5,000 damages. I hope and trust that we shall recover the full amount claimed. Resistance to. the tyranny of railroad understrappers is so infrequent, that when displayed, it merits the warmest encouragement."

"I see that one man's injuries are worth more than another's," said the judge. "In a recent trial in Massachusetts, for damages to the person in a railway collision, the jury were instructed to consider, in awarding the plaintiff damages for permanent injuries: his health for the period of life thus far spent; to take him as he had stood with all his accomplishments, professional, intellectual, and other, and to say what diminution the injury has produced in them, and to give him compensation therefor, in dollars and cents. The plaintiff was a Dr. Breck, of Springfield, a physician in large practice, and of remarkable powers of endurance. The jury awarded him $10,000. He claimed $40,000. This is a small measure of damages for such injuries as would incapacitate a physician from doing more than a fraction of his former work, but the point was clearly settled that one man's injuries are worth more than another's."

At this juncture, the conductor brought a message from the ladies, asking the judge and our lawyer to step into the dining car and settle a dispute. The gallant gentle-

11

men went at once, for both had wives among the merry
party.   It transpired that the ladies had been discussing
the subject of railway accidents, and the possibility of
making a railway company pay for the loss of a lady's
wardrobe, lost or ruined in a railway collision.

The legal gentlemen decided that the case was quite
clear, the lawyer citing a suit in point :

"Mrs. Dorothy Rawson sued the Pennsylvania Railroad, and recovered $4,000, for her baggage, personal
ornaments, wearing apparel, etc., a large part of which
were gifts from her husband. The railway company
made a defence on two points :

" ' That her husband and not she was the proper person to sue.

" ' 2. That the company had made a condition in the
ticket that they would not be liable for more than $100.'

"The Court overruled both points, and decided in
favor of Mrs. Rawson. No two principles of law are
more clear than those upon which this decision was
based. I give them for the benefit of those people who
are not lawyers, but who are much imposed upon in this
direction :

" ' 1. The jewels, ornaments, and wearing apparel of a
woman are what the common law calls her paraphernalia, and are held to be her own against all the world.
It would be hard if a married woman could not own some
personal property of her own, even against her husband.
So the common law holds that the dress and ornaments
of a woman, however valuable they be, though one
should be the Koh-i-noor diamond, are sacred to herself.
The attorneys for Mrs. Rawson, therefore, judged rightly
when they brought the suit in her name. It was herself
and nobody else who was injured. Now to understand a
little more of this : the reader who is not a lawyer should
know that by the common law the *personal* property of

the wife becomes the husband's. It was on this ground that the attorney for the defendant (the Pennsylvania Railroad Company) resisted the right of Mrs. Rawson to sue. But they were mistaken in this. The *paraphernalia* of a wife (her dress and ornaments) belong to herself alone.

" ' 2. The Pennsylvania Railroad Company undertook to *limit* their responsibility as common carriers, by stating that they had given *notice* that they would not be responsible for more than $100. What did that notice amount to? Nothing. And why? Because the Pennsylvania Railroad Company are *common carriers*, and they cannot avoid their obligations *by any act of their own*. This is something all travellers ought to know, for railroads, steamboats, stages, all common carriers, are trying to avoid their responsibility by notices of this sort. It cannot be done ; for as they undertake to carry persons and freights for hire, the law makes them responsible for damages, and they cannot avoid it.' "

" How impatiently we take all railroad delays," remarked the preacher to the timid traveller. " No matter what may be the cause, no difference how well conducted the road, we fret and work ourselves into a fever of ridicule, coarse jests, and untimely remarks of all kinds, for the gratification of ourselves and other belated travellers. Or, if given to the poetical, we pencil our vituperations upon the walls of depots, and immortalize our sarcasm. The Bungtown Railway Company may run twenty daily trains over a single track of two hundred and fifty miles in length ; they may have to wait at some meeting point for delayed passenger trains, detained on any part of the route from New York City, a trip of twelve hundred miles, and by any of the mishaps that may arise in any business. It may be that some parts of the track have become suddenly unsafe for the usual rate of speed, or the thermometer sinks to 15 degrees below zero, during a night trip; or some part of the machinery gets out of order, as even stationary machinery will do; or perhaps some accident, more or less serious, has occurred, through the universal anxiety among people and railroad companies to brook no delays or tardiness. All this makes but little difference to our fretful, selfish selves, if we have made up our minds to go somewhere 'on time.' We curse the road and the officers, the engine and route.

"A few years ago, we could ride seven hours over the worst of roads in a cold, wintry day, with cold feet, bumped about in an old lumber wagon or a stage-hack, glad to reach the railroad, and were comparatively satisfied with such locomotion. Now we can't wait the fourth part of that time in a comfortable depot-house, without showing our pertness or irascibility."

"Yes!" responded the timid traveller; "but if that old stage-hack had stalled for a day in the snow, within twenty miles of that railroad and comfort, what then?"

"When I took up this line of march," said the colonel, "the newspaper batteries all along the line of the Ohio and Mississippi Railway, from St. Louis to Cincinnati, were belching forth their editorial fire, composed of squibs and diminutive thunder, at that corporation, for not renewing the passes of editors. Every paper we bought of the train-boys had its load. But strange to say the trains went on as usual, apparently unawed by the terrific cannonade of harmless shot and shell. I went over the same road the year before, and found that the line, with all its officers and men, were perfection with this very class of editors. The papers we bought on the road then slopped over with puffing and praise. But since the first of a certain January, these gentlemen lack all the essentials of conducting a popular railway. The Ohio and Mississippi Road has never been a paying concern, and if the management, for the sake of economy, saw fit to change their regulations, they had a right to do so. As far as I was able to judge, most of the officers and conductors of that year have been retained, and they manifest a most courteous and obliging spirit. In fact, Miles, Fields, Wise, and all their colleagues, are models of what a conductor should be, and I doubt if their superiors can be found. I mention it because it is the first instance that has come under my notice, of a railway corporation aiming a blow at the dead-head system, which, born of courtesy, has developed into a disgraceful abuse."

"There is a prospect now of being rid of another nuisance," rejoined the judge. "By an act of Congress passed at the last session, 'train-boys' on railway cars are not permitted to continue the avocation of vending cigars to passengers, unless they take out a pedler's license, and give bonds in $200,000 to the Government. The authorities have already proceeded to take cognizance of any cases that may come to their notice."

"I wish they could be abolished altogether," said the timid traveller—"I mean the rascally train-boys."

"The stuff they sell is rank poison," added the consumptive.

"There is a new swindle out," said the doctor, "and as we have a reporter on board, perhaps he will give it as a warning to the travelling public. This swindle takes the form of a lady, tall, interesting, refined in manners, and not younger than thirty. She dresses in the deepest mourning, and passes as a widow of a clergyman."

"Lord forgive her," interrupted the preacher.

"She frequents cars, hotels, and depots, and her game

consists in feigning great distress, and the loss of pocket-book or railway ticket, and solicits aid from travellers to defray her expenses to her destination. She obtains many loans, some gifts, and the proceeds of her eloquent appeals doubtless amount to a generous sum each day."

"Well," said the lawyer, "this is an age of progression, and woman must needs show her equality with man, no less in rascality than in honor and uprightness."

"There is a station on the Erie Road, in New Jersey," said the merchant, "called Sufferns. It is a suburban station, the home of many a city merchant. A reasonable walk from the villages of the valley, you will find an American community, with nearly the least possible that is human, save the form ; without civilization or organization of the lowest order, even as much as gypsies ; without art above the art of savages—hunting, charcoal-burning, and making baskets, wooden brooms, and the like. They are without hope, or enterprise, or industry for anything better or beyond the instant demands of the animal nature. Without a line of the simplest literature, or the least idea of written language or numerals ; without a trace of the Bible, of Christianity, or of any sort of religion or deity ; nay, almost without language, their *patois* being so scanty as well as disorganized, that only the commonest of facts are communicated by it, and those with difficulty. There is, of course, nothing worthy the name of marriage or family among them. Three surnames, it is said, suffice for three-quarters of the race. Their bearing is abject and spiritless, their faces stolid, their glances furtive, and their conduct timorous. Nobody knows or cares how they live, how they are born. or by what means they die, or how they are buried, in their savage isolation."

"Do not our missionaries go among them?" asked the preacher.

"No," the merchant replied, "they are too near home, too near civilization, and besides, they make their own flannel underwear, and have no use for bandanna handkerchiefs. Distance, you know, lends enchantment to the missionary's views."

"Too true; we have neglected heathen all about us."

"If your friend is travelling abroad," began the judge, "send him a copy of Mr. McElrath's letter. Mr. McElrath is the appraiser, you know, or was, and his letter is a manifesto to ten thousand Americans. He tells the travelling and travelled American that he knows what the law is, and that it shall be enforced. Mr. McElrath is quite clear upon that point indeed.

"No traveller in Europe will deny, that the inspection of his personal luggage by the custom-house officers at every frontier, was one of the chief annoyances of his journey. It has been some little time since I made the grand tour, but I remember this very well. Upon reaching the Austrian line, as I approached Salzburg, I had a slight difference of opinion with the royal imperial inspector, whom I conceived to be a royal imperial ass! He fumbled long and earnestly and vexatiously, in a very small travelling-bag, to find contraband articles. During this official search, he ingeniously contrived to disturb the cork of a modest bottle of ink, which consequently bedewed all the contents of the bag. The veterans of travel at that day, admonished by much sad experience, always declared that their shaving-soap and slippers contained nothing contraband, and displayed a five-franc piece as conclusive evidence, which was always accepted as proof. It is a misfortune, certainly, that this relic of barbarism continued so long as a part of our own practice, and that the American who used to swear at this vexation all through Europe, returns to encounter it in its worst form at his own door.

"Still Mr. McElrath, the appraiser, is perfectly right. It is a law of the land, and he properly insists upon executing it. He probably knows as well as anybody that the surest way of getting a bad law changed is to insist upon executing it to the rigorous letter. He very justly will not wink at its evasion; and as the travelling members of the human family seem to suppose that there is no harm in smuggling, and that the detective officer of the customs cannot be really in earnest, the appraiser issued a letter in which he defines the requirements of the law in the matter of personal luggage, and informs whomsoever it may concern that if they wish to avoid detention and trouble, they will not try to smuggle silks and woollens partially shaped into clothes under the name of wearing apparel. This is horribly vexatious, but if the free and enlightened American does not like it he must change the law. He cannot fairly complain of his own action. The appraiser is his officer executing his will. The account of dissatisfaction is to be settled with himself, not with the appraiser.

"The appraiser expected that ten thousand persons would return to the United States that year, bringing with them various articles, such as new clothes and fancy goods, worth two millions of dollars, the regular duties upon which would amount to about one million. To the ten thousand Americans about to retreat, he desired to say 'beforehand, that every dollar of these duties will be exacted, and must be paid before their trunks and packages can get through the hands of the customs officers.'

"The ten thousand might bring their combs and brushes if in actual use: their fine-cut tobacco, if it had been once chewed; their coats and trousers partially worn; their professional books and tools of trade, not machinery; also pictures and statues by American artists abroad; also jewelry when worn, and evidently intended to be worn by the bearers; also one pair of slippers if well down at the heel; also household plate and effects if they have been in use one year abroad. Everything else was to be carefully stated in writing by the ten thousand, and upon their arrival the duties, amounting to about fifty per cent., would be levied. The duties must then and there be paid, and every one of the noble army could step proudly ashore upon the land of the free and the home of the brave.

"I give this to the reporter, because I see by the papers that we are on the eve of an important Presidential campaign. Mr. McElrath's letter is one of the most powerful free-trade documents that I have seen.

"One of the principal hotel nuisances in America and elsewhere, is, that no one on entering an establishment knows what will be the amount of his bill, until he leaves it, or what are his privileges while there. It is rarely found that the bill tallies with the notices tacked up so modestly behind doors; and it is to be regretted that hotel proprietors do not expose a more satisfactory prospectus in some conspicuous place. I have a sample here, which I found in the entrance-way of a hotel at Lahore, East India:

"'Gentlemen who come in hotel not say anything about their meals they will be charged for and if they should say beforehand that they are going out to breakfast or dinner, etc., are if they say that they have not

11*

anything to eat they will not be charged, and if not so, they will be charged, or unless they bring it to the notice of the manager of the place, and should they want to say anything, they must order the manager for and not any one else, and unless they bring it to the notice of the manager, they will be charge for the least things according to hotel rate, and no fuss will be allowed afterward about it. Should any gentleman take wall lamp or candle light from the public rooms they must pay for it without any dispute its charges. Monthly gentlemens will have to pay my fixed rate made with them at the time, and should they absent day in the month they will not be allowed to deduct anything out of it, because I take from them less rate than my usual rate of monthly charges.' "

The conductor, who had reported progress from time to time, now entered with the welcome intelligence that in an hour the track would be clear.

XXIII.

THE COLOSSUS OF ROADS.

BUCK NORTON was a cripple,
  Of two off toes bereft,
A twelve-foot leap had fix'd him,
  With just his right foot left.
That is, his south foot yielded
  To a bender up above,
All through a bigger bender,
  That time at " Mickey's Cove."

You're mightly right in that, sir,
  Was never known to flinch ;
Lost half a foot at Mickey's,
  But never gave an inch.
He spread some when he hobbled,
  Was loose, when he got tight,
But once upon the foot-board,
  That left foot came out right.

He likes to tell the story,
  For he's heavy on the stump ;
And jokes about mementos
  Of that rather famous jump.

How he engineer'd it thro', sir,
   And liked to kick the pail;
When his right foot got in limbo,
   And his left foot gave leg bail.
No flag was swung at Mickey's,
   And the freight was coming blind;
He put his best foot for'ard,
   And came out a foot behind.

When the toes began to heel, sir,
   He put that best foot down,
And swore they'd keep on workin',
   Wherever they were thrown.
For no lazy bones were ever
   Known to hang about his train;
And dead broke as now they were, sir,
   They would live somehow again.

His left knee somehow weakened
   When he tried to say his prayers;
And the other out of practice,
   So he stopped them for repairs.
Since they fell out there at Mickey's,
   They don't fall in quite so strong;
The left seems short of feeling,
   And the right feels much too long.

Not on his last legs yet, sir,
   Though his rivals tried a ruse;
Gave out that he was dying,
   Just to fill Buck Norton's shoes.
They put their own foot in it,
   For Hammond said to Moore:
"There's more behind his nozzle,
   Than there ever was before."

With one foot on his engine,
   And the other on the land,
We'll call him our Colossus
   Of Roads—you understand?

To foot it up, our cripple
  Stands high, as well he may:
His engine draws like "60,"
  And Norton draws big pay.

XXIV.

FIVE MINUTES BEHIND.

A SWITCHMAN'S STORY.

 ROUGH cabin of logs in the midst of dense woods, and shut in by the precipitous crests of rocky hills. No neighbors, save at the red farmhouse some few miles in the valley below. It was only on the clearest days that I could see the dim wreath of smoke curling up from the Wycliffe chimneys.

I had been struggling to ward off the iron grasp of poverty, and here was employment ready to my hand. Why should I mind the solitude?

John Walker had also applied for the situation of switchman at Branhill Station. Rumor had it, that pretty Barbara Wycliffe had herself gone in to headquarters, and used her influence in Walker's behalf. I had been taken with the girl myself. There was something in the tropic glow of her dark Spanish beauty, and the sparkle of her brown eyes, that was strangely attractive to me. Walker was a sullen, reticent fellow, with a bad look out of his eye, and somehow I didn't like the idea of her becoming his wife. True, they said she had—but who cares what they said?

The sun was creeping slowly up the leafless woods and sombre stretches of black-green pines that covered the eastern hill one sparkling March afternoon, as I came leisurely in after half an hour's brisk work at wood-cutting down in the hollow. The instant I entered I became conscious, by that peculiar magnetic influence which all have experienced, of the presence of some one else in the little apartment. Nor was I mistaken. John Walker was lounging in the rocking-chair by the one window, reading a week-old newspaper.

"Halloo, Walker! how came *you* here?"

"Through the back-door. I've just strolled up from Wycliffe's. And how are you getting along, old fellow?"

"Oh, first-rate. What are you doing?"

"Nothing just at present. I am looking for a place on the E—— Road as brakeman until something better turns up. Upon my word you've got things pretty snug here, Reuben. Does the Company give you the place?"

"Yes."

"Comfortable, though not gorgeous," he said, looking carelessly around. "Nice warm walls, chimney, big enough to roast an ox—two, if you want 'em—furniture neat—clock on the shelf—what's that for, eh?"

I smiled as I confessed the clock's utility.

"Not having yet attained the dignity of a watch, I depend on a clock to inform me of the time."

"Ah, that's it! Switches changed often?"

"Twice a day, when the down Lightning meets the up Accommodation, on the Branch, and the Way Mail on the Branch leaves the main track."

"Late?"

What a lounging, indolent sort of way he had, as he put

the questions indifferently to me! I looked rather sullenly at him, but he was not at all disturbed by my gaze.

"Well, yes, late and early. Nine in the morning for the Branch, seven in the evening for the Lightning."

"Pretty easy life of it, Eyre?"

"Not hard, only one has to be prompt."

"Yes—yes, to be sure. Seen much of old Wycliffe's folks here, eh?"

"Occasionally."

"Well, I'm off; if I go on the E—— Road, don't make love to Barbara!"

During all this, his cold gray eyes wandered uneasily about the apartment, and he never once looked at me with the frank, fearless gaze that is most appropriate between man and man. It was a forced smile that met his last remark, and I could have knocked the coarse jester down.

The next day was one of those brilliant bits of sunshine and brightness, that occasionally diversify the early weeks of our Northern spring. I had been down in the woods piling up the logs I had cut the day before, and on returning up the narrow path, I saw the light flutter of a scarlet shawl cross the window of my little dwelling from the inside.

"More company," I thought, with a quick, electric bound at my heart; for I knew there was but one woman for miles around who would be likely to visit me, and then, besides, Barbara Wycliffe's sweet eyes were like lodestars to me, and I felt it must be her. I sprang up the slope with a movement as light as my heart, and entered at the wide-open door.

"Barbara," said I, holding out both my hands, "this is an unexpected pleasure."

She had been crimson when my footstep first sounded on the threshold; now she turned deadly pale, with a whiteness that startled me.

"Oh, is it you, Reuben—Mr. Eyre? I'm so glad you have come. I—I—" She stammered and stuttered painfully, and was much confused. "I—I was looking for our stray guinea-fowls in the woods above, and I went farther than I had any idea of. I was very tired, and I thought I would stop in a minute and rest."

"And you are as welcome as flowers in May, Barbara; but you *know* you are."

For she had smiled up in my face with an arch, half-doubtful look. There was no question of absent color now; her cheeks glowed like—like—like the velvet petals of a "Giant of Battles" rose, I suppose the poets would say; but I thought of the red glare of the locomotive's head-light, which was always beautiful to me.

"And did you find the runaways?"

"No. I think they must be down in the maple swamp. I shall look for them there to-morrow. But, Mr. Eyre, I wanted to say, besides—" She hesitated and hung down her head.

"Well, Barbara, what?" I asked.

"I don't know," she said, convulsively. "I don't know what. But I came to—to warn you—"

Again the deathly pallor came over her face. There was a strange, startled look in her brown eyes.

"Warn me, Barbara! Of what?"

"Of him—of that man—John Walker."

I had felt, when she said she came to warn me, that it was of that man. She was surprised that I was not startled, and asked me, hurriedly:

"What was he doing here, to-day, Reuben?"

I did look at her in astonishment this time.

"Has he been here to-day, Barbara? You are think-ing of yesterday evening?" I suggested.

"No, I am not," she answered, impetuously. "I am *not* thinking of yesterday evening. I mean to-day; not an hour ago."

"What makes you think he was here, Barbara?"

"Because I saw him; because I—I *followed* him. I know he was bent on mischief, and mischief against you."

I shook my head doubtfully.

"Are you quite sure you are not mistaken? For if he had been here, would he not have stayed to see me? When did you see him here, and where?"

"I tell you it was but a little while ago. He means you mischief, Reuben; be sure of that. I *saw* him put a large knife in his breast, as he left the house, and I fol-lowed him—followed him until I saw him reach the door. He stopped by the door, and stood still a minute or two, as if he were listening."

"Perhaps he was listening to hear if I were at home."

"I was sure of it, and started on a run to the house to warn you; but I was so agitated I could not move fast. I saw him enter, and I tried to scream, but could not. I felt he would do you an injury with that knife."

"Well?"

"Well, he went in and closed the door behind him; but he did not remain there more than two minutes; for as I ran I saw him come out again, and strike right into the woods to the left."

"That is the short cut to the railroad switch. Perhaps he expected to find me there."

"Perhaps he did," said Barbara.

"Or possibly"—the "green-eyed monster" was reasserting its presence once more, and trying to smile, I said—"possibly he knew you were out, and hoped to meet *you* somewhere in the vicinity."

Barbara's long lashes drooped for a moment; then there was a flash in her eyes; and then she answered, carelessly, with just a perceptible sneer:

"It is just possible that he did, though why he should arm himself to meet me, is beyond my comprehension. At all events, he went the wrong way.   Good-evening."

"Surely you are not going yet?"

"I must, thank you.   Father will certainly think I am lost if I don't hurry home."

I saw by the clock that it was only half-past five. "You will let me walk with you as far as the bridge, Barbara?"

She would have hesitated awhile on any occasion, and have refused my escort.   This little rustic maiden of the wilderness possessed all the impulses and wiles of a drawing-room coquette, and seldom missed an opportunity of tormenting me.   My allusion to Walker had offended her, and she grew serious.   Had I deemed it possible that she could experience personal fear, I should have fancied that she was afraid of something or somebody, for her hand trembled, as she laid it on my arm. Then I thought something in the melting darkness of her eye appealed to me with a voiceless cry for help!

"What is it, Barbara?" I questioned, instinctively.

She looked wonderingly at me—the look had all gone out of her eyes now.

"Nothing.   I did not speak."

"But what ails you?   Why are you so depressed in spirits?"

"I feel there is something wrong—that man—you have escaped him this time, but I want you to be wary of him."

"For your sake?" I ventured, stutteringly and hesitatingly.

"For your own sake," she answered; and then both of us were silent for some time.

What a delightful, dreamy walk that was, down to the bridge, whose rude planks spanned the shallow, brawling stream, with the low sun hanging like a ball of gold above the purpled woods, and the air full of fragrant breathings of the spring-tide, whose coming footsteps were already sweet upon the hills! Pleasant in spite of warning and Walker. Barbara's softly-spoken "Good-by!" sounded like saddest music as I turned away from the bridge, regretting that I could not prolong the rambling *tête-à-tête* to an indefinite length.

A few paces higher up I turned once more to watch the scarlet gleam of Barbara's wrappings through the column-like trunks of the leafless trees ; and as my eye rested on this one bright glimpse of color, a tall figure emerged with a stealthy air from the thickets beyond, and joined her.

It was Walker! How the sharp pang of jealousy shot through my heart as I saw him bend over her little hand, and still hold it in his own, as he walked by her side. Was it a preconcerted interview ? Had she told him to meet her, as soon as I, the deluded dupe, was well out of the way ? Did they make my home a rendezvous to escape the eyes of her father ? Did they—

Hark ! Surely that was a cry, wild and startling— a cry from Barbara Wycliffe's lips ! From my post on the higher ground, I could see that she had started back from him, and drawn her hand away. My first thought, was to spring down into the ravine, but desisted when I saw him take the hand once again. I could see tnat he was speaking in an eager manner, pointing in my direction, with frequent and impulsive gestures, and then I saw him grasp her hand again. I saw his arm around her waist—her head upon his shoulder, and worst of all —she did not repulse him !

"Glad I did not make a fool of myself," I muttered bitterly, turning away with long irregular strides up the hill. "Let them go on their way. It is the last time I shall be duped by the bright eyes of a heartless coquette. I am glad I have discovered her in her true light at last."

But I was not glad. There was a pang gnawing at my heart as I slowly returned to the cabin ; and as I entered the room, I looked up involuntarily, with the instinct that grows from constant habit, at the clock. The hands indicated the hour of six. Somehow I fancied it was later than that. The sun had dipped down behind the purple line of woods ; the long shadows of the tree-trunks stretching out across the brown turf in front of my door-step had vanished, and just in the warm orange glow of the west a great golden star flamed and quivered like a solitary eye of fire.

"It can't be that the sun sets earlier than usual," I said to myself, half doubtfully, and yet—

Standing there hesitating—I knew not why—I heard the bell of St. Mark's at Branhill—the church-bell of the far-off village. It could be heard only on the stillest days, when the wind set in a peculiar direction ; but now the strokes rang out with marvellous distinctness :

One—two—three—four—five—six—seven !

Like invisible writing suddenly flashing into view at the

magic action of fire, the whole chain of circumstances became frightfully, diabolically clear.   John Walker's mysterious presence in my cabin but two hours since was sufficiently explained now.   He had writhed in, deadly and noiseless, like a serpent, to work my ruin, and elevate himself upon the wreck of my good name and trust. His hand had moved backward the indices of my timepiece upon the dial with a motive too horrible for me to contemplate without a shudder.   He knew (for had I not myself told him?) that the Lightning Express, going North, met the Branch-road train at seven o'clock, and that it rushed wildly forward without stopping, with only a whistle of warning.   The switch was set to the Branch road; it must be changed at a quarter to seven, or the Lightning Express would leave the track and collide with the " Accommodation," calmly waiting it in fancied security. Yes ; John Walker had deliberately laid his plans to ruin me ; and Barbara—could it be possible that Barbara's sweet frankness, her unwonted presence, her warning, were part of his fiendish conspiracy to divert my attention, and wile me away from the post of duty?   Was Barbara in his interest ? and had I been doubly deceived ?   As I stood there perfectly motionless, with cold drops oozing out upon my brow, and a frozen sort of rigidity at my heart, I could almost see the shattered cars, the shapeless, splintered ruin, the crushed machinery, the ghastly faces upturned to the glowing purple of the fair twilight sky ; I could hear the shrieks and groans and dying gasps through the dull, continuous roar that seemed to surge across my brain !   And *I—I* should have been the unconscious murderer, the guiltless criminal !   O God of all mercies ! Was there no way of averting the impending shadow of this awful catastrophe ?

FIVE MINUTES BEHIND
PAGE 263.

All this was thought in a second; and before the chimes had ceased ringing the final stroke of seven, I bounded from the room. My usual route down to the switch was a foot-path, steep and narrow, that skirted the edges of the precipitous hills; but there was a nearer and much more direct way, through dense undergrowth and matted briars and bushes, through which I plunged, heedless of tearing thorns and tangled branches, which seemed to impede my progress with almost human malice. As I ran my speed was accelerated by the shrill whistle of the approaching Accommodation train. I did not mind that —the Accommodation would stop on its track and wait for the Lightning Express to pass; but I had not a second to spare, for usually the whistle of the Lightning was heard as if it were the echo of the other, so nearly simultaneously were they due at Branhill Junction. As I neared the track with breath that came in short, panting sobs and laboring pulses, I saw, as it were, through a scarlet mist of blood, the white, starry gleam of the signal lamp in its accustomed place—the " all right" token to the engineer of the Lightning train !

Whose hand had so foully lighted that treacherous star of doom ?

As I ran I had searched for the key of the switch-lock. It was safe. I sprang to the track, hurling down the signal with a vehemence that shivered the strong glass to a thousand atoms. I thrust the key into the lock and unlocked the switch. Great Heavens ! the lever was immovable ! The villain had done his work completely, and with a small wooden wedge driven firmly between the lever and the iron framework of the switch, had made the movement of the former impossible. The loud shriek of the now approaching train gave me additional strength in vain, for I could not move the rails. Walker and Barbara Wycliffe had neglected no one link in the chain of their detestable plot. One instant I stood, in the utter abandonment of despair. In the same terrible instant the glare of the thundering train flashed on the track and lighted it up with painful brilliancy, and I saw, as I knew, that the rails were wrong. While my mind seemed to give way before the terrible doom which I had no power to avert, a breathless, gasping voice sounded close in my ear, and a heavy iron implement was thrust into my hands. I did not see her, but I knew who it was. I did not see the implement which I grasped, but I knew there was strength in it.

"Reuben! Reuben! Quick! it is the crowbar!"

Before the words were finished I had formed my plan of action. With a powerful blow I struck the iron rod of the switch—the stem which connected the lever and the rails, but which now prevented them from moving. A single blow was enough. I heard the sharp twang of the iron rod as it snapped. I leaped to the side of the track. I placed the crow-bar as a lever under the rail, and was about to move the switch with a laugh of relief, when I felt both my arms grappled from behind, with a hold as firm as steel, and I was thrown violently back, dropping the crow-bar as I fell.

"Not so fast, Reuben Eyre," hissed the hated voice of John Walker close to my ear. "I will be revenged yet, though pretty Barbara has played me false."

I struggled to free myself from his clinging grasp, with a strength that afterward seemed supernatural, but in vain. He had drawn me, I suppose, unconsciously on to the track, and I could already feel the thrill and tremble of the earth beneath my feet—a sure sign that the approaching train was nearing us. I thought of the unsuspecting passengers whose fate hung in the balance. Were they to perish when help and rescue lay almost within a hand's-breadth of me? They talk of the bitterness of death—this was the bitterness of life ; and in that moment of horrible suspense I drank the loathed cup to the very dregs.

But, thanks to God's providence, help was nearer at hand than I had dared to hope. With surprising courage and presence of mind, Barbara Wycliffe had seized the crow-bar, and forced the rails into position. Brave girl! It did not require more than a woman's strength, but at that moment she needed more than a man's courage. It wasn't nerve and sinew she needed, but the heart to do it. The train did not slacken its speed. The engineer had failed to notice the absence of the signal, and dashed wildly on! It did not matter now; the switch was all right and the danger past.

No, not past! You forget that while I saw all this; saw Barbara's act ; saw the rails move ; saw them rightly adjusted; saw the engineer's mistake—actually reflected that it was the result of his firm confidence in me—I had never failed him before—can you believe that all this time —this crowded instant—I was engaged in a struggle for life with John Walker? Mind and matter were totally distinct. Mentally I was absorbed in Barbara's work; physically, I grappled with John Walker! The train and its precious freight safe, mind returned to matter, and Walker soon found I was more than a match for him. My first reflection was to drag him and myself from the track, across which we were struggling. It was the work of an instant. Then with a superhuman effort I endeavored to free myself from his grasp, and I threw him violently from me.　He staggered back a pace or two, vainly endeavoring to recover his equilibrium, and then fell.

Fell, great Heaven! directly across the iron track!

I made an instinctive step forward to save him, but Barbara Wycliffe's arms were clasped tightly around me, Barbara's voice was crying out wildly,

"Reuben! Reuben! for *my* sake!"

And in the same breath the Lightning Express rushed over the track like a fiery serpent, and I knew that John Walker's accounts with Time were closed forever.

The engineer and fireman of the Accommodation train, which was standing on the Branch road, had, in the glare of the locomotive, witnessed the struggle, and heard Barbara's screams, and now came rushing forward.　In awed silence they removed the body from the track where it lay, fearfully crushed and mangled, with glazed eyes upturned, and brow still contracted with the scowl of mortal rage.

So the man died, and there was no living soul to mourn his death.

As the engineer of the Accommodation comprehended the situation, and explained it to the wondering passengers, he turned to me as I mechanically readjusted the switch to allow the Accommodation to pass, and said :

"Lucky for you, old fellow, that the Lightning was five minutes behind time."

Five minutes behind time—and those five minutes had held the destiny of life and death within their pulsing seconds!

As the last crash and rattle of the vanishing train, which now sped on its way, smote upon my ear, my duty for the night wholly done, all the fictitious strength that had lent vigor to my arm, and nerve to my limbs, seemed taken from me. My friendly crow-bar dropped with a dull sound from my hands, the far-off crests of the purple hills seemed to reel and tremble, and I fell like a log to the ground, weak and fainting, with Barbara Wycliffe's sweet face bending over me, like the face of an angel.

When thought and sense returned to me once more, days after, I was in my little cabin, and the Wycliffes, father and daughter, were ministering to me. And the farmer told me how the people from all about the country had come to look at the dead man, and hear the verdict of the coroner's jury, and to see how narrowly the passengers of the two trains had escaped the doom that had come down upon *him* like an avenging spirit.

"And I tell ye, it made their blood run cold," said the farmer. "They called my little girl a heroine, and I ain't sure but that they're right!"

"Barbara," said I, when the old man had gone to the spring for water, and we were left alone together, "how did it happen? How did you know that *he*—"

"He told me himself," said Barbara, in a low, troubled voice.

"When?"

"That evening, after I had left you at the bridge."

"And you, Barbara, what did you say?"

"At first I screamed with terror. Then he told me he had done it for love of me; that when he got your place he would marry me. What could I do? I dared not turn back to you, for there was murder in his eyes, and he would have stabbed you—perhaps me, too, long before I could have reached you; so I let him fancy— God forgive me—that I would be his accomplice in his wicked schemes and his wife afterward. He told me all he had done. So when he left me I went straight to where I had seen my father's crow-bar lying by the track ; and oh, Reuben ! it seemed as if I never should be able to drag its weary weight through the woods to your post. Every rush of the wind in the tree-tops seemed like the train coming, and every rustling leaf was John Walker's step ! "

She bowed her head in her hands with a shudder. But Farmer Wycliffe's footfall was on the frozen earth outside, and I had not yet learned quite all I wanted to know.

" Then, Barbara, I was wrong when I thought you loved John Walker."

" Wrong—altogether wrong ! "

" And it was not he—but—but *me* you loved all the time ? "

The roses came to her cheek, and the small head was royally poised.

" Because, darling I have loved you these many months. Tell me my fate quickly—your father is close at hand. · Is it yes or no ? "

And Barbara whispered—" Yes."

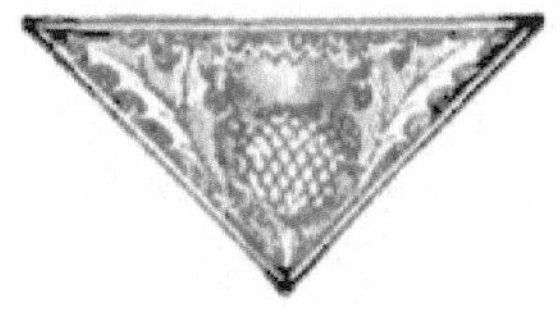

XXV.

UP AND DOWN THE RAIL.

BY AN OFFICE-MAN.

 AM in the employ of the what-d'ye-call-'em Central Railway; but it does not concern you whether I am a director, superintendent, conductor, or brakeman. My purpose is simply to put down a few remarks concerning the machinery by which this great line is worked, and thereby ease my mind of a nightmare which has weighed upon it for some time.

The august and all-powerful body of directors, as a matter of course, come first; but of them we can say little. They are of the gods, and sit above the thunder, and it is with mortals that we have now to deal. To the vast body of officials and employés on this our railway, the board of directors is a sort of mythical assembly, which they hear frequently mentioned, but which they seldom or never see. They hear of them in the reports —those puzzling compilations of facts and figures which not one person in a thousand can make head or tail of, or they see "By order of the Board of Directors," printed at the foot of something or other; but further than this, the acquaintance does not extend. Sometimes, indeed, as Mr. Brown happens to be traversing the platform, a friend will take him by the button for a moment, and with a mysterious nod will whisper, "Do you see that stout gentleman with the thick walking-stick? Well, that is Mr. Pompous, our chairman." Or, "Do you see that thin person walking with his hands behind him? That is Mr. Crœsus. He is one of our directors, and said to be worth half a million of money." Mr. Brown, who is one of us, you know, will gaze for a moment with hushed reverence, and then, hurrying to the office, tell his fellow-clerks what he has seen, adding that he should like to have told old Pompous a bit of his mind about the horrid low salaries and overwork in our department.

The heads of departments are, with rare exceptions, the only portion of the executive with whom the board comes in contact. They are not without their cares, these directors, their lofty position notwithstanding; especially if the traffic for a given time does not show well, or any of their transactions on behalf of the Company prove unfortunate; for in such cases stockholders are liable to turn rusty and put awkward questions at the next general meeting, which must be answered in a more or less straightforward manner.

Next to the directors in point of precedence comes the president or general superintendent. Most managers of large railways have some special point about them for which they are noted more than another. Some are known as skilful diplomatists; dexterous in drawing up agreements; far-seeing in their plans for the future; not to be outwitted by the stratagem of hostile lines. Others have a talent for developing the home traffic of their lines by creating a trade where none existed before ; for swelling the returns and realizing a thumping dividend at the close of the fiscal year. These are the men whom the shareholders delight to honor. Other managers there are, in secondary positions, who are known as close shavers and economists; who cut down the expenses to the lowest figure ; who are continually finding out some morsel of cheese that needs paring ; payers of starvation salaries ; detested in secret by all whom they employ ; who think by such penny wisdom to make up for their pound foolishness in other things. Here and there we have still an ornamental sub-manager, a mechanical figure with clock-work brains, placed on its pedestal by patronage or accident ; not destined to remain there for any length of time, but soon to run down and be displaced by something more practical. The origin of our big railroad men is as various as their talents. Some have risen to the elevation they occupy from the humblest positions on the Road, by aptitude, force of will, or good fortune. These are generally your best men. As a rule superintendents are well paid.

We may compare the general superintendent in his cabinet to a spider seated at the nucleus of his web, controlling from that point a hundred diverging threads, and itself scarcely seen, keeping ceaseless watch over the whole. But, unlike the spider, who does all its business by itself, our superintendent is obliged to employ sundry subordinates, division or assistant superintendents, master mechanics, road masters—to keep his web in working order. Each takes one or more threads, and being responsible to the spider-in-chief for their management.

To the road-master belongs the maintenance and renewal of the permanent way; the formation and alteration of branch lines, sidings, tunnels, bridges, viaducts, etc. He must see, indeed, that the line is kept in thorough repair from one end to the other. He has assistants, of course, stationed up and down the line.

The secretary is, on most roads, the official representative of the Company. He keeps the stock and share accounts, issues all dividend and interest warrants, acts as treasurer, and receives all moneys. The auditor has the management of the accounts of the line. The general freight agent has charge of the traffic of the line, and the general ticket or passenger agent, the management of the passenger traffic. There is no class of men connected with railways on whom greater responsibility rests than on station agents. There are numerous small stations on every road, where one man performs the whole of the duties—freight agent, ticket agent, express agent, telegraph operator, and switchman, all for a mere pittance per month, and a small house. The agents of the larger stations are generally recruited from among the more intelligent clerks, or the agents of smaller stations whose business talents have attracted attention at headquarters.

From wiper to fireman, and from fireman to engineer, is the scale which must be ascended by those who aspire to the dignity of running a locomotive. A practical acquaintance with their duties is thus insured in those to whose care and vigilance thousands of lives are hourly intrusted. There are no dirtier stations than those of wiper and fireman. They have to clean out the engines, light the fires, keep the brasses clean, and get everything ready for the engineer. What with the steam, the oil, and the dampness of the atmosphere, it is a difficult matter to keep a locomotive thoroughly bright and clean.

Engineers and firemen, when on the road, may often be seen to take advantage of a spare moment to give the brass a rub, or to bring out an oil can with a long nib, and lubricate the interior of the iron monster under their command. The engineer becomes much attached to his locomotive, and frequently gives it the endearing name of " wife " or " sweetheart."

It is a pleasant change when our fireman is made engineer. For some time at first he is set to drive a yard or construction engine, and is not intrusted with the lives of men until his experience has been thoroughly tested. The engineer is generally a sociable, easy-going fellow. He earns his money readily, and spends it freely. The healthy out-of-doors life he is forced to lead influences his tastes in several ways. He is fond of company, fond of his pipe, sometimes of his glass. He is a good husband and father, and whatever his wife may be at home, he likes to see her in fashionable attire on gala occasions. He himself, when he is spruced up of an evening, is a very different individual from the black, greasy-looking person in overalls, who brought you in by the four o'clock train this afternoon. Long habit has made night and day alike to him, and he will get up at midnight as readily as at noon. He gets a good meal at home before he sets off ; for the rest he takes some coffee in a can and warms it over the boiler, as an accompaniment to a few sandwiches or some bread and butter ; though he is not above a steak grilled over the glowing embers as he rides along.

Brakemen and conductors occupy the same position relatively as firemen and engineers, though not one brakeman in twenty ever becomes a conductor ; still each of them may hope to be one of the fortunate. There are two classes of brakemen and conductors—passenger and

12*

freight. A combination of vigilance, honesty, firmness, courage, and courtesy, is required to form a good railway conductor or brakeman. Happily for the public, the combination is by no means rare. He must wink at an occasional cigar or pipe, if not too openly displayed, especially if there be no lady in the offending car. In case of any break-down or accident, he must have his wits thoroughly about him, and see at a glance how the disaster may be soonest remedied.

As to consolidations, let us run over the great Central route, from the depot at Philadelphia to Pittsburg : from Pittsburg, on the Steubenville, Columbus, and Pan-Handle road, to Columbus ; from Columbus to Union City, and branching to the left, to Indianapolis ; from Union City to Logansport ; from Logansport to the Illinois State line, and the latter point, by the Toledo, Peoria, and Warsaw Railway, complete to the Mississippi river, and thence onward, maintaining a midland course to the Pacific ocean. This great central combination, having its base on the Atlantic, and its principal depots at New York, Philadelphia, Washington, and Baltimore, which are easily accessible—New Jersey by the Lebanon Valley and the Baltimore Central, and the latter by the Baltimore and Ohio—open a continuous avenue on a single longitudinous line everywhere from the Atlantic ocean to the western terminus of the Pacific Railway. Wonderful progress indeed is all this, and it may well lead government makers of New York to reflect a little upon the point, whether it is either wise or possible to interdict consolidations. It occurs to me, that such interdiction is of near kin to that which would forbid the inventor to put together the parts of his machine to answer the ends of his discovery. For illustration, the greater number of roads on a given line, the greater must be the expense, delays, and the higher the rates. Consolidation is but an expression of practical energy and economy. Twenty roads here referred to are thrown into two or three, practically into one. For instance, from the Illinois State line eastward—the Toledo, Logansport, and Burlington; the Union and Logansport; the Columbus and Indianapolis; the Indiana Central; the Piqua—making 362 miles —are made into the Indiana Central Company; and so of the entire line. Consolidations have taken the whole route from Pittsburg to the Mississippi river at Keokuk or Warsaw, **under a single name, covering a distance of 680 miles.**

XXVI.

 RAILWAY detective got on Hod. Hale's train, on the Erie Road, at Batavia, having bought a ticket for Avon. He kept the ticket and paid his fare. When they reached Avon, the end of Hale's run, he produced the ticket with the remark, "Here's a ticket I found on the platform," expecting Hale to put it in his pocket. "Here's what we do with those fellows," replied Hale, taking the ticket, punching it and putting it in his pocket, "and now I'll show you what we do with *you* fellows."

Hale then invited him to join him at his residence, where he exacted from him the following confession :

"Up to the commencement of the present year I have been employed as a railroad detective. Having found a more honorable employment, and by way of penance for the past, I feel desirous of making some amends to that class of men that I have heretofore aided, unjustly in many cases, in vilifying, by giving a few facts of the workings of that unscrupulous gang known as railway detectives, so as to open the eyes of our railroad officials to the injustice of condemning innocent men upon the word of such as now belong to that gang.

" Any railroad company can ascertain that nine-tenths of the conductors accused of dishonesty are accused unjustly. The plan is, when a contract to work on a road is taken, to first select a victim, to suppose at once that he is guilty, and, reversing the maxim of the common law, to either find or manufacture material to establish the premises. A miracle alone can save him. The reputation of the men set to watch him is at stake, and they feel that it is incumbent upon them to bring him in guilty of fraudulent practices.

" One dodge is to get one to ask a conductor to change a bill for accommodation, while another witnesses the operation and swears—and swears technically true—that he saw the conductor receive money, and neither return nor punch a ticket. Another plan is to buy two tickets at the office in one day, present one to the conductor and retain the other, reporting that the conductor took it but did not punch it. In the meanwhile, the unsold ticket is given to the confederate, who will start the next day on the same train for the same place, and presents the ticket sold the day before to the conductor, who, if he did not notice the date, is trapped. It is a very successful plan, as it hangs both the conductor and the agent.

" Another dodge is this : several 'spotters' crowd around the conductor, calling for tickets, and offering money for different points on the road. The one who pays for the point farthest off will manage to get the ticket from the conductor that belongs to the one paying for the nearest point. Some of the gang then get off at the nearest station, leaving the tickets in the hands of one or two who go the whole distance, giving up the long tickets

and holding the short ones as evidence against the conductor.   Here a case is made, and the conductor cannot
make a satisfactory explanation.

"These are a few of the nefarious and rascally schemes
used by detectives.   I do not say that conductors, as a
class, are any more honest than any other class ; but the
really dishonest ones are often in the 'ring,' and are seldom reported.   These are facts, and I could, were it expedient, give you the names of parties whom I know have
been unjustly dealt with.   I have done all in my power
for them, have been to the executive, and in one case
have succeeded in having reinstated a man whom I believed to be strictly honest.   And I now take another
step in the vindication of those wronged in the public
prints.   Let the managers of railroads see and think, that
an evil may be remedied.   Let them first select honorable men for this responsible position, and then treat
them as men."

XXVII.

THE FOUNDER OF THE RAILWAY SYSTEM.

A BIOGRAPHICAL SKETCH.

AMONG the ashes and slag of a poor colliery village, near Newcastle-on-Tyne, in the unplastered room, with a clay floor and garret roof, that was the entire home of the family to which he was born, there came into the world, on a June day, ninety years ago, one of its best benefactors. The village is named Wylam. In the year 1781, the family occupying one of the four laborers' apartments contained in the cottage known as High Street House, was that of Robert Stephenson and his wife Mabel, their only child being a two-year-old boy named James. On the ninth of June, year just named, a second son was born to them, whom they called George. That was George Stephenson, the founder of the Railway System.

His father, known as "old Bob" by the neighbors, was a fireman to the pumping engine at the Wylam colliery, earning not more than twelve shillings a week. Little George carried his father's dinner to the engine, helped to tug about and nurse the children younger than himself, and to keep them out of the way of the chaldron wagons on the wooden tram-road that ran close before the threshold of the cottage door. If Mabel had been a Pythoness, she might have discovered, as she stood in the door, lines of fate in the two wooden couplets on the road. But they only warned her of danger threatening her children while at play.

The coal at Wylam was worked out, and old Bob's engine, which had "stood till she grew fearsome to look at," was pulled down. The poor family then followed the work to Dewley Burn, where Robert Stephenson waited as fireman on a newer engine. Little George—Geordie Steevie, as he was called—was then eight years old. Of course he had not been to school, but he was strong, nimble of body and of wit, and eager to begin the business of bread-winning with the least possible delay. In a neighboring farm-house lived Grace Ainslie, a widow, whose cows had the right to graze along the wagon road. The post of keeping them out of the way of the wagons, and preventing them from trespassing on other persons' liberties, was given to George. He was to have a shilling a week, and his duty was to include barring the gates at night after the wagons had all passed.

That was the beginning of George Stephenson's career, and from it he pushed forward inch by inch upward. Of course he had certain peculiar abilities, but many may have them, yet few do good with them. George Stephenson made his own fortune, and also added largely to the wealth and general well-being of society. In climbing the hill Difficulty, he was content to mount by short, firm steps, keeping his eyes well upon the ground that happens to lie next before his feet. It is not our purpose to follow the details of his career, though no gossip would be more interesting and instructive. At the age of fourteen he was promoted from the position of driver of the gin-horse, to the post of assistant fireman to his father at the Dewley engine. He was then so young that he used to hide when the owner of the colliery came round, lest he should think him too small for the place. At fifteen he was promoted to the full office of fireman at a new working. At the age of eighteen he could not read or write his name. He was then getting his friend Coe to teach him the mystery of braking, that he might, when opportunity occurred, advance to the post of brakeman, next above that which he held. He became curious also to know, definitely, something about the famous engines that were in those days planned by Watt and Bolton. The desire for knowledge taught him the necessity of learning to read books. He was promoted to the position of brakeman, and subsequently became engine-wright to the colliery at Killingworth, at a salary of one hundred pounds a year. He had now opportunities of carrying still further his study of the engine, as well as turning to account the knowledge he already possessed. The locomotive was then known to the world as a new toy, curious and costly. Stephenson had a perception of what might be done with it, and was beginning to make it the subject of his thoughts. The father entered him as a member of the Newcastle Literary and Philosophical Institution, and toiled with him over books of science borrowed from its library. Various experiments had been made with the new locomotive engines. One had been tried on the Wylam tram-road, which went by the cottage in which Stephenson was born. He was now thirty-two years old, still brooding on the subject ; watched their failures, worked at the theory of their construction, and made it his business to see one. He felt his way to the manufacture of a better engine, and proceeded to bring the subject under the notice of the lessees of the colliery. He had acquired reputation not only as an ingenious but as a safe and prudent man. Lord Ravenswood, the principal partner, therefore authorized him to fulfil his wish ; and with the greatest difficulty, making workmen of some of the colliery hands, with the colliery blacksmith as his head assistant, he built his first locomotive in the workshops at Westmoor, and called it "My Lord." It was the first engine constructed with smooth wheels, for Stephenson never admitted the prevailing notion, that contrivances were necessary to secure adhesion. "My Lord" was called "Blucher" by the people round about. It was first placed on the Killingworth Railway on the twenty-fifth of July, eighteen hundred and fourteen, and though a cumbrous machine, was the most successful that had been constructed up to that date.

At the end of a year it was found that the work done by Blucher cost about as much as the same work would have cost if done by horses. Then it occurred to Stephenson to turn the steam-pipe into the chimney, and carry the smoke up with the draught of a steam-blast. That would add to the intensity of the fire, and to the rapidity with which steam could be generated. The power of the engine was by this expedient doubled.

He had already made up his mind that the perfection of a travelling engine would be half lost if it did not run on a perfected rail. Engine and rail he spoke of, even then, as "man and wife," and his contrivances for the improvement of the locomotive always went hand in hand with his contrivances for the improvement of the road upon which it ran. We need not follow the mechanical details. In his work at the rail and engine, he made progress in his own way, inch by inch. Every new locomotive built by him contained improvements on its predecessor; every time he laid down a new rail he added some new element of strength and firmness to it. The Killingworth Colliery Railway was the seed from which sprang the whole system of railway intercourse.

One of Stephenson's chief pleasures, in his latter days, was to hold out a helping hand to poor inventors who deserved assistance. Inch by inch he made his ground good in the world, and for the world. A year before his death, in 1848, somebody about to dedicate a book to him, asked him what were his "ornamental initials." His reply was, "I have to state that I have no flourishes to my name, either before or after ; and I think it will be as well if you merely say, George Stephenson."

XXVIII.

ANECDOTES AND INCIDENTS OF THE RAIL.

"Fifteen Years for Refreshments"—"Gum Drops"—A Mistake
—An Accident—"Is this Seat occupied?"—"I'm going to
get out!"—An Intrusive Stranger—"Golly, Boss!"—How the
Clergyman put it—A Spread—"Give us a Chaw!"—A Victim
—The Lady and the Boy—Twenty Minutes for Dinner—The
Lady Smoker—A Touching Scene—Suspected Larceny—Three-
Card Monte—"Your Fare, if you please"—"It is a Male!"—
A more Successful Attempt—The Naturalist and the Deacon—
"Not Good on this Line"—A Special Train—A Little Sermon
—A Pleasant Travelling Companion—Swindlers Outwitted—A
Thrilling Scene—Married on the Platform—A Ventriloquist
Aboard—The Metamorphosis—Sunshine and Storm—The Back
Seat.

 RETURNED traveller empties his portman-
teau, and enters upon his Diary the anecdotes
and incidents he has gathered by the way:

We had on our train a keeper who was taking two convicts to the State Prison. When the train
stopped at Sing Sing, he called out: "Step out, gentlemen, fifteen years for refreshments!"

The train-boy came along with his basket of candy and corn, and approaching an old gentleman near me, said: "Pop corn! Pop corn!" "Haven't got any teeth," angrily replied the old man. "Gum drops! gum drops," called the smart boy.

I rode a short distance with the governor of one of the Western States, a gallant and jocose man. He sat in the same seat with a friend, when two young men came in, escorting two young ladies. There were no vacant seats, and the governor and his friend surrendered their own. What was their astonishment to see the young men occupy the seats and take the young ladies on their laps! "What a mistake," exclaimed the governor; "we might have done that!"

I rode from Hartford with a friend of the late Mr. Heaton, who repeated the remark made by that gentleman in 1839: "I have been watching the stages. I find that the average number of passengers in Hartford and New Haven stages is twenty-seven. If anybody wants to invest $3,000,000 in a railroad between these two cities, I am willing they should go ahead. I won't invest!"

We were coming into Charleston, South Carolina, when the locomotive ran into a mule team. We were thrown from the track, and getting out, found the cart destroyed and the driver fatally injured. The mule calmly stood by and watched the proceedings with a pleasant smile.

"Is this seat occupied?" asked an exquisite of an elderly lady of rustic design in the cars at Norwalk on one occasion.

"I don't know," said she, hastily running her hands, with a great deal of solicitude, over the surface. "It feels mostly like plush, but you can't most always tell!"

A young lady entered our crowded car at a certain station. An old gentleman arose at the opposite end as she approached. "Oh, don't rise," said the lovely girl, "I can just as well stand."

"I don't care whether you sit or stand," he replied, "I'm going to get out!"

Every time a train approaches a station called ——, on a Connecticut road, a man sits on a fence near the depot. He had done so daily for fifteen years. He had an old mare so frightened by the pesky "kears" once, that she died of convulsions. He is now daring those "kears" to try their darned noise on him. If they serve him as they did the mare, he is just going to have the whole infernal thing stopped!

There is always an intrusive stranger aboard. He asked a little girl sitting by her mother as to her name, destination, etc. After learning that she was going to Philadelphia, he asked: "What motive is taking you thither?" "I believe they call it the locomotive, sir," was the innocent reply. The intrusive stranger got another seat.

A smart young commercial tourist, who rides on the rail a good deal in Wisconsin, has a habit of jumping off the cars at stations where opportunities offer, and "kissing his sister." He apologizes when he discovers his mistake. I was on the train when he made his last venture. The damsel raised her veil and exclaimed: "Golly, boss, what you 'bout dar?"

Detained over the Sabbath in a railroad centre, I attended divine service. I wrote down the following metaphor from the clergyman's sermon:

"At the death of the just, the locomotive of his soul, driven by the coal of faith and the steam of hope, dashes along the rails of charity toward that immovable depot where is found the eternal symbol which is God."

A woman in Boston is trying to recover five thousand dollars from a horse-railroad company, in part payment for sundry breaks, jars, and fractures received on account of having a lot of passengers fall upon her. The rails sprung, and the car sprung from the track. The Company acknowledge the "spread" so far as the track is concerned, but why they should be held responsible for the passengers "spreading" themselves over the plaintiff, they are at a loss to know. She says if they don't pay she will never ride in one of their cars again. So, now!

I had just bought a morning paper, when a large and powerfully-built passenger exclaimed:

"Who dare spit tobacco juice on the floor of this car?" at the same time stalking down the aisle, frowning upon the passengers.

"I dare," said a burly-looking fellow, as he deliberately ejected a quantity of the noxious saliva upon the floor of the aisle.

"All right, my friend," said the first speaker, slapping the other in a friendly manner upon the shoulder, "give us a chaw!"

There was a horrible catastrophe on the Dijon Railroad, over in France. We came along the next day, and stopped to view the wreck. An old man presented himself at the place of disaster. A workman, who was collecting the *débris* and clearing the track, inquired what he wanted:

"Monsieur, I am one of the victims."

The workman looked up, and seeing a man without injury, inquired, "Whom have you lost, then—your wife, your child, and friend?"

" No, monsieur, I have lost my umbrella."

The workman searched among the broken cars, and by a singular chance found the umbrella.

"There," said he, giving it to the peasant, "you are lucky to get out of the scrape that way."

"You call that lucky," returned the man ; "look here, they have broken two whalebones !"

We were on the 4.30 train from New York, and as we reached Stamford, an antique-looking dame thrust her head out of the window opposite the door of the refreshment room, and briefly shouted, "*Sonny !*"

A bright-looking boy came up to the window.

"Little boy," said she, "have you a mother?"

"Yes, ma'am."

"Do you love her?"

"Yes, ma'am."

"Do you go to school, dear?"

"Yes, ma'am."

"And are you faithful to your studies?"

"Yes, ma'am."

"Do you say your prayers every night?"

"Yes, ma'am."

"Can I trust you to do an errand for me?"

"Yes, ma'am."

"I think I can too," said the kind lady, looking steadily down on the manly face.

"Here is five cents, get me an apple. Remember God sees you!"

"Twenty minutes for dinner!" shouted the brakeman as we approached Xenia.

Arrived there, I entered the dining-room and inquired of a waiter:

"What do you have for dinner?"

"Twenty minutes," was the hurried reply.

I told him I would try half a dozen minutes, raw, on the half-shell, just to see how they went. Told him to make a minute of it on his books. He scratched his head trying to comprehend the order, but finally gave it up and waited upon some one else.

I approached a man who stood near the door with a roll of money in his hand.

"What do you have for dinner?"

"Half a dollar," says he.

I told him that I would take half a dollar well done. I asked him if he could send me, in addition, a boiled pocket-book stuffed with greenbacks, and some seven-thirties garnished with postage-stamps and ten-cent scrip. Also a Confederate bond, done brown, with lettuce alone (let us alone). I would like to wash my dinner down with National Bank Notes on "draft."

He said they were out of everything but the bank-notes, and he then ordered a waiter to go to the bank and "draw" some.

One night, passing from Wilmington to Florence, Alabama, our car was filled with gentlemen, only one lady being present. After we had proceeded some way, it was proposed to have a smoke. So when the conductor came through, he was asked if he would allow us to smoke. He pointed to the lady and replied, "If she has no objections, smoke away." I went to the lady, and bowing, asked if it would be offensive to her. "Not at all, my dear sir," she answered, politely. "I am so lonesome, if I had a cigar I would smoke myself." She was supplied with one, and we were a set of happy fellows.

We were on the night train of the Atlantic and Great Western Railroad, when a touching scene occurred. An old lady, an invalid, was in the cars, and watched over with tender care by her daughter and son-in-law, to whose city home she was going for the benefit of her health. One of the sections was comfortably arranged, so that the old lady said she should rest as well as if at home. Before retiring the young people sang a hymn in an under-tone, the mother seeming to enjoy it thoroughly, while she gazed out into the dim twilight. Several times during the night the daughter went to her mother's side to see that she was resting well; but about four o'clock she spoke to her mother, and no answer was returned. A wild cry was heard: "Mother's dead!" and the startled passengers became aware that the aged invalid had passed to the spirit land without a struggle. When the old lady left her own village home she had said: "Tell my friends, if I slip away on this journey, that I was ready and willing to go."

I was called upon to interfere in behalf of a Sacramento lady on one occasion, who had been arraigned for larceny under suspicious circumstances. She was riding in a crowded railway car, and occupied a seat with another lady passenger. Like a great many other women of the present day, she wore curls—her own hair, of course, but it wasn't fastened on strictly according to Nature's programme. By and by, as the train jolted along, she felt something falling about her face and neck, and in a second it flashed across her brain that her curls had become detached. The predicament was a shocking one, but she endeavored to save herself as much as possible by quietly passing the capillary ornament into her pocket, thanking her stars that she was almost at her destination. At the station she hastened to the dressing-room to repair damages to her toilet, when, behold! the mirror reflected back the fact that her curls were in their proper position, and an examination of those in her pocket showed that they were not hers, but of a different color, and belonging to the lady who sat by her side in the car.

I was on the Kansas City, St. Joe, and Council Bluffs train, and when between Leavenworth and Kansas City, saw a party of three-card monte men fleece a New York drummer out of $1,300. The victim was a German, and fell in with one of the "cappers," who was likewise a German. The German confederate represented the Texas cattle-drover to perfection, and managed, by his frank and unsophisticated demeanor, to enlist the confidence and co-operation of the New York commercial representative in a venture to capture the funds of the monte men. The "commercial man" won several times, and always received his winnings in counterfeit bills. At length he lost all his greenbacks, and put up a draft for $1,000, which he had just received at Kansas City, and the draft followed the cash into the pockets of the monte rascals. The victimized "drummer" retired from the game quite overwhelmed with despair. The draft belonged to the firm which the commercial man represented; and when the victim found that he had not guessed the winning card, he walked at once to the rear car of the train, took a seat, and gazed out of the window for a moment, and then went out upon the platform.

I heard that he was picked up next day, with his throat cut from ear to ear.

"Your fare, if you please, madam," said the conductor to an elderly lady who had got aboard at a way station. The elderly lady looked up, and, drawing forth a letter, spoke with a voice that was shrill: "Two of Mr. ——'s children is dead, and they've writ me to come to the buryin to-day. Isn't it terrible!" The conductor looked as shocked as possible, and expressed sympathy. "And," continued the old lady, "I want you to let me ride free." "I can't let you ride free unless you have a pass," returned the conductor, mildly. "*Not to go to a funeral?*" said the old lady. "No, madam," replied the conductor. "I'm sorry to say that the rules of the road are very strict, and I am not allowed to discriminate." "Well, I think you oughtn't to charge toll for going to a funeral," persisted the old lady. "If we let everybody going to funerals ride free," again spoke the conductor, "it wouldn't pay. Besides, it would be encouraging the funeral business in a way that would cast a gloom over the entire country. Your fare is a dollar and a half, madam." "Well," retorted the old lady, drawing out a well-filled purse, "I think you might let me go free, 'specially as I'm going to a *double* funeral. Mr. ——'s children is both dead, and they'll be buried in the same grave, I reckon. Oh! it's a *turrible* blow!" And the old lady, wiping her eyes, paid her fare. As the conductor moved on, she turned to a passenger and remarked, with some indignation, "These railroaders is the most *unfeelin'* folks I ever seed."

An elegant lady entered the car, addressing the conductor who followed.

"I won't go except in a ladies' car; the regulations oblige you to have one, and you *shall*."

"Certainly, ma'am, certainly. I'll order one immediately; but that baby can't go in it, ma'am. It must stay in the gentlemen's car; it is a *male!*"

I made a note of a more successful attempt that came

under my observation at a busy junction on a Wisconsin road. A clean, well-dressed man attempted to enter the rear car of the train, but was stopped by the brakeman, and told to go to the next car forward, as the rear one was reserved for ladies and gentlemen accompanied by ladies. A merry twinkle was in the young man's eye, as he stepped from the car to the platform. He walked straight to a robust and somewhat remarkable female representative from the land of shamrock, and very courteously offered to assist her in transporting her bundles, which were neither few nor slight, to the train. The words "May the good Lord bless your honor," were the only ones that reached me ; but it was evident that his offices were accepted. Then, after some conversation in an under-tone, the pair who had so recently, and in plain view of Mr. Brakeman, become travelling companions, approached the forbidden car. When about to enter, the brakeman interposed his person, and directed him to go to the next car. The man insisted that *his lady* and himself had, under the rules laid down, a right to enter. The brakeman replied,

"It is *not* your lady."

The traveller, turning confidentially to his new-found appendage, asked, in the most winning way:

"Arn't you, my dear?"

(The woman had cheeks like a cheese-rind and a nose like a piece of decayed beefsteak.) Clearly, and to the point, came the answer:

"Shure I am, darlint."

There was no resisting such proofs, and the pair marched in triumph to a seat, amid roars of laughter from the passengers, who had been attentive spectators of the scene.

I fell in with a naturalist and a Baptist deacon on the Union Pacific Road, only last autumn. They made a deal of sport, but one incident will perhaps suffice.

"Do you see that pretty woman in there?" asked the naturalist of the deacon. The speaker pointed to a neatly-dressed, modest-appearing lady, who was eating with the other passengers at one of the feeding stations.

"Yes, what of her?"

"Oh, nothing, only I'll bet you a new hat that I'll go in and kiss her."

"That's nothing; anybody can kiss a woman."

"But I never saw her before. I'll agree if she makes any fuss about it, to pay for the hat."

"Don't you know her, honest?"

"Upon my word."

"Never saw her before?"

"Never, so help me."

"It's a bet."

The naturalist walked up to the lady, put his face down to hers, and then kissed her squarely on the cheek. To the infinite surprise of the Baptist deacon, she did not hit him with a water pitcher, or scream "murder." She simply glanced up at him, blushed a little, and then called for another bit of the sliced ham.

"Is the naturalist among women what Rarey is among horses?" was the mental inquiry of the Baptist deacon, in connection with the probable price, in coin, of a $7\frac{1}{2}$ hat in San Francisco.

I took the New York and Harlem Road at Fourth avenue and Twenty-sixth street one day, and shared a seat with a well-known Doctor of Divinity. He is a positive man, and resents an insult as vehemently as a man of the world. Engaged earnestly in conversation, he handed the conductor a ticket, as he came to collect the fare. The conductor did not move on. As he remained studying the ticket, the doctor's attention was attracted toward the official, who appeared to be highly interested in the piece of pasteboard. He read it, smiled, shook his head, and finally said to the doctor:

"This may all be very well, but the ticket is not good on this line."

"What's the reason it's not good, I should like to know?" said the testy doctor; "I bought it not half an hour ago!"

"I guess not," said the conductor. The altercation drew the attention of all the passengers. "This is very good advice, but it will not pass you over this line," and the conductor read: "Thou shalt not take the name of the Lord thy God in vain."

An explosion followed, amid which the doctor paid his fare. He has concluded to keep his religious tickets in a separate packet.

I give the next incident a prominent place in my Diary, because I was a party in the adventure.

A Portsmouth, New Hampshire, man hired a special train in Boston for $75.00, and upon reaching Newburyport, was joined by a clergyman and several ladies, who entered the car without invitation, apparently thinking it a regular train. The rightful tenant of the train said nothing, except to ask the ladies' permission to continue smoking. The minister was highly incensed at this, and after reading a long homily on the evil effects of tobacco, branched off on the impoliteness to his "fellow-men and wimmin," in thus smoking in a public conveyance. The smoker making no reply, the minister became enraged, and started for the depot-master. This official entered the car and told its occupants that it had been hired by the gentleman who was using the weed, who could smoke, drink, chew, or stand on his head the whole journey, if he pleased, and if the people in the car didn't like it, they could wait for the regular train, which was coming on behind. The dominie apologized, amid the titter of the ladies.

At a certain railroad station on our route, one of those beautiful lessons which all should learn, was taught in such a natural, simple way, that I shall never forget it. It was a bleak, snowy day ; the train was late, the ladies' waiting-room dark and smoky, and the dozen women, old and young, who sat impatiently waiting, all looked cross, stupid, or low-spirited. Just then a forlorn old woman, shaking with the palsy, came in with a basket of little wares for sale, and went about mutely offering them to the sitters. Nobody purchased, and the poor old soul stood blinking at the door a moment, as if reluctant to go out again into the bitter storm. Presently she turned and poked about the room, as if in search for something, and then a pale lady in black, who lay as if asleep on a sofa, opened her eyes, saw the old woman, and instantly asked in a kind voice—

" Have you lost anything, ma'am ? "

" No, dear. I'm looking for the heating place to have a warm 'fore I go out agin. My eyes are poor, and I don't seem to find the furnace anywhere."

" Here it is ; " and the lady led her to the steam radiator, placed a chair, and showed her how to warm her feet.

" Well, now, ain't that nice ? " said the old woman, spreading her ragged mittens to dry. " Thankee, dear ; this is proper comfortable, ain't it ? I'm most froze to-day, bein' lame and aching; and not selling much made me sort of down-hearted."

The lady smiled, went to the counter, bought a cup of tea and some sort of food, carried it herself to the old woman, and said, as respectfully and kindly as if the poor old soul had been dressed in silk and fur, "Won't you have a cup of hot tea? It's very comforting such a day as this."

"Sakes alive! Do they give tea at this depot?" cried the old lady in a tone of innocent surprise, that made a smile go round the room, touching the glummest face like a streak of sunshine. "Well, now, this is just lovely," added the old lady, sipping away with a relish. "That does warm my heart."

While she refreshed herself, telling her story meanwhile, the lady looked over the poor little wares in the basket, bought soap, pins, and shoe-strings, and cheered the old soul by paying well for them.

As my companion and myself watched her doing this, we thought what a sweet face she had, though it seemed very plain before. We felt much ashamed of ourselves, that we had grimly shaken our heads when the basket had been offered us, only a moment before. As I saw a look of interest, sympathy, and kindness come into the faces around me, I wished that I had been the magician to call it out. It was only a kind word and a friendly act, but somehow it brightened that dingy room. It changed the faces of a dozen women, and I think it touched a dozen hearts, for I saw many eyes follow the pale, plain lady with sudden respect. When the old woman with many thanks got up to go, several persons beckoned to her and bought something, as if they wanted to repair their negligence.

I was the only gentleman present to be impressed by

13*

the lady's kind act ; so it was not done for effect. No possible reward could be received for it, save the thanks of a poor old woman. But that simple little charity was as good as a sermon, and I think each traveller resumed the journey better for that half-hour in the dreary station.

The 10.40 morning train on the New York Central is the express, and on this occasion it was in charge of Mr. Frank Klock. Two men got on board at Canastota, and one of them had his face so muffled up, that it was impossible to catch a glimpse of any portion of his visage, save his eyes. He took his seat, and after awhile, paid his fare to Utica. Just in the rear of the muffled individual, sat a gentleman occupied with his newspaper. As Klock took the fare the reader looked up and asked :

"Conductor, what is it that smells so ? "

" I don't smell anything yet, sir," was the reply.

"But I do. Perhaps it is this paper just bought of the newsboy." (And he smells the paper.) "It smells as if —if some one were sick !"

The conductor left the car, and thought little more of the matter, but the passengers took the suggestion, and commenced snuff, snuff, snuff, and the most uneasy one of all was the inquiring gentleman who sat in the rear of the muffled passenger. The conductor returned, and as he opened the door, he too was struck with the singular odor that now pervaded the car. The small-pox was then raging in some of the Eastern cities, and the unpleasant suggestion at once flashed upon him : " Possibly that muffled man has the disease." The car was very warm, yet the fellow never disturbed his wrappings. The train was just leaving Oneida, and the odor grew stronger. Klock approached the man and inquired :

"What ails you, sir?"

"Nothing, sir."

"Are you not sick?"

"No, sir!"

"But your face is broken out," continued Klock, "and I believe you have the small-pox, and that you are the cause of this sickening smell in the car. It is my duty to inform the passengers that I think you have the small-pox, that they may protect themselves." And he sang out—

"I think this passenger has the small-pox, and gentlemen had better obtain seats in the other cars."

This was enough. The inquiring man who had "snuffed" the most cleared the back of his seat at a single bound. In his haste and terror he attempted to take a bee-line for the door through a very fat old lady who was aiming in the same direction. The remainder of the passengers also hurried to the doors, and some thirty seconds elapsed before Klock and his patient were left alone. At Rome Mr. Klock telegraphed to Utica that the city authorities might arrange to receive their distinguished visitor with proper attention. But none of the authorities appeared, and the Central cut the Gordian knot by switching the car from the train on a side-track, where Mr. Small-pox was left alone. The Board of Health finally took him in charge.

At a point about 280 miles east of Kansas City, an elderly and clerical-looking individual engaged a sleeping berth on our train for that city. He selected the lower berth of a section, the upper half of which had been engaged by two dapper-looking individuals, who, shortly after the train started, came back from the smoking-car and took seats in their section. The trio soon struck up a travelling acquaintance, and judging from the pleasant expression of the three countenances, this acquaintance was mutually agreeable and profitable, as will presently be seen.

The elderly gentleman, who may be known here as Mr. Greene, was a retired merchant from Central New York, on his way West to invest in corner-lots and Kansas lands. He was one of those benignant old sun-flowers whose smiles beam alike upon the just and the unjust; whose well-filled pocket-book is always forthcoming to change a ten or a twenty for some casual companion who doesn't happen to have any small bills about him; and whose worldly goods are but as legitimate spoils for the confidence gentry—that is to say, judging from the way he appeared to me. His companions, whom I will call Sharpe and Ketchum, were of that class to be met with all over the railroad world, fashionable vagrants, who travel on their shape.

By and by the conductor of the Pullman Palace Car came around to collect his fare for berths.

The elderly gentleman, being first in order, produced a pocket-book, at once well-worn and well-filled, and paid his little fare, and then came the turn of the other two. Now, Sharpe had plenty of money, while Ketchum, though laden with exchange on New York and Buffalo, had run out of currency. Sharpe paid his small bill, but Ketchum ransacked his pocket-book and vest pockets in vain. Sharpe very generously offered to pay his companion's bill, but the latter wouldn't hear of any such sacrifices on the part of his friend. He would, however, gladly accept cash for one of his drafts, if Sharpe would be so kind, but under no circumstances would he accept any other favor. It transpired that Sharpe would be so kind. So Ketchum produced a draft purporting to be drawn to his order on the "Commercial National Bank" of Buffalo, amounting to $157.40. But Sharpe could not make the change. Would the elderly gentleman be so unutterably gracious as to break a fifty for him. Of course he would—but he couldn't. But a happy thought struck Sharpe. If his companion had such delicate scruples about permitting him to pay his bill, perhaps the elderly gentleman would purchase the draft. Certainly he would do that, but investigation revealed that he had nothing smaller than a one-hundred-dollar bill, except some desultory change the conductor had given him for a five when he paid his bill. Finally Sharpe and Ketchum laid their heads and their finances together, and succeeded in making up a purse of $203.40, including the draft for $157.40, and $40 currency, whereat the elderly gentleman gave them two $100 notes and his $3 in change—they generously "throwing in" the 40 cents—wherewith Ketchum paid his bill, and the conductor went on his way rejoicing, while the financiers prepared to retire by having their bunks "made up."

Morning revealed the fact that Sharpe and Ketchum had found it convenient to step off at some casual station during the night, though the elderly gentleman quietly enjoyed his regular rest. The conductor, fearing from indications that his passenger had been swindled, approached him and said :

"I am afraid that draft you got last night was a fraud."

"Well," was the bland response of the imperturbable Greene, "I presume it is, but if it's any bigger fraud than the two $100 notes were, why then I ain't $53 in good money ahead, which I think I am."

He added that he was not in the habit of passing counterfeit money, but he happened to have them with him, and having measured the two chaps who had attempted to swindle him, he had quietly determined to beat them at their own game.

"If you want anything more," said he, "to make this affair satisfactory, I can give you good references, either in Kansas City or New York, where I reside."

We didn't demand the references.

This was on the Omaha express, east, on the Chicago and Northwestern Railway. As the train stopped at Round Grove, a small station about ten miles west of Sterling, Illinois, two ladies, one of them carrying a baby about eight months old, got aboard the train, and took seats in the ladies' car. As the train was about starting again, a German, whom we subsequently learned was named Henry Bohlman, the husband of the woman with the child, stepped aboard, and entered the ladies' car. Passing along the aisle, until opposite the two ladies, he suddenly drew a revolver, and fired at his wife, who still held the child in her arms. Fearing he had not succeeded in his hellish work, he attempted to fire the second time, but was seized by one of the passengers and a brakeman, and the revolver taken from him. He was secured and taken into the baggage-car, where he was carefully guarded until the train reached Sterling, when he was handed over to the proper authorities. On examination it was found that the lady was uninjured, but the murderous ball had pierced and gone entirely through both thighs of the unfortunate child, causing a very serious, though not fatal wound. The man expressed himself as very sorry that he had missed his wife and hit the child. Conductor Wilcox afterwards informed us that

Bohlman was actuated by jealousy and the usual sus-picion.

A young friend in Paris was telling me how he came by his German wife. While travelling in that country, he took the road from Strasbourg to Berlin. In the car-riage he selected were four other persons, two mammas and two daughters. The two mothers were face to face in one corner; the young man took the opposite, and found himself face to face with the young ladies. He put on a careless and absent air. The collector came to demand the tickets. The young man paid no attention at all, when the request was many times repeated. Roused at last from his reverie in presence of the ladies, he had recourse to a *ruse*, to avoid exciting ridicule.

"What are you saying," said he. "Why do you not speak French?"

The collector then explained by signs, the ticket was examined, and the young man returned to his reverie; but not to enjoy it long, for this time the young ladies roused him. They began in full voice:

"This young man is a very handsome one," said one.

"Hist, Bertha!" said the other, in a sort of affright.

"Why, he doesn't know a word of German," said Ber-tha. "We can talk freely. What do you think of him?"

"Only ordinary," was the reply.

"You are difficult to please. He has a charming figure and genteel air."

"He is too pale, and besides, you know I do not like dark men."

"And you know I prefer dark to fair. We have noth-ing but fair faces in Germany. It is monotonous and commonplace."

"You forget that you are a blonde."

"Oh, for woman it is different. He has nice mustaches."

"Bertha, if your mother should hear you!"

"She is busy with her talk to your mother; besides, it is no harm to speak of mustaches."

"I prefer the light mustaches of Albert."

"I understand you and Albert are engaged; but I, who am without a lover, am free to exercise my opinions, and as free to say that this young man has beautiful eyes."

"They have no expression," returned the other.

"You do not know. I am sure he has much spirit; and it is a pity he does not speak German; he would chat with us."

"Would you marry a Frenchman?"

"Why not, if he looks like this one, and was spirited, well-born, and amiable? But I can hardly keep from laughing. See, he doesn't dream what we are saying."

The young traveller was endowed with a great power of self-control, and he had preserved his absent and inattentive air all the time; and while the dialogue continued he thought what curious results his attempts to avert a laugh, by pretending not to know German, had brought about. He looked carefully at Bertha, and his resolution was taken. At the next station the collector came again for the tickets, when the young man, with extra elaboration, and in excellent German, said:

"Ah! you want my ticket. Very well—let me see: I believe it is in my *portemonnaie*. Oh, yes; here it is!"

The effect was startling. Bertha became nearly senseless, but soon recovered under the polite apologies of the young Frenchman. They were pleased with each other; and in a few weeks Bertha ratified her good opinion of

the young man, and gave a practical proof of her willing-
ness to wed a Frenchman.

I found that they have a queer way of doing things
matrimonial, down in Cave City, where, just before our
arrival, the Grand Duke had taken his Kentucky hash.
David Brown is a rollicking son of Kentucky, a true type
of the independent village or country youth, who is just
entering upon his maturity. Maria Martin is, or was, a
village maiden of some charms, and a good deal of spirit
and Kentucky grit. David and Maria courted and loved
and agreed to marry ; for the fair lady told us all about
it herself. For some reason, David put off the sol-
emnization of the nuptials from time to time, until Maria's
patience became exhausted. Meeting her lover one day,
she said to him, with more emphasis than elegance :

"I tell you what it is, Dave ; you've got to dry up this
nonsense, and quit this foolin.' It's about time we was
married ; and I want you to come to time."

"Dave" thought he would come to time ; but as the
parties had met on the platform of the depot at Cave
City, David was at a loss to know where he and Maria
would have the ceremony performed. Maria's wits were
sharp enough for the emergency, and so she told David
she would provide a place, and started him off to the
county clerk for the necessary license.

During his absence, Maria entered the depot, and
asked the station-agent for the privilege of being married
on the platform in front of the depot.

"Certainly," replied the polite agent ; "or right here
in the depot, if you prefer. But here comes the passenger ; hadn't you better wait till it goes by?"

"No, not if ' Dave ' hurries up ; can't wait for nothing.
We'll take the platform here."

David soon returned with the license, accompanied by his brother, who swore the wedding should not take place. We arrived and were informed of what was going on, just as the brother was using cuss words, and drew a pistol, which fairly riled David, who also flirted out a revolver. He would have demolished the interfering brother but for the interposition of the passengers, who hustled the offender into the baggage-room, away from the scene.

The marriage then took place, the parties standing out in the cold upon the platform, while the ceremony was being performed. David rather enjoyed the novelty of the affair. "By gosh, this is bully, ain't it, Mariar?" he exclaimed. "You bet, Dave," responded Maria, and then the happy pair went on their way rejoicing. Long life to them, and may their tribe increase.

On the cars going from Providence to Boston, we found a well-known magician and ventriloquist, whom I will name Fritz. The conductor came around to collect the fare. The magician, who was busily engaged reading a newspaper at the time, did not notice what was going on, until he heard the words, "Your fare, sir." He quietly put his hand in his pocket, and drew forth a silver dollar, of a peculiar denomination, and quickly handed it to the conductor, that being the amount of the fare. The conductor, pleased at coming in possession of so acceptable a pocket piece, placed it hurriedly in his pocket and moved on. On his return, Fritz stopped him and said:

"In passing you my fare, sir, I made a great mistake. I was busy reading, and did not notice that I gave you a silver coin, which was given me as a keepsake, by an intimate friend. Please redeem it, and I will pay my fare in currency."

"Certainly, sir, with the greatest of pleasure," at the same time reaching in his pocket. After fumbling around there for some time, and not finding it, he changed color and was much embarrassed, lest the passenger might think he was deceiving him. The other passengers, seeing the conductor looking so confused, began to gather around to see what the excitement was about. After the magician had puzzled him for some time, he placed his hand in his own vest pocket, and brought forth the same silver dollar. The conductor was thunderstruck.

"I would like to know, sir, how you got that piece out of my pocket, without my knowledge?"

"You did not put it in your pocket," was the reply; "I took it from your hand before it reached your pocket."

The conductor was puzzled, and warned the passengers to avoid the man. At this juncture, one old man cried out—"Gentlemen, I am robbed of every dollar!" "Begorra," yelled an Irishman, "sthop the train; Biddy's money is gone!"

A green-looking Yankee, on his way from Chicago to Vermont, sings out on looking at his pocket-book: "Well, I'll be gol darned, what became of my two dollars and sixteen cents, I had when I left Chicago? I thought I left all thieves there, but there's some of 'em on this train."

An old woman sitting in the rear of Fritz, on discovering the loss of her money, cried out: "My God, what shall I do? I am a ruined woman." Then the children set up one of the most unearthly yells that I ever heard. Taking all together, there never was such a scene on a train of cars before. After the cunning showman had advertised himself sufficiently, he turned to the conductor with the remark:

"I guess there has been no passengers sacked; I

was merely testing my ventriloquial powers;" at the same time pulling out his pocket-book to pay his fare and redeem his silver dollar.

A young English lady who was in our party on the Continent, being called upon for a concluding tale of the train, communicated the following adventure :

"Although," she commenced, " I am often compelled to travel without a companion, yet have I such a dislike for sick folk and babies, that I never made a journey in a ladies' carriage. Only once, however, have I suffered any inconvenience through my unprotected condition, and that exception occurred on this very line. After I had taken my seat one morning at Paddington, in an empty carriage, I was joined just as the train was moving off, by a strange-looking young man, with remarkably long hair. He was of course a little hurried, but he seemed besides to be so disturbed and wild, that I was quite alarmed for fear of his not being in his right mind, nor did his subsequent conduct quite reassure me. Our train was an express, and he inquired eagerly, at once, which was the first station whereat we were advertised to stop. I consulted my Bradshaw, and furnished him with the required information. It was Reading. The young man looked at his watch.

" ' Madam,' said he, ' there is but half an hour between me, and, it may be, ruin. Excuse me, therefore, for my abruptness. You have, I perceive, a pair of scissors in your work-bag. Oblige me, if you please, by cutting off all my hair.'

" ' Sir,' said I, ' it is impossible.'

" ' Madame,' he urged, and a look of severe determination crossed his features, ' I am a desperate man. Beware how you refuse me what I ask. Cut my hair off close to the roots—immediately, and here is a newspaper to hold the ambrosial curls.'

" I thought he was mad, of course, and believing that it would be dangerous to thwart him, I cut off all his hair to the last lock.

" 'Now, madam,' said he, unlocking a small portmanteau, 'you will further oblige me by looking out of the window, as I am about to change my clothes.'

" Of course I looked out of the window for a very considerable time, and when he observed, 'Madam, I need no longer put you to any inconvenience,' I did not recognize the young man in the least.

" Instead of his former rather gay costume, he was attired in black, and wore a gray wig and silver spectacles. He looked like a respectable divine of the Church of England, of about sixty-four years of age.   To complete that character, he held a volume of sermons in his hand, which might have been his own.

" 'I do not wish to threaten you, young lady,' he resumed, 'and I think besides, that I can trust your kind face.   Will you promise me not to reveal this metamorphosis until your journey's end?'

" 'I will,' said I, 'most certainly.'

" At Reading, the guard and a person in plain clothes looked into our carriage.

" 'You have the ticket, my love,' said the young man blandly, and looking at me as though he were my father.

" 'Never mind, sir; we don't want them,' said the official, and he withdrew with his companion.

" 'I shall now leave you, madam,' observed my fellow-traveller, as soon as the coast was clear.   'By your kind and courageous conduct, you have saved my life, and perhaps even your own.'

"In another minute he was gone, and the train was in motion. Not till the next morning did I learn from the papers, that the gentleman on whom I had operated as hair-cutter, had committed forgery to an enormous amount, in London, a few hours before I met him, and that he had been tracked into the express car at Paddington. Also, that, although the telegraph had been put in motion and described him accurately—at Reading, when the train was searched, he was nowhere to be found."

As the Sabbath is a living subject of speculation and thought among us, it should be recorded here, that Sabbath-keeping pays. All honor to the Pennsylvania Central Railway Company, in the attempt of its directors to give its employés the blessings of the Sabbath.

We left Cincinnati on Saturday morning for a rapid journey to New York, and return. Before midnight on Saturday, Altoona was reached, and there we were to rest on the Sabbath-day, according to the commandment. This is the city where locomotives keep Sabbath —where freight trains rest on the Lord's day, and, as a consequence, where engineers, and brakemen, and railroad hands of all grades, are both permitted and encouraged to enjoy Sabbath repose and its needful relaxation.

It is as grateful a feeling as it is strange, to awake on a Sunday morning in quietness—scarcely a sound stirring —amid a population of twelve thousand, who all the week are driving the immense work of the Pennsylvania Central, or hurrying in attendance on trains which pass every few minutes, both day and night. On Sunday the laboring air is still ; those terrible shrieks and whistles of locomotives, which tear the atmosphere to pieces all the week, are hushed. There is no roar of trains, no roll of engines, no groaning of escaped steam. The Sabbath stillness is scarcely broken, except by Sabbath bells. One passenger train passes, I believe, each way in the early morning and in the evening ; but we saw no freight trains moving. We counted thirteen freight trains standing on the tracks in front of the Logan House.

The result of this policy is according to God's law and promise, but, of course, equally according to a natural law. Workmen of a higher moral calibre are secured. The men are faithful, have more physical endurance, and more spirit than when their powers are overtaxed by seven days' labor in every week. An accident on this road is very rare ; and the profits are rolling up by millions. It is not my purpose to encourage people to keep the Lord's day *because* of the profit it brings, although there is no question about it. God's word never has failed, and never will. His sanction of Sabbath observance is merely an interpretation of an invariable natural law. But all that I desire is to put the facts side by side. Railroad men can decide for themselves how nearly they are related as cause and effect.

My Diary would be incomplete without a brief sketch of the Railway Hog; the small-souled, selfish brute, who pays grudgingly for one seat, and strains his wits to hold two. "This seat is taken, sir," tells his story. My particular hog wore a plug hat with a genuine Boston gloss, and enamelled shirt, with closely cropped, iron-gray beard. I know his kind. He is an eminently respectable beast, who always pays his debts promptly, takes an interest in Sunday-schools, administrates his dead brother's children out of their patrimony, is the president of joint-stock companies, and has biographical eulogies published in the papers when he finally kicks the bucket. I knew the hog lied when he said, "This seat is taken, sir," and watched him to see how many times he would reproduce the falsehood. The coach was rather full, and, would you believe it, that miserable hog told sixteen separate and distinct lies in order to gratify his mean selfishness. Enough to sink a healthier soul to perdition. He varied the formula; one time it was a wave of the hand and look to the rear of the car, to indicate that the holder of the seat had gone for a drink of water and would be back soon.

When questioned another time, by a timid, mild-mannered passenger, he replied by a stolid stare, and then spreading himself a little wider, he resumed the perusal of his newspaper. I was tempted to crawl behind him, and say in his ear, "You're an awful liar;" but my revenge came by and by.

A big, red-faced two-hundred-pounder, in a dirty linen coat, came in at a way-station. He was sweaty to a fearful degree. His feet smelt like a valerianate of ammonia and rotten fish, and his breath was a hot, stinking sirocco, based on bad whiskey and onions. This fiery and fragrant behemoth preferred to settle himself in the seat that was taken. "This seat is—" began the hog. "Well, I guess I'll take it till the other fellow comes," returned the sweet-stinking heavy-weight, and down he plumped, partially crushing the hog in his descent. The latter frowned and began to bluster, but the red-faced ruffian soon took that out of him with a threat to swallow him whole—to chaw him up and spit him out—to pitch him out of the window—to go through him like a dose of salts, and to make various dispositions of him in case he didn't simmer down. Our porcine friend simmered, and then the barbarian grew good-humored. He told funny anecdotes and poked the hog in the ribs. He wanted to know where he came from and where he was going. He spat quarts of tobacco juice across him out of the window, spattering his shirt-front, between his boots and all around. He offered him a "chaw," every time he took out his plug of navy. The hog perspired freely, and shivered with disgust. Finally he crawled out and stood up for forty miles, until another seat was vacant.

We were on the Overland train, bound for San Francisco, with Littlejohn as conductor. Among the passengers was a young man, possessed of a judicious spirit of economy and a pardonable share of vanity. The judicious economy was made manifest to the other occupants of the car, by the fact that the young man wore plain clothing and a single Cheviot shirt, all the way from Chicago. How the pardonable vanity became apparent, is where the joke comes in. He had been to the East on a visit, and the girl he left behind had been notified in advance of his approach, and in company with a few other friends, was to meet him at Niles station.

Visions of rapture floated through his brain, and seating himself in a secluded corner of the car, he poured forth his spirit's gladness in a rush of melody, somewhat as thus :

> " Home again, home again,
>   From a foh-hoh-reign shore :
>   And oh ! it fills my so-o-ul with joy,
>   To me-he-eat my friends once more."

Suddenly he hushed his notes of joy, and reached forward for his carpet-bag.

The appalling idea flashed across his mind that the shirt which had done him so much good service—which had clung to him during the toilsome journey across two thousand miles of mountain, plain, and desert—was not exactly the thing to appear in when one wished to intensify an already good impression. It certainly wouldn't be the clean thing, he said to himself—it wouldn't be justice to the shirt. So he resolved to change. But how? The car contained several lady passengers, and they watched everything that was going on around them, with an assiduity that did honor to the sex. "Ah! ha! str-rr-rategy, my boy!" said this resolute young man unto himself. "The tunnel—we are approaching the tunnel. With good management I can do the deed in the long tunnel just beyond Sunol;" and with a heavenly smile upon his manly features he gracefully lifted his carpet-bag from the floor, unlocked it, and drew forth a snowy shirt, with nice frilled bosom. Then from another recess he drew a little packet containing a pair of handsome sleeve-buttons and a set of studs, which were quickly adjusted in their proper places. Casting a careful glance from the window, he saw that the train was not far from the tunnel where the metamorphosis was to take place, and so he turned his back upon the other passengers, and began to loosen sundry buttons—in short, prepared to shuck himself. Presently the eventful moment came. The iron horse plunged into the dark recesses of the tunnel, and the car was shrouded in impenetrable darkness. Presently a ray of light gleamed in fantastic shapes along the rugged wall of the tunnel, and by its faint glimmer a struggling figure was discernible in the direction of the young man's seat. As the light became stronger, its gyrations grew more frantic. Its great long arms, incased in white, thrashed wildly about as though in the agony of despair; and finally when, with a shriek of joy, the engine dashed out into the dazzling sunlight, it sank down into its seat, apparently crushed with mortification and cha-grin.

The ladies screamed with terror, and hid their blushes at the unusual apparition. Strong men crushed their handkerchiefs into their mouths, and nearly choked with emotion. The figure reclined motionless upon the soft cushion, until some one with more courage than the rest advanced to ascertain who and what it was. Finally the terrible truth was revealed. The white covering was lifted, and from beneath appeared the features of our young friend, clothed with carnation's richest hue. The mystery was soon explained. He had gotten the Cheviot off, but alas ! in his hurry and excitement he had forgot-ten to undo the collar fastening of the elegant white-frilled front. Horror ! it would not go over his head !

On my way from Providence to Boston I came across what struck me as a very singular genius. This was a stout, black-whiskered man who sat immediately in front of me, and who indulged from time to time in the most singular manœuvres. Every now and then, he would get up and hurry away to the narrow passage which leads to the door in these drawing-room cars, and when he thought himself secure from observation, would fall to laughing in the most violent manner, and continue the healthful exercise until his face was as red as a lobster. As we neared Boston, these demonstrations increased in violence, save that the stranger no longer ran away to laugh, but kept his seat, and chuckled away to himself, with his chin down deep in his shirt collar.

But the changes those portmanteaus underwent ! He moved them there, here, everywhere ; he put them beside him, in front of him, and beneath. He was evidently getting ready to leave, but as we were yet 25 miles from Boston, the idea of such early preparations was ridiculous. If we had entered the city then, the mystery would have remained unsolved, but the stranger at last became so excited, that he could keep his seat no longer. Some one must help him, and as I was the nearest, he selected me. Suddenly turning, as if I had asked a question, he said, rocking himself to and fro in his chair, and slapping his legs—

"Been gone three years! Yes, been in Europe. Folks don't expect me for six months yet, but I got through and started! I telegraphed them at the last station; they've got it by this time."

As he said this, he changed the portmanteau on his left to the right, and the one on the right to the left again.

"Got a wife?" said I.

"Yes, and three children." Then he got up and folded his overcoat anew, and hung it over the back of the seat.

"You are pretty nervous over the matter, ain't you?" I said, watching his fidgety movements.

"Well, I should think so," he replied; "I hain't slept soundly for a week. And do you know," he went on, glancing around at the passengers and speaking in a low tone, "I'm almost certain the train will run off the track and break my neck, before I get to Boston. Well, the fact is, I've had too much good luck for one man lately. The thing can't last; 'taint natural that it should, you know. I've watched it. First it rains, then it shines, then it rains again. It rains as hard, you think it's never going to stop; then it shines so bright, you think it's always going to shine; and just as you're settled to either belief, you are knocked over by a change, to show you that you know nothing about it at all."

" Well, according to this philosophy," said I, " you will continue to have sunshine, because you are expecting a storm ! "

" It's curious," he replied, " but the only thing that makes me think I'll get through safe is, because I think I won't."

" Well, that is curious," I rejoined.

" Yes," he replied, " I'm a machinist—made a discovery—nobody believed in it—spent all my money trying to bring it out—mortgaged my home—all went. Everybody laughed at me—everybody but my wife—spunky little woman—said she would work her fingers off before I should give it up. Went to England—no better there—came within an ace of jumping off London Bridge. Went into a shop to earn money enough to come home with ; there I met the man I wanted. To make a long story short, I've brought £30,000 with me, and the best of it is, she don't know anything about it. I've fooled her so often, and disappointed her so much, that I just concluded I would say nothing about this. When I got my money, though, you better believe I struck a bee-line for home."

" And now you will make her happy ? " said I.

" Happy ! " he replied ; " why, you don't know anything about it. She worked like a dog while I have been gone, trying to support herself and the children decently. They paid her thirteen cents apiece for making coarse shirts, and that's the way she'd live half the time. She'll come down there to meet me in a gingham dress and a shawl a hundred years old, and she'll think she's dressed up. Oh she won't have no clothes after this ; oh no, I guess not." And with these words, which implied that his wife's wardrobe would soon rival Queen Victoria's, the stranger tore down the passage-way again, and getting in his old corner, where he thought himself out of sight, went through the strangest pantomime ; laughing, putting his mouth into the drollest shapes, and then swinging himself back and forth in the limited space, as if he were walking down Broadway, a full-rigged metropolitan belle.

And so on, until we rolled into the depot, and I placed myself on the other car, opposite the stranger, who, with a portmanteau in each hand, had descended on the lower step, ready to jump to the platform. I looked from his face to the faces of the people below us, but saw no sign of recognition. Suddenly he cried, " There they are !" and laughed outright, but in an hysterical sort of a way, as he looked over the crowd. I followed his eye, and saw some distance back a little woman in a faded dress and well-worn hat. She was crowded out, as it were, shouldered away, by the well-dressed and elbowing throng. As she glanced rapidly from window to window, as the coaches glided in, the face was almost painful in its intense, but hopeless expression.

She had not yet seen the stranger, but in a moment after she caught his eye, and in another instant he had jumped to the platform, with his two portmanteaus, and making a hole in the crowd, pushing one here and there, and running one of his bundles plump into the perspective of a very fat old gentleman in spectacles, he rushed toward the place where she was standing. I think I never saw a face assume so many different expressions in as short a time, as did that of the little woman while her busband was on his way to her. She was not to say handsome, but somehow I felt a big lump rise in my throat as I watched her. She was trying to laugh, but God bless her ! how completely she failed in the attempt. Her mouth got into position ; but it never moved after that, save to draw down the corners and quiver, while she blinked her eyes so fast, that I suspect she only caught glimpses of the broad-shouldered fellow who elbowed his way toward her. And then, as he drew close, and dropped those everlasting portmanteaus, she just turned completely around with her back toward him, and covered her face with her hands. The strong man then gathered her up as though she had been a baby, and held her to his breast.

There were enough gaping at them, Heaven knows, and for a moment I turned my eyes away. Then I saw two boys in threadbare roundabouts standing near, wiping their eyes and noses on their little coat-sleeves, and bursting out anew at every fresh demonstration on the part of their mother. When I looked at the stranger again, he had drawn his hat down over his eyes. But the wife was looking up at him, and it seemed that the pent-up tears of those weary months of waiting were streaming through her eyelids.

I had occasion to make a hurried professional trip to the next city on our line. There had been an accident up north somewhere, a broken engine, if I remember correctly, so that when the train arrived at our station behind time, there were few seats for the accommodation of the crowd that awaited its arrival. Then followed, what is witnessed in no other country, a grand American rush !

The experienced traveller never rushes ; so I found myself obliged to take a back seat ; that uncomfortable little affair near the door, originally devised for the bewildered foreigner, unused to travel. It was the first time that I had occupied a back seat in all my travels, and I found that, after all, it was not without its advantages. From this back window I obtained a wide, new outlook into the world. Away behind, my native mountains, shifting into new beauty of shape, as the track twisted this way and that. There was a fascination in watching this track unroll itself from beneath the speeding cars, and spreading away in the distance. Now into the deep gorge, then out over high embankments, through the arches of bridges, over rivers and streams, and here almost touching the corner of the old farm-house, built before railroads were thought of at all.

Then the after-glimpses of the people we had just left—bits of human nature, entirely lost by the occupants of the front seats. The young man who kissed his hand from the back platform, and the girl he left behind him waving her 'kerchief in response. The old gentleman getting slowly into his empty wagon, gazing wistfully after the train, that was whirling his only son off to the greedy West. The young mother with a child in her arms, whose lips were still moist with the father's parting kiss. The lazy loungers at the depot, picking up their feet and sauntering off; the men ploughing in the fields; the women hanging out clothes; the laborers on the track, leaning on their shovels, until we passed; runaway horses, sobering down; all this had escaped me before, and no doubt many another traveller had treated the same commonplace affairs with silent contempt.

"So like life," said my better self; "so we come and go. A little stir, a little brief importance, then we are gone, and the world goes on just the same."

You notice from the back seat how everything seems to catch the infection of hurry from the train. The dead leaves whirl and leap in the air; the very sand flies on the breeze; the sober trees in the wild old woods wave and toss their branches, as if anxious to be off—their arms stretched out imploringly, saying, "Take us from this silence and solitude out into the busy, hurrying world, to which you go!"

Bringing your eyes and your thoughts back into the crowded car, you pity the gayly-dressed young man with the bloated face, in one of the best front seats on the shady side; how intently he looks out of the window, whenever a woman enters from a way-station; and the fat old gentleman near by, who secures the same end, by burying his face in his newspaper. And the portly gentleman, raising the window at regular intervals, to squirt filthy tobacco juice at the changing scene without. How much they were losing, I thought! All this beautiful, changing scene of life, and beauty, and human nature, going on around them, and they, shut up in their own selfish selves, none the wiser or better for it.

Thinking of all I had been through during these years of travel, I wondered if the people who take the back seat in life have not the best of it, after all. The people who are not in a fret or a hurry; ready to push down and trample upon their fellow-travellers, in order to secure the best positions and places; the first notice the front seats generally. The people who do not expect much, seldom think of themselves, and are not eager to thrust themselves forward. That there is a deal of serenity always attendant on the back seat; a leisure from one's self, that gives abundant room for much outside living. The journey is so short, too, and so swift, that really the seat one occupies is of but little consequence. And looking again, one finds such a vast material about him for love and society and friendship, which giving him no heed, leaves him at his journey's end. Material for life-long friends, if the conductor would only make one acquainted; but the travelling tricks of bad women and worse men have made us suspicious of each other, until one can scarcely offer a common civility to a lady upon the cars, without being met with a look of suspicion or an expression of alarm. But I see from the back seat faces before me of culture and refinement; countenances expressive of sympathy and kindness; interesting and entertaining people, who may be my "long lost brothers and sisters," but between whom and myself no word or sign of recognition will ever pass. Each has his own world and a separate path, all reaching, however, to the great depot Beyond.

The people in the back seat reach the journey's end just as soon, and once there, no one asks how they came. Let us be good-natured, unselfish, and helpful to our fellow-passengers, and possess our souls in peace.

XXIX.

THE DEAF COVE.

A DETECTIVE'S STORY.

MYSTERIOUS murder had been committed, and a large reward offered for the capture of the guilty parties. Alarmed at the extraordinary excitement which followed, disreputable and suspicions characters of all kinds fled the city. Detectives were sent in all directions, and being an old member of the force, I received especial instructions from Pinkerton, and one wet November evening, was set down at the Great Western Railway depot, to await the starting of the night express. My luggage consisted of a single travelling-bag, and getting a check for that, I had nothing to do but stroll about until the train should be made up.

I have a natural dislike for the waiting-room at a railway station, so lighting a cigar, I walked the platform outside, watching the faces of those who were already going aboard the train to secure good seats. There was the usual bustle of a crowded depot on this occasion. The wet had driven all the apple-women and pea-nut venders inside, who were vociferously shouting the merits of their wares to every customer. Hackmen were blustering, as they always are on rainy nights, and porters were swearing, as only porters can. The engineer and fireman were getting into their oil-clothes and glazed caps, and the sharp-voiced bell was speaking out its warning to delinquents.

I became interested at once in two strangers who were evidently to be my fellow-travellers. I need not explain why, after seeing them, I failed to look at any others. They were walking back and forth like myself, apparently waiting for the conductor's " all aboard," before giving up their liberty. An elderly gentleman and a young girl— at least, the iron-gray hair of the one, and the silken brown curls of the other—said as much. I am not good at a yarn, or I would have said before, that I was still a young man, and had been often selected to work up female cases, on account of my good looks and gentlemanly manners.

Under the pretence of examining the time-table, I stopped short, and got a very good view of both countenances. The gentleman was sixty or thereabouts, with a seamed, weather-beaten face, like that of one who has followed the seas. The girl I cannot describe as she appeared to me then. An ordinary observer would have seen a fair, oval face, like the faces of those born under southern skies. She smiled at something her companion was saying, revealing teeth as white as pearls. If I have a weakness for any particular charm, it is for perfect teeth. Without such a charm, no woman can be lovely. Her hands were ungloved, and upon the left forefinger sparkled and burned like fire a single diamond set in gold.

My theory of love at first sight came to be a real thing

at the moment I beheld her face. I felt the assurance in every nerve—the assurance which has never left me, from that day to this. The couple passed on before me again, and I·followed them, taking note of every minute detail. The crimson robes that encircled the girl became sacred to me. I wondered that I had never before known what constituted the acme of perfection in a woman's dress.

In turning back for the tenth time in my promenade, I noticed one person whose appearance at once arrested my official gaze. A tall, slightly stooping man, wrapped in a heavy cloak of a military pattern. His gait was that of a lithe, active individual of thirty; but his gray hair, and the cane on which he leaned, or pretended to lean, gave him an elderly appearance. I was unable to get a fair view of his face, but it was plain that the gleam of the cold gray eye—furtive, yet alert, like that of a greyhound—was not the eye of an infirm old man. In short, the appearance of age was a disguise assumed for some purpose, a discovery that recalled the business in hand. While setting my detective wits to work, my eye singled out another individual, who excited my curiosity even more than the first. This person was leaning against a peanut stand, crunching the filberts the boy was cracking for him, and like myself, perhaps, taking note of those around him. He was short, thick-set, and muscular. He wore a suit of plain black, a white neck-cloth, and carried a book under his arm. I got behind him and read its title : "Barnes' Notes on the Gospel of St. Paul."

Was he a clergyman ? I asked my professional self— then took a second look. His face was red, as though the parish in his charge had stocked the cellar of the parsonage with generous wine. His features were coarse and repulsive, so far as I could see, for the lower part of his physiognomy was entirely concealed in a heavy growth of reddish-gray beard. I could form no opinion of his eyes, for they were sheltered behind green glasses with very respectable gold frames.

It occurred to me in a moment that there was some sort of a collusion between these two men, though why I should indulge this fancy I could not determine. Even with the horrible murder still fresh in my memory, and a city at my back searching all its avenues for the murderers, I did not for a moment imagine that either of these mild-mannered and unsuspicious persons were in any way connected with that bloody affair. Neither can I explain why, now. It was one of those psychological phenomena which occasionally occur to the most matter-of-fact of men, and wholly inexplicable through the medium of language.

I felt a little nettled with myself for observing either of these men, when I might look at the young girl instead. Presently the last bell sounded, and my old gentleman assisted the young girl to a carriage. I sprang after them, determined if possible to keep near her ; but to my chagrin I found that every seat in that car was occupied. I went to the next one behind, with no better luck.

The next carriage I entered was a compartment car, at the rear of the train, I judged. The first compartment was empty ; and congratulating myself on that circumstance, I took a comfortable position, with my feet on the next seat, and resigned myself to dreams of her, and, perhaps, by and by, a little sleep. For the train was express to Beaunier—I give only fictitious names—and I should not be troubled for my ticket or check until just before reaching there.

Just as the train had got under way, and I was indulging in a rapturous waking dream of those hazel eyes I had seen beneath that scarlet feather, the door of my retreat was opened, somewhat cautiously, it appeared to me, and the man I had seen at the depot, in the military cloak, looked in.

I felt insufferably annoyed, for I concluded he was hunting for a seat, and I did not care to have my pleasant thoughts disturbed by his conversation. A sudden idea came into my head. I would feign deafness, and thus be spared the infliction of being obliged to keep up a civil show of sociability. He addressed me in a manner which was polite and gentlemanly.

"Do you object to company, sir?"

"Eh!" said I, in a loud voice, and putting my hand to my ear in the way most deaf persons have.

I found the man looked relieved, but it might have been only a fancy.

He repeated the question in a tone so loud, that I wondered if the people in the next car would not hear it and take alarm.

I shook my head in a dissatisfied way, took a slip of paper and pencil from my pocket, and gave them to him.

"Write," said I.

He wrote the question in a bold, free hand.

"Do you object to having company, sir?"

"Certainly not," I replied, after reading it, though I told as arrant a falsehood as I was capable of in two words.

He stepped to the door, and spoke to some one outside. I heard the words distinctly.

"Come in, Dick. Thar's only one fellow here, and he's as deaf as the ——. He wouldn't hear Gabriel's trumpet if it should sound this moment."

Dick stepped inside, and, as I had fully expected, he proved to be the short, thick-set clerical gentleman I had seen at the peanut stand. He took a survey of me through his spectacles.

"Humph!" said he, "rather an intelligent-looking chap. Are you sure he's deaf?"

"Try him, and see," responded the other.

"I hope we do not incommode you, sir?" said he, in a tone which seemed to me a sort of cross between a steam-whistle and a clap of August thunder.

I replied by giving him my pencil and paper.

He looked satisfied, and wrote rapidly—

"Let us become acquainted. My companion is Dr. Severance, of Baltimore, and I am the Rev. John Smith, of the same place."

I read the lines, and took from my pocket a printed card, of which I always carried a varied assortment. He took it and read it aloud with an amused twinkle creeping about the wrinkles at the corners of his ambushed eyes :

JOHN D. SMITH,

DEALER IN DRY GOODS AND EMBROIDERIES,
Galesburg, Ills.

Dr. Smith laughed, as his friend remarked, "Your namesake, my Rev. John!"

"Another John Smith! by Jupiter!" cried the reverend gentleman. "If I was the genuine and original John Smith, I'd have my name patented, and every pretender should be prosecuted according to law!" and then he wrote a line or two for my perusal, to the effect that he was happy to meet me, and that he deeply regretted my infirmity, because it would deprive him of the great pleasure of my conversation.

After this complimentary courtesy they left me to myself, and I subsided into my corner of the seat, drew my hat over my eyes, and simulated sleep.

"It's deuced lucky," said the man called Dick, "that this car happens to be so nearly empty; Providence favors us. That is clerical language, isn't it?" with a loud ha, ha! at his irreverent wit.

"Decidedly lucky," responded the other. "That chap is of no more consequence than a dead log. But are you quite sure that Starkey will not fail us?"

"Sure? Yes, sir! as sure as that we are here. He knows Dick Turner too well, to trifle in a matter of this kind. He stands in fear of his fate," and the villain significantly touched the butt end of a pistol which protruded from an inner breast-pocket.

"It is a ticklish undertaking," said the other; "one, the plan of which does you infinite credit as a prince in your profession. You ought to be prime minister to his Satanic Majesty in the next world."

"Well, when I am," replied Dick, "I'll be sure to speak a word to his highness in favor of my friend Jack Mortlan, alias Dr. Severance."

"Don't waste words in compliments, Dick. Let me be sure that I fully understand the plan."

"Certainly, I will detail it to you if you like, though I thought you were thoroughly posted. The facts in the case are these. Old Capt. Van Luce has been master of a privateer—or, what amounts to the same thing—has served his country gloriously in this great and wicked rebellion."

"Nonsense! don't go into the spread-eagle style. Speak English!" responded Jack, testily.

"Anything to oblige. The old gentleman was rich

before the war, he is richer now, and what is more to the point, he is going to his home in B——, and has his prize-money, a cool hundred thousand, in his possession. Also, he has his daughter, and she having been on a visit to New York, has her diamonds, which are worth fifty thousand more, among her luggage. The entire plunder is contained in the black-leather valise that is stowed away at this moment under the seat the father and daughter occupy, whar he can keep his foot on it, and be ready to seize upon it at a moment's notice. By Jove, Jack! the girl is a beauty! I don't wonder you feel sore over the way things have turned out! Didn't she look handsome in that black-velvet hat, with the scarlet feather in it, and that crimson shawl over her shoulders? Gad! Florence Van Luce is a splendid-looking woman, and she will be quite handsome enough without diamonds."

You may well believe that I could hardly keep from starting to my feet, as I listened to this conversation; but, by an effort, I controlled myself to hear what more might be said.

"It was a cruel hit for you, Jack, when she failed to see your manifold attractions, and mittened you as coolly as she would have exterminated a troublesome mosquito."

"Hush!" said the other, fiercely, "you shall not jest upon that subject! Her rejection made a demon of me! Before that I was only a fast young man, with as many virtues, and no more vices than the average; but ever since I have been a fiend! She might have been my salvation—you needn't sneer, Dick Turner—but instead she has been my ruin. And yet I'll do her the justice to say, that she tried to avoid me always; and when she rejected my love she was kind. Kind! my God! how I hated her, because I thought pity made her kind! I tell you, Dick, no woman who thoroughly knows Jack Mortlan will ever dare his hatred with impunity! I loved her once, now I hate her!"

"Softly, softly, Jack. What if yonder blockhead should wake up? He'd see from the expression of your face that something was agog. Let the girl go! such as her are not for you and me. And yet we were both gentlemen once! But never mind! We will be again, when the old man's money is ours!"

"You have selected Hanly as the place, I understand?"

"Yes; there could not be a better place for such an accident (?) if it had been made to order. This train is express to Beaunier—the only stoppage it makes is at Tylerville, twenty-five miles beyond Hanly, for wood and water. Just beyond Hanly village there is a long cut, and the train runs in on a curve. It is two miles from the covered river bridge. The cut is always dark; it will be darker still to-night, and the lamps won't light the track a rod ahead, the fog is so thick. In the middle of this cut, ten lengths of the rail will be taken up when the whistle for Hanly village is heard. Starkey is there now, I'll warrant ye, ready to operate the moment he hears the whistle. Of course, there will be an accident, and some people will be killed, and some will be hurt; but that's not our look-out. If people want to be out of danger, let 'em keep out of railway trains—particularly those that are express! But the cream of the joke, and decidedly the wittiest thing in the whole plan is this: you and I shall run no risk from the smash; for, hark ye! *we* are in the very hindmost car; and just as we pass Hanly village I shall take the liberty of unshackling this car from the train; and as it has a brake of its own, we shall manage to run quite up to the scene of the catastrophe, and be there ready to lend our assistance, which will be rendered by seizing on old Van Luce's black valise, and any other valuables which may be lying around loose. I have marked just the position of the old fellow in the car—he's a careful traveller—just exactly in the middle, fourth car from this; and if he's not killed, it will be very easy to snatch the valise and light out. Starkey is to have a carriage and horses waiting behind the hill for us; and in two hours we shall be on board the L—— train, speeding back to New York. How d'ye like the scheme, my friend?"

"You are a trump," responded Jack, "only I wish I was sure that Florence would not be hurt. Much as I hate her, I am not sunk so low as to feel just right about putting a woman in danger."

"Tush! don't be spooney. Take a drink of this, and it will set you all right."

My blood was fairly on fire. A hundred vague plans flitted through my brain, among the most tempting of which was the desire to take my revolver from my pocket, and shoot the villains dead where they sat. But they were armed and desperate; and besides, the men of the train would take me for a madman, if I communicated even the substance of the story I had heard. So, as there was yet some seventy miles between us and Hanly, I sat still and awaited further developments.

"What if our interesting companion should take exception to our uncoupling the car?" ·

"Pshaw! He sleeps like a top. If he wasn't, there's nothing strange about a couple of passengers going out to smoke."

Meanwhile, the train rushed on through the darkness; and even now I sometimes awake with a start on stormy nights—the grinding roar of the wheels on the rails seeming yet to ring in my ears, just as I heard it that night, when every revolution brought us nearer and nearer to doom.

"Come, come, Jack," said Turner, "let's go out into the air and have a smoke. I'll just turn the key on this chap, to be sure in case he has been shamming."

The two men went out, and I was a prisoner!

The brain works quickly in such moments, if it works at all, and very soon I had formed a plan by which I hoped to save the train. Much upon the road upon peculiar duty, I had become familiar with the interpretation of the locomotive's whistles; and just at this moment the engine shrieked out on the thick night air. Two sharp, quick cries, and then a shrill, prolonged scream. We had made unusually good time, and now Bellevue was distant only twenty-two miles! Not to be mistaken, I took out my note-book. Yes, I was right. Two quick whistles and a prolonged one meant a station; and my time-table gave the distance and the name. How fortunate, too, that I knew the road so well!

I had not then a moment to lose. Putting my hand on my revolver, lest my fiendish fellow-travellers should suddenly return, I stole to the rear door of the car, only to find it locked! Probably they had prepared this car before leaving the depot. But I was not to be thus thwarted. The windows were wide, and with one blow of my heavy boot, I crashed both glass and sash, and climbed through. There was no foothold outside, save the iron brace which ran around the car. Standing upon this, and clinging to the window-frame, I looked out through the gloom.   It was a fearful night ; a thick mist was falling, and the wind felt like the breath of a tomb.

A few rods from Bellevue, the line crossed a deep though narrow river, upon a " pile bridge." The signal of " all right " at this bridge was three lights, two red and one green.   Leaning out as far as I dared, I soon caught the gleam of the lights, and almost simultaneously, we were thundering over the bridge.   Uttering a brief but heart-felt prayer to God, I let go my hold and leaped forward !

An intolerable sense of suffocation, succeeded by a coldness like ice ; and then I seemed to sink down to unfathomable depths.   Presently I rose to the surface of the water, and struck out for the shore.   I was very near it, and almost instantly my feet touched the bottom. Breathless and dripping as I was, I ran with all speed to the station-house, rushed into the telegraph office there, and found the operator dozing in his chair.   He stared at me in blank dismay.   Telegraph instantly, I exclaimed, to stop the train at Hanly village.   Tell them to arrest two men who are travelling in the rear car.   One is tall, with a slight stoop, gray hair, and lightish eyes.   The other short, thick-set, red hair and whiskers.   I repeated this rapidly, at the same time writing it down.

Still the man stared at me.

" I do not understand," he said.   " This line is only used by the train despatchers and officers of the road, from whom all orders must be received.   I have no authority to stop trains."

" There is danger ahead," I almost screamed.   " Beyond Hanly village the track is up.   Send the message instantly."

" I cannot, sir ; it is against orders, but I will communicate with headquarters. In the meantime, let me ask, are you mad or drunk ?"

"But the message ?" I yelled.

"The message has been sent from headquarters, and the despatcher orders the express stopped at Hanly vil-. lage. Also the arrest of the parties with yourself. If you are a lunatic, as I suppose, they will take you all to-gether."

I steadied my voice.

"I beg your pardon, sir, for behaving in such an un-heard of, and perhaps rude manner. But I dared not stop to explain until you had sent the message. God grant it may be in time ! " And as briefly as might be, I made the amazed operator acquainted with what the reader already knows.

"We will go on to Hanly village at once," he said. " I am anxious for the *dénoûment;* and besides, it will be necessary that you should be there to accuse these cow-ardly rascals."

He put a bottle of wine and some glasses on the table, and told me to make myself at home ; and though I am not much of a "wine-bibber," I think the two glasses I took that night were a benefit to me ; for I was so nearly distracted with fear in regard to the train that contained Florence Van Luce, that I needed something to steady my overstrung nerves.

The operator, whose name was Morgan, now left me, while he went out to arouse the road-master to get his permission to have a locomotive "fixed up" to take us to Hanly. He returned in fifteen minutes to say that all was in readiness. The road-master accompanied us, and I venture to say, none of us ever travelled at the rate of speed we made that night. Morgan ventured to remonstrate with the engineer, but he looked admiringly at the high pressure of steam registered by the guage, and replied with something like triumph—

"She can stan' it, sir! Gad! there aint a machine on the road that can run with old *Forty-two.*"

At last we saw the signal light of Hanly station, and the "Forty-two" uttered a shrill cry to notify the station people of our approach. In a moment three sharp whistles in quick succession were returned.

"That's the *Twenty-four*," said our engineer. "Should know that whistle among a thousand—and the Twenty-four's the machine that allers draws the night express. They're pulled up at Hanly village, you may bet your life on that."

I remember that I put my two hands together, and said to myself, "Thank God! thank God!"

We drew up behind the express train, and alighting, made our way to the depot. The utmost confusion prevailed. Half the village, aroused by so unusual a circumstance as the stoppage of the night express, had turned out, and were gathered in little knots around the station, discussing the singularity of the whole affair.

My whilom fellow-travellers were held in custody by the railway police. Dick was inclined to bluster, and protest his innocence of every real and imaginary sin that ever was dreamed of; Jack was stolid and sullen, and maintained a rigid silence.

As we entered the room, Dick was saying,

"What in the deuce are we stopped here for? I'll have satisfaction out of somebody for this! Detained like two criminals! The Company's pockets shall smart for it! By whose authority was the train stopped? Just tell me that, will ye?"

"We received a telegram," said the station-agent. "Keep cool, sir; if you are innocent of the charge which some party will bring against you, you will be set at liberty."

"Who sent the telegram?" demanded Dick, fiercely.

"I had that honor, sir," said I, pausing in front of him.

"By —— The deaf cove that pretended to be asleep in the compartment-car! By Jupiter! he was shamming I told you so, Jack!"

"Is there a magistrate present?" I inquired, looking around on the sea of inquisitive faces.

And an elderly gentleman, stepping out from the crowd, announced himself qualified.

"I wish to be put upon oath," said I. "I deem it no more than justice to myself that all the travellers by the express should listen to my statement, that I may be exonerated from blame in having been the means of bringing their journey to so abrupt a termination for the present."

And under oath, simply and briefly as might be, I gave a narration of facts as the reader already knows them, though I confess to skipping that portion touching the love of Jack Mortlan for Florence Van Luce. I thought the story just as complete without that.

Just as I had finished my statement, one of the messengers sent forward to look for the danger of which my telegram had given intimation, returned. He was breathless and agitated, and announced the track torn up for some lengths in the middle of Hanly "cut," and also the discovery of a pair of horses and a carriage, secreted in a clump of bushes a few yards from the line.

I had not the remotest idea of being made a hero, but the people would insist on shaking hands with me, and thanking me for the service I had rendered ; and among the warmest thanks of all were those of Capt. Van Luce.

And when he had said all he could think of, he called his daughter to finish for him.

" Florence, my dear, come hither, and—and—hang it ! do the thing up as it ought to be done. Shiver my timbers if I know what to say to the man who has saved my life, and that of my darling ! This is my daughter, Florence, Mr.—Mr. —— Well, I declare, I don't happen to know your name."

" I beg your pardon. My name is simply Martin, George Martin, and I reside in B——"

Florence laid her dear little hand in mine and I took it gladly enough, resisting with an effort the impulse of my heart to take her to my bosom.

My wife, whose name is Florence. looks over my shoulder and says my story is done. Every one who has had any romance in his life will guess the conclusion.

Dick and Jack were tried and condemned to imprisonment for life. Jack subsequently committed suicide in his cell. Pinkerton, our chief, said it was the best case I ever worked up, as it was the last.

XXX.

THE HOTEL CLERK OF THE PERIOD.

MY DEAR DUKE: I am very glad to see you again; indeed the more so, since I have seen nothing to compare with you in all my travels. Nothing to equal the charms and grace of your person, the perfection of those ambrosial curls, and the extent and magnificence of your jewelry. Nothing to approach that kingly air with which you deal out your princely favors to the plebeians who beg and cringe at the foot of your throne. True, I have met impostors and pretenders, who, coming into the position by inheritance, became selfish, giddy, and tyrannical by a too sudden assumption of its vast power and influence. Imitations abound, too, in monarchical countries, where a traveller asking for accommodations is treated as an equal rather than a mendicant; where a vagabond, entering with portmanteau in hand, is permitted to approach the Presence without a formal introduction.

I recall a glaring instance of this apostasy in France.

The keeper of a tav—my dear Duke, I beg your pardon —the proprietor of the principal hotel in the Rue de ——, really announced to the public, that his guests would be welcomed with kindness and attention ! Think of that, my friend, and condole with human depravity ! Fresh from America, I called to inspect the novelty.   I found there a ser—your pardon again—a gentleman of plebeian birth behind the count—that is to say, in the office—who had just opened a stock of patience and courtesy.   He was in plain attire, and actually without a jewel or other insignia of rank.   I was even permitted to converse with him, so far had he forgotten the dignity of his position.

You, who know so well what belongs to the dignity of a first-class serv—as I should say—clerk, would have blushed with mortification at this prostitution of a noble profession.   He descended to the level of the citizen at once.   As the crowds rushed in to inspect his stock of patience and courtesy, he spoke in humble tones, and gave a ready and pleasant answer to every comer.   What surprised me more than all, was to see him descend from what we in America recognize as a throne, and actually *mix* with those low people, and attend in person to their wants !   One instance, my dear Duke, I shall never forget.   This was a not to say tidy gentleman, who called for a front chamber on the second floor, and complaining of fatigue, requested to be shown there at once.   The servant not answering the bell promptly, this clerk really left his post, and accompanied the party to his very door ! For impudence on the one hand, and conde- scension on the other, I have never witnessed the like be- fore or since.

But, my dear Duke, this is not all.   I learned that in

that house, porters, waiters, and chambermaids were treated as human beings—men and women—instead of the outcasts we know them to be everywhere ; that this clerk really regarded himself as a servant with the rest, an employé on the same train, as we travellers would say. He answered their questions with the same courtesy and attention that was bestowed upon the wealthy patrons of the house, and sent them upon errands with the air of one who begged a favor, rather than exacted the performance of a duty. I noticed, too, that he received his "guests," as he styled them, with a desire to extend them every accommodation, instead of giving them to understand that he was the master and they the suppliants. The modest tradesman who sought a night's lodging, was as kindly received as the parties of the respectable classes who swept in from carriages. Disgusted with all this, I took occasion to assure him, that in America his house would not last a day. He replied, that hospitality should be impartial. That every man who stopped with him once, should be treated with such courtesy that he would remember it with gratitude, and come again.

When I came over, my dear Duke, I was not surprised to hear that this hotel was the first that the Communists destroyed.

Is it any wonder, my dear Macomber, that I welcomed the change upon my arrival last night? To see you standing there, dressed in the height of fashion ; blazing with brilliant jewelry, and moistened, as it were, with the rarest exotics ; as calm and serene before that crowd of noisy travellers, as a real Duke in his reception-chamber, was to forget the French hireling and all his disgusting surroundings. You were there to command as the Patron, not the servant of mankind. To give every one to understand, that they are inferior beings, permitted to receive your patronage and never to question either its quality, quantity, or mode of delivery.

As this crowd of hungry, soiled, and weary passengers came in from the late trains, how you enjoyed the opportunity! One old gentleman, evidently a thief in disguise, peered at you through gold spectacles. I could see that a consciousness of guilt caused him to approach you with an abject and cowardly air. The low crowd moved aside to give him entrance to your gracious presence.

"I am too old and feeble to go far, sir; will you give me a room on a near floor?"

To see you gaze over their heads as if you failed to hear, with that princely air which is indeed charming, and remark—

"*Sir—Move on!*"

I tell you, my dear Duke, that was a master-stroke of genius! And then, as question after question came from the dastardly offenders, to have you answer all with that ill-suppressed contempt, which is the highest charm of your profession! I tell you, sir (as I have a right to say to any friend who attains to greatness in his calling), such rare skill comes only of deep study and careful practice.

Courtesy, indeed! A lot of miserable travellers asking for a night's lodging? Do the hounds imagine that the pittance they pay entitles them to more? Shall a serv—(that is to say, a gentleman of your parts, Mr. Macomber) be forever bowing and scraping, and making fine speeches to people whom he never expects to meet again?

Your power, my friend, is of a piece with that of the railway conductor who has just brought us through.

The comfort of scores of your fellow-passengers on the World's train is in your hands every day. You may make yourself a valuable servant—for we are servants all —and your house popular and profitable, if you will. You are placed there to serve your guest with that for which he is ready to pay, and it becomes you to see to it that it comes to him from polite and willing hands. Every traveller recognizes you at once. You may send him away as a friend or an enemy, and every man has his influence. Let it be your aim then, my friend, to send down into his heart some pleasant memory of his stay. Some kindly action—a word—or even a smile !

THE END.